Trouble Always Finds Me

JAMES TAYLOR

story by JAMES TAYLOR & MARCO SPARKS

Trouble Always Finds Me

Print ISBN: 978-1-7330662-2-8
eBook ISBN: 978-1-7330662-3-5

Cover artwork by Michael Manuel

First Edition, 2020

For mentors and teachers

Table of Contents

Chapter One

The Good Twin

NO MATTER HOW MANY TIMES SHE READ IT, THAT FIRST ENTRY IN Nurse Bennett's journal never failed to give her the shivers.

> "March 10. Trouble in the ER last night. Pregnant girl blew in with the storm. Soaked to the bone, wild-eyed and screaming, barely 23. Says Valerie Valentine is trying to kill her. Delivered just after midnight. Surprise surprise, it's twins."

Five days later, that pregnant girl would be dead.

Mom...

She'd been thinking a lot about narratives lately. It was hard not to around her sister. Sometimes, it was like things fit too perfectly to be chance. Did Mom sense that her story was coming to an end? Would she? Was it happening right now?

"How did you find me?!" the Fortune Teller screeched, pulling the paper bag off her head and punching her in the face.

Something popped, and white novas of pain exploded in her hazy vision. For a panicked second, she thought her orbital bone had fractured. It was the Fortune Teller who cried out, though, wincing and recoiling and cradling her wrist. Good. Now if the room would just stop spinning…

Her brown eyes squinted through the bangs of her crimson wig—Drew's favorite—as she fought against the dull pressure gnawing away at her consciousness. Drugged. Goddamnit, the tea had been drugged—and she'd drunk it like an amateur, not even waiting to see how Drew reacted first. How embarrassing. And she was supposed to be the smart one.

Her dim surroundings swam into focus. A haggard lady with a rats nest of gray hair loomed, her jaundiced pallor that spoke of methamphetamine abuse. Walls draped in black velvet, crystals and curio cabinets, a single light floating above. Drew Porter, her burly sidekick and *Trouble* super-fan, face-planted on the scrying table next to her with a Raley's bag over his head. Like her, he was bound to his chair at the wrists with several loops of twine. Unlike her, he was still out cold.

"Some bodyguard you are," she said to his prone form.

They were in the backroom of The Mystic Madame, a cheap psychic joint in a forgotten corner of a forgotten strip mall in Petaluma. The muffled patter of January rain drifted in through the ceiling. She knew from too many YouTube videos that there would be a footswitch under the Fortune Teller's chair that killed the light and made the crystal ball glow. A nice parlor trick, and a better distraction, if she could just reach the switch.

"Answer me! Or I'll do for your other eye too!" her captor shouted again, breath like a rancid diaper.

"What are you, like 90? Go on, break your other wrist."

That earned her the back of the Fortune Teller's uninjured hand.

This was the sort of shit that Jenny Valentine—aka Trouble, the pint-sized girl detective who never found herself in a jam she couldn't mischief her way out of—practiced for. Lived for. But she wasn't Jenny Valentine. She was the other one. The ace in the hole. The secret twin.

> "March 12. Her name is Laura Onishi, the new mom. It seems Dad is Valerie Valentine's husband. Laura is absolutely paranoid that Val is out to get her, refuses to let her babies leave her sight. Being difficult. Younger twin Elizabeth has an infection, needs the incubator. Doctor Singh is losing patience. I told him not to worry, didn't he see the birth certificate? "Danger" is this baby's middle name. He didn't appreciate it."

For most of her life, Eliza—as she preferred to be called these days—believed that her mother was a Jane Doe who died in childbirth at Santa Rosa Memorial Hospital in California. A silver-haired nurse from the ER named Rose Bennett took pity and adopted her. Shortly after, they left the North Bay behind for a suburb in East Sacramento. Eliza never had any reason to question this narrative, and honestly, she didn't really care who her father was. It was just the two of them, and she was content; the brainy little adopted half-Japanese girl who idolized Hermione Granger and wanted to be a doctor when she grew up.

Nurse Bennett had seen 52 winters and lacked the energy to keep up with Eliza after long shifts in the Med Center emergency room. So from an early age, they struck a deal. Eliza would behave, pull down good grades, and practice a hobby. In return, she'd get all the best privileges: the giant box of crayons, a Happy Meal every Friday, a TV in her room. She even got to skip school to go to midnight releases of the last two Harry Potter movies. When she got straight

A's for a whole year in Third Grade, Nurse Bennett bought her a new American Girl doll and *all* the accessories. Over the years, she took piano lessons, learned to juggle, did ballet, even earned a black belt in Taekwondo. Life was good.

Until four years ago, when Nurse Bennett violated the deal and got herself diagnosed with Alzheimer's, then, everything changed.

"Honestly, it wasn't that hard to find you," Eliza said, glaring at the old lady. "It only took a while. I guess RJ didn't have time to war-drive to every two-bit Psychic in the North Bay on Yelp. You should have switched Tarot decks."

It was still weird, thinking of RJ Valentine, the late and legendary author of the *Trouble: Girl Detective* book series as *Dad*.

> **"March 13. Laura has relented and let Baby Danger stay in the incubator. Infection should clear up in a few days. She's still paranoid about being followed, but I assured her I hadn't seen anything out of the ordinary in the ER. Except for her, that is."**

Nurse Bennett had been getting increasingly absentminded for a few years already, with Eliza picking up more and more of her slack. Reminding her adoptive mother when to pay the bills. Buying groceries with the family debit card. Pretending it was a private inside joke when her mom couldn't remember a neighbor's name. The first time Nurse Bennett forgot who Eliza was, it was terrifying. She kept saying, "Danger. Danger."

After the diagnosis, Nurse Bennett had to retire. They sold the house and moved to a smaller place in the Auburn Foothills to save money. Trips to Disneyland for a flawless report card were no longer on the table. No more Shakespeare Camp, no more archery lessons. Eliza was to be "homeschooled," which meant keeping an eye on her mom while taking classes online.

The tests were easy; Eliza's attention wandered. She grew restless and reckless, cooped up in that shabby house with all the responsibility now, and none of the reward. Her old friends had drifted away, but the internet was always there to shock and horrify and entertain her. At night, she delved deep into the dark corners of the web: X-rated tumblrs, troll forums, K-pop fandom. She brigaded shitty gamer dudes, traded memes, and invented new online personas, relishing in the chaos she could cause. Years passed in quiet desolation.

A week before her 15th birthday, Nurse Bennett sat her down. It was time, she said. There was a very important secret that needed telling, and she'd better tell it while she still remembered.

Eliza could still recall the moment, sitting on the couch under that scratchy throw blanket she always hated. She was only half-listening, worried this was another delusion. According to Nurse Bennett, Eliza's actual birthday was today! Eliza's birth mother wasn't a Jane Doe after all. She was a grad student who'd had an affair with an English professor and aspiring author named RJ Valentine. Yes, *that* RJ—

"Valentine?" the Fortune Teller sucked in a breath through missing teeth and leveled a cold, deadly stare at Eliza. "He got what was coming to him."

"What, he fuck you over or something? What was your beef with him?" asked Eliza.

"I'm going to have to kill you both," the Fortune Teller said absently, glancing around the room with calculating eyes that sent a chill down Eliza's spine. She was far too detached, like maybe she'd done this before.

"Hey hey hey, enough of that talk!" Eliza said, writhing in panic under the rough twine that restrained her. "Have you seen how big this guy is?" She jutted her chin at Drew's passed-out bulk. "Let's work something out."

"Don't matter how big when he's unconscious," said the Fortune Teller, opening and closing drawers in a nearby armoire.

"That's not what I mean. You're not thinking this through," Eliza said, her mind racing ahead of the stiletto dagger her captor had just produced. "Do you know how hard it is to get away with murder when there's a body? Can you even imagine how many pieces you're gonna have to chop this guy into before you can carry him to Lake Berryessa in small, watertight, durable plastic bags, weighted down with lead fishing tackle?"

The Fortune Teller was appalled. Drew groaned.

"What the fuck, Jenny?" came his muffled voice from under the paper bag.

> "March 15. I shouldn't have told her. A friend works at Blackbird Springs General, says Valerie Valentine just gave birth to a son of her own. When Laura found out, she wouldn't wait any longer, even with Elizabeth still recovering from the infection. She packed up the other baby and looked me dead in the eye and said: "No matter what you hear, no matter how much it might seem like an accident, if something happens to me or my baby, it's murder. If I don't come back, you take Lizzy, and you hide her from Valerie Valentine!" Insisted I swear on it. Sure. Fine. Anything to calm her down."

Narratives. Mom knew hers was coming to an end. Knew Val was involved. She told Nurse Bennett so that one day, Nurse Bennett would tell Eliza, and Eliza would have her revenge. If that was the story, Eliza should make it through this, right? She still had a story of her own. Or was framing Val for murder already vengeance served?

"Who told you to wake up?"

With surprising speed, the Fortune Teller yanked Drew upright and pulled off the bag covering his face. His normally golden-brown skin had gone ashen from whatever they'd been dosed with.

"How much did you give him?" Eliza asked, more panicked than she wanted to admit.

"Not enough," said the Fortune Teller.

Drew barely had time to blink in surprise before the Fortune Teller grabbed his chin and forced more tea down his throat. He spit it back in her face, the magnificent bastard. Eliza's heart fluttered as Drew growled in defiance and said, "I prefer hot chocolate!"

He was such a dork! She could kiss him, but in a heartbeat, the stiletto was back in the Fortune Teller's injured hand, this time its needle-sharp point twitching an inch from Eliza's neck.

"Drink!" the Fortune Teller commanded, holding up the cup of tea to Drew's mouth with her other hand.

Drew threw desperate glances at Eliza and the dagger.

She was doing the math, trying to figure their odds with Drew unconscious again when a familiar pattern from her Apple Watch tapped her on the wrist.

"It's okay," Eliza said to him. "Give us a little time for some girl talk."

Drew scowled. "Jenny—"

"Trust me," she said.

He flared his nostrils and gave the Fortune Teller a feral grin. "You have no idea who you're dealing with," he said, rather ironically, and drank the tea.

Within seconds, his eyes were drooping. The Fortune Teller covered his head with the paper bag again and Drew face planted back into oblivion.

"So RJ," Eliza said, picking up the thread and hoping to keep her captor occupied. "Come on, I never met him. Tell me, what did Daddy do to you?"

> "March 16: Oh my god! On KRON tonight, 'Deadly
> Traffic Accident on Highway 12.' They showed a
> picture, and it was her, it was Laura Onishi! She's dead!
> Did Val really have her killed?? No mention of the other
> twin, Jennifer. Oh my god, what do I do?"

Nurse Bennett's secret was out, and Eliza couldn't help but snort in derision. It was a joke, right? You couldn't just *hide* a person. That was impossible. But as Nurse Bennett told it, she'd made Eliza's mom a promise and felt honor-bound to keep it. With the help of Doctor Singh, they fabricated a death certificate for Elizabeth Danger Valentine. Then, a new birth certificate for a Jane Doe baby that Eliza was to become.

Just in time, too. The next morning, a stranger in a black suit and overcoat had come to the hospital, asking about Laura's other child. Officially, Eliza had died from a neonatal infection. They turned the stranger away, Nurse Bennett adopted the Jane Doe infant, and they moved to another city at the first opportunity. From then on, not a word was spoken of Eliza's real parents.

Not for 15 years.

Not until Nurse Bennett's memory was fading and time was running out. After Eliza laughed it off, Nurse Bennett opened her antique wooden jewelry box and reached inside. Eliza had been borrowing shiny bracelets and necklaces from it for years and somehow never noticed it had a false bottom. Out came several pages of a journal, still ragged at the edges from the diary they'd been hastily ripped out of, and a pink and blue document. Eliza's real birth certificate. Eliza's real middle name.

What about her twin sister? Was she killed in the accident too? Nurse Bennett didn't know or couldn't remember. What were they talking about again?

"It was at the county fair last spring," said the Fortune Teller, gently stroking her injured wrist, her eyes far away. "Valentine was there, signing books. My husband and I had a booth nearby. Every few hours, Tomas would walk down the line for RJ's autograph and do a cattle call, and I'd do some cold reads to drum up business."

She hissed, still aggrieved about what came next.

"I did a reading on some young lady. I guess it was his daughter."

"Wait—Tori?"

"She was a real superior bitch." The Fortune Teller licked her lips. "Didn't like my read. Said I'd insulted her. Excuse me for smelling the vodka on her breath. She went and complained to daddy. The next time I went out for a show, RJ was waiting." Her voice caught in her throat. "He somehow knew that Tomas had an old warrant and got the sheriff to arrest him. Then he dismantled me. Exposed me. Gave away every trick I had in front of a huge crowd. Even pulled off my turban and wig, said I was from Turlock and 'cultural appropriating.' And everyone laughed and laughed, because he was RJ Valentine, the Gentleman Sleuth, just showing off for his fans.

"It was humiliating. He ruined us. We couldn't work in Blackbird Springs after that. We were broke, and Tomas couldn't afford the legal fees, only saw one way out." She sniffled. "The dumb idiot didn't even check the insurance policy first. It wouldn't pay out for suicide, so it was all for nothing." She studied the tip of the blade, her dark eyes full of scorn and hatred. "So yeah, RJ got what was coming to him."

"Where were you on the night of August 10th? Last summer?"

Eliza asked.

The Fortune Teller laughed.

"I was waiting for him, you know? The night of the Gala?"

Goosebumps prickled on Eliza's arms. "Go on."

"Who do you think this was for?" she said, fingering the dagger. "I'd been watching him. I knew he had a room at the Crow's Nest he liked to keep secret. Figured he'd show up after the Gala. The Fairmont was only a couple blocks away." Her shoulders collapsed in resignation. She set the dagger down. "But he never showed. Turns out Valerie Valentine did for RJ herself. Who's laughing now, you arrogant prick?"

"So, you *didn't* kill him?" Eliza deflated, letting out a breath she'd been holding. "Damn. I just lost a bet."

> "March 10. You'll be 15 today, Elizabeth. Maybe I should have told you sooner. Maybe I should have tried to track down your mom's family. She said they disowned her, but maybe they've changed. I think she had a sister named Michelle. But you've brought me so much joy. Joy I never knew I was missing. I'm sorry if I did the wrong thing, but I'd do it again. I love you."

Nurse Bennett was never the same afterward. Slowly, inexorably, the only mom Eliza had ever known was fading away, a frightened, helpless stranger emerging in her place. She wasn't the only one. After years of increasing isolation and a shocking birthday surprise, Eliza was a stranger to herself. Or maybe this was growing up. She found new hobbies more befitting of her namesake. She pilfered cash. She learned to drive. She prepared.

It took her nearly a year to find Jenny. She hadn't even known to look for her. There were a dozen women named Michelle Onishi in the Bay Area, but none with a dead sister named Laura. After many fruitless Google searches and some embarrassing phone calls, Eliza chanced one night upon a user on the r/TroubleNovels subreddit with some very odd and spiteful personal opinions about RJ Valentine's wife Valerie. Stalking her profile, Eliza discovered that she lived down south in Glendale, CA. A quick search revealed a Michelle Onishi who lived in Glendale and taught at a local high school.

In a rush of adrenaline, she'd spent $60 using a dummy profile to buy Glendale High's most recent yearbook. When she got it in the mail, she flipped immediately to the teachers' mugshots and found Michelle Onishi. The Asian woman with the shoulder-length bob certainly *could* be her aunt. Eliza checked the index and found another page listing for her maybe-aunt. Michelle Onishi was also the Assistant Adviser of the Asian-Pacific Club, and from the club photo, shorter than half her students. Eliza was short too. Her eyes wandered over the picture. She was pondering how to contact this Michelle when suddenly—and quite shockingly—she found her own face staring back at her. A face with short, punky hair and a shady grin, but it was unmistakably *her*. The name in the caption, first row, third from the left: Jennifer Valentine.

A month later, Nurse Bennett passed. When CPS came to place Eliza with a new family, they found an empty house. Eliza Bennett had ceased to exist. She'd squirreled away $20,000 of Nurse Bennett's retirement fund and gone off alone to find her twin sister.

Speak of the devil.

Eliza caught a flicker of movement behind the Fortune Teller. She managed to keep her face neutral as her sister Jenny crept into the room and reached for a heavy amethyst crystal sitting atop the armoire.

"No," said the Fortune Teller. "I didn't kill RJ Valentine. But you…" The Fortune Teller's hand drifted to the dagger again. "Oh, I've heard about you. Saw your photo in the paper. The 'pint-sized girl detective' who can't keep her nose out of other people's business. Just like your dad."

She wrapped her wizened fingers around the stiletto blade and raised her fist to strike. Eliza's foot brushed over the floor switch under the table.

"Looks like you picked the wrong mystery to solve this time," said the Fortune Teller with a loathsome grin.

Eliza pressed down on the floor switch.

The room plunged into darkness just as Jenny swung the big hunk of crystal at the Fortune Teller's head.

"What can I say?" said Eliza as the blow connected with a satisfying crunch. "Trouble always finds me."

Chapter Two

Game Face

"I GUESS SHE DIDN'T SEE *THAT* COMING," JENNY SNICKERED, cutting her sister free. Eliza rubbed her wrists for a half-second before turning to check on Drew, their trusty sidekick.

"Is he still out?" Jenny whispered in her sister's ear, appraising Eliza's darkening black eye. They were identical twins, though this new shiner would make them easy to tell apart. That wouldn't do at all.

Eliza lifted Drew's arm and let go. It thumped on the table, completely limp. Good. As far as Drew knew, there was only Jenny, even though half the time they hung out, he was actually hanging with Eliza instead.

"Still has a pulse at least," Eliza said, her tone nonplussed.

"I got here as fast as I could!" Jenny said, deciding to leave out that she'd been in the middle of a delirious make-out session with Dinah when she'd gotten the S.O.S. She was up to 1,074 kisses with her girlfriend now, and yes, she was counting them.

"Did that include doing a bump of coke?" Eliza asked, pointing to her nose with a judgemental glare.

Jenny wiped under her nose, and white powder came off on her finger.

"Relax, it's just Adderall."

"Sure, that makes it better."

"It's my same dose!" Jenny rolled her eyes. "I just needed it to act faster. For you. I read about it on one of your websites, you know."

Eliza's shoulders slumped, and her face softened into a grateful smile. "Thank you."

"That's what big sisters are for," Jenny said with a wink. Her sister still looked a little dazed, so Jenny dug in her bag for some black pills, Trouble's favorite poison remedy. "Here. Activated charcoal. Like in *Trouble on the Orient Express*. Should help with whatever she dosed you with."

"I'm not sure if this actually works like in the books." Eliza smirked. "How much did you hear?"

"Enough to know we're gonna have to start on another clue," Jenny said. "And: I won the bet!"

Which meant they'd be keeping their hair short instead of growing it out.

"I was right about her wanting RJ dead, at least."

"*Dad* was right when he made that tarot card a clue," Jenny said. "Still, the thing about the room at the Crow's Nest is interesting. I wonder if Trouble, Inc. is still paying for it."

"Something to check with Mr. Webb on," Eliza said. She rolled her neck and flexed her hand into a fist. "All right, let's get this over with before we call the cops."

Jenny groaned.

"Do we have to?"

"I don't think makeup is gonna cover this up," Eliza said. She touched her eye and winced.

"You can just lie low for a while," Jenny said. "I'll do the statue ceremony thing this weekend."

"Can't. You have a PreCalc final. It's like 30 percent of your grade."

Her twin was the math genius of the family and had been taking most of Jenny's PreCalc tests this semester. They had a set rotation for school, trading places every other day, and even though Jenny tried to keep up with her PreCalc work—with Eliza doing her best to tutor Jenny—she didn't trust herself to pass the final.

"Ugh. Fine," Jenny said. "At least this is the last math class we need for college."

Jenny's new school, Blackbird Springs Academy, was on a block schedule, which meant that in another week, her least favorite subject would never trouble her again.

"We still haven't figured out how we're both going to get into college," said Eliza, bringing up a sore subject.

"We're rich now. We'll figure something out."

When their father, the famous mystery novelist RJ Valentine, died suddenly five months ago, his will left the *Trouble* publishing fortune to whichever of his seven named heirs solved his murder. Each heir was given a cryptic heirloom clue to follow.

RJ's wife Valerie Valentine—emphatically *not* the mother of Trouble and Danger—received a priceless bottle of wine.

Jenny received an old photo of Dad with their mother, Laura Onishi.

Local Sheriff Blake Lockhart got a noose, seemingly in reference to the famous Casey Klein murder case.

Dad gave Yvonne Griffin, editor of the local newspaper, an old book called *The Stranger of Sausalito*.

A small statue of an onyx blackbird went to their half-brother Jack Valentine.

Shifty Declan Dillion's clue, a tarot card of Death, proved prophetic when he was murdered himself a few weeks later by Dad's own killer.

Finally, there was Alicia Aaron, the mercurial one-legged, red-haired wallflower. Jenny couldn't figure out why Dad had left Alicia a skeleton key, and if Alicia knew, she was keeping it to herself.

Jenny had solved the mystery of Valerie Valentine's wine bottle clue, but it didn't lead to RJ's killer. With Aunt Shelly threatening to move back to Glendale, Jenny had no choice but to frame their hateful step-mother for Dad's murder, anyway. Now they had possession of the sprawling Valentine mansion and over $230 million in assets. If Elizabeth Danger Valentine's existence was ever revealed, their frame job on Val would fall apart, so they continued to share Jenny's identity. But the real killer—who had adopted the identity of *The Stranger*, the villain from Dad's *Trouble: Girl Detective* junior readers book series— was still out there and targeting Jenny next.

Her sister had followed Declan Dillion's tarot card clue here, and though she'd found another person who wanted their father dead, it seemed the Fortune Teller, too, was another bust. Back to square one, with nothing but black eyes to show for it.

Eliza got herself into a fighter's stance, showing off her years of self-defense training. Jenny closed her eyes, already dreading the pain.

"Aunt Shelly is going to kill me," she said. "Dinah is going to kill me."

"Oh, she loves this shit," said Eliza with a smirk. "She'll be dying to kiss and make it better."

Jenny's cheeks warmed at the thought. "Like you'd know, you're always avoiding her."

"For *obvious reasons*, Trouble."

The whole sharing-an-identity thing had gotten a lot trickier when Jenny started dating the head cheerleader, Dinah Black.

"You ready?" asked Eliza.

Jenny sighed and pulled the crimson red wig off of Eliza's head. Eliza rubbed her short black hair as Jenny fitted the wig onto her own pixie-cut locks.

"Do your worst," said Jenny.

Eliza gave her a savage right cross to the face.

As shiners went, Eliza gave her a real beauty. Jenny's eye was still puffy and purple for the statue ceremony on Friday night, much to Aunt Shelly's chagrin.

"You know, I swore I would never become my mother, and it's like you're trying to call my bluff," said Shelly.

"I'm helping you self-actualize," Jenny said. "You should thank me."

"Couldn't you at least try to cover it up with makeup?" Shelly asked, fussing with Jenny's new wig. She glanced over her shoulder at the row of photographers stationed in the press bullpen to the left of the VIP seats. "They're taking your picture, and you look like a criminal."

"You sound like my PR lady, Stacy," Jenny said. She swatted Shelly's hand away and repositioned a lock of chestnut hair over her black eye. It had cost an obscene amount of money to get a wig in the exact style and cut of Tori Valentine's hair, but what was money to a quarter-billionaire when you wanted to stick it to your mean stepsister? "Anyway, you haven't even disowned me yet, so you're way ahead of Obaasama."

Old anger rippled over her aunt's face, forcing her to take a calming breath. "Your grandmother didn't disown you. I suppose I should take comfort that you don't listen to your publicist either. It's nice to know it's not personal."

"Aww, Shelly." Jenny rested her head on her aunt's shoulder. "With you, it's always personal."

Shelly gave her a reassuring squeeze. The only downside to winning Dad's fortune was all the attention it brought with it. You couldn't really stay anonymous when you got RJ Valentine's wife arrested for his murder and inherited all his money and the rights to the *Trouble* publishing empire.

She blew on her hands and tucked them into the sleeves of her purple Burberry trench coat. It was dusk, and the temperature was 41 degrees and falling, not the best time to be sitting in folding chairs in the Town Square Park. Silver and gold lights twinkled from the gnarled oak tree branches above. Deputies Mack and Calderon patrolled on horseback, keeping the mass of onlookers outside the VIP area from ruining the foliage. It would be charming if this weren't all Val's doing.

After Dad died, the Valentine Foundation commissioned a statue of him for the park in Town Square. A place for all *Trouble* fans who made their pilgrimages to Blackbird Springs to pay their respects. Val hadn't included Jenny in the planning, so she had no idea what it looked like. Jenny would have the last laugh, though, since Val was stuck on house arrest and couldn't attend.

"Your brother looks nice," said her aunt.

She nodded to the small stage in front of the old City Hall building where her half-brother Jack was sitting in a chair, legs crossed above the knee, wearing a perfectly tailored black suit with a golden tie. He'd spotted her too, those shimmering blue eyes darting away to avoid her smile. Her heart sank. He'd have to forgive her for his mother's arrest eventually.

No Tori up there, though, Jenny noted. Interesting.

The Mayor cleared his throat into the microphone, and everyone settled down.

Jenny's Apple Watch tapped her thrice on the wrist. In the code she and Eliza had worked out, it meant *I'm here*. Since they'd arrived in Blackbird Springs in September, it had begun to mean something more: *I'm with you*. Or perhaps: *I love you*. Somewhere, on one of the roofs surrounding the park, her sister was watching. Jenny tapped three times back in reply.

"Ladies and Gentlemen," the Mayor said, gazing out at the crowd. His body language screamed "anxious," for reasons Jenny couldn't understand until he spoke again. "May I introduce... Valerie Valentine."

Flashbulbs and shutters popped in staccato bursts on her left shoulder. A cacophonous roar of boos and cheers rang out from the crowd as Val took the stage in a brilliant white Vera Wang gown, her chestnut hair swooped to one side like a model. Val would be gorgeous if she didn't smile like someone who'd just smelled a fart. Jenny's lips tightened, twin storms of guilt and rage warring in her gut.

Somehow Val had sweet-talked the judge into letting her out of her penthouse suite at the Crow's Nest hotel to preside over this farce of a dedication. Apparently, His Honorable So-and-So didn't care about jury pools or the message it sent having the Mayor share a stage next to the lady his DA was prosecuting for murder.

Did they believe Val? Did they suspect, with some sixth sense, that Jenny's solution to the mystery was a fake?

She had to fight back, had to show confidence. So she stood up and dramatically stomped off, letting the murmurs and whispers wash over her exit.

"Thank you," said Valerie over the PA speakers behind her. "Thank you to all *true* citizens of Blackbird Springs who came out to remember my husband, Jonathan Valentine, who you knew as RJ."

"They're dragging this bitch on Twitter," said a buxom, raven-haired girl to her friends, watching from behind the VIP ropes. Jenny locked eyes with her for a moment. Her voice was familiar, but Jenny couldn't recall where she'd heard it before. The other teens flanking her snickered and stole glances at Jenny. These girls, Jenny knew: a popular clique from school that she avoided. One of them whispered an insult, and the rest laughed.

Suddenly, she was back in Glendale again, cheeks burning in humiliation from the mean jokes and snide remarks her old classmates would make. This was bullshit. She was rich now. Jenny switched course and headed for Sheriff Lockhart, who was talking to some redhead.

Val continued behind her. "When the Valentine Foundation ordered this piece, we—well, I don't think any of us expected to end up where we are now."

Val stuck out her right leg to show off her ankle bracelet, resting just above her Jimmy Choo pumps. Nervous titters rippled through the VIP section.

"She does wear it better than you, Trouble," said Alicia Aaron, turning away from the Sheriff to face her. Jenny did a double-take, her jaw hanging open at Alicia's new look.

After Jenny won the game, she'd offered the other contestants two percent of the Valentine fortune to smooth over any ill feelings and keep them from asking questions. The money had just cleared, and Alicia, it seemed, had not been frugal with it. Gone were the dumpy skirts, black lipstick, and drab red hair, replaced by what Jenny could only describe as Goth Chic: a black tartan skirt, red corset top, tight leather jacket, and choker necklace with an Ankh pendant dangling from her neck. Since Eliza promised to, Jenny had purchased Alicia a fancy new prosthetic leg, which was apparently so functional that

Alicia could wear her new thigh-high boots over it. She'd gone to a real hairstylist and gotten an undercut and a fresh dye job—a lush red, like a glass of *Ressort Rouge*.

She looked kinda hot, Jenny had to admit.

Jenny made a mental note to go shopping with Dinah ASAP. She couldn't live with Alicia possessing the cuter wardrobe and better hair.

"RJ's books brought happiness to so many girls out there," Val was saying up on stage. "I know he would never want to cause you all any distress. But my husband was *murdered!*"

The word echoed through the park, bringing all side-chatter to a halt. Val's lip quivered as she paused to command the crowd's full attention.

"He was murdered by a coward. Who is still out there, and is *laughing*, because they're getting away with it!" Val let her face flush, selling the righteous anger as she stared directly at Jenny. "And I will not rest until his true killer is brought to justice!"

"Smart," said Alicia. "She doesn't profess her innocence so much as beg the question."

"We already have some promising leads, but we need your help," said Val. "The Valentine Foundation will offer a five million dollar reward for information leading to the capture of the real killer."

Someone whistled. A fresh wave of rumors spread through the audience.

"Fuck me," said Lockhart.

Jenny's heart plummeted. She and Eliza had made good progress with the tarot card, but with a bunch of eager vultures crowding the investigation…

"Interesting gambit," said a cultured voice in her ear. Hamilton Webb, Dad's lawyer—and acting President of Trouble, Inc.—had materialized at her right elbow.

"Is the Valentine Foundation allowed to do that?" Jenny asked, feeling ill.

"Unethical, perhaps, but she is the Foundation President," said Mr. Webb.

"I'd also like to invite you all to the charity festival we'll be throwing right here in downtown Blackbird Springs next month," Val said. "On Valentine's Day, natch. We'll be having a parade, games, and prizes for all. Proceeds will go to Friends of the Library. Now, let's have a look at this wonderful statue."

Val brightened, moving to a large object draped in red velvet. Jack stood up to help with the big reveal.

"By the way," Mr. Webb said, leaning over. "I checked our records for this hotel room you think John was keeping. The only payments we're making to the Crow's Nest are for Val's penthouse, per the will terms, and a conference room now and then for business meetings."

Jenny nodded. If only Eliza had gotten a room number from the Fortune Teller before Jenny knocked her out.

"Of course, your father did go off book from time to time. Even from me."

Val gripped the velvet with both fists. "RJ will always be a part of Blackbird Springs," she said. "If you're ever feeling lost, come have a seat. He loves to chat."

She and Jack pulled away the red velvet to reveal a new park bench. It was built extra long to accommodate a bronze statue taking up a seat on one side. The likeness was uncanny. There was Dad, immortalized exactly to scale in burnished golden-brown metal, crossing his legs, an arm resting on the back of the bench as he turned with his trademark coy smile to the open space next to him.

The crowd erupted in applause. Jenny vomited onto the grass. Nobody seemed to notice except Alicia, who leapt back to save her new boots.

Jenny coughed and spit a few times, her puke steaming in the cold night air as she wiped her mouth. "Hypothetically speaking," she said, turning to Mr. Webb.

He raised an eyebrow.

"Hypothetically. Say Val pays someone off to fix her alibi or something?"

"The evidence you presented precludes that," said Mr. Webb.

"Right, but just say. What if she gets off?" Jenny's throat burned, and not just from the bile.

"There's a contingency," he said tersely, taking off his horn-rimmed glasses and polishing them on his tie.

Already, people were rushing to take selfies with "RJ" on the new park bench.

"What is it?" Jenny asked.

"The game resumes," said Mr. Webb.

"But—what about the money?"

"If the mistake is determined to be in good faith, 90 percent of your inherited assets shall transfer to the new winner, or a trust, if no new winner is confirmed," said Mr. Webb. "This was all in the paperwork you signed."

Fuck. Jenny had already given away 10 percent to Drew, and that was before two percent each to Yvonne Griffin, the Sheriff, and Alicia. A horrifying vision blossomed in Jenny's mind. She and Eliza, forced out of the mansion with the Stranger waiting for them, and millions of dollars in debt to boot.

"But it won't, right?" Mr. Webb raised an eyebrow. "You've got Val in possession of the murder weapon, at the scene of the crime, with no alibi."

"Right." Jenny stared ahead in a daze, barely noticing when Aunt

Shelly found her. Lockhart, still tentative around her aunt since their ugly breakup, quickly busied himself directing traffic, shouting into a megaphone for folks to form a line.

"Let's get you home," Shelly said.

Jenny tapped out a code on her watch. Two taps, then one, then two again. *I need you.*

She was heading with Shelly to a gap in the crowd when something tickled the back of her neck. She spun, glancing around. A *frisson* was erupting in the media pen, reporters pointing at their phones and jabbering at each other in disbelief. As though they could sense her gaze, they suddenly looked up and rushed her way.

"Shit. Come on," said Jenny, trying to find an escape through the throngs of onlookers.

The reporters were sprinting now, only 20 feet away. Jenny spotted Yvonne Griffin, local editor of the *Blackbird Times*, gaining on them with the long-striding closing speed that had earned her an invite to the WNIT at Pepperdine. The press mob was ten feet away, then five—

And then they ran right past Jenny and shoved their phones into Sheriff Lockhart's face.

"Sheriff Lockhart, have you spoken to Campbell Klein yet?!" asked one.

"Do you plan on resigning?" shouted another.

"What? Why?" Lockhart asked, his voice amplified by the megaphone still clutched in his hand.

"Sheriff, do you have any comment?"

"About what?" he said.

"Napa Valley PD just held a press conference," Ms. Griffin said, her face grave. "They're saying Casey Klein's killer has struck again."

Chapter Three

Casey's Walk

RAIN POUNDED ON THE GREENHOUSE ROOF. ELIZA WAS WAITING in the dark next to the secret passageway into Valentine Manor, watching streams of water flow over the transparent glass panels above her. Her sister had made good on her threat to Valerie, hiring a landscaper to renovate the entire conservatory. Gone were the giant ferns, the sickly sweet crimson and black roses, and the oppressive, humid atmosphere. In their place: cherry trees, clusters of bamboo, and a little bed of daisies.

"Whatcha thinking about?" her sister's voice called softly behind her.

"Monterey," Eliza said, still studying the ceiling.

"Really?"

"The water on the glass," said Eliza. "It makes me think of the aquariums. Have you ever gone?"

"No."

"I went once, with Nurse Bennett. We should go sometime."

"That'd be nice," said Jenny. "Maybe after Val buys herself an alibi, and they take the mansion away."

"We're fine," Eliza said, turning away from the glass. "As long as I stay hidden, the frame job on Val is airtight."

"What if someone comes forward? Whoever sent Val that note to meet them here the night of?"

"If they wanted to, they would have done so by now," Eliza said. "Besides, who would believe them? We already have Val on tape trying to pay you off in this very room. She's not credible anymore."

"Then why is the mayor letting her come out and play?" Jenny slumped onto one of the stone benches to sulk.

Eliza had no response to that. It was clear Val was juiced in with the local power brokers, but enough to get away with murder? "Stop it. You'll make us both paranoid. That die is already cast; let's focus on a problem we can solve. Did you get a chance to watch the Napa PD press conference on Casey Klein?"

Jenny yawned. "No, sorry. Shelly made me eat some noodles. Oh—here."

She dug in her pocket and tossed Eliza a box of Pocky. Eliza snorted. "Thanks. So, they found a body in the sloughs. Sarah Ortiz, 13. Been missing for days. Apparently, there's physical evidence that matches the Casey Klein case. They're calling him the 'Hot Springs Hangman,' cause Sarah had a noose around her neck, like Casey."

"Is that their physical evidence?" Jenny frowned. "Anyone can make a noose."

"No, they said it's something else, something indisputable, but they won't reveal exactly what to protect the investigation."

Jenny lay down on the bench, a far off look in her eyes as she ruminated.

Eliza munched on a Pocky stick and tried to recall what she could of the murder. Casey Klein's body wasn't discovered until months after she'd gone missing, with a white rope noose around her neck and a receipt for an oil change in her coat pocket. Cause of death: strangulation. The receipt belonged to a local gardener named Oscar Manuel, who worked two doors down from the Klein home. He had no alibi, and some strands of Casey's hair were found in his truck. Case closed. Except RJ Valentine was sure the police had gotten it wrong. He even talked Blake into disinterring Casey's body, claiming he could prove Oscar Manuel was innocent. But he couldn't.

"Killing little girls is kinda dark for the Stranger," Jenny said. "He was more of a consulting criminal. But he has been quiet for a while. If they're right about the evidence, it can't be the guy they convicted. The gardener. He died in prison a couple years ago."

"The noose was in the will, which means Dad thought it could be a clue to his own killer. Maybe the Stranger wants revenge for Oscar Manuel being wrongfully imprisoned?" Eliza asked.

"Why go after Dad, then?" Jenny shook her head. "He was trying to get him out, right? If they wanted revenge, they'd go after Lockhart."

Sheriff Blake Lockhart, then just a deputy, got the big break in the case when he followed a tip line call and discovered Casey's body in a ditch near Guerneville.

"Unless Dad was onto something, and getting too close," said Eliza. She took the bench opposite Jenny and lay down herself, staring up at the turbulent sky through the glass roof. Like being in the Great Hall at Hogwarts, she thought to herself with a smile. "What do you think? Dig deeper on Casey Klein, hunt for that secret hotel room the Fortune Teller mentioned, or try buying Alicia's heirloom like Drew suggested?"

"Mr. Webb said there's nothing on our books about the room. I was gonna swing by the Crow's Nest tomorrow," said Jenny. She turned onto her side to face Eliza. "There has to be a reason Dad was so convinced Oscar Manuel was innocent, right?"

"We should talk to Penny," said Eliza. "Her mom wrote a book about Casey."

"Lockhart, too. He had to have known Dad's theory."

"*I'll* talk to Blake," Eliza said. "He likes me better." Jenny smirked and gave her the finger. "You should talk to Mason, too. See if he can get us the original police report."

"Already texted him. Why didn't we hear about it in the news?" asked Jenny. "That Sarah Ortiz was missing?"

"Because she was undocumented," Eliza sighed. "Her parents were afraid to report it."

"Fuck. Fuck that!" Jenny sat up, that familiar, reassuring fire in her eyes. "Stranger or no, let's get this bastard."

THE NEXT MORNING, JENNY GOT UP EARLY AND WENT JOGGING WITH Aunt Shelly. Things had been good between them lately, but ever since they moved into the sprawling mansion, it felt like they'd been seeing less and less of each other. Especially now that Shelly was dating Mr. White, the journalism teacher. He was a goober, and the endless string of Boston sports clothing he wore couldn't match Lockhart's tight, form-fitting uniforms, but at least he wasn't using her aunt to spy on Jenny like the Sheriff did.

They'd reached downtown and done a couple laps around the park when Jenny's watch vibrated.

"Okay, ring's closed!" she said, coming to a stop and clutching her knees.

"Coffee?" Shelly asked, panting.

"Hell yes."

They lucked into an open outdoor table at Basque Boulangerie Cafe and got lattes and lemon bars. The mixture of caffeine and steamed milk, cold weather, sugar, exercise, and sweat had Jenny's nerves firing in all the best ways. She felt alert and alive and ready to solve a new mystery.

"You seem better today," Shelly said, a concerned smile behind her cup as she sipped.

"I'm fine," Jenny insisted. "Last night was just… weird."

"If you're having panic attacks again, maybe you should go back on your medication."

"It wasn't a panic attack," said Jenny. "It was just disgust. I hate that statue. Fucking hate it!"

Annoyed cafe patrons turned their way at the commotion. Jenny stared them down, daring anyone to say something.

Shelly studied her with stern scrutiny. "I'm ordering you some Xanax, just in case."

"Fine. Great."

"You're not…" Shelly lowered her voice. "You're not pregnant, are you?"

"What?! No!" Jenny felt her cheeks flush. "First of all, Dinah and I aren't—not that it's your business, but second of all, like, duh, wrong plumbing."

"Okay, jeez," said Shelly. "It's just… I see the way you look at Drew in class sometimes."

Fucking Danger and her horny-ass crush on Drew.

"He's just a friend, oh my god," Jenny said. "You should be happy, you're always telling me I could make friends if I were nicer to people."

"Well, you're making friends, at least."

"I can be nice. Hey, Ojiisama's law firm did immigration stuff, right?" she asked.

"Uh, more corporate law. Trade stuff," said Shelly. "Hah, I was supposed to get a law degree and work there with Dad."

"But didn't you say they worked on visas and stuff too?"

"Sometimes. Pro bono. Why?"

"The family of that girl they found, they might have some trouble," said Jenny. "Would it be okay if I had Mr. Webb contact the firm to help?"

Shelly cocked her head, pleasantly surprised. "That would be nice, yes. More philanthropy, less troublemaking. Agreed?"

"I'm turning over a new leaf," Jenny smiled sweetly.

Shelly tossed her cup in the trash and groaned, stretching down to touch her toes. "The run back is always worse."

"You go on, I'm meeting Penny," said Jenny.

"Be home before dark," Shelly said. "And be smart. That girl they found, she wasn't much younger than you."

"Don't worry." Jenny withdrew a collapsible riot baton from her purse, its weight a comfort in hand. "I'm not defenseless."

PENNY WASN'T EXPECTING HER FOR AN HOUR, SO JENNY HEADED OVER to the Crow's Nest hotel. She figured a bribe of $100 ought to get her a look at the room bookings, but the Maître D' was surprisingly uptight.

"Okay, how about a thousand?" Jenny countered when he sniffed at her initial offer.

"Young lady!"

"Come on, you know who I am, don't you?" she asked. "Trouble? Girl Detective?"

The Maître D' sneered.

"Okay, that sounds douchey, but you knew my dad, right? I just need to know if he kept a room here."

"The Crow's Nest takes the privacy of our guests very seriously," he said, and even pronounced the priv in privacy like shiv, so he def meant business. "We would only disclose a roster of our current lessees to actual law enforcement, not girl detectives."

"So… you're saying the room he kept is still being leased?" she guessed.

His ears turned bright red, and he called for security. In the end, the best Jenny could get from him was a suite on the fourth floor, and only after getting Mr. Webb to call and authorize it, since they wouldn't book to a minor. It was no penthouse suite like where Jack and Val lived, but it got her access to the building to snoop around, and it wouldn't hurt to have a safe house in town.

After a quick shower, Jenny was back in Town Square, taking a moment to stroll through the park and appreciate her hometown. The air was crisp with the scent of pine and chimney fires. She wished she could visit the ducks, but they'd gone south for the winter. Their loss. LA could only dream of smelling this good.

At the curb, the latest issue in the Blackbird Times newspaper rack screamed, "KLEIN KILLER RETURNS?" Jenny stopped to take a photo, switching her Instagram to the official Trouble account. It had taken a lot of begging and convincing of Stacy in PR to get access, and she was under strict orders to only publish wholesome *Trouble* content. She applied a filter to the headline photo and added a hashtag.

#OnIt

It was *Trouble*-related. More or less.

"This is bullshit," said a man nearby.

Jenny looked up to see Officer Peña writing a parking ticket for a white Hyundai economy car. The driver looked young, with a short-sleeve button-up shirt and black frame glasses.

"I've been parking there all week," he said in a hoarse voice.

"Emergency street cleaning," Peña said. "All the residents got emailed."

"I don't live here," he whined.

Peña shrugged, hiding a grin. "Talk to the Sheriff."

The man seethed—until he saw Jenny approaching. "Hey! Are you Jennifer Valentine? I need to talk to—"

"She's a minor," Peña said, stepping between them.

"Yeah, piss off, Warby Parker." Jenny brandished her baton.

That sent him packing. She beamed at Officer Peña.

"I've got more of these if you don't behave," Peña remarked to Jenny, tapping her ticket pad.

"Aww, I was hoping for handcuffs," said Jenny with a wink. Officer Peña cut her hair short recently, and Jenny had maybe developed a tiny crush on her.

"What do you want?" Peña asked, ignoring the flirtation behind her mirrored aviators.

"Who was that?"

Peña glanced over her shoulder and said, "Says he's a reporter."

"Why did you lie about the street cleaning?" Jenny asked.

"Above my pay grade," Peña said. "Like I told him, take it up with Lockhart."

"Hmm. What can you tell me about Casey Klein?" asked Jenny.

"Nothing. Stay out of it."

"Have you ever had to fire that gun?"

"Move it along, Miss Valentine."

"Fine, fine. I like your new haircut," Jenny called back with a grin as she ran off.

WOODHALL ELEMENTARY SCHOOL WAS ABOUT A HALF-MILE FROM Blackbird Springs Academy, in the priciest part of town. Dinah lived right down the street. The school seemed tiny compared to the high school, the few buildings dwarfed by the 12-foot-high metal fence that surrounded the campus. Jenny wondered if the fence was there 13 years ago when Casey Klein went missing. Or was it the knee-jerk response of a frightened community to a shocking murder in their midst?

She couldn't blame them. She'd ordered a ton of security improvements after the Stranger broke into Valentine Manor and defaced the Big Board last fall.

"Since when are you in the True Crime Club?" Penny Griffin asked, warily glancing around as she walked up.

Penny was at least the second smartest in their year, a friend of Drew's, her brother Jack's girlfriend, and deeply mistrusting of Jenny.

"Right. About that."

Penny groaned. "There is no True Crime Club meetup today, is there?"

"No, but please don't go," Jenny said. "Look, I know Jack is angry with me—"

"He's not the only one," Penny said sharply, glaring down at her. She was much taller than Jenny, her high-knotted, braided ponytail only increasing the effect.

"Fair. All I can say is I'm sorry. I shouldn't have kept you in the dark about that call to Val," said Jenny. Part of her frame job on Val was getting her evil stepmother to show up at a storage locker, which Penny facilitated with a fake phone call, not knowing Jenny's true intention. It wouldn't have been so awkward if Jack hadn't stubbornly refused to believe his mother was guilty. Penny was forced to choose between her new boyfriend Jack, and the sketchiest girl in school. Jenny couldn't blame her, really. "I'm still getting used to not working alone, but that's on me. Mea culpa and shit."

"And shit."

"I mean, your mom and my dad were friends. It feels like we should be too."

Penny sighed. "I assume that you didn't just call me here to apologize? Which I do appreciate, by the way."

"I did not," Jenny said.

"You really think you can solve it?"

"With your help? Maybe."

It was exactly the sort of enticement that Penny couldn't resist. Despite claiming that she wasn't a *Trouble* fan, Penny clearly loved a good mystery.

"Okay, I'll bite," said Penny. "But no lies or games—and keep my boy Drew out of harm's way this time."

"Drew's fine, he likes danger," Jenny said, smirking to herself.

"He's going through a midlife crisis," said Penny.

"What do you mean?"

She snorted. "You'll see soon enough. I don't want to ruin it. Anyway, what do you want to know?"

"I want to return to the scene of the crime," said Jenny.

"Hmm. Sure." Penny clicked her heel, pivoting to face the elementary school. "Flashback to April 3rd, 13 years ago. At 3:03 PM, the bell rings, and Casey Klein leaves school, heading east on MacArthur Street. She is, by all reports, walking alone."

Penny walked east. Jenny followed, and together they retraced the last steps of a doomed little blonde girl.

"You sound like you've done this before," Jenny said.

"'Casey's Walk' is sort of a true-crime ritual," Penny said. She squared her shoulders, beaming with pride. "It's what mom named her book."

Jenny looked to her right and caught her breath. They were passing

Black Rock Cemetery.

"Oh, sorry," said Penny. "I guess he's in there."

She placed a hand on Jenny's shoulder. Jenny patted it, grateful, and nodded. "Casey's in there too, right? Andy and Dave said so."

"Do you want to go see?"

Jenny shivered. "No."

They walked past the cemetery in silence.

"I wonder if she whistled," Jenny said.

They arrived at an intersection.

"At approximately 3:10 PM, Jason Fullmore, a classmate, remembers seeing Casey turn right, as she typically would, heading home." Penny led them south down Fifth Street.

They passed by custom houses that managed to seem modest and decadent at the same time. None had more than three or four bedrooms, but Jenny knew, from studying Zillow, that each of these properties went for over $1 million, easy.

"Another neighbor, Claudia Wright, recalls seeing Casey walk by, out her kitchen window, at about 3:15 PM." Penny pointed out a house on the corner of Pear Tree Court. "So far, pretty normal, right?"

"Mmhmm," Jenny said, checking her watch. They'd been walking for only a few minutes.

"Well, depending on what theory you subscribe to, that could be about to change."

They walked on, soon making another right at the next street, Eastin Drive. A wide median forked the exit from Eastin to Fifth here, with a big, gnarled oak tree growing between the left and right lanes. Fancy decorative masonry on either side of Eastin identified this street as an especially ritzy neighborhood. All the houses were vaguely gothic, with tall, vertical windows and steep, slanted roofs recalling Blackbird Springs's Germanic roots. Each lawn was immaculate, every building made of stone.

"Damn. What did Casey's parents do for a living?" Jenny asked.

"Reed Klein was a C-suite exec at some financial firm in the City," said Penny. "Campbell didn't really work then. She was a 'photographer,' the way rich white ladies do."

She stopped them in front of a broad one-story house made of brick.

"Casey is last seen here," said Penny. "Brett Klinger, a high school student, saw her walking by as he parked his car. According to him—and this is where things get weird—it was 2:18 PM."

"Hmm," said Jenny. "That doesn't seem possible."

"Exactly," said Penny. "The most obvious explanation: April 3rd was the day after Daylight Savings. He probably forgot to reset the clock in his car. But you'd better believe there are a lot of theories online about that phantom hour."

They continued down Eastin, turning left at the next opportunity. The house on the corner here was massive, wrapping all the way around the turn in the road. There were two driveways—and between them, a row of topiary sculptures.

"They say these were Oscar Manuel's specialty," said Penny, pointing to the hedges carved to resemble penguins and raccoons.

"Which means that Casey's house…" Jenny leaned out, looking ahead.

"Yep."

They passed another sprawling one-story castle and arrived at a slightly less resplendent house on the corner of Eastin and Denmark Street.

"The Klein house," said Penny.

"Do the parents still live here?" Jenny asked.

"No."

Jenny followed the sidewalk around the corner to get a look at the front entrance. "So somewhere between Brett Klinger's house and here is the scene of the crime." She glanced around. The neighborhood was silent and placid, though she couldn't shake the sensation that she was being watched. "Not a lot of foot traffic or cars. Big lawns, houses set way back from the road. If ever there was a place you could disappear in broad daylight, I guess this is it."

"Casey normally made it home by 3:30 PM at the latest," said Penny. "Her mom was inside, developing photos in the darkroom. At 3:25 PM, she came out here to wait for Casey, as she always did. But Casey never showed up."

"Does the dad have an alibi?"

Penny nodded. "At work in SoMa. Many witnesses. Oscar Manuel claims to have been hiking up in the foothills, but he was alone, and no one can vouch for his whereabouts."

"My dad thought he didn't do it," said Jenny.

"Sometimes, the simplest explanation really is the best one," said Penny. "I'll be real, this isn't the most popular of true crime murders. Other than the Daylight Savings Time wrinkle, there's not much to work with. Mom's book never sold well. 'The gardener did it,' just isn't scary enough."

"Except now the police are saying the killer struck again," said Jenny.

"The smart money says it's a copycat."

"Maybe," said Jenny. What would Dad have seen that she was missing? She walked to the edge of Casey's old house. Down Denmark Street, the land was more rural, with fewer houses, open fields, and rows of grapevines. "To just disappear like that, she probably knew her abductor. Trusted them. Would she have trusted Oscar Manuel?"

Penny shrugged. "Who knows? Let's talk about my fee."

"What fee?"

"For giving you this tour," Penny said. "Mom wants an interview. Or at least a few good quotes."

"Yeah, sure," Jenny said distantly. Something had caught her eye on the bright sidewalk. She knelt down to confirm that her eyes were not mistaken: it was the butt of a clove cigarette with black lipstick on the tip. Alicia Aaron's brand.

"What is it?" Penny asked.

She palmed the cigarette butt. "Nothing. Yeah, I'll email your mom. But um… On a scale of one to ten, how mad would you say Jack still is with me?"

"Like a six?" Penny bit her lip. "The thing is—don't tell him I told you this—he's only good at holding grudges if you let him. He hates confrontation. If you can get him talking, I think he'll come around."

Jenny hoped so. Never mind the cops, she wasn't the only heir on this case. It was time for baby brother to stop sulking and join the family business.

Chapter Four

Warmer

A T SEVEN STORIES, THE CROW'S NEST WAS THE TALLEST BUILDING in the city. Quite high enough for Jenny as she rode up to the penthouse in a gaudy, gold and glass elevator, pointedly avoiding the view out the windows. Even accessing this floor required a keycard, but it turned out Jenny and one of the maids had a mutual friend named Benjamin Franklin.

The elevator car glided silently to a stop, and the door chimed as it opened. Jenny crossed the hallway to the door marked **PH**, and knocked. Mere seconds later, the door swung open, and she found herself face to face with her half-brother Jack. They shared their father's razor-sharp cheekbones, but he had nearly a foot in height on her. Right now he was shirtless, wearing workout shorts and Beats wireless earbuds. She must have caught him on the way to the gym. He didn't seem happy to see her.

"Hi, Jack," she said softly.

He stared at her with his piercing blue eyes for a good 10 seconds before muttering, "I'll call you back," and tapping one of his earbuds. "What do you want?"

"Is Tori here?" she asked, hoping it would annoy Jack if she wasn't here to see him.

"No."

"Junior, who is it?" called his mother's voice from inside. Jenny's eyes narrowed.

"Just the towel service," he replied, still glaring at Jenny. "I'm going to the gym."

Jack reached to the side, grabbing a compression shirt, and stepped out into the hall. Since he wasn't actively shunning her, Jenny followed along as he pulled on his shirt and led them to the elevator.

"How've you been?" she asked, again averting her eyes from the view.

"You mean since you kicked me out of my house and had my mother arrested?"

He jabbed angrily at the button for the second floor.

"It seems like you're both doing just fine for yourselves," Jenny said, rolling her eyes. "Have you ever even made your own bed a day in your life?"

"Not that it's relevant, but yes," he said, unable to stop his lip from curling. "Housekeeping only comes once a week for residents here."

"Oh shit, I didn't realize I was standing next to the salt of the fucking earth." A lightbulb flickered. "What day does the maid come?"

"Monday. That's not the point. Mom could go to jail for life!"

"Only if she's guilty," said Jenny.

"She's not. She would never do that to Dad."

"Are you sure?" Jenny asked. "Cause I never got the impression—"

"That's right, you didn't," he snapped at her. "You don't have any impression of my mom and dad, because you didn't know them!"

The door chimed and rolled open.

"Only because your mother wouldn't let him see me!" she yelled, all her old wounds reopening.

"Uh oh," said a voice. It was that reporter in the Warby Parker glasses from earlier. He was smirking at them in front of the elevator door. "Do I detect a bit of sibling rivalry amongst the Valentine Clan?"

"Shut up!" they both yelled to him in unison. The reporter recoiled, and Jenny swore she detected the barest hint of an RJ smile at the corners of Jack's mouth. They walked in silence until the reporter was out of sight.

"Look, I didn't come here to fight. Have you seriously not seen Tori?" Jenny asked.

He shook his head and guided them into the hotel health club, grabbing towels from the attendant.

"Come on, you can spot me."

Jenny followed him to the free weights, watching in fascination as her brother put a couple big disc plates on either side of the bench press bar and sat down.

"I'm not gonna be able to lift this if you drop it," she said, feeling suddenly nervous. It felt like Jack had finally cracked the door open for her a tiny bit, and she didn't want to screw it up.

"You won't have to. You're just there to help."

He began dipping and lifting the bench press bar with smooth, easy motions.

"Shouldn't Mason be here to spot you?" Jenny asked. Mason Lockhart, the Sheriff's son, was the closest thing her brother had to a friend.

Jack let out a heavy exhale, grimacing, and did another rep.

"He's busy with Drew today," said Jack.

Jenny's eyes narrowed. "Doing what?"

"Drew didn't tell you?" he asked.

"No. Tell me what?"

Another rep.

"He and Mason bought guitars with the game money. They're forming a band."

Jenny laughed so hard she almost fell over.

"Hey, come on!" Jack barked at her, struggling with his last rep. Jenny recovered enough to help him re-rack the bar.

"Sorry. Sorry."

"Can you please talk Drew out of this?" Jack pleaded. "I get douche chills every time Mason sings."

"*He's* the singer?!"

Jack nodded in pain as he sat up and wiped off the bench.

"Let's be real, Drew's got bass player written all over him," said Jack.

Jenny tried to picture it and simply could not. She giggled some more.

"Your turn," said Jack, nodding to the bench.

"There's no way I can lift that," she said, shaking her head.

"Then we'll take some off," he said. "Come on, Valentine, you gotta do more than jog if you want to get cut."

So they swapped the heavy weights out for a couple light ones, and Jenny did her best not to embarrass herself.

"I hope you don't mind that I took your old room," she said between reps.

"Whatever," he said, his eyes hardening a bit. "I guess Dinah will be used to it."

"Uhh." Jenny's face burned.

"Jesus— Not like that!" Jack's face was reddening too. They'd never really acknowledged that Jenny was dating his ex until now. "I didn't mean—"

"Change of subject! Change of subject!" Jenny shouted.

"Yes, please!"

"Casey Klein!" Jenny said, willing her brain to forget the last 10 seconds. "Did Dad ever tell you about his theory on that case?"

Jack shook his head. "Why are you still trying to solve the heirloom clues?"

"It's my nature," she said, doing another rep. "Any chance I could buy that Onyx Blackbird statue off you?"

"No."

"What about Tori?" she asked, pausing with the bar at her chest to rest. "Do you think Dad might have shared his theory with her?"

"Maybe. Probably. Those two were always thick as thieves."

"You really don't know how to reach her?" Jenny pushed hard to lift the bar back onto the rack and let out an exhausted breath. "Gimme something I can work with, Junior, or I'll tell Drew you want to play the drums."

Jack's nostrils flared at the suggestion, but he rubbed his chin, thinking. "Tori used to volunteer at the local no-kill shelter," he said. "She might still."

"See, I knew you weren't useless." Jenny stood up and wiped down the bench.

"You know Casey is kind of a sore subject with my sister, right?"

"She is? Why?" asked Jenny.

He bit his lip, hesitating. "I guess you wouldn't have known. Casey Klein was Tori's best friend."

MONTHS AS TROUBLE'S UNDERSTUDY HAD TAUGHT ELIZA THAT BEING a good Girl Detective meant waiting around for hours and hours. Waiting and watching closely.

It was getting late. She had perched herself on the roof of the Poison Pen, a spot she'd discovered during Jenny's brief stint as a stock girl at the bookstore. Back in Auburn, when Nurse Bennet was still around, Eliza would sneak out at night to climb the water tower behind their house. She enjoyed being up high—not like Trouble, who was afraid of heights and refused to admit it.

All the restaurants had closed; the streets were vacant. Soft jazz trickled up from hidden speakers. Eliza imagined she was in Cittàgazze, alone in a town abandoned by the grown-ups. Blake's Police Tahoe was still parked out in front of the station; he had to leave sooner or later. Sooner, she hoped. The temperature was about to drop below freezing.

Finally, the station lights switched off, and Eliza made her move, shoving the camera in her knapsack, sliding down the fire escape behind the building, and hurrying down a side alley. She'd timed it perfectly. Blake was just getting into his Tahoe when she reached the sidewalk in front of the station.

She made a dash for it; the engine started; Eliza yanked open the passenger door and hopped right in.

"What the—" Blake was about to go for his pistol, so Eliza raised her hands. Recognition dawned on his face, and she belatedly remembered that she was in disguise, wearing a dirty blonde wig, pulled back in a ponytail.

"You," said the Sheriff, his handsome face bristling with a familiar exasperation. "What are you doing? You shouldn't be out after dark."

"You need a shave," Eliza said, frowning at his stubble. Now that she noticed it, his whole face looked worn, tired. She thought she detected the sour tang of alcohol on his lips.

"Noted," he said. "Can I help you?"

"Casey Klein."

"No. Out!"

"I didn't even ask you anything yet!"

"We are not having this discussion," Blake said, putting the car back in park and killing the engine.

"Drive me home, at least," she offered, pulling on her seat belt. "You wouldn't want me out alone at night with a killer on the loose, would you?"

"Fine," he grunted and started the engine again. Eliza allowed a satisfied smile as he put the truck in gear and left the curb. "For a price."

"You already got your two percent."

"Tell me how you found that Fortune Teller when I have Declan's tarot card locked up in evidence."

Eliza laughed. "Do you?"

Blake's jaw clenched. "Impossible. You couldn't have gotten in there."

"Of course not. That would be illegal." Unbeknownst to Blake, his son Mason had borrowed the card for Jenny. She'd discovered a secret about Mason last fall at his cabin. A secret big enough that Mason would use his dad's access to steal evidence if it kept her quiet, making him a handy, if unreliable ally. But in the meantime, the Sheriff's scowl demanded an answer. "I have an excellent memory. Your turn. What's with your cops shaking down that reporter in town?"

"That guy? Habitual line-stepper," he said. "Stepped one time too many. Take care to learn from his mistake."

Eliza chewed her lip, annoyed. They turned onto Highway 12 toward the mansion.

"Speaking of mistakes, how'd RJ talk you into digging up Casey's corpse? What was his theory?"

"Why don't you ask him," Blake said with an unkind smile.

"Fuck you," said Eliza, her temper flaring. "I'm trying to help!"

"I don't need your help!" he shouted at her. "This is not a game! You got extremely lucky at Pinefall. You should probably be dead. If I told you the things Oscar Manuel did to that girl's body, you'd have nightmares for a week!"

Tires screeched as he took the turn onto Cellar Drive much too fast. Somehow, he adjusted the steering wheel in time to keep them on the road.

"You think I don't already have nightmares?" Eliza screamed back at him. "What if he comes for me next? I need to know what I'm up against."

"He's dead. Besides, you're not his type," Blake said. "And yes, I mean that in all the awful ways you think—though you might want to take that wig off."

Eliza swallowed her reply, repulsed.

"And if I find out you're harassing Oscar's mother, so help me I'll—"

"Look out!" Eliza shouted.

Blake slammed on the breaks.

Up ahead, before the gates to the mansion, something was lying in the road.

"What the—"

"Quiet," Blake ordered. He flipped on the spotlight mounted on his side mirror and aimed it at sprawled form.

It was a young girl, lying prone, with a white noose around her neck.

THE GIRL'S DIRTY BLONDE HAIR RIPPLED LIGHTLY IN THE NIGHT breeze. Her head was turned away, hiding her face. There was no blood that Eliza could see in the harsh glare of the spotlight. Her skin was so pale.

"Is this a prank?" Blake asked, his face deadly serious. "Did you set this up?"

"No," Eliza whispered.

Blake eased his door open, one hand on the holster of his service pistol. "Stay here."

"Hell no," said Eliza, unbuckling her seat belt.

He didn't bother to argue, drifting closer to the body with careful, cautious steps. Eliza followed, moving behind him and checking their flank. All she could see was Blake's Tahoe and the rustling leaves of the grapevines that lined the road to the mansion.

"Are you kidding me?" Blake said. Eliza turned to find him kneeling by the body. He reached out for the head, rotating it—

"Don't," she said, feeling sick.

He didn't listen, twisting the face around to stare at Eliza with lifeless eyes and frozen alabaster skin. Eliza frowned. The eyes were *too* lifeless, the skin *too* smooth.

"It's a doll," she said, realization dawning. Eliza knelt next to the figure. There was a note pinned to the doll's dress.

You're getting warmer

"I ought to arrest you," Blake said quietly.

"Wait! I didn't do this!" She was sure Jenny would not have either. She spun around, scanning the vineyards.

"So maybe Drew or Penny did," he said, stalking back to his truck. "I know how you work."

"Where are you going?"

"Home," he snarled. "And the next time you pull some shit like this, I'll charge you with obstruction of justice." He slammed the door and started the engine.

"What about me?" Eliza called, rushing back to the passenger side.

"You can walk!" he shouted from inside the cabin. He gunned it in reverse, spinning out as he flipped the car around to point south, and tore down the long driveway back to Cellar Drive.

In a matter of seconds, she was alone again before the Valentine Manor gates. Alone, save for the doll body in the road. A gust of wind blew up, making Eliza shiver. In the distance, she could hear the train whistle as it passed. She was on the wrong side of the gate to be lingering. She tried not to let her imagination run wild and send her into a panic as she knelt to lift the surprisingly heavy doll over her shoulder. The noose rope trailed behind her, slapping the back of her legs as she hustled to the gate keypad.

After the Stranger infiltrated the mansion to leave his **KiLLROY WAS HERE** threat on the big board in the study, Jenny had upgraded the security on the mansion. The fence was electrified, motion sensors blanketed the grounds, and there was a night watchman on duty. This made it trickier for Eliza to get in and out of the mansion from the treehouse, but would theoretically keep the Stranger out too.

This doll had to be his work. Even if he didn't kill Casey Klein, he wanted them on the case. He did this in the books sometimes. Leaving sinister little clues to prod Trouble in the right direction, lording his knowledge over her. It's why some fans theorized that the Stranger was actually Trouble's dad, helping his daughter solve the mysteries. Jenny did not subscribe to this theory on principle. Eliza thought it had too many holes to stand up, and RJ was a meticulous plotter.

Once inside the gates, she followed a memorized path through the vines and then across the grass field to the east. Jenny paid the security contractor extra to leave holes in the motion sensor coverage. This string of dead spots led her to a small side gate through the fence on the west. From there, she headed for the copse of oak trees where her treehouse awaited. Eliza popped in her AirPods and called Jenny as she made the trek.

"How'd it go?" her sister asked.

"Not great, Trouble," Eliza said.

She relayed the events of the drive with Blake and the doll waiting for her at the gates.

"The Stranger wants us on the Casey Klein case," said Jenny over the phone. "Good."

"Is it?" Eliza had arrived at the treehouse. Rather than climb the ladder, she walked to a nearby fire pit. Leaning over, she dumped the doll in, grateful to be free of the weight.

"We did the tarot card next because it seemed like maybe the Stranger was trying to keep us away from that clue," Jenny said. "But that turned out to be a total bust. So maybe he wants us following the right clue instead of the wrong one."

"I wouldn't count on the Stranger for help," said Eliza, fishing out a bottle of lighter fluid from a stash of supplies.

"I'm not," said Jenny. "But he's playing the game as much as we are. It's our move now."

Eliza sprayed lighter fluid all over the doll, tossing the bottle into the fire pit when it was empty. "Blake slipped up. He said not to harass Oscar Manuel's mother."

"Oh, I didn't even think of that," said Jenny. "Dad might have told her his theory if he thought Oscar was innocent."

"Yep." Eliza used her zippo to light a cigarette she'd been saving all day.

"Are you smoking? I thought we agreed," Jenny admonished in her ears.

"No, I quit," Eliza lied. Her sister grumbled. "I swear!"

"When are you coming in? We need to plan our outfits."

Eliza took a long drag, savoring the feeling of the smoke filling up her lungs. She really had quit, more or less. A single cigarette didn't count, and she needed something to take the edge off after finding that doll. There was an idea that wormed its way into her brain sometimes if she didn't fight it. That this was Trouble's story, not hers. That she was the expendable one.

"Okay," she exhaled, willing her anxiety to drift away on her smoky breath. She tossed the lit cigarette into the fire pit. In a moment, flames spread lazily over the doll, following the sprays of lighter fluid. "I'll be right in."

Chapter Five

The Ghostwriter

IT RARELY SNOWED IN BLACKBIRD SPRINGS, BUT ON MONDAY morning, it hailed. Jenny was delighted and showed it by greeting Dinah with a snowball. She wasn't expecting her aim to be quite so good, or Dinah to be caught completely flat-footed and not duck. So she kinda nailed her full in the face.

"I'm sorry!" Jenny pleaded as Dinah drove them both to school, her girlfriend's demeanor gone as icy as the weather. "I've never seen it hail before."

"If I get a bruise…" Dinah seethed. The right side of her heart-shaped face already looked a bit puffy.

"Then we'll match," said Jenny, still sporting a fading black eye of her own. "And everyone will know you're mine."

She leaned over and smooched her girlfriend on the forehead. 1,075. Dinah only stared ahead at the stoplight, her jaw set in displeasure, and Jenny feared she'd really messed up. But when she tried to lean back into her own seat, Dinah grabbed the back of Jenny's neck and devoured her mouth in a glorious kiss. Jenny savored the playful rovings of Dinah's tongue, the taste of her cinnamon lip balm—

A car horn honked behind them.

Dinah pulled away, wiping her lips with hungry satisfaction. "I missed you this weekend. What number was that?"

"1,076," Jenny said, her toes curling, barely hearing Dinah tease her for still counting kisses.

They drove on, Jenny in a daze until Dinah parked in a spot right at the front of the lot. It was reserved for the Student of the Month, an honor that Dinah had won for the second time this school year. Pulling up right next to them—in a disabled spot—was a lifted jeep: Mason. He could park there because he was the sheriff's son, and thus, immune to parking tickets.

Everyone piled out. Drew was riding shotgun with Mason, with Jack and Penny in the backseat.

"Sup, scissor sisters," said Mason, leering at them. Penny and Drew both glared. Jack grimaced. Thunder rumbled in the distance.

"You anger the gods, Mason," said Dinah.

"What's wrong with your face?" he replied.

Dinah shot a told-you-so glare at Jenny.

"Guys, it's too early for this," said Jack, yawning behind his Wayfarers.

"You need to get to bed on time," Penny said, snuggling up to her boyfriend.

"Hey, so who's got English first period?" said Drew, desperate to change the subject. He'd long harbored a crush on Penny, his childhood BFF. They dated for like a day before she called it off. He claimed he was cool with Penny and Jack going out, but Jenny could tell it bugged him.

"Mine's second period," said Penny. "Mr. Hooke."

"Same," said Jenny.

"Oh, me too," Dinah smiled.

"Is Mr. Hooke cool?" Jenny asked.

"I was his TA freshman year," said Dinah. "He's all right. I mean, he's read *Twilight*, and not just to make fun of it. He tries."

The boys all had English first period.

"Great, total sausage fest," said Mason.

HONK!

They were all interrupted by a gunmetal Ford Mustang laying on the horn behind Mason's jeep. Alicia Aaron was behind the wheel, glaring at them.

"She does have a better claim to the disabled spot than you do, Mace," Jack said.

"Fine! Jeez! I guess *I'm* the asshole!" Mason stomped over to his jeep and got in, barely giving Alicia time to move out of the way before he backed out and sped off to find another spot in the student parking lot.

"A Mustang, how basic," said a voice behind Jenny. She turned to see a clique of girls in designer brands, clutching Starbucks cups in their manicured hands.

"Americans are so embarrassing," said their leader, a girl with wavy, black hair and what was clearly an American accent. "In Paris, owning a car is, like, so gauche."

These were the girls from the statue ceremony the other night. A brunette with sanguine, dewy cheeks, and alert eyes seemed to be the second-in-command, flanked by a copper-skinned beauty with tight curls and a freckle-faced girl with red hair.

"Meghan, you're back, what a treat," said Dinah, smiling without a hint of kindness. "How was Europe?"

"Très magnifique. Way better than this dump," said the raven-haired girl who must be Meghan.

Drew and Penny exchanged nonplussed glances.

"Did you visit the Louvre?" Jenny asked though she didn't really care. It was back again, that feeling like she knew this girl Meghan from somewhere.

"Pssh, museums are for tourists," she said. Her posse laughed.

"You *were* a tourist," said Alicia, limping up.

"I was a student," Meghan snapped. "In Paris, if you're looking for real culture, you go to Marais." She turned to appraise Jenny with a critical eye. "Damn, Jack, I'd heard Dinah traded in her Valentine for this year's model, but I guess I figured she'd be…"

"Prettier?" offered the brunette.

"Taller," said Meghan. "The heart wants what it wants, I guess," she added with a liar's smile.

"You must be Meghan May," said Jenny, clutching Dinah's hand in support. She turned to the other girls. "And her Bitchy Brigade. Right?"

Meghan sneered. The brunette's face turned bright red. Drew covered his mouth to hide a smile.

"No one calls them that to their faces," Penny whispered.

"Très déclassé, Valentine," said Jack.

"You just made yourself an enemy," said the girl with the ebony ringlets.

"Four enemies," said the redhead.

"My enemies tend not to last long," said Jenny.

Meghan stepped closer. "Yeah?"

Dinah gave her a warning squeeze. Mason was giving her a weird, worried look. Jenny closed her eyes, forcing herself to relax.

"Sorry," she said. "I didn't realize that wasn't a nickname you self-applied."

"We prefer the 'Slay Squad,'" Meghan hissed.

"Yas queen," Drew deadpanned.

"You must tell me all about Europe sometime," said Jenny. "I hear we might go there for the class trip this summer."

The bell saved Meghan from having to reply. Her posse all twirled on their heels and marched into school.

"Do I even want to know?" Dinah muttered in Jenny's ear. Her hot breath on Jenny's neck snapped Jenny back into the present. She rubbed the wrist she'd broken a few months back.

"I feel like I know her from somewhere."

First period for Jenny meant American History with Mrs. Cortez. Jenny yawned through the usual syllabus-reading and ice-breakers, already making a mental note to let Danger take the wheel on this class. Then it was off to English with Mr. Hooke, one door down from the Journalism room. Jenny finally got to share a class with Dinah, but on the downside, the whole Bitchy Brigade was in this class too.

During roll, Jenny learned the names of Meghan's clique and looked them up. Charlie Zaleska, the brunette, had a semi-popular makeup tutorial channel on YouTube, which explained her gorgeous skin. Freckle Face Lily Geist posted lots of pictures of her dog and her cleavage and gave Jenny a real hanger-on vibe. The black girl, Shani Wolf, had done a little modeling—or at least paid for a photoshoot. Her parents had high finance jobs in the City. Whatever. They could have their dumb squad, Jenny would just ignore them.

Or so she thought until she felt a sharp sting in her back, through the purple wool sweater she was wearing.

"Ow!" She turned around to see Charlie giving her an evil grin, the pen she'd just poked Jenny with between her teeth. "Do you mind?"

"What?" Charlie said, feigning innocence.

"Cut it out, Charlie," Dinah whispered.

The rest of the Bitchy Brigade giggled. "So protective," said Shani.

Jenny took a deep breath and tried not to lose her shit, focusing on what the teacher was saying for once. Mr. Hooke was stroking his bushy red beard—the only hair on his head—and was talking about the two valedictorian hopefuls in his class, Penny and Dinah. He was expecting great things on today's assignment: they were to complete a one-page essay about their favorite book before class ended.

"To be clear," he said, "I'm not looking for you to impress me with your literary taste. This is about embracing your passion and expressing it on the page. In other words, anyone who claims *The Great Gatsby* is getting an F."

"Is it all right if I do mine in French?" Meghan May asked.

"Is this French class, Miss May?" Mr. Hooke replied in a tone that stopped just short of annoyance.

Everyone snickered.

"I'm particularly interested to find out what book *you* pick, Miss Valentine." Mr. Hooke turned to her now. "My daughter's an enormous fan. Nearly choked on her cornflakes this morning when I told her you'd be in my class this semester."

Everyone laughed. Jenny smiled, inwardly cursing her new English teacher. She immediately sensed that the Bitchy Brigade would never let her hear the end of it if they found out she picked a *Trouble* book. Fine. Dinah had given her a copy of *The Miseducation of Cameron Post* for Christmas, and she'd read most of it. Well, some of it, at least.

She hunkered down to write, trying to recall enough details to fill a page. Charlie poked her again. She ignored it, peaking at Dinah's paper instead. She'd picked *Pride and Prejudice* because her girlfriend was classy like that. Jenny pulled out her phone under her desk and surreptitiously googled the wiki page for *The Miseducation of Cameron*

Post. She tapped through some image galleries; it was hard to stay focused. With everyone quietly writing, she could just make out Mr. White teaching the Inverted Pyramid in his journalism class next door. Most important, to least. Her mind kept drifting to Casey Klein. Walking home from school one minute, bound and gagged in Oscar Manuel's truck the next.

What was the most important detail there? The receipt in Casey's pocket? The place where she went missing? The timing? If Tori was her best friend, could she have provided Dad with some critical detail that figured into his theory?

"Pencils down," said Mr. Hooke.

Jenny stared down at her paper. It was a mess of vague statements and half-baked thoughts about the lesbian teen experience. She grimaced and prayed Mr. Hooke wasn't a harsh grader. He moved down the aisle, collecting papers. Jenny's thoughts turned to lunch. Her watch tapped her with an alert. She hoped it was burrito day. Not that this place could match a good LA taqueria, but—

A shiver ran down her spine. Dinah's phone was buzzing too; she could hear it. And Charlie's behind her. And Penny's... Half her classmates were pulling out their phones, frowning.

"Come on, girls, no phones during class, you know the rules," said Mr. Hooke. "You can wait one more minute for the bell."

Someone snorted. Murmurs of laughter rose around her.

"Wow, uh hey, Mr. Hooke, how's your wife?" said Lily Geist.

"What?!" their teacher snapped, frowning at Lily.

"You should check your email, dude," said Meghan May.

Jenny relented and pulled her phone out. She had a new email message.

From: gh0stwrit3r@hotmail.com
To: jtvalentine@bsacademy.k12.ca.us.edu
Subject: some tea

"Sad" is getting left by your wife for her spin class instructor. "Pathetic" is when it happened a year ago, she took the kids and moved to San Jose, and you're still pretending you talk to your daughter every day because you're too embarrassed for your colleagues to learn the truth. Your ex has moved on, Mr. Hooke. Isn't it time you did too?

— The Ghostwriter

P.S. There's a lot more tea to spill. Worried you might be next? Rat on your classmates, and I'll spare you instead. Or pay $200 to this bitcoin address (1HesYJSP1QqcyPEjnQ9vzBL1wujruNGe7R). Choose your poison.

Mr. Hooke had finally pulled out his own phone and was reading the email. His whole head turned an angry shade of purple.

"It was you, wasn't it?!" Meghan May shouted. Jenny glanced over, and her heart froze to the core. Meghan was pointing an accusing finger directly at her. "Yeah, you guilty bitch, I can see it in your face. Jenny's the Ghostwriter!"

"I'm not the Ghostwriter," Jenny told the Vice Principal. "And if I was, I certainly wouldn't tell you."

Vice Principal Carter tented his bony fingers, judging her behind reading glasses hanging from the end of his nose. The last time Jenny was here, she got suspended for a week, which inadvertently led to Declan Dillion's death. This time…

"Mr. Hooke says Meghan May saw you on your phone before the email went out," he said in that reedy, commanding voice of his.

"I already showed him my Sent mailbox—"

"She could have deleted the message," Mr. Hooke cut in.

Jenny glanced at Mr. Hooke, hovering behind Mr. Carter's desk. His swollen anger had drained away, leaving him small and sallow and humiliated. The Ghostwriter, it seemed, knew just where to twist the knife.

"Sure, but you're asking me to prove a negative." Jenny rubbed her temples. "Besides, if I were the Ghostwriter, I would have used ProtonMail or something secure. Also, I'm rich. Why would I be shaking down students for $200?"

"Maybe you just like causing tro—" the Vice Principal hesitated.

"I don't always go looking for it, you know," Jenny said.

"What were you doing on your phone then?" Mr. Hooke asked.

Googling screen caps of Chloe Moretz.

"I was researching something for my essay."

"Ah, which is cheating, isn't it, Harvey?" the Vice Principal asked.

"Yeah. It is," Mr. Hooke said. "Electronic devices are prohibited during class."

Jenny's watch vibrated, the screen lighting up with a message from Danger. She angled her wrist to glance at it.

> **D:** No dice on the animal shelter, it's been closed for months.

"You have somewhere to be?" the Vice Principal asked.

"I'm already there," Jenny sighed.

"Wonderful." The Vice Principal clapped his hands together. "Well, we can't let cheating go unpunished, so how about Saturday School detention? One month of it."

"Oh, come on!" Jenny did not have time for this bullshit.

"We take discipline very seriously at Blackbird Springs Academy, Miss Valentine," the Vice Principal said. "Yes, make your crude hand gestures, but this is not your first infraction. Now, I would be amenable to a reduction in punishment if you were to help me put a stop to this Ghostwriter character."

Jenny cackled. "So that's what this shakedown is for? You know Trouble doesn't charge, *'If the cause is worthy.'* But I've got my plate full with the Hot Springs Hangman right now."

"Why don't you stick to something more your age level?" said Mr. Hooke.

"Why don't *you*—"

"Watch it," the Vice Principal growled.

Okay. Okay. Be chill, she told herself. Mr. Hooke was not her enemy. Jenny took a few calming breaths and stood up, retrieving a copy of *My Name is Trouble* from her bag.

"Why don't you send this to your daughter." She used Mr. Carter's pen to sign the inside cover and handed it to Mr. Hooke. "I'm late for Shop class."

Saturday school. What a joke, she'd just send Eliza.

"No way, go yourself," said Eliza. She wrapped a pillow around the blender they'd installed in the bathroom and hit the Max Blend button.

"I have that earnings meeting on Saturday with Mr. Webb," Jenny said over the muffled drone of frozen strawberries and ice liquifying in the Vitamix 5200.

"I can go to that," Eliza said.

"Come on, it's the first one."

"Ugh. Fine," Eliza said, easing off the blend button, but keeping the pillow held tight. It was after midnight, and Aunt Shelly should be asleep, but it was still prudent to be careful.

"Besides, you never had to go to Japanese school. I've lost so many Saturdays already. Karmically, you're due."

"I don't know, Japanese school sounds kinda neat," said Eliza. "Can't be worse than trying to learn with Rosetta Stone."

Along with sleuthing, tutoring, and being Jenny half the time, Eliza had been trying to cram some basic Japanese before their grandparents returned from Okinawa.

"You don't know what you're saying," said Jenny, rinsing off the cutting board and paring knife in the sink. "I didn't learn anything there anyways."

"Isn't that because you got kicked out after two months?"

"That was the first one. Shelly threatened to sell me to carnies if I didn't last at least a couple years in the second one."

"And that worked?" asked Eliza.

"I had a bad experience at the circus once, okay?"

Jenny produced chilled rocks glasses from the mini-fridge underneath the sink, and Eliza poured them both daiquiris.

"I put some kale in here, you know, for nutrition," Eliza said. "And Malibu, for fun."

They both giggled and clinked glasses.

"We are geniuses," said Jenny. "Let's watch Trouble conspiracy videos on Youtube."

"No! I can't take any more of those." Eliza sipped her drink, letting the cool, tart flavors mix with the warmth of the rum on the way down her throat. She didn't like to get drunk, but catching a little buzz helped her sleep.

And made her cocky.

She picked up the paring knife. "Let's play the knife game."

Jenny squeaked and yanked her hand behind her back.

"Scaredy-cat."

"What do you think Jack used this fridge for?" Jenny asked, suddenly fascinated by the appliance.

"Pssh. Who knows? Probably freezing his own semen."

Jenny nearly spit out her daiquiri.

"I mean, he would, right??"

"He's not so bad," Jenny insisted. "You just need to spend more time with him."

"Well, I'll be seeing him tomorrow. And your girlfriend. You guys are still doing the no PDAs thing at school, right?"

"Yeah yeah. Don't worry, you won't have to kiss a girl," said Jenny.

"I love that you think that's what the issue is," Eliza said. "What if we just switched after lunch? So you always have mornings with Dinah?"

"But then I have to do all of American History by myself," Jenny moaned.

They moved back to the bedroom. Jenny had kept the green-gold wallpaper and Slytherin aesthetic, replacing Jack's posters with canvas prints of the Trouble covers, and a giant map of Blackbird Springs. Eliza perched by the window facing the courtyard, rolling the knife in her fingers. Jenny settled into a nest of pillows on the giant bed.

"Look, you don't even need me anymore at school," said Eliza. "PreCalc is over. I can just go back to my online homeschooling."

"You told me you hated that. Besides, don't you want to help solve the Ghostwriter mystery?" Jenny asked.

Eliza allowed herself a smug laugh. "I already solved it."

"What?" Jenny asked. "How?"

"You're not the only girl detective in the family," Eliza said, basking in the radiance of her sister's jealousy. "The internet is kinda my thing. It's how I found you."

"Well, who is it?"

Eliza hesitated. "Okay, I'm like 90 percent sure."

"Mmmm, here come the caveats."

"Let's play a game," said Eliza. "There's no hurry, right? This Ghostwriter is not the Stranger; they can't hurt us." She snatched up a piece of Valentine stationery and grabbed a pen. "If I'm correct," she said, writing something down on the paper, "then 'Jenny Valentine' has a one-time bi moment with Drew."

"Hell. No."

"Okay, fine," Eliza said, slicing off the corner of the page and folding it up into smaller and smaller pieces. "If I'm wrong, I go to History for you all semester." She tucked the folded paper into the tiny cavity in her silver locket. It was a gift from Jenny for Christmas. Inside, on one half, there was an engraved *D*, and on the other, a picture of their mother. Jenny had an identical locket with a *T* instead. "And if I'm right, you buy me a car. A Jeep Rubicon, soft-top, in silver."

"And I thought I was the lesbian," Jenny said.

"Shut up, they're cool!" Eliza threw a pillow at her.

"Can you even drive?" asked Jenny.

"I taught myself the basics, back when Nurse Bennett..." Those last days with hospice weren't a memory she liked to revisit. "I'm out of practice, though."

"Think of something better, I was gonna buy us cars anyway," Jenny said, grabbing her iPad and typing as she spoke. "Did I tell you Alicia Aaron got herself a new Mustang?"

"Why does it seem like she's the only one enjoying Dad's money?"

"She's gonna burn through it." Jenny pressed a finger to her chin. "Actually, I think I'll have Mr. Webb order a fleet of Jeeps. Like a half-dozen, so we can expense them for the vineyard. No one will notice if we borrow one now and then."

"Okay, how about this," Eliza said, a devilish new idea occurring to her. "If I'm right, I get to go on the class trip this summer."

Jenny screwed up her face in a scowl. "But Dinah's on the planning committee for that."

"Come on, Trouble-chan, put some skin in the game."

Jenny laughed.

"Finish your Rosetta Stone already so I can teach you the good swear words."

"You're stalling."

"Fine. Deal." Jenny stuck out a hand, and they shook on it. "But let's put your guess in my locket so you can't change it. There's no way you already solved it."

Eliza shrugged and handed her the little folded up paper.

"No peeking."

"If I peek, I forfeit. Trouble's honor." Jenny closed her locket around the paper.

"I'll start packing for Europe," Eliza said with a smirk. "Oh, that reminds me, I've got the address for Oscar Manuel's mom."

"Nice. Is it far?"

Eliza turned to the big map on the wall, flicking the paring knife across the room and embedding it east of Valentine Manor, on the proverbial wrong side of the tracks.

"It's uhh… you might want to bring Drew."

Chapter Six

Alkali Estates

JENNY WOULD HAVE TO WAIT UNTIL AFTER SCHOOL TO VISIT Oscar's mom. In the meantime, the Ghostwriter didn't wait long for an encore. Blackbird Springs Academy was buzzing with the latest scandals when Jenny and Dinah arrived the next morning. Penny gave them the scoop.

After the school blocked mass emails, the Ghostwriter established a Facebook page and made three posts. The first alleged that the Senior Class Treasurer was pilfering funds to feed an Oxy habit. The second one was kinda weak: some freshman named Tommy Baxter never took his gym clothes home to wash them.

Those were just opening acts, though. Meghan May was the star of the Ghostwriter's third and final post of the morning, in which she was accused of wearing old clothes that fellow Bitchy Brigader Charlie Zaleska had donated to Goodwill. The Ghostwriter went savage on Meghan's try-hard desperation, bad taste, and—most damning of all—thrift, including quotes directly attributed to Charlie, talking mad shit about her supposed BFF.

Jenny and Dinah made identical *yikes!* faces as they read the post.

"'She doesn't even pay for her own coke.' Holy shit!" said Dinah.

Mason brayed with laughter.

"The Slay Squad is in turmoil," said Penny.

"Yas queen," said Drew.

"Charlie denies it all, of course," Penny added. "Thing is, I have to guess it's at least a little bit true for Meghan to get so worked up. Touched a nerve, maybe."

"Lead shark knows if she swims too slow, they'll eat her first," said Dinah.

"Mmmhmm," Penny said, holding Dinah's gaze in challenge. Dinah smiled back, the hint of a feral grin curling her pretty lips.

"Ladies, you shouldn't gossip," said Jack, deigning to join the conversation. "Especially when you don't know the good shit, not this fake clout chasing."

"Oh, do tell, baby brother," Jenny replied.

The slick prick gave her a condescending head shake. "Sunlight is no time for nocturnes," he said, retreating behind his shades. Drew was nodding along sagely.

"Pssh. What do you know?" Mason elbowed him.

"I'll just say this," Drew said with an odd confidence. "The clothes thing is whatever. But that drug talk? A good Christian girl like Meghan is bound to get in *trouble*."

Mason rolled his eyes. "Put a bass guitar in this fool's hand, and he thinks he's Han Solo."

"Meghan and Charlie don't even wear the same size," said Alicia Aaron.

Had that little mouse been sitting there this whole time?

"Ugh, am I gonna have to make a Facebook account?" Dinah asked.

Jenny already knew the Meghan thing was fake, of course—she was the one who sent the Ghostwriter the story. She wanted to find out how much the Ghostwriter really knew, and where he drew the line.

Her watch tapped her on the wrist three times. Danger was near.

"I gotta run to the ladies," Jenny said, peeling herself away from Dinah.

"I'll come with," Dinah said, skipping over to join her. It was sweet but inconvenient. Jenny tapped her watch twice: *hide.*

Inside the girls' room, Jenny let Dinah take the open stall, pretending to fix her lipstick in the mirror. Today's ensemble was one of Jenny's new favorites. Black & white Chuck Taylor high-tops, black skinny jeans, and a white tank top with **Girl Detective** printed on it in a bubbly font. Officially licensed, of course. Her lavender cardigan kept her warm, and her Prada pink-gold shades kept the early morning sun at bay.

With a soft click, the last stall door eased open behind her. Jenny slipped in.

Eliza was sitting on the toilet lid, wearing an identical outfit and holding a backpack with a change of clothes. This was what they'd worked out so Eliza wouldn't find herself in an awkward make-out session before first period on the drive to school.

When Dinah exited her stall to wash her hands, there was "Jenny," just coming out to join her. The two left shortly, never giving a second glance to the girl with the big coat and bushy hair at the far end of the counter. After nearly five months, the twins were magicians at the old switcheroo. Now Jenny was free to get to work.

WELL, SHE WAS FREE AFTER SHE WENT BACK TO SLEEP FOR A COUPLE hours, first. Mrs. Rivas would be cleaning her room in Valentine Manor right now, so Jenny walked to the Crow's Nest and crashed in her suite until noon. *Then* it was time to get to work.

Despite her hands-off approach with the publishing company, they still managed to fill up her inbox every day. Jenny skimmed through the messages on her iPad. There was one from Stacy in PR asking just what the "#OnIt" Instagram post was supposed to mean. Like she didn't already know. Jenny flagged it and a few others to come back to later and fired off an email to Mr. Webb.

> Hi Mr. Webb!
>
> Need a favor, ASAP. I'd like to get six Jeeps for the vineyard/mansion. See specs below, nothing too fancy, but silver, if you please. Expense them to Trouble, Inc. in whatever way is most agreeable, etc. Oh, but no logos or signage on them. Just in case 💀🏴
>
> Also! Can you get in touch with my grandfather's old law firm? I'd like to hire an immigration lawyer to look in on Sarah Ortiz's family, in case they're having any trouble with ICE. On me.
> Thank you,
>
> -Trouble

After a few more messages, she emailed Yvonne Griffin with some quotes about Casey Klein and Val's upcoming Valentine's Day gala thing. Once caught up, she switched to her Maps app and pulled up the address for Oscar Manuel's mom.

Just outside Blackbird Springs city limits, in unincorporated Calistoga County, was a trailer park called the Alkali Estates. Rent was cheap there, and—according to local gossip—so was meth, weed, and any other vice you could think of.

It was also where the people who made the wine that made Napa Valley famous could afford to live, so maybe that reputation was a lot of prejudiced nonsense from the local bourgeoisie. Still, she shouldn't go alone. She texted Drew.

> **Jenny:** Trouble requires her sidekick. Meet me in the parking lot after school, Drewboo.

And then, Eliza.

> **T:** Meeting Drew for Alkali Estates. Better lay low for a while.

Jenny was Mr. White's TA during last period, so Eliza would have to hide in the bathroom for a half-hour after school, just to be safe.

In the meantime, she walked the floors of the Crow's Nest, applying a small piece of transparent tape to the bottom of every door. If what Jack said about housekeeping on Mondays for residents was correct, and Dad's secret room was still paid for, no one should be going in or out of it for the next few days. She finished taping the sixth-floor doors with minutes to spare and hurried back to campus to meet her driver just as school let out.

"I have to be back for practice by four," Drew said as he got into Jenny's town car.

"That's fine, shouldn't take too long." Jenny filled him in on their next target on the ride to the trailer park.

"The Hot Springs Hangman." Drew turned over the words carefully. "I guess that's the obvious meaning of Sheriff Lockhart's noose heirloom."

As far as Drew knew, they were hunting down the other heirloom clues for fun and good civic duty. He didn't know the real killer, the Stranger, was still out there.

"We should start a new Big Board," Jenny said. "I'll order a new projector screen and have it shipped to you. Just be sure to pick it up before your parents see it."

"If you still had time for your old pal, you'd know I sent them on vacation," Drew said.

"Right. I remember now, geez. I've been busy," Jenny said. "All expenses paid to Spain, right? How long?"

"A month."

"Nice. Shelly wouldn't let me stay home alone for a single weekend."

"Good son privileges," he said with a coy grin. "I even get to drive Mom's Subaru to the store for groceries."

"Wow. I'm a holy hell to my aunt, and I just bought six Jeeps," said Jenny. "Nice guys *do* finish last."

"Hey, if getting a 10 percent cut of your fortune is finishing last, I'll take it. You still owe me those ass-jets, though."

"Have you even spent any of it on yourself?"

He shrugged. "Bought a new catcher's mitt. And uh, some audio equipment."

Jenny wanted to tease him about this band he and Mason were forming, but the driver was already pulling over at their destination. Alkali Estates was a half-mile strip of trailers nestled between Alkali Creek and a steep ridge reaching out from the Castle foothills. There was the obligatory car up on blocks out in front of a double-wide, a sad, rusted merry-go-round, and a Slavic dude sitting in a fold-up lawn chair, vaping.

"Ugh. I hate this place," said Drew.

"Don't be a snob," Jenny said as they got out.

"It's not that," he said, frowning at some far off memory.

"What?"

He let out a ragged breath. Jenny pulled the story out of him on the walk to the gates. It turned out Mr. Porter, Drew's dad, had grown up in the Alkali Estates.

"So, I got busted for shoplifting once," he said. "Third Grade."

"*Good son.* What'd you steal?"

"A fucking Twinkie—and a magnifying glass. It doesn't matter. My dad was furious. He drove me out here and was like, is this where you wanna end up? You wanna be one of them? Just on and on about how he'd worked his ass off from fry cook to head chef to leave this place behind, and blah blah blah. I don't know, it was kinda shitty. I mean, it's not like these people did anything wrong. Anyway, he made me spend four hours here every Saturday for a month, picking up trash."

Jenny patted him on the shoulder. "Wow, a whole month of Saturdays, you poor thing. I hope you left a good impression. The guy they convicted of Casey Klein's murder: his mother lives here. Let's see if those kids know her."

She pointed to a couple Latino kids who had stopped shooting hoops on the asphalt half court to watch them.

"Hola," said Drew, followed by a comment in Spanish. The kids chuckled.

"What'd you say?"

"Nothing." His smile suggested otherwise. He asked them a question that included "Señora Manuel."

One kid shrugged, the other went back to shooting hoops.

"Yeah, they're not saying," said Drew. "We should have brought Mason. He says he buys his black-market Viagra here."

"Every word of that sentence is cursed," Jenny said, rummaging in her backpack. She pulled out a stack of papers. "We'll have to try the flyers trick. Also—how is it that I've never seen any of this cavalcade of girls Mason claims to be romancing?"

"He says they go to Harbor High."

"Sure they do."

They moved down the rows of double-wide trailers, placing flyers for the school play in each mailbox. Jenny's fictional counterpart pulled this move in *Trouble Comes Knocking*. The mailman had just been through, which meant most people hadn't checked their mail yet, and Jenny could peek at the addresses on delivered letters to look for a Mrs. Manuel.

"You realize there could be more than one Manuel here," Drew said.

"I think we'll know when we find the right one," she said, checking an overstuffed mailbox full of junk mail, all addressed to a Jorge Lopez.

"Here we go," said Drew, pointing to a utility bill for Mary Manuel.

"First time's the charm?" Jenny said, grabbing the envelope.

Mary Manuel lived at 4518 Crescent Lane. They located the trailer and walked right up.

"What's the play?" Drew muttered as she knocked on the door.

An elderly woman with a polite smile greeted them in Spanish.

"Mrs. Manuel?" Jenny said, holding up the utility bill.

"Si. Y tu?"

"My name is Jennifer Valentine. I think you knew my father." Drew translated.

A shadow passed over the woman's face. The smile vanished. She replied with a few brusque words.

"She says we'd better come in," Drew said.

THE TRAILER WAS SURPRISINGLY WELL-APPOINTED, WITH LINOLEUM that approximated bamboo flooring, an oversized sectional, and a legit 4K television mounted on the wall. Jenny and Shelly never had to live in a trailer, but they'd never owned a KitchenAid before either. A propane space heater glowed in the corner, keeping them toasty.

Mrs. Manuel handed them mugs of hot cocoa. Jenny sunk deep into the couch next to Drew.

"You're Oscar Manuel's mother," Jenny said. Drew translated.

"She's asking why you don't speak Spanish like your father," he said.

"Because the girl I had a crush on took French," Jenny sighed, wistful. "Don't actually tell her that."

The old woman moved to the window as she spoke, peeking through the blinds. Drew replied in Spanish again, then waited for her reply.

"She says we shouldn't be here. RJ isn't—wasn't very popular around Alkali Estates.

"Because of Casey Klein?" Jenny said.

"Because of Rita Thomas," Drew relayed.

"Who?" Jenny asked.

Mrs. Manuel harrumphed and spoke a word in English. "*Exactly.*"

Drew teased the tale out slowly. Mrs. Manuel seemed both eager and reluctant to unfold the story of Rita Thomas, a young Latina girl who went missing from Alkali Estates three days before Casey Klein's disappearance.

"She says Rita attended an ESL school," Drew translated. "Not like Casey, the smiling gringo daughter of a wealthy family. When Casey went missing, it was all over the news. No one mentioned Rita. I guess she got lost in the news cycle."

Mrs. Manuel went on. Drew nodded, occasionally interjecting with brief questions.

"RJ thought the two girls might be part of a pattern," said Drew. "The police didn't think so. Casey went missing in broad daylight on the way home from school. But with Rita, no one could say exactly when they'd last seen her, and runaways weren't uncommon in migrant communities. Then Rita's body washed up in the north shoals a few weeks later, and the official story was that she'd drowned in the creek and been swept down toward the bay."

He paused, eyes tilted up as he pondered. "I guess that checks out if she went down the east fork. Anyway, the cops moved on to other leads. RJ didn't. He kept poking around the trailer park, asking questions about Rita and other residents."

Mrs. Manuel added another few sentences.

"At first, people didn't mind," Drew said. "He could speak fluent Spanish, and he wasn't a cop. He seemed like he cared."

Jenny couldn't help but think of the Rosetta Stone Japanese lessons she'd given Eliza for Christmas. Their grandparents would be back from Okinawa in a few weeks, and Eliza wanted to be prepared. She wondered if her sister was as nervous about the meeting as she was.

"Huh. Turns out RJ was watching her son even before Lockhart found Casey's body," said Drew. "When Oscar was arrested, she expected RJ to be smug. Instead, he kept coming back, walking along the creek, talking to Oscar's friends. He was sure that something connected Rita and Casey, and since Oscar had an alibi for Rita, then he must be innocent of Casey's murder too."

"What did *you* think, Mrs. Manuel?" Jenny asked.

Drew relayed the question. The old woman bit her lip to stop it from quivering. Her voice cracked with deep emotion as she spoke, and afterward, she wiped her eyes.

"She says—" Drew cleared his throat, sounding a bit husky himself. "She says, 'Oscar was always a little wild, but he was a good boy.' She can't believe it. She never will. And now they're saying the killer struck again. They didn't give her so much as a 'Sorry.' It sounds like no one's even contacted her. Until us. That's fucked up."

He asked another question in Spanish.

"I asked her about the receipt they found on Casey," Drew said. "'She doesn't know. She doesn't know. RJ thought it could have been planted.'"

Drew stroked his chin while Mrs. Manuel blew her nose. Jenny frowned. "Ask her why people around here didn't like my dad," she said. "It sounds like he was trying to help."

"Hmm," said Drew after listening to the reply. "It was hard for Rita's family to move on when RJ kept coming around every few weeks. He thought the real killer might be from here too, and they could have used Oscar as a patsy. Sounds like he talked the Sheriff into doing a few raids. It didn't go well. They never found anything about Casey or Rita, but there was some drug stuff, and a couple people were undocumented. It just wasn't the kind of attention they needed."

"Did she ever get a name from my dad? His suspect?" Jenny asked.

Mrs. Manuel glanced out the window again as she spoke.

"He would never tell her. Very secretive, your dad," said Drew.

"Was this before or after they disinterred Casey's body?" Jenny asked.

Drew raised an eyebrow but haltingly repeated her question. Mrs. Manuel blanched. "I don't know the word for 'disinterred,'" he said, glaring at Jenny. "You're making me sound tactless."

The woman smiled, somehow understanding that Jenny was the asshole here, and replied.

"Before," Drew translated. "He thought a second autopsy would show a link between Rita and Casey. It was… inconclusive. After that, she didn't see him much."

"He'd have been on his book tour," said Jenny. "First *Trouble* book came out that fall."

Mrs. Manuel went on. Drew listened, tilting his head in interest.

"Quote: 'It became my own dark hobby for a while.' She would read deep in many local newspapers. Go looking for Missing person posters. Check the milk carton each week for someone new. It's not unusual for a couple girls a year to disappear in the North Bay. Always from poor neighborhoods, Bosnian refugees, day laborer communities. Places where they wouldn't be reported. Like she said, runaways happen."

A car engine thrummed outside as it passed by. Mrs. Manuel continued.

"But so many of them right around Casey's age. Rita's age." Drew said. As he spoke, Mrs. Manual pulled out a binder from her shelf. It was full of grainy, black and white photos—all little girls.

The car engine died. Jenny stood up and walked to the window. There was no one out front except a van idling across the street. A man with a hard, weathered face sat behind the wheel, smoking a cigarette. He made eye contact, and Jenny quickly looked away. Mrs. Manuel spoke again behind her.

"She doesn't want to seem ungrateful," said Drew. "She appreciates all RJ's done for her. If you're here to tell her that things have changed, she understands."

"Huh? What does she mean?" Jenny asked, turning from the window.

At that moment, a figure in a dark, hooded trench coat entered through the rear door of the trailer.

"Lo siento, llego tarde, Mary. Había una gran fila en el banco," said a clipped, cultured voice in a mid-Atlantic accent. The stranger tugged off her hood, and wavy chestnut hair spilled out. "Ya comiste—"

Jenny stiffened, at a loss for words. Staring at her from across the compact living room was Tori Valentine. In her elusive step-sister's left hand was an open bank envelope stuffed with US currency.

"Jennifer," said Tori, finding her voice first. "What the bloody hell are you doing here?"

Chapter Seven

Valentine Girls

THE HEATER BUZZED IN THE CORNER. NOBODY SPOKE FOR HALF A dozen heartbeats.

"I was about to ask you the same thing," Jenny said, shifting her gaze to the envelope of money in Tori's hand.

"You shouldn't be here," Tori said, setting the money on the table. "Mary, ¿qué les has dicho?"

Drew relayed the conversation: "'What have you told them?' 'Sorry, I thought they'd come in your place.'"

Tori growled, unappreciative of Drew's bilingual skills. Jenny pointed to the money. "So what's that? Hush money?"

"We should get going," said Drew, standing.

"Wait. Stop," said Tori. "You can't, not yet." She moved to the window by the front door, peering out. "There's a reporter out there. I was wondering what he was up to. He must have followed you two bozos here."

Jenny joined her at the window, peeking through the blinds. A white sedan was parked out on the main road, behind Jenny's town car. It looked cheap and rented. That young reporter in the black frame Warby Parker glasses was leaning against the hood, pretending to look at a fold-out map, but really watching Mrs. Manuel's trailer. In the distance, a train whistle blew.

"What do you think he's gonna write when he finds out you and I were both here to see Mrs. Manuel?" Jenny said.

"Nothing, if he's smart," Tori said. "He's not here for a story."

"What then?" Jenny asked.

"My mother's reward. It's bringing all these types—your types—out of the woodwork. I warned her this would happen."

Mrs. Manuel asked a question.

"Tea, por favor," Tori replied. "Earl Grey."

"Hot!" Drew chirped.

Tori had her phone to her ear now. "I need a favor, darling." Jenny guessed from Tori's contemptuous smile that the other person was asking about her. "Not this time. There's a journalist skulking around Alkali Estates. White Hyundai. Be a dear and send a Black & White over to run him off... Never you mind." She hung up and rolled her eyes. "Five minutes."

"Isn't Sheriff Lockhart a little old for you?" Jenny said.

"Your powers of deduction continue to disappoint." She extended a slender middle finger in Jenny's face. Her nails were trimmed short and manicured with clear polish; she wore a silver Tiffany ring.

"Mrs. Manuel, would you mind if I had a look at that binder?" Jenny asked. The old woman had been holding it earlier, but it seemed to have vanished when Tori arrived.

Drew translated. Mrs. Manuel's eyes darted to Tori for a millisecond. Her reply was curt. Drew snorted. "'What binder?'"

"I can pay more than she can if that's what this is about," Jenny said. "Put you up in a nicer neighborhood."

"Uhh." Drew hesitated.

79

Tori spoke in rapid Spanish with the woman. Mrs. Manuel gave Jenny a repulsed frown, an edge creeping into her voice.

"She likes it here, thank you very much," Tori relayed with heavy condescension.

Jenny turned back to the window, hiding her embarrassment.

They waited in silence while Mrs. Manuel made tea. A few minutes later, a police SUV pulled up next to Warby Parker's car, out on the main road.

Jenny leaned over, speaking softly to Tori. "So you and Dad have been taking care of Mrs. Manuel, eh? That's cool. I can handle that, though, if you want."

"Your charity overwhelms," Tori said through her teeth.

"Just trying to lighten the load, seeing as how Dad didn't leave you anything in the will."

"I can manage it."

"Hmm. Too bad about that no-kill shelter you used to volunteer at," Jenny replied. "Guess they couldn't manage it. Those poor dogs. If only they had a new benefactor."

"Now, that's more like it. You monster."

"What can I say, I like cats. But I could be a dog person. For a price."

"And what price is that?" Tori asked.

"What was Dad's theory about the murder? Who was his suspect?"

Tori's cheek twitched. "Sorry, he never told me."

"Lie," said Jenny. They regarded each other stiffly, Jenny's muscles bracing for a fight. Tori held her stare long enough to make a point. "Answer me this, then," Jenny said. "Where were you?"

"Hmm?"

"You were her best friend, supposedly. So, where were you when Casey was walking home that day?"

Hollow cheeks sagged on Tori's pained face. Jenny knew that look, she saw it every morning in the mirror: guilt. But was it survivor's guilt, or something else?

Tori stepped closer, her breath hot in Jenny's ear. "Leave it alone, Jennifer. The noose is not your clue."

"It's not yours either."

Her stepsister didn't reply, but Jenny could practically feel the hatred radiating off of Tori. She was saved when the white Hyundai outside drove away. Jenny nodded to Drew. It was time to leave. He thanked Mrs. Manuel for both of them.

"Don't come back here," Tori said, opening the door for them to go. "I mean it."

"Tell me," said Jenny, standing on the small porch. "Who do you like for the murder?"

"Dad's? Or Casey's?" Tori asked.

"Casey's." She belatedly caught the implication. "Your mom killed my dad."

"Sure she did," said Tori. True darkness radiated behind her blue eyes. "But Casey... Oh, I don't know," she said after a while. "But if your dumb ass somehow gets there first... Well, no one wants another trial."

SCHOOLWORK AND TIME WITH DINAH WOULD KEEP JENNY BUSY FOR a couple days. She was up to kiss number 1,165 now. On Wednesday, she sent Eliza to Drew's garage to set up the new Big Board. Her sister had been on edge ever since the doll thing. Jenny hoped she'd feel better if she got back into the process of sleuthing with Drew, though with no suspects, the case still felt amorphous and incomplete.

Apparently, Drew wanted to pull the records for anyone who lived at the Alkali Estates when Rita Thomas went missing, but that felt like a huge time sink. Also, Jenny had no idea how one would even acquire such information.

No, Jenny was feeling impatient. Or maybe that was the Adderall. Truth be told, she was on edge too. Her encounter with Tori had unsettled her more than she wanted to admit. Tori knew something Jenny didn't. She was following some kind of instructions from Dad. And she breezily assumed Val's innocence. If Jenny thought about it too much, the embers of a panic attack would stir deep in her chest. Jenny refused to go back to that life, so she'd taken to popping a Xanax when the feeling arose.

It helped, but it wiped her out. To compensate, she'd had to double her Adderall dose—which might have sharpened her up a little too much. Still, fuck real estate research. It was time to light a fire under an asset who was dragging his feet. If he burned, he burned.

Jenny pulled out her phone and opened the ProtonMail app…

WHEN DINAH PULLED INTO HER STUDENT OF THE MONTH PARKING spot the next morning, Mason was waiting for them. His head looked especially swollen and roided out today, with an unkind frown and flaring nostrils for Jenny as she got out.

"Oh no, it's an angry thumb," said Dinah.

"We gotta have words, bastard," Mason said. His voice was coarse and desperate.

Dinah's brow crinkled in suspicion. Jenny gave her a reassuring smile and nodded to the school entrance. "It's all right. I'll see you in English."

Her girlfriend gave Mason the evil eye for a beat. "Behave yourself," she said to him before striding away in a darling pencil skirt.

"Hey, wait, can I borrow your lip balm?" Jenny called after her. Dinah tossed it to her, and Jenny held her gaze, forcing Mason to watch as she rubbed it over her lips. "Thanks. I wanna taste you during History."

She was rewarded with a rare blush from Dinah, something to savor as she put up with the expected tantrum.

Once she was gone, Mason held his phone up, reading from a certain Facebook page. "'Blind item. There's a secret baby daddy among you—you'll never guess who. Stay tuned.' WHAT THE FUCK!?"

"Quiet, idiot!" she hissed. "Or they're gonna figure out it's you."

When Jenny had spied Mason growing weed at his dad's cabin last fall, she also got him on video taking a newborn baby from some blonde, and feeding the infant with a bottle. He'd been keeping the child a secret from everyone, even his own father.

"I thought we had a deal," he said, stepping into her personal space.

"Do we?" Jenny replied, taking a step forward into his and forcing him back. "Cause where I sit, you're falling down on the job. Get that goddamned Casey Klein file in my hand, or the Ghostwriter gets another scoop."

"He'll know it's gone missing," Mason whispered as Alicia Aaron limped by. "He checks it every night. Gets it out, kills a fifth of vodka, and just stares at it."

There was a hint of something behind his eyes she'd never seen in him before: concern. "Look, you wait till he gets the file out, cause a distraction, then get in there and take pictures of every page you can. If you wanna help your dad, help me."

"Why do you care?" he asked. "You solved the mystery, you've got your money. Hell, *I've* got some of your money. Can't we all just chill?"

"Every heirloom my dad left is a debt. A wrong that he didn't have time to right. And I can't rest—he can't rest—until that debt is paid." Jenny was surprised to realize, halfway through her off-the-cuff bullshit, that she actually meant it.

"No more tips to the Ghostwriter," Mason said.

"Do your job, and there won't be," Jenny said. "You have till Monday."

His eyes flashed, but he was powerless to protest. "Fine."

"Oh, and Mason?" she stopped him before he could stalk off and rummaged in her purse. Making sure no one was watching, she pressed a *Trouble*-branded pacifier into his palm. "For Lilah," she said with a wink. "Maybe someday you can introduce me to her mom."

WHEN JENNY GOT CALLED INTO THE VICE PRINCIPAL'S OFFICE ON Friday, it felt uncomfortably like karmic retribution. She'd made no real progress on the Ghostwriter—other than learning that he'd post literally anything that you sent him—and now it was her turn to get squeezed.

"We've had three fights already, and someone slashed Kenny Anderson's bike tires," Vice Principal Carter said, passing a hand through his thinning hair.

"Was that the kid with the secret neo-Nazi Twitter account?" Jenny asked. "It seems I've lost all my fucks to give for his stupid bike."

"Do you want another month of Saturday detention?"

"I'm working on it." Jenny gave an exasperated huff. "I've got a few leads, but no proof yet."

"Work harder," the Vice Principal said. He tapped some keys on his keyboard. "I'd expect a little more urgency after this latest post."

"What?" she said.

He swung his desk monitor around to show her. A red wave of

fury crested between her temples as she read the Ghostwriter's latest missive.

"That son of a bitch."

Jenny prowled through the cafeteria, looking for a certain angry thumb. She found Mason eating pizza with Jack, not far from Meghan May's table of popular girls.

"I know that was you!" she yelled, jabbing a finger at him.

"What do you mean?" Mason said, pretending to stifle his stupid, oafish laugh. Jack was watching her cooly with mild disinterest.

"Are you a part of this?" Jenny asked.

"Of course not," Jack said, biting into a slice of pizza. The box was from The Red Grape, a pricy local joint.

"Wait, did you get that delivered?" she asked.

He smirked and shrugged. "I like a good buffalo mozz on my pie."

"'Blind item!'" Mason shouted, reading from his phone with glee. "'A certain nouveau riche heiress is lying about her parentage. Somebody check that bastard's papers and demand a DNA test.' Wow, whoever could that be referring to?"

"I do not need this bullshit," Jenny said, stealing a slice of their pizza. "Do you know what kind of hassle this will cause if it gets beyond the school? We've barely gotten the reporters to stop calling us!"

"Hey Jenny, is it true you had plastic surgery to look more like Jack?" called Lily from Meghan's table. The rest of the Bitchy Brigade snickered.

"What, are you afraid they'll find something?" Mason said, inquisitively tilting his head.

"I mean, what are the odds he'd really have a kid named Trouble?"

said Meghan. "Who only showed up after he died, claiming to be his heir?"

"Oh shit, look at her face," Charlie said. "Do you think she's gonna cry?"

Jenny was absolutely not about to cry. "You know, Meghan, I didn't believe it when the Ghostwriter said you had bought Charlie's leftovers from Goodwill, but it sounds like you're taking everything he posts as fact, eh?"

Charlie seemed to lick her lips as Meghan flushed.

"That was a lie!" Meghan said.

"And so is this!" Something tickled the back of Jenny's mind. She frowned, but the wisp of an idea was already gone.

"You just can't trust anyone on the internet these days," Jack said. "Whither your journalistic integrity, Ghostwriter? Alas."

Charlie had drifted over, and boldly made a move for Jack's pizza box.

"Is there garlic on this?" she asked Jack.

"Of course," said Jack.

She gagged and retreated.

"Thanks for the support, by the way," Jenny told her brother.

"Mason, stop calling Jenny a bastard," Jack said, straightening his posture. "You've got money now. We call them 'natural children.'"

Jenny twisted her head around to glare at Mason, the implicit warning burning in her retinas. He was still watching her with a doltish head tilt.

"Well, I guess we know you're not the Ghostwriter," Mason said.

"Like I would be so lame." Jenny shoved a massive bite of Jack's precious buffalo mozzarella pizza into her mouth and plopped down next to her brother. "No Penny today?"

"Her mom took her into the City for the weekend," he said.

"Yvonne's doing a bunch of spots on the networks for the Klein murder thing. Now that Dad—well, she's the foremost civilian expert on the case."

"Huh," Jenny said, a side mission taking shape in her head. "They're gone the whole weekend?"

THE FIRE ESCAPE SQUEAKED UNDER ELIZA'S WEIGHT AS SHE HAULED herself up onto the landing. She tensed and held her breath, waiting for a sign she'd been noticed. None came. After a minute, she allowed herself to exhale and went to work on the window into Penny's bedroom. The industrial-strength magnet made quick work of the latch on the other side of the glass, just like the cat burglar from *Trouble in Paris*. It felt kind of shitty to break into her friend's apartment. Jenny didn't want to miss the opportunity to get a peek at another heirloom clue, though.

Eliza slipped inside, rolling onto Penny's bed. If her luck held, she hadn't just tripped a silent alarm. Her ensemble was pure stealth tonight: all black pants, black gloves, a slinky black shirt, and a black stocking mask. No point in a wig when you were doing second-story work.

Penny and Yvonne Griffin lived in a small apartment above the offices of the Blackbird Times. In theory, that old hardcover copy of *The Stranger of Sausalito* was somewhere in this building. With a little luck, she'd find it. With a lot of luck, she'd have a chance to snap a photo of every page.

She crept to the bedroom door and peeked out. The hallway was pitch black; she'd have to risk a light. "Lumos," she whispered. With a click, her hand-light blazed to its lowest setting, which still seemed blindingly bright. Thank god Penny didn't have a dog.

Yvonne's room was across the hall. Eliza hurried for the bookshelf on the far wall, feeling another pang of regret at the sight of an unmade bed. This was a violation, being here in this private space. She ran her flashlight over the book titles once, then twice. Mostly non-fiction, several sports bios, and a full collection of the *Trouble* series. *The Stranger of Sausalito* wasn't here. She checked the nightstand drawers: nothing.

Eliza was halfway to the door when a clattering, ringing alarm bell pierced the silence.

Her heart skipped a beat. So much for her good luck.

She retreated to the hallway and was about to head for the fire escape when she spotted another cluster of shelves in the living room.

Grimacing, Eliza hurtled the couch and rifled through the books. She found lots of Joan Didion and Toni Morrison—and a surprising amount of V. C. Andrews, which must belong to Penny—but not the heirloom book she'd come for.

A loud thud sounded from the floor below. Eliza's hand darted to the small knife on her waistband. Someone else was here. Time to leave. She hurried back to Penny's bedroom and out the window.

Intuition tugged at her. Told her to go up, not back down. She climbed the fire escape up to the roof, and not a moment too soon. Flashing red and blue lights strobed. A police radio crackled below.

Eliza had spent enough time on the roof of the Pen to know you could cover a lot of distance up here if you were brave enough to risk the 4-story drop between buildings. Was she a Gryffindor or what? She took off at a sprint, moving parallel to the street below. B&Es were more Trouble's thing, but Danger was *her* middle name.

The alley up ahead had to be a dozen feet wide. With a last burst of speed, she leapt out over empty space.

It was impossible not to grin.

Her landing was almost perfect, barely stumbling, easily clearing the alley with a couple feet to spare. She ran on, leaping over shorter gaps until she finally came to Broadway Avenue. It occurred to her, as she psyched herself up to slide down the drainpipe, that a white Hyundai had been parked on this corner when Eliza first clambered up to Penny's window. Retrieving her 18-speed now, it was nowhere to be seen.

Chapter Eight

Trouble, Inc.

THE SUN WASN'T EVEN UP YET WHEN TEGAN & SARA ERUPTED FROM Jenny's phone. She groaned and hit snooze, burrowing deeper under the covers. A minute later, without warning, the bedroom door burst open with a thunderclap.

"I thought we had an agreement!" said Aunt Shelly, her unbrushed hair a storm of crackling rage.

"Jesus Christ!" Jenny bolted upright in a panic, glancing around. "Can you fucking knock?!"

"Language, Jennifer!" Aunt Shelly was dressed in workout leggings and a tank top, either just back from a run or about to take one.

"I could have been like—naked or something!"

"You know I used to change your diapers, right?"

"That's not the point! I deserve my privacy! Oh my god!" Jenny said.

"Okay, okay, I'm sorry," Shelly said. "I'll knock next time. Why are you back in bed? And what the hell is this?"

She thrust a tabloid newspaper in Jenny's face: "HEIRESS SPEAKS" declared the headline of the latest edition of *The Blackbird*

Times.

"What?" Jenny asked, too innocently.

"'I caught my father's killer, and now I'm coming for the Hot Springs Hangman,'" Aunt Shelly said, reading from the article. "Sounds like someone didn't turn over a new leaf. Maybe a few weeks restriction would help."

"Shell, I—I was just messing around." Perhaps Jenny had been feeling a little overzealous when she sent those quotes to Yvonne Griffin. "I thought it would be funny to stick it to Lockhart. He's taking it in the shorts over the Klein case right now."

Shelly's hair relaxed a little, from pure rage back to high-key annoyance. "You don't need to do that."

"He deserves it. And worse."

"No, no, he doesn't." Her aunt sighed. "I've forgiven him. Just… just leave him be."

"Wait, you and he aren't—" Jenny crinkled her nose at the idea of Blake and Shelly dating again.

"No, jeez," she laughed. "Peter's taking me horseback riding today, and I don't want to be late."

"*Peter.* Gross, he's Mr. White."

"You've got 30 minutes to get dressed for Saturday school. Don't dawdle."

Her aunt spun and marched out. At least she closed the door behind her. A dozen heartbeats later, Eliza stepped out of the bathroom, dressed in a t-shirt and boy shorts, drying her hair with a towel.

Jenny sagged into her pillows, relieved. "That was too close," she said.

"Sorry, you were asleep when I came in last night," Eliza whispered. "I must have forgotten to lock the door."

"How'd it go?" Jenny asked.

"Do you want the bad news or the worse news?"

Jenny groaned. "Let me shower first."

Fortunately, there was still plenty of hot water left. After five minutes under the scalding rainfall jets, Jenny was almost awake. Eliza filled her in on the failed attempt at Yvonne Griffin's apartment while Jenny dressed.

"You're sure it was that reporter's car?" Jenny asked.

"Well, not a hundred percent, but it was a white Hyundai. Whose else would it be?" Eliza frowned at her. "Hey, has that always been there?"

Eliza pointed at her back. Jenny checked over her shoulder in the vanity mirror, just able to see the old white scar in the center, peeking out from under her bra strap.

"Oh, yeah. Childhood injury."

"I guess it's one-pieces for us this summer," Eliza said.

"You mean when I'm lounging by the pool on our class trip?" She shot a greedy smirk at her sister.

"Not if I'm right about the Ghostwriter," said Eliza. "You sure you don't want to go to Saturday School? Look for some clues at school?"

"Maybe *you're* the Ghostwriter," Jenny said, fingering her locket. "And no, I have a meeting. It's earnings day."

TWO HOURS LATER, JENNY SAT ON A PARK BENCH IN TOWN SQUARE, under a steel-gray sky that threatened rain. A dozen tourists milled about, shooting the occasional dirty look her way. Because this wasn't just any park bench, it was the one with Dad's bronze statue sitting on one side, a welcoming arm resting on the back of the seat. Jenny kept out of his reach, hugging her knees to stay warm. She'd worn her translucent purple rain poncho, which looked good with her black tank top underneath but wasn't much against the chilly weather. Her bangs spilled out from under the hood. They were getting long; she was due for a cut.

She checked her last texts from Eliza.

> **D:** Ugh, that mean girl Charlie is here
>
> **D:** Mr. Hooke is taking our phones fuck this
>
> **T:** Don't do anything I wouldn't do 😊 2 da loo!

The back of her neck prickled. Someone was watching her. She looked around casually, pretending to stretch. There, across the street. A man was staring at her, half-hidden behind a lamppost. Grizzled, Latino, tall and lanky, with muscular arms and hands almost black with soot or grease. There was something familiar about him.

"Excuse me," said a woman.

Jenny nearly jumped with a start. When she looked back, the strange man was getting into a big white van and driving away. She made a mental note of the sign on the back: **Calistoga Farrier**.

"Would you mind if we got a picture?" the woman asked.

She had approached with her daughter. No older than six, wearing a purple coat and a too-big red fedora. Who couldn't smile at that? Jenny brightened up and waited expectantly. The lady and her daughter just stared at her.

"I don't think she meant a picture with you, Miss Valentine."

A tall man with a hawkish nose and horn-rimmed glasses circled around to the front of the bench.

"Wait—Trouble?" asked the woman. But Jenny was already up and walking away with Mr. Webb.

"How long did it take?" Mr. Webb asked. "Before someone finally asked you to move?"

"Half hour or so," Jenny said.

"Is it because Valerie Valentine had it made?"

She glanced back at the mother and daughter. The little Trouble fan was already snuggling up under the arm of the bronze RJ Valentine as her mom used a selfie stick to get them all in the shot. What a happy family.

"No," said Jenny, forcing her lip to stop quivering and popping an Adderall. "That's not why I hate it."

TROUBLE, INC. HELD ITS QUARTERLY RESULTS MEETING IN A conference room at the Crow's Nest. A half-dozen of dad's money men and women were in attendance. Accountants, publishing reps, merchandise guys: everyone who had a stake in the business of a certain internationally beloved, precocious girl detective. They all shook Jenny's hand, offering condolences and fealty, and an unspoken plea to not screw up their gravy train.

They gave Jenny a binder full of financial data and a seat at the head of the table. Mr. Webb guided them through the report page by page, enumerating various operating expenses, profits, losses, charges, and fees. Jenny really tried to keep up, but it was so deadly dull.

"Are we at the part yet where I can start making decrees?" she asked Mr. Webb, after a particularly baffling debate about prepaid debit cards between Mr. Gregory in Marketing and Stacy Loeb in PR.

The suits shifted uncomfortably.

"Soon," Mr. Webb said.

"Can you just, like, point to the number here that matters to me?" she said, tapping her binder.

He leaned over and used a $500 Montblanc pen to circle a 13 with two commas after it.

"Holy shit."

"As you can imagine, the holiday season, combined with RJ's tragic passing, generated a lot of demand for the brand," said Mr. Webb.

"Speaking of which, can we sync up on the next book?" asked the lady from Penguin. "If we want it out for Q1, we're gonna want to spin up the marketing push soon."

"What book?" Jenny asked.

"We've got a few different concepts," she said. "*Trouble in Camelot, It Takes Trouble to Tango, Zero Dark Trouble.* All ghostwritten, obviously. You're welcome to read them if you'd like—as long as you sign an NDA."

"Wait, wasn't Dad's final manuscript part of the will?" Jenny asked Mr. Webb.

"It was," he said with a sigh. "But he died before he could tell me where he was keeping it. Presumably, it's hidden somewhere in Valentine Manor."

"Or Val has it." Jenny set her jaw, a familiar rage awakening.

"I asked her, but she said she had no idea," Mr. Webb said.

"We'll see about that." She closed her binder. "I'm gonna go 'sync up' with my wicked stepmother. Great job, everyone, keep stacking that bread up. Give yourselves all a $20 grand bonus on me. No new books unless they're written by RJ for real."

"But the next holiday season—" the Penguin lady said.

"Just do a box set or something," Jenny said.

"We already did one last year."

"We'll figure something out," Jenny said. "Maybe I could do some readings. Like, fan events."

"Oooh, yeah, the market research on that isn't great." Mr. Gregory winced. "Probably best for you to keep a low profile."

"What about this Valentine's Day parade thing?" Stacy asked. "Maybe a commemorative giveaway?"

"No. I don't want Trouble, Inc. having anything to do with that," Jenny said. She turned to Mr. Webb. "How are my jeeps coming along?"

"Getting detailed at the dealership as we speak," he said.

"Good. You know that animal shelter over on Second Street? Figure out who we need to write a check to in order to get it reopened. And then do it. Thanks."

She stood and pulled on her poncho.

"Be good, Trouble," Mr. Webb said with a Cheshire cat grin.

Jenny surveyed the wary suits gathered around the table with a devilish smile of her own. "Who wants to read about that?"

BEFORE HEADING UP TO VAL'S, JENNY TOOK A CIRCUITOUS ROUTE through every floor below, checking to see if any of the tape she'd left on doors remained unbroken. She found three possible candidates for Dad's secret room: 237, 308, and 525. Now, how to narrow them down without arousing the Maître D's suspicion? Maybe Eliza would have an idea. Right now, Valerie Valentine required her full attention.

The elevator chimed, and Jenny stepped out into the penthouse hallway. She steeled herself and pounded on the door.

A minute went by with no response. Jenny knocked again.

"I know you're in there, Val!" she shouted. "Open up, we need to talk!"

The door sprung open immediately.

"Come to say you're sorry?" said Val.

"Jesus," Jenny said, getting a look at her evil stepmother. Gone was the glamorous evening gown and perfect makeup from the ceremony last week. This Val looked blotchy and haggard—and she kinda smelled. Her hair was in a messy ponytail, and she was wearing *sweatpants* for christ's sake. Jenny sniffed. "You should really get out more."

"What do you want? I'm missing *Vanderpump Rules*."

"Can't a girl just have a chat with the lady who killed her dad?"

Val drifted back into the foyer of the penthouse suite, leaving the door open. Jenny took it as an invitation to follow.

"We both know I didn't do it. I can't decide if you framed me yourself, or you're just a useful idiot."

The suite was decked out with an expensive leather sectional, marble tile, and thick linen curtains. Val had certainly made herself at home. Takeout boxes overflowed the small wastebasket, and one of her bras draped haphazardly over an armchair.

"Coffee?" Val shouted over the ad for detergent blaring on the TV.

"Sure," Jenny said, finding the remote and muting the television. She moved the bra and took a seat in the chair. "No underwire?"

"Tommy John, they're amazing," Val said, joining her with two steaming mugs.

Jenny smiled and took her mug and poured it out into a nearby potted plant.

"Where's my manuscript?"

Val rolled her eyes. "There is no manuscript."

"Bullshit," said Jenny. "It's in the will. Everyone knows he was working on something big."

Val laughed and sipped her coffee. "Sure. Five years he spent: farting around in his study, drinking scotch, and pretending to work on his next masterpiece. I never saw a single page. You can call that writing, I call it functional alcoholism."

The retort caught in Jenny's throat. It couldn't be true. Val was just trying to get under her skin.

"That's a really messed up way to speak of the dead."

"Oh no, you don't get to play that card," said Val. "He was my husband. We loved each other since before you were even born."

"And yet here I sit."

Val's reply was a sad, droopy smile. Jenny couldn't stand her pitiful appearance any longer. She stood up and paced into the suite's kitchen, casually glancing around for clues. There was an itinerary for the Valentine's Day festival on the counter and what looked like a schematic of the parade route nearby. A cheesy "#1 Student" magnet pinned Jack's essay from English class to the fridge.

"You know, when you're convicted, you're gonna need a kind word at sentencing if you want to avoid the needle," Jenny said, scanning Jack's essay. His favorite book, predictably, was *The Catcher in the Rye*. Mr. Hooke gave him an A- on the paper. At this moment, Eliza would be rewriting Jenny's essay in detention. Probably about some Harry Potter book. She turned back to Val. "Hand over the manuscript, and maybe we can… come to an arrangement. For the love you bore my father."

Val laughed. "No, that's not why you're here."

"Hmm?"

"You don't want the manuscript," Val said, approaching her.

"Yes, I do," Jenny said.

"No," said Val, stepping close and setting her mug on the counter. "You want absolution. You *did* frame me."

Jenny swallowed. "Dream on."

"I know that look. I saw it once before, on your mother's guilty face. Do you know what she said to me when I confronted her?" A shiver of dread ran up Jenny's spine. Val stepped closer. Even without her customary three-inch heels, she towered over Jenny. "She said, 'Don't worry, Val, he doesn't want your money.' Hah! So magnanimous. Like *I* was the one who needed to worry. Who's laughing now, *La La?*"

Without thinking, Jenny threw a right cross and punched that smug smile right off Val's dumb face—

Or at least, she tried to. Val somehow caught her fist and held it there in a freakishly strong grip. She regarded Jenny for a moment, a snake sizing up its lunch, before digging her nails into the back of Jenny's hand.

"Ow!" Jenny yelped.

"Let's get something straight." Val moved to the foyer, dragging Jenny along by her hand. "You do not get to ruin my life and then act like you care."

"Same!" Jenny hissed.

Val opened the door and yanked her out into the hall, smashing the elevator button with her free hand. "Learn from your mother, Jennifer, and stay the fuck away from my family."

A chime sounded, and she finally let go of Jenny's hand, shoving her into the elevator. Blood wept from the puncture wounds. Jenny was too stunned to reply.

"Oh, and try that again, and I'll see that you join her," Val added as the elevator doors closed between them.

She shouldn't have looked out the window. In her rage, Jenny spun around and stared down at the town below. By the time Jenny reached the lobby, she could hardly see straight. Darkness pressed in from all around. It felt like her body was too small to contain her rage, like it would just erupt out of her at any moment. It felt like—Jenny gripped the railing in the elevator car—it felt like another panic attack.

She slid to the floor, fighting to breathe. For months she'd been okay, but Val could see right through her false confidence and knew just where to stick the knife and make it hurt.

The elevator car dinged, and the doors slid open, revealing Sheriff Lockhart leaning against the far wall with crossed arms and a cross face.

"Productive chat?" he asked.

Jenny struggled to force air into her lungs. "She basically admitted to killing my mother," she gasped, fumbling for the bottle of Xanax in her purse.

Lockhart frowned and stepped into the elevator car, hitting the Emergency Stop button. "She couldn't have, she would have been in the maternity ward with Jack." He slid down into a catcher's crouch against the side wall, wincing as his knees popped. "You know, your father would get these attacks. Usually before a live reading. He said it was stage fright, but now… I wonder if maybe he was terrified he might see you in the audience."

Jenny labored through another breath. "Go to hell."

"Big breaths. Focus on this." He held out a folded piece of paper.

They sat for a while as Jenny got her body under control. Lockhart waved off hotel guests to the next car over. The dark vignette that had encircled her vision slowly withdrew.

"What is that?" Jenny reached out for the folded paper, but he withdrew it and wagged a finger at her.

"A present," he said. "You okay to stand?"

Jenny held out her hand. He covered it with a big, meaty paw and lifted her back on her feet like she weighed nothing.

"Hold your hands out." He gestured with the folded up paper.

She held out her hands, curious. But instead of giving her the paper, he shackled her with handcuffs.

Jenny sighed. "Is this necessary?"

"No." He grinned.

Lockhart walked her out into the lobby, taking care to pass by the front desk so all the staff and wealthy hotel guests would see. That bastard, the Maître D' had a big shit-eating grin on his face.

"That's right, get an eyeful, you rich pricks. Blackbird Springs's number one badass coming through."

Officer Peña was waiting outside with Mr. Webb, blowing into her gloved hands and looking extra cute in her uniform with earmuffs on.

"That reporter is up my ass, would you please call him?" Peña said to Lockhart.

"Hi Darcy," Jenny said, rediscovering her smile.

"That's Officer Peña to you," she replied. Lockhart grumbled and pulled off her earmuffs. She scowled. "Aww, come on, Blake."

"You need your ears," Lockhart said.

He handed Mr. Webb that piece of paper. Mr. Webb read it aloud. "Jennifer Valentine, by order of the court, you are not to come within 500 feet of Valerie Valentine, under penalty of arrest, etcetera etcetera. Well, that took longer than I expected, honestly."

"Good day, ma'am," Lockhart said, walking to his truck.

"Don't forget these," Jenny said, tossing him the handcuffs and rubbing her wrists.

"How did you—?" Lockhart stared dumbfounded at the unlocked cuffs.

Officer Peña chuckled. "You forget to tighten them, boss?"

The sheriff studied Jenny with eyes full of doubt. "That court order is serious. Don't test me."

"Yeah, yeah, get lost. I need to confer with my lawyer," said Jenny.

Lockhart ground his teeth but left with Peña. She waited until they were out of earshot.

"How much would it take to buy Val out of that penthouse?" Jenny asked. "There's gotta be a number, right? Where the hotel would kick her out if I paid enough?"

"I think that would constitute harassment," Mr. Webb said, looking over the restraining order. "Before you go, I have something for you."

He snapped his fingers, and a business card appeared in his hand. On the back was a handwritten name and an address for somewhere up in the hills.

"She's asked to meet you," Mr. Webb said. "I think it's a bad idea, but she insisted."

"Who's Campbell Batori?" she asked.

Mr. Webb tsk-tsked her. "Batori is her maiden name. She changed it back after the divorce."

Jenny shrugged.

"If you'd done more research before running off to visit Mary Manuel, you'd know her as Campbell Klein," said Mr. Webb. "Casey Klein's mother."

Chapter Nine

Survivor's Guilt

After what felt like an eternity, Saturday School was finally over. Eliza grabbed her phone and bolted from the classroom as soon as Mr. Hooke released them, eager to put some distance between herself and Charlie Zaleska.

Bored out of her mind in detention, she'd let Charlie talk her into being a makeup guinea pig to practice on. There were worse ways to spend a morning, and it was sort of like going to Sephora with money. And it was, for a while.

Thunder rumbled, and the wind howled, whipping the tresses of her blonde wig all over. It would rain soon. She tapped her phone screen and got bombarded with new texts and voicemails. Eliza hopped into the waiting town car and caught up on the morning's developments on the ride back to the mansion. Trouble had been busy living up to her namesake.

As soon as they parked, Eliza rushed up the front stairs, a first giant raindrop splashing on her head. Bad news for Shelly's horseback riding date. Hopefully, her aunt hadn't come home early. Eliza traded her shoes for house slippers and padded to Jenny's bedroom in the east wing.

No sign of her sister. Good. She could wash this makeup off. She reached for the bathroom door—

—and walked right into her twin. A tortured yelp escaped her lips.

"Oh! Sorry," said Jenny, stepping to the side. Eliza tried to duck past, but Jenny missed nothing. "Hold up."

Eliza winced and turned around. Jenny's eyes sparkled.

"You look… amazing."

"It's nothing," said Eliza.

Just some liquid foundation, lash extensions, light contouring, jungle red lipstick, "and a little trade secret for that dewy, JBF look," Charlie had said with a laugh and a leer of her hazel eyes.

"No, seriously, you're a babe," said Jenny.

"Why thank you, identical twin," Eliza said.

"Is this what you did in detention?" Jenny smiled. "Are you dating the school jock now?"

"Hah, hah. We got bored and killed time."

"Who's we?"

She glanced away. "Some… freshman girls."

"Lie," Jenny declared. "Who?"

Eliza grimaced. "Charlie Zaleska. I let her practice on me. I hope that doesn't, like, lower your social status or anything."

Jenny snorted. "I'm surprised she didn't give you a unibrow or something. She's good. Maybe I should usurp Meghan and recruit Charlie to my own squad."

"I wouldn't trust her that far. I think she was just happy to have someone else to practice on," said Eliza. She left out the part where she gave Charlie her number for homework and maybe gave her the wrong impression with all that unavoidable eye contact. Jenny Valentine was dating Dinah Black; she wasn't supposed to be having a moment in detention with Charlie Zaleska. And Eliza… well, Eliza didn't know what she was supposed to be doing anymore.

"Are you okay?" Jenny asked.

"Oh, yeah. How'd it go at the earnings meeting?"

Jenny grimaced. "Well…"

She listened as Jenny recounted her run-in with Val.

"You should have let the Undertaker poison her when we had the chance," Eliza said.

"If I had, we couldn't have framed her. Don't worry, she's on the list. We just have to figure out how to get a P.I. to look into Mom's last days without discovering *you*. Anyway, speaking of murder mysteries, how'd you like to meet with Casey Klein's mom while Dinah and I go shopping?"

Eliza wrinkled her nose. "I wouldn't."

"Would it make a difference if you could drive there?" Jenny said, producing a set of car keys from nowhere and spinning them around her finger.

Eliza's eyes lit up. "The jeeps?"

"There's one in the garage." Jenny tossed her the keys. "Webb should have the rest here by Monday."

The skin on Eliza's forearms prickled with anticipation. The freedom of an open road was in the palm of her hand. "What's the address?"

THE FIRST THING ELIZA NOTICED, AS SHE GINGERLY MANEUVERED down the muddy road on Campbell Batori's property, was the statues. She'd thought the brown owl perched on the gate post was real—and about to offer her a side quest—until it dawned on her that it wasn't moving. Further in were two bronze German shepherds, nipping at each other in the tall grass. A vagrant hitchhiker sticking out his thumb, a ballerina, a sad clown with a balloon, a giant tortoise ambling along. All cast in metal with a deep, burnished brown patina.

Ms. Batori's house was a great big barn. It sat amidst a meadow up in the hills north of town, enclosed on three sides by a forest of oak trees and manzanita, and a babbling creek on the other. The place must have cost a cool $2-3 million. Clearly, she'd done all right in the divorce. A wide concrete slab out front served as a driveway. Eliza drove onto it and stopped, searching for the parking brake.

The afternoon rain had slackened to a heavy mist. She killed the ignition and watched her windshield go hazy with moisture. To the west, the sun peaked out on the horizon, below the cloud layer— golden hour. Confidence swelled within her as she caught her reflection in the mirror. She took a selfie. She looked great. Maybe she'd send it to Charlie later. The makeup artist would appreciate her handiwork in this lighting.

A loud, metallic shrieking rang out from the side of the house. Eliza hopped out and followed the noise around the corner to an open pair of massive wooden doors. Inside, someone in an oversized protective mask and respirator was attacking a steel rod with an angle grinder, sending a stream of sparks shooting across the shop floor.

The metal shrieking stopped, and they stashed the angle grinder, yanked out some white earbuds, and reached up to pull off the heavy safety mask. The only picture Eliza had seen of Casey's mother was a family portrait back when Casey was alive. Blonde and beautiful, with perfect white teeth and a conservative neckline on her navy dress. Happier times. The woman before her was unmistakably the same but from some alternate *Days of Future Past* timeline. She'd cut her hair short—even shorter than Jenny's—and let the blonde fade to silver. Eliza suddenly felt childish covered in makeup and a luxuriant, golden wig next to this badass woman who had lost all fucks to give when she'd lost her daughter.

Ms. Batori pulled off her work gloves, paused her iPod Nano, and shrugged out of a heavy canvas jacket to reveal a messy white tank top and arms rippling with lean muscle underneath. She sauntered over in a loose gait—she even moved like she didn't give a fuck—and studied Eliza with lively, intelligent eyes.

"Yeah, you're John's, all right," said Campbell Batori. "I heard you were Trouble."

A very RJ-esque grin tugged at the corner of Eliza's mouth. No, but close.

Ms. Batori used a blowtorch to heat her kettle for some tea. It seemed a bit much—like she might be showing off. Cool, though. The workshop had to be at least 30 feet on a side, full of power tools and hammers and chisels, scraps of wood and metal and wax, plaster casts, and half-formed blobs of melted bronze strewn about.

"I remember those," Eliza said, pointing to the ancient iPod with headphones wrapped around it, which Ms. Batori had deposited on top of a welder. "My mo—my aunt had one."

"I'm not a crabby old Luddite, I swear," she said. "If I get careless with a plasma cutter, these are a lot cheaper to replace than my phone."

"Right. What do you listen to?"

"Trade secret," she said with a flinty grin. "Did you like the piece I made?"

"What piece?" asked Eliza.

"You know, your father. The bench," she said.

"Ohhh. That was you? You made the statue of RJ?" Eliza blushed. Of course she had, bronze work surrounded them. "Wow, um, yeah.

It's—it really captures him."

Ms. Batori nodded. "You hate it, don't you?"

"Oh—no! Ms. Batori, it's great!"

"Please, call me Campbell. And it's all right," she said with a grim but caring smile. "I tried to talk Valerie into something else, but she insisted, and the commission was too good to pass up."

"I mean, the craftsmanship is amazing," Eliza tried, blushing harder.

Campbell snorted. "So amazing, you threw up when you saw it, I hear."

Eliza fumbled for words and found none.

"I get it, I really do," Campbell said.

"I guess it's just weird to see him like that," Eliza offered.

"I know."

Silence hung between them until the kettle whistled. Campbell killed the blow torch.

"I made one of Casey once," she said, swallowing a lump in her throat. "After she... After. Carved it in wax, then cast it in silicon, then investment, then bronze, the whole deal. I polished it all up till it was perfect. Looked just like her. It made me want to fucking kill myself."

Eliza nodded, fascinated. She'd been expecting a tongue-lashing from an angry rich lady, pickled in high-priced rosé and grief. Instead, Campbell Batori was raw and open and honest. Jenny would like her, Eliza thought. Eliza decided she liked her too.

"What'd you do with it?" she asked.

"Took a plasma torch to it," said Campbell, walking to a small shelf holding teacups and dishes. "I think most of the bronze ended up as a kid in a wheelchair out in front of the new wing at Santa Rosa Memorial Hospital."

"Oh," said Eliza. "I was born there, actually."

"I remember," she said with a smirk, cleaning two small cups in a big industrial sink.

"Really?"

"I must confess, the girls and I were talking a lot of trash about your mom and dad back then," Campbell said, her eyes lighting up with youthful vigor at the memory. "Valerie had always been so smug about him. But then the accident happened, and, well, you know the rest."

Eliza nodded like this was true.

"But that was a different Campbell," she said. "Mrs. Klein." She wiggled her bare ring finger, and the spark in her eyes faded. "I hear you're going to catch my daughter's killer." She gestured to a copy of the *Blackbird Times* on a small table in the back of the shop.

Right to the point, then.

"Oh—sorry," said Eliza.

"Don't be sorry, catch the bastard."

Campbell poured her a cup the old-fashioned way, with the tea leaves at the bottom. Eliza breathed in the aroma, thinking of Professor Trelawney and her dour premonitions.

"So, you think Oscar Manuel was innocent?" Eliza asked.

A flicker of pain flashed across Campbell's pale face. "I always wanted him to be," she said with a sigh, taking a seat across from Eliza. "This will probably sound stupid. It never made any sense to Reed, but I—it just seemed so *unfair* for it to be Oscar. An act of such evil—it couldn't be this dimwitted gardener—this idiot with a pedo fetish that my Casey just had the dumb luck to cross paths with. I needed the killer to be the devil himself. Hannibal Lecter and Keyser Soze. I needed it to mean something. But it never did."

"Who do you think did it?"

She shrugged and looked away. "I don't know."

"Come on, I know you've got an idea. A theory, at least."

"Your dad had one for a long time," Campbell said. "He could never get enough evidence."

Eliza waited for more, but that seemed to be all that Ms. Batori had to say on the subject.

"See, the thing is, RJ kinda took that theory to the grave," Eliza said. "If I'm gonna catch this guy, I need to know what he knew."

"Did you talk to Oscar's mom?"

Eliza nodded. "She's got a binder full of missing girls. No one's even said 'sorry' to her. Did the cops talk to you after they found this new girl?"

"I got a courtesy call. Blake assures me it's probably just a copycat, but that didn't stop Napa PD from holding that ridiculous press conference. I'm gonna be honest, Jenny, there's a chance we're both getting our hopes up over some inter-departmental dick-waving."

"But if we're not," Eliza said, giving Campbell a pleading look. "Trouble needs to know where the scent went cold."

Campbell pursed her lips, hesitating. "I'm trying to remember how to think like a mother, here," she said. "I got the impression this guy was on the unsavory side. You need to be careful."

A jolt ran through Eliza's spine. Was RJ, perhaps, not careful enough? Could this be what put the Stranger on his trail? "Can I get a name, at least?"

"John never gave me one. He wanted me to stay pure, in case I needed to testify. I know he was focused really hard on the timing of everything; when Casey was last seen."

"Because of the Daylight Savings Time thing?"

Campbell smiled. "I see you've read Yvonne's book." She stood up. "Let me show you something."

Curiosity piqued, Eliza followed Ms. Batori inside the main part of the house and into a dusty office that appeared seldom-used. On the wall, Campbell had made a Big Board of her own, with pictures of Casey, Oscar Manuel, Blake Lockhart, and others, surrounding a large map of Eastin Drive, where Casey went missing.

"Here's the problem with the DST theory," she said, pointing to her house on the map. "At 2:10 PM, I put a batch of film into developer in my darkroom. I know, because there was a clock in there that I used to time things."

"I take it photography was your thing back then?" Eliza asked.

"Yeah," she said. An old ache rippled across her face. "We'd just built that darkroom. That was gonna be my new hobby." She blinked, willing the memory away. "Old Campbell. Anyway, right after I put the film in, I went to talk to Helen Wagner." She pointed to the house on the corner—the one with all the topiary statues, where Oscar Manuel had worked. "I went to the front door here, around the corner. It was for some PTA thing. Helen had a check for me for a school trip we were fundraising for."

"Weren't you guys all rich?"

"Well, we... I guess it was more about the sense of community than the money," Campbell said with a shrug. "Anyway, we talked at her door for a few minutes, then I came inside to help her move an end table. Couldn't have been in there for more than 5-6 minutes, tops. But the point is, if Brett Klinger says he saw Casey at 2:18 PM here." She pointed to a house further east. "Then I should have seen her too when I walked around the corner here."

"Is it possible she slipped by while you were inside?" Eliza asked.

"I doubt it. Helen's house has those big bay windows in the front. We would have seen her." Campbell sighed with old frustration. "Plus, Casey would have never left school early, regardless."

"Also, there were the other witnesses who saw her after 3:00 PM," said Eliza.

"Oh, you don't know about the Cynthia theory?"

Eliza shook her head, unfamiliar with the name.

"Cynthia Spade," said Campbell. "Another girl who went to Woodhall. Fifth grade. She had blonde hair too. From behind, she might have looked like Casey. The idea was, the other witnesses saw her instead of Casey. But even if that were true, I still would have seen her if she'd walked past the Klinger house at 2:18 PM. And Brett lived on our street, he would have been able to tell them apart."

She turned away from the map, rolling her neck. "Which means I was probably waiting out front, just around the corner, an hour later when her killer picked her up. So close…"

Eliza studied the map, searching for another explanation to this riddle.

"What was she like?" Eliza asked. "Casey, I mean."

"She was… I don't remember," Campbell said, a sudden sob escaping her throat. "It's awful. All I can see now is this perfect little girl, when I know there were times when she'd argue with Reed, or refuse to clean her room, or get in trouble at school for gossiping with Tori or whatever. But I can't see that anymore. All I see is that perfect bronze statue, and that's not who she was. She was real, and she was mine, and I can't even remember her voice anymore."

She turned away, tears flowing freely. Eliza sniffed, overcome herself, and tentatively reached out to place a hand on Campbell's shoulder. "I um—I can't even begin to imagine what you went through," Eliza said. "But I know what it's like to lose someone. I guess it never gets easier."

Campbell turned, wiping her eyes. "I'm so sorry, how insensitive of me. You just lost your father."

She patted Eliza's hand.

"Actually, I barely knew him," Eliza said. "But there was this woman—kind of a friend of the family—who helped raise me. She got sick a few years back, and every day it was like there was a little less of her. I told myself it made it easier. Like she was easing herself out of my life in the gentlest of ways possible. And when she passed, I was so busy for a while, I didn't even feel it. But lately, I see something that reminds me of her, and it's just a punch in the gut."

They stood together for a while, Ms. Batori patting Eliza's hand over and over before slowly drawing away. She brushed aside a lock of the blonde wig with her hand. "I know I'm supposed to have something wise to tell you," she said. "All I've got is: cherish every moment."

"Tell you what," said Eliza. "Skip the wisdom and give me anything you can about RJ's suspect."

"Right," Campbell nodded. "I'm pretty sure they worked at a metal shop in town—Geno's. RJ asked me a lot of questions about that place. I had been visiting there to take pictures. It was kind of my industrial phase. At least once, I brought Casey to the shop with me to watch."

"Hmm. Geno's. Got it."

"Be careful," she warned. "Those guys aren't the type to appreciate strangers poking around. Some of them got pissy when I asked to shoot there. Concerned about their 'civil liberties,' if you take my meaning. They could be dangerous."

"So am I," Eliza said.

Campbell walked her to the jeep under an umbrella. It was twilight, and the rain had picked up again.

"Oh, I forgot to ask!" Eliza shouted above the storm as she got in. "How'd my dad ever talk you into disinterring Casey?"

"That other girl, the Mexican one from the trailer park!" yelled Campbell. She lowered the umbrella, heedless of the deluge. "She had tiny flecks of sawdust in her lungs! Blake and John thought if they could find the same material in Casey's, it would link the crimes. But it had been too long before we found her. Between that and being buried, there just wasn't—wasn't enough left."

"I'm sorry! Thank you!" Eliza said. "I'm on the case!"

Campbell gave the jeep's side-panel an encouraging double-pat.

"Come by anytime, I can always use an extra pair of hands!"

Eliza smiled and drove off. Jenny was out with Dinah tonight, and they might come back to the mansion for a while, so she would need to crash in the treehouse or the Crow's Nest suite in town.

Actually, now that she had a car, maybe there was something else she could do. Jenny wouldn't need her till Monday, and Eliza needed a vacation from Trouble, if just for a day. She pulled onto the highway and went East instead of West. There was something she'd been putting off for far too long.

Chapter Ten

The Glass Slipper

THE STYLIST AT BELLA BOUTIQUE PINCHED HER CHIN BETWEEN her thumb and forefinger, fixing Jenny with her full, professional attention in a manner that Jenny found hard not to take as a threat.

"I'm just not sure that purple is your color," she said.

The nerve.

Jenny looked over at her girlfriend. Green was Dinah's color tonight. She'd dyed her hair tendrils to match her emerald t-shirt dress, complemented by a broad brown leather belt and matching knee-high leather boots. It was date night, and they'd agreed on shopping and dinner downtown, but Dinah had been distant from the start. Even now, she was faking a cough and avoiding eye contact. Jenny would have to deal with the stylist herself.

"How do you mean?" she asked through gritted teeth.

"Well, you run warm," the stylist said. "So I'm thinking we want some bold colors. Royal blue, crimson, maybe pink. Like shocking pink, not millennial. I have the perfect outfit!"

She hurried over to a rack of coats and flipped through them.

Jenny caught Dinah's eye. "Hey. What's up?"

Dinah's lip curled in a wan smile. "I got an A-minus in American History."

"Nice."

"No, not nice. Penny Griffin got an A-plus. She's ahead of me for Valedictorian now, and Thanh Trân is nipping at my heals too." Dinah's voice went hoarse, her eyes glossy.

"Oh, baby." Jenny reached over and squeezed her hand. "It's okay, it happens."

"Not to me!"

The stylist returned before Jenny could say something further. Dinah turned away, pretending to examine some strappy Louboutin pumps.

"This is so you," said the stylist, holding up a thigh-length red and black tartan coat. "We'll get a black belt and leggings. It's got that old school cool with a modern flair."

"Uh, great." Jenny glanced to Dinah for approval but found the back of her blonde head instead. Her shoulders were riding high and rigid. Stressed. "Do you like those shoes? We can get em."

"Nah," Dinah said, moving further away to examine another pair.

"Box a pair up for her," Jenny whispered to the stylist, nodding to the pumps. "Size 8."

"Did you want the outfit?" the stylist asked.

Jenny shrugged. She didn't, but Eliza would.

"Sure. I'll take two."

They hit BeBe and Ulta before calling it quits. Jenny's personal goal of maxing out the $25,000 limit on her Discover Black card would have to wait. The rain was pouring in earnest now, so she called her driver to take their shopping bags back to the mansion. Sensing an opportunity for romance, they walked on foot to the new Mexican place Dinah picked out, huddled close under a giant umbrella.

"This isn't one of those fusion places, is it?" Jenny asked, dubious.

"It says they have 'bulletproof street tacos,' whatever that means," said Dinah.

"It's an LA thing."

"We can go somewhere else."

"No! No, this is fine. It's your pick," Jenny said. "I just want you to have a good time."

She snuggled closer to Dinah under the umbrella. She was just getting comfortable when a girl shrieked, and they both leapt apart, startled.

Jenny's head darted around for the source of the alarm. Dinah let out a soft groan of disgust as Jenny spotted two girls running their way, hurrying to get out of the rain. Both looked utterly impractical in their loose blouses, A-line skirts, and sequined flats.

"Do you mind?!" Meghan May asked, not waiting for an answer as she and a soaked Lily Geist ran up and huddled under their big umbrella.

Dinah's hand, Jenny noted, slowly withdrew from her purse, empty. "Hey," she said to the girls.

"Can we pretty-please get an escort to Rosie's?" asked Meghan.

"Oh my god, are you Link? I love Zelda," Lily said, looking Dinah up and down. "Are you cosplaying?" She turned to Jenny. "Which one are you?"

"Trouble," Jenny said, stepping in front of her girlfriend when Dinah's hand darted back into her purse.

"Pleeeeaaase?" Meghan pleaded. "In Paris, they cover all the sidewalks, I forgot you can't just walk anywhere in the rain here."

"We're going to Yaco, we can take you that far," said Jenny.

"Nice, I know the manager there," said Lily.

Jenny threw an arm around Dinah, who relaxed and offered an

exasperated eye roll. They matriculated down Broadway, taking small steps crammed in under the umbrella while Lily kept up a seemingly endless monologue about the best service staff to score party drugs off of.

"God, I miss Declan," Lily said as they arrived at Yaco.

"We can take em all the way to Rosie's, can't we?" Jenny asked Dinah.

"Noooo!" Meghan protested. "You guys are on a date. Don't mind us." She pulled Lily away, ducking under an awning. Before they went inside, Meghan stopped Dinah. "I just want to say, it's really brave to get out there and stand by your girl like this. Au revoir."

"What was that about?" Jenny asked once they were indoors.

"Ehh, I'll tell you later. Can we get something on the veranda? They have heaters."

Jenny had to admit, this was a cool restaurant, even if lobster and avocado tacos weren't precisely what she'd call "bulletproof." They were up on the second story deck, under a waterproof canopy. The winter chill warred with gas braziers, creating a thermal confusion that her body didn't know what to do with, leaving her skin flushed, and her mood, well, horny.

"I'll bet this place is great for people-watching," Dinah said, squeezing some lime over her taco. "You know, when it's not cats and dogs."

They had a table near the edge of the deck, giving them a good vantage of the corner down below without being too high up.

"It's not bad for people watching now," Jenny said, locking eyes with Dinah and putting as much of her current mood into her gaze as she knew how.

Dinah did a little bashful pose for her that made her toes curl. Still, something nagged at Jenny.

"Have I been—I'm not distracting you, am I?" she asked. "Keeping you from studying?"

"No!" Dinah said quickly. "Well, I mean, yes, but I don't think that's it. Not entirely, at least."

"A good distraction, I hope," Jenny said, feeling crappy.

"Of course," said Dinah. She reached across the table and gave Jenny's hand a comforting squeeze. Some of the tension melted away.

"Sounds like Jack needs to be more of a distraction for Penny," said Jenny. "Though I suppose he wasn't much of one for you, either."

Dinah blushed hard. "Dude!"

"Oh shit, I made it weird again, didn't I?" Jenny's mortified smile was so wide it hurt, her cheeks aflame.

"We need like a code word for this," Dinah said. "Any time we're too close to something one of us *really* doesn't want to get into, we just say 'danger zone,' and change the subject, no questions asked."

"Uhh, not that word," said Jenny. "How about this: Shelly dated this complete weasel David for two years back in LA. Afterward, we wouldn't even say his name, just 'Dryden Street,' cause that's where he lived. I'd say, 'Why can't we eat at Brick and Flour anymore?' and she'd say 'Dryden Street.' She'd ask where the stain on her winter sweater came from, and I'd say, 'Dryden Street.' Truth be told, that was actually me, but still, fuck that guy."

"So, if you ask me to make out in the disability elevator in the HUM building, I can say…?" Dinah winced.

"Dryden Street?" Jenny asked with chagrin. "Seriously?"

"Dryden Street!" Dinah squealed. She was smiling for real now, though. Much better.

"Perfect," said Jenny. "But before we start, I have two questions. Not Jack-related."

Dinah hesitated before nodding. "Okay."

"First, what's in your purse?"

Dinah smiled, unsurprised, and pulled out a heavy black thing with metal points on the end. A stun gun. "My dad got it for me after my girlfriend ended up in the newspaper connected to a murder for the—what—fourth time?"

"Fair enough. Do you know where he got it? I want one."

"I'll check. What's your other question."

Jenny tried to ask as casually as possible. "What are you really upset about tonight? Cause it's not just your history grade."

Dinah's eyes hardened. She picked up her phone and tapped it, then turned it around to show Jenny a Facebook post.

Trouble in Paradise?

And underneath, a photo of Charlie Zaleska with her face almost touching Eliza's. One could imagine they were about to kiss. It must have been taken this morning at Saturday school.

"The fucking Ghostwriter?" Jenny scowled. "Who even took this?"

"Can we address the bigger issue first?" Dinah asked.

"Look, I swear to God, I was just letting her practice doing makeup on me," Jenny said, trying not to acknowledge the odd look of yearning on Danger's face. "We were bored and killing time. Nothing happened."

"Be honest. Do you think she's pretty?"

"I mean, sure, but in an 'I'm jealous of your perfect skin' way, not in an 'I'm attracted' way." She wrapped her hand around Dinah's. "What can I say, I prefer blondes."

Dinah leaned over and they kissed for a while, exploring the contours of each other's tongues.

1,190… 1,191…

"Good," Dinah said when she came up for air. "That little slattern needs to learn her place."

Her mind went all fuzzy for a while, heat blossoming deep in her core. Hearing Dinah drag bitches with 50-cent words *did things* to her.

"Oh, so that's what Meghan was talking about," Jenny said, her brain finally catching up.

Their phones both vibrated at once.

"What's this, more Ghostwriter?" Dinah said, grabbing her phone. Jenny checked hers. Eliza had sent her a long text. Casey's mom didn't have a name, but Dad's suspect might have worked at Geno's Metal Shop in town... Also, Eliza was in Sacramento... She read the message twice, concerned about her sister when she noticed that Dinah had gone quiet.

"What's up?" she asked.

"My mom—ugh." Dinah's expression was pained. "They're going to this dad rock concert at the Fillmore tonight, and they forgot to let Lancer out." She bit her lip. "Would you hate me if we left early?"

Jenny frowned. Dinah's dog was an older pup and needed frequent bathroom breaks. "I guess tonight's not our night, huh?"

"Sorry."

"It's fine. Lancer would never forgive me if I kept you." With her night suddenly open, Jenny's thoughts drifted to the metal shop Danger mentioned. "You go on, I'll call the driver for you. There are a couple errands I want to run since I'm down here."

"Oh. Okay. You sure?" Dinah asked.

"Yeah, it's fine." Jenny pressed her lips to the back of Dinah's hand. "We'll call this 'To be continued.'"

Before she left, Dinah came around the table to give her a good long taste of her cinnamon lip balm.

"Do you need to borrow this?" Dinah asked, patting the heavy stun gun inside her purse.

"No, nothing like that," Jenny lied. "Gotta pick up some supplies for Shop class."

After Dinah left, Jenny sat at their table for a bit, nursing her tea and ruminating on Eliza's text. Did her sister miss home? Was Jenny not enough of a home for her? She always got weird about Jenny and Dinah. Whatever. She checked her Maps app. Geno's Metal Shop was about a mile away. Not far from The Cellars, where Declan Dillion met his end. It was some sort of co-op, and they were open till midnight. Should she go in disguise? Or openly, as Trouble, picking up the trail where Dad left off…

It was five minutes before the epiphany hit: maybe alone, defenseless, and in the dark wasn't the best way to visit this place. It took her 10 minutes to realize she should have offered to go with Dinah, and 10 more to compose a breezy semi-apology text.

She tapped **Send** and sighed, running a hand through her bangs. The rain had thankfully calmed to a misty drizzle. Down below on the corner, locals hurried about. Jenny lost herself in the patterns of their movement, counting umbrellas and raincoats, sensible shoes… a pair of sparkly flats caught her attention. She followed their owner's legs up to a curvy chest and drenched red hair. It was Lily Geist, sans Meghan, walking back up the street. Off to score some molly, perhaps.

Jenny felt, more than heard, the rumble of the train passing. Her watch tapped her wrist.

> **Dinah:**   Send me a cute selfie and I'll forgive you.
>
> A distracting one 😏

Crisis averted. Hoping no one was looking, she pulled down the neck of her tank top, exposing her bra. She'd distract Dinah, all right. Jenny bit her lip and snapped a pic. It was trashy in precisely the way she wanted.

> **Jenny:**   B+ here you come!

She popped a Xanax, tucked a C-Note under her tea saucer, and sent the photo.

Before calling her driver, she ducked into the market across the street. They sold dried pineapple slices, and Jenny was absolutely craving them after the spicy meal. Dessert in hand, she made her way toward Town Square, letting the crystalized fruit dissolve in her mouth. It was past 10:00 PM now, and the sidewalks were mostly empty.

Movement to her right caught her eye. She turned to find herself in front of the Poison Pen, still closed while the remnants of the Carnegie family dealt with their legal issues. Maybe it was just her reflection, but she could swear something had moved inside the bookstore.

Jenny approached the storefront window and held up her hands to peer inside the dark building. All the books were gone, along with the familiar tall bookshelves, leaving only a bare countertop by the front and a few random cinderblocks behind.

In the back, she could see the outline of the door to the stockroom. It appeared to be half-open. Movement flickered behind it. The stock room door closed, and Jenny's heart froze to the core.

Someone was inside the Poison Pen.

She stepped back and looked at the entrance door: it was slightly ajar. A tiny wooden shard, easy to miss, was wedged between the door and frame, up at the top of the doorjamb. Unable to stop herself, compelled by instinct, she reached for the door handle and pulled.

The door swung open, the little wooden wedge falling with a soft clatter to the sidewalk.

"That's far enough," said a gruff voice behind her.

Jenny spun, doing a double—then triple—take at the source. Deputy Calderon had somehow snuck up on her, which wouldn't be so bad if he hadn't managed it while riding a horse.

"How the—" Jenny paused to catch her breath. "Does that thing have stealth mode or something?"

"Ole Ricochet's got a creep to her," Calderon said, rubbing the horse's neck. "That and rubber horseshoes. You wanna explain what you were just about to do?"

"Oh! Right, shit! Someone's in there!"

"Inside the bookstore?"

"Yeah! I think they were about to leave when I noticed them, so they slipped out the back instead."

"Okay, sure, that's plausible," Calderon said. "But so what? Why does that mean you need to break in and follow them?"

"I wasn't—the door was propped open." Jenny tossed her bangs in annoyance. "Look, I snoop, it's what I—"

She was interrupted by something falling to the sidewalk between them. Calderon's horse neighed, reeling back.

"Tranquila, chica!" he said, slipping out of the saddle.

Jenny beat him to the object: a woman's flat. Sparkly with sequins.

"Don't touch it!" Calderon barked.

He was staring straight up, color draining from his face. Jenny followed his gaze. At the top of the building, a woman's leg was dangling over the edge. It wasn't moving.

Calderon swore and looped Ricochet's reins around a parking meter, then his revolver and flashlight were out. Jenny wasn't about to stick around out here alone, so she followed him inside the dark bookstore.

They crossed quickly to the stockroom door. The deputy charged in, but the room was empty.

Jenny pointed to the exit in the back. "There's a staircase to the roof through there. It's a back hallway that all the shops share."

He nodded and led on. The hallway was empty, too, as far as the light from the flashlight could reveal. They hurried up the stairs, finally bursting out onto the roof three flights up.

It was hard to say if it was the height up here, or the body lying atop the parapet that made Jenny's knees shake. Calderon raced over, but Jenny already knew what he'd find. She'd known as soon as she saw the shoe.

Lily Geist's lips were still curled into an O, stunned terror frozen on her face. A white rope noose coiled around her neck, and someone had shoved her pretty red hair under a blonde wig.

Calderon checked for a pulse and grimaced. "Still warm. Can't have been more than 15 minutes. Fuck!"

Jenny peeked over the edge and immediately regretted it, fighting off a rush of vertigo that threatened to disgorge her lobster tacos. A memory flashed.

It was freezing up here on the hospital roof. She'd never felt so cold, and so alone...

Jenny blinked and pulled away, crouching below the parapet ledge. She'd only meant to limit her view when something in Lily's left hand caught her eye. Jenny produced a black latex glove from her back pocket.

"No touching!" said Calderon. "You shouldn't even be here."

Jenny handed the glove to him, exasperated, and pointed to Lily's hand. He blinked twice.

"No wonder you keep Blake up at night."

"She's holding something."

He relented and put the glove on, carefully prying Lily's hand open and extracting a $20 bill. He frowned and sniffed it.

"Bleach." He rose and lifted her other hand to smell it too. "He wiped her down."

Calderon reached for his shoulder radio and called it in, motioning for Jenny to stand back. Her phone vibrated. Dinah calling. Jenny answered it, unable to look away from Lily's body.

"Oh my god, did you take that photo at Yaco's?" Dinah giggled over the line.

"Hey, bad news," Jenny said. "Better tell your dad I'm up to five now."

"Five what? What do you mean?"

"The Hot Springs Hangman," Jenny said. "He just killed Lily Geist, and I think he wanted me to find her."

Chapter Eleven

Dirty Blonde

N EWS TRAVELED FAST. WHEN JENNY KNOCKED ON DREW'S FRONT door the next morning, he answered with a Louisville Slugger in hand, eyes darting around behind her, as if the Hot Springs Hangman might jump out from behind a potted cactus at any moment.

"It's just me," she said.

"I'm surprised your aunt let you out," he said.

"Well, she doesn't know I was the one to find Lily," Jenny muttered. "Calderon let me give a statement and get out of there. So keep that on the QT."

They headed to Drew's garage. Inside, the baseball tee and tarp had been tucked into the corner, replaced by guitars, a synthesizer, and a sparkly red and chrome drum kit. Jenny laughed and grabbed the drumsticks, generating a cacophony of percussion until Drew gave her a look.

"I should be your drummer!" she announced.

He shook his head ruefully and pulled down the retractable screen to reveal their new Big Board.

"I already did the honors," he said, pointing to a print-out of Lily

Geist taped up next to Casey, Rita Thomas, and Sarah Ortiz.

"Did you have to use that photo?" Jenny asked. He'd printed out an Instagram photo of Lily in a bikini, sitting by the pool with her Jack Russell terrier.

"What? I like dogs," Drew said with a pervy grin.

"You're such a boy sometimes."

While searching for a better photo, Jenny recounted last night's events, from walking with Meghan and Lily, dinner at Yaco, then finding Lily on the roof of the Poison Pen.

"It's weird," said Jenny. "Lily's 17, those other girls were younger. And they were found weeks or months later. With Lily, it was like the Hangman wanted me to find her."

"To scare you," said Drew.

"It's because you called him out in the newspaper, Trouble," said a squeaky voice from behind.

She spun to find Alicia Aaron standing in the doorway.

"What the fuck?" Jenny scrambled to roll up the Big Board.

"Don't bother," Alicia said. "I already saw the entire thing yesterday when Drew went to the bathroom."

"*Drew.*" She glared at her sidekick. "Why is she here?"

He stammered for a reply.

"Band practice," Alicia said. She sat at the drum kit and tapped out a crisp beat on the hi-hat and snare.

"*She's* your drummer??"

"I love how we can have whole conversations that go in one ear and out the other," Drew said. "I told you last week."

Eliza had failed to mention this. "My mind palace must have been full that day," Jenny said.

"Where's Mason?" Drew asked Alicia.

"Coming." Alicia nodded at the Big Board. "Are you trying to solve

128

all the heirloom clues?"

"Eventually," Jenny said. "Don't suppose you'd like to sell me yours?"

"I don't know," Alicia said, patting the skeleton key hanging from a gold chain around her neck. "Seems like cheating."

"Is $300,000 enough to ease your conscience?" she asked.

"Oh, it would need to be at least a million," Alicia said. "Plus, you have to publish my first novel."

"Hah, dream on."

"Fine, I'll keep it. But would you mind not publicly challenging serial killers? At least the ones who hunt girls."

"Don't act so superior, I know you're on the case too," Jenny said.

With a bang, the door flew open, and they all flinched.

"Y'all ready to rock out with your cocks out?!" Mason shouted as he sauntered in.

"Don't be gross, Mason," said Alicia.

"Sorry." Drew grimaced. "I forgot that we practice earlier on Sunday. Did you want to meet later?"

"Oh, I wouldn't miss this for anything." Jenny smiled, pushing aside the drill and center punch on the workbench and hopping up to sit and watch. Drew strapped on his bass, and the three did some unstructured jamming as they tuned their instruments and checked their mic levels.

"What are you guys called?" Jenny asked when there was a pause in the noise.

"Dirty Blonde," said Drew.

"No, 33 Percent Mike," said Mason, twisting a tuning peg on his Fender.

"None of you is a Mike," Jenny pointed out. "Or blonde."

"See, no one gets it, Mace," said Alicia, twirling a drumstick and looking—for the first time Jenny had ever seen her—comfortable and at ease. "We should be Crash and the Girls."

"Oh, because that's not obscure and inscrutable," said Mason.

"Guys, 'Bring Me to Life!'" Drew shouted, cutting off all conversation with some bars on the synthesizer. Shortly, Alicia joined in on her mic. Mason waited for his cue to come in with a crunchy guitar, and they did a passable, if sloppy, version of the Evanescence song.

Jenny wanted so badly to make fun of them, and it was a supremely cheesy performance, but something about their confidence, their willingness to put themselves out there and look stupid, kept her mouth shut. If it kept the image of Lily's frozen O lips out of her mind, what was the harm? Even Mason seemed sorta cool, lunging and stomping as he played, crooning into his mic like a troubadour. By the end of the song, Jenny found herself clapping in reluctant applause.

"What'd you think?" Drew asked, tweaking some knobs on the mixer.

"We're hoping to play the Valentine's Day thing in a couple weeks," said Mason.

"I'm honestly shocked you can play your instruments," Jenny said. "It was good."

"We should work on 'Shallow,'" Alicia said, sipping from a water bottle. She'd taken her jacket off and had a bare-shouldered corset top on underneath. Drew was, Jenny observed, paying Alicia the kind of attention he usually reserved for her. It was a good thing Eliza wasn't here to witness this.

Mason drifted over to look at the Big Board, plinking strings on his guitar.

"Lily's probably a copycat," he said.

"You think?" asked Drew.

It was Mason's turn to give Jenny a smug grin. "I caught a peek of my dad's file on Casey Klein. They didn't tell the media, but Casey's head was shaved when Dad found her body."

Jenny glared, helpless to shut him up. This was how he took his revenge: by blabbing it all with Alicia right there.

"How's that make Lily a copycat?" Alicia asked.

"I'm getting there," he said. "So, the Napa PD cops. When they found Sarah Ortiz, she was wearing a blonde wig. It was made out of Casey's hair. DNA was a perfect match."

Jenny shivered, picturing the dozens of missing girls in Mary Manuel's binder, each taking their turn in the wig. "So because the wig on Lily was a fake, you think it's someone else? But how would they know about the wig in the first place?"

"How do *you* know about a wig on Lily?" asked Alicia.

Before she could concoct a decent lie, an ear-piercing electronic squeal interrupted them. All their phones were blowing up at once. It wasn't a text. It was an emergency broadcast alert.

> **A city-wide curfew is declared for all residents under 18 years old. Blackbird Springs will be on partial lockdown, effective at sundown. Visit blackbirdsprings.org/alert for more info.**

AUNT SHELLY WAS IN THE MAP ROOM, WHICH SHE'D UNOFFICIALLY claimed as her office. Old charts and tapestries and nautical trinkets lined the walls, with a gigantic table in the center where she was "grading papers," but mostly engrossed in the local news about Lily's murder on one of the mansion's ubiquitous retractable flat-screen TVs.

When Jenny entered, Shelly swallowed hard with glassy eyes.

"Shell?"

Her aunt blinked, holding up a sheet of paper. It was an Econ quiz. Lily's quiz.

"It's just—I can't believe it," said Shelly. "I just saw her."

"I know. Me too." Jenny grabbed the remote and switched the TV off. "Come on, this isn't the night for this."

"I don't want you going anywhere without permission," Shelly said, wagging a commanding finger at her. "From now on, you're on lockdown."

Wonderful. Whether it was the Hot Springs Hangman's intent or not, he was making it harder for Jenny to investigate. It wasn't helping that the Ghostwriter's latest post was an insane conspiracy theory about Lily's death being a marketing hoax to hype the release of the next *Trouble* novel.

There was nothing to be done with Eliza in Sacramento, though, so she dragged Shelly into the Screening Room, ordered sushi from the kitchen, and put on *Groundhog Day*, as was tradition. This year, they watched with Japanese dubs and English subtitles. Her grandparents would be home in a few weeks, and she was out of practice.

"Don't you wish you'd paid more attention in Japanese school now?" Shelly asked in Japanese, testing her.

"No. I just don't want them to think that you raised a delinquent," Jenny replied in the best Japanese she could muster as a montage of Bill Murray's character killing himself played on screen.

"A what?"

"A delinquent," Jenny said in English.

Shelly snorted. "You mean, *Sukeban?* And you are a delinquent."

"I just mean, they shouldn't hold it against you. Do they know about—about the hospital? Last year?" Jenny asked.

"They do," said Shelly. "I had to ask them for money to help pay for it. Don't worry, they're not going to hold it against you. They're excited to see you."

This made Jenny feel better, but something still troubled her. "Then why didn't they ever come to visit?"

"It's not that simple," Shelly glanced over at Jenny, a hint of sadness on her face. "It was never just one way; I had a lot of anger towards them. Still do."

"About Mom?"

Shelly flexed and stretched her arms, calming herself with a deep breath. "I can't blame them for everything. But if Laura hadn't felt like she had nowhere else to turn, she never would have been on that road. Some of that is my fault. I was so wrapped up in my own shit in college. If I could live that day over…"

Jenny leaned her head on her aunt's shoulder.

"I could have taken a quarter off," Shelly said. She used to sound so bitter whenever Mom came up, but since returning to Blackbird Springs, that pain had faded to sad regret. "Maybe she would have gotten better prenatal care, and Lizzy would have been born healthy."

Jenny nearly choked on her California roll. Aunt Shelly almost *never* mentioned her supposedly deceased twin.

"What would you have done if there were two of us?" Jenny asked as casually as she dared.

"Oh God, I can't even imagine. I barely managed with just you. Probably marry some loser, just to have someone else around to help out."

"Dryden Street."

"For real," said her aunt.

"Talking of which, how was the ride with what's his face?" Jenny asked. "Did you get caught in the rain?"

A touch of scarlet bloomed on Shelly's cheeks.

"You know what, forget I asked."

"In Japan, you'd say 'kinishinaide,'" said Shelly.

"Tell me more about Mom," said Jenny.

"Well, let's see. Her Freshman year in college, she was in a play where she did a nude scene. Mom and Dad refused to attend…"

THE NIGHTMARES RETURNED THAT NIGHT. SHE'D MANAGED TO disassociate from the horror all day, but in dreams, she couldn't hide from Lily Geist's haunting face. Sometimes Jenny was back on the roof of the Poison Pen, sometimes she was at the hospital. Sometimes the noose was around her own neck, in a wig of Casey's hair…

Jenny awoke early and swallowed a Xanax. Dinah messaged to say she was skipping, but with Shelly on high alert, Jenny had no such option.

The morning bell was a haze of grim pageantry. Students crying in the quad. Open Campus privileges for upperclassmen revoked. The remaining Bitchy Brigaders dressed all in black. "Grief counselors are on hand," etc. etc. This was supposed to be Eliza's day of school, but her twin was late in getting back. Jenny sleepwalked through American History, dying for caffeine—or something stronger.

The rail of Adderall she did at break overdid it. Now it felt like everyone was staring at her, blaming her. Everywhere she turned, she could feel their judgment. Jenny had stepped to a serial killer, and now their friend was dead.

"Could you show some respect and look somewhere else?" Shani said.

Jenny blinked. How long had she been staring at Lily's empty desk?

"As if I'd ever date a psycho," Charlie hissed in her ear, her mouth always too close to Jenny's neck.

"Don't flatter yourself, I only date hot chicks," Jenny replied.

"You wish." Charlie gave her the finger, but there was an unmistakable hint of disappointment behind her lash extensions. Jenny desperately needed to sit Eliza down and go over exactly what those two talked about in detention.

At lunch, she sought out Mason in the cafeteria. He and Jack were slouching on the indoor bleachers with JeRay Crawford and Lai Saechao and some other jocks from the baseball team. The vibe was grim, not the usual grabass that surrounded Mason and his bros. Jack looked up from poking at his chicken nuggets to fix Jenny with a stern glare.

"Someone broke into Penny's place and tried to steal her mom's book. You know the one."

"Well, it wasn't me, if that's what you're implying," Jenny said.

Lying was easy when you were telling the truth. It was Eliza who broke in.

"Interesting that you would assume so. Does she seem a little defensive?" Jack asked Penny next to him.

"She does," Penny said, mistrustful eyes on Jenny.

"She does indeed." Jack squinted at her. "And I did tell you that Penny and her mom would be out of town last Friday."

"I really don't need this," she said. "I'm under a lot of stress right now."

"Playing chicken with a killer of women," said Jack.

"If I wanted that book, I'd just write Ms. Griffin a check."

"She'd never sell it," said Penny.

Jenny searched for a reply. They were all still staring. Mason especially had a queer look in his eye. She needed to give them something.

"Look, I didn't mention this before, didn't want you to worry," Jenny said, leaning closer and dropping into sotto voce. "There's this guy you should watch out for. I thought he was only following me, but maybe not. He's a reporter, or at least posing as one. Jack, you saw him at the hotel when we went to the gym, remember?"

Jack's brow crinkled. "Kinda plain-looking guy. Black frame glasses?"

Jenny nodded. "Drives a rented Hyundai, white. He followed me and Drew the other day, and I spotted him poking around near the Blackbird Times building last week. I think he's been trying to talk to your dad, too," she added, nodding to Mason.

"What's his deal?" Penny asked.

"There's a $5 million reward for anyone who can give Valerie Valentine an alibi. What do you think?" she said.

Her watch tapped her on the wrist three times. Eliza was near.

"I gotta run to the loo," she said, turning to Mason. "You guys want to know a secret about Mason?"

He scowled and rapidly tapped his phone. A moment later, her watch vibrated with a new email. Casey's file, finally.

"What?" Penny and Jack asked.

"He can do a killer cover of 'Call Me Maybe.'"

Jack burst into laughter, slugging Mason on the shoulder. Penny and the other guys were cracking up. Even Meghan May, in mourning at a table nearby, smiled.

"Shut up, it slaps!" Mason replied with a dead-eyed smile. He pointed a finger gun at her. "One of these days, bastard. When you least expect it."

Jenny curtsied and hurried to the bathroom across the quad.

To Danger.

Once the Girl's Room was empty, Jenny ducked into the last stall to find a blonde Eliza in a black coat and floral print skirt.

"Sorry, I didn't know what you were wearing today," Eliza said softly.

"You all right?" Jenny asked.

"Yeah," she said brightening. "Yeah, I needed that. Thanks for the wheels. Did you get the report from Mason?"

"Yeah." Jenny pulled up the email. "Let's take a look."

They swapped clothes as they read. Casey's file—or the photos of three pages Mason had been able to snap of it—was illuminating, and also frustratingly unhelpful. The first was a timeline of events the day she disappeared: nothing new there. The second photo was of Page Five of Casey's autopsy report: an analysis of trace evidence found on her body. Someone—probably Blake—had circled a detail: horse hairs on Casey's skirt.

"Horse hairs," Eliza repeated as she pulled on Jenny's jeans. "Weird. What else?"

"Uh, head shaved," Jenny said, swiping to the next photo. "Memo from Napa PD about the wig and the DNA. Fuck, we already know all this. That asshole is holding out. I should leak something to the Ghostwriter about his kid."

"Let's see how the Metal Shop goes first." Eliza held up a calming hand. "BTW, you're gonna need to hop the fence, Deputy Mack was out front in a police cruiser," said Eliza.

Jenny adjusted the blonde wig. "I guess this is the Hangman's color."

"Hold up," Eliza said, examining Jenny's fingernails.

"Oh, I splurged at Ulta," Jenny said, pulling out a bottle of silver nail polish. "There's, like, bits of pure silver in here."

"We classy. I'll trade you." Eliza took the nail polish and rummaged in her purse. "It's not silver, but as requested." She held out a slender black object with twin metal points at one end. "I got one too, but let's hope we won't need them."

Jenny squeezed the stun gun trigger and lightning arced between the contact points. Not so defenseless anymore. "Let's hope we do."

THE ROAR OF MACHINERY AND STACCATO HAMMER BLOWS reverberated from within Geno's Metal Shop. Jenny kept one hand on the new stun gun in her purse and entered through a battered screen door.

Her nose immediately itched from the acrid ozone smell. Most of the noise, she saw, was coming from mechanical hammers lining the wall to her right, where a couple burly ironworkers were flattening out yellow-hot ingots of steel in showers of sparks. In the back, a ponytailed man in a leather apron was beating on some metal with a hammer and anvil. Jenny instinctively sensed he was in charge from the way he repositioned himself to watch her as she approached.

"Are you Geno!?" she shouted over the din.

He hesitated for a beat before swinging one last blow of the hammer and shoving the metal back into a gas-fired forge. With a hand free, he gestured to the front door and followed Jenny, yanking out his earbuds once they were back on the street.

"Ilya," he said in a soft, accented voice. "Geno's dead. What do you want?"

"Do you work here?"

"Well..." His fingers flexed around the hammer handle that he'd made a point of bringing with him. "It's a Co-op. We all pay dues and share the space."

"Did you work here 13 years ago?" Jenny asked.

"Why don't you come to the point?"

"I'm just trying to get an idea of who would have worked here then," Jenny said.

"Lots of guys. Farriers, blacksmiths, bladesmiths. Some coopers."

Jenny frowned at the word.

"Barrel-makers," he explained. "You know, for the wine."

"What's a farrier?" she asked.

"They shoe horses."

Lightning arced in her mind's eye, pulling together two nagging details.

"Horse hairs…" Jenny blinked, recalling that strange man watching her the other day at the statue. He'd been watching her at Alkali Estates too, she realized, in the van across the street from Mary Manuel's trailer. And the sign on the van… "Does a guy from Calistoga Farrier come here?"

Ilya's face darkened. "Look, I already told RJ a hundred times: we don't vet our membership. You pay your dues and follow the rules; we don't ask questions. That's how guys here like it!"

Her jaw hung slack. She pictured a specter of her father, standing on this very patch of sidewalk, waiting for Jenny to finally catch up.

"When was the last time you saw RJ Valentine?" she asked in a faltering voice.

"It was the day of that big party, the charity thing, last August," said Ilya. He paced away and cursed, slamming his hammer into a tree trunk. The blacksmith returned, pulling out his wallet. "How the fuck did he know?"

"Know what?"

"He told me, 'Someday, a teenage girl might come snooping around, asking about Jorge Lopez. And if she does, give her this.'"

He held out a small piece of paper, the size of a playing card. It was worn and bent from its time in Ilya's wallet. On one side was the little peeking man in a hat.

On the other, a message for her.

Warmer?
Find Jorge Lopez at Bottle Shock. Ask him about Sonya.

And below, his signature, with the big V flourish. RJ was here.

Chapter Twelve

Dressed to Kill

"**Y**OU SURE ABOUT THIS," ELIZA ASKED. HER FINGER HOVERED over the **Call** button on Charlie Zaleska's contact. "She just lost her friend."

"Looked to me like she wanted us as a new one," said Jenny.

"Fuck it." She hit **Call**, turned on speakerphone, and held a finger up to shush her sister.

It picked up on the second ring.

"Hey, Jenny, what's up?" came Charlie's voice. She sounded hoarse like she'd been crying.

"Hey," Eliza said, unsure how to respond as her sister. "You sound like you could use a distraction."

"Desperately," she said, perking up.

"I need you to make me over like a totally different person," Eliza said. "Like right now. I'll pay you a hundred dollars."

"Shoot, I'll do that for free."

"Text me your address, I'll send a car over."

Jenny hit **End Call** before Charlie could respond. Eliza raised an eyebrow. Jenny raised one right back.

"Sorry, am I salting your game?" Jenny asked.

"Shut up," said Eliza. "It's okay to be nice to people sometimes, you know? Half the school is terrified of me. You. Us, whatever."

"Fear can be useful."

"Trouble isn't mean," Eliza said, causing her sister to frown.

"I'm not mean," Jenny said. "Unless I have to be."

"10 points to Slytherin," she said under her breath.

"Huh?"

"Nothing. It's just... it doesn't always feel good. It's hard to be you sometimes."

Her sister let out a melancholy breath and reached over to take Eliza by the wrist. With her index finger, she tapped three times. "Believe me, I fucking know, Lizzy," Jenny said. "I couldn't do this without you."

Warmth bloomed in Eliza's breast. Sometimes, she just needed to hear it. The weight that she'd been feeling—that even a trip to Sacramento hadn't lifted felt a little less smothering. "Let's go over this again."

They were in the treehouse after school, digging into the latest clue.

"It's like it was all right there," Jenny said, looking at the background check they'd run on Jorge Lopez. "Lives in Alkali Estates, criminal record, works with horses, had probably met the victim at that metal shop."

"Except, none of that is hard evidence." Eliza bit her lip. "Do you think we should wait? Maybe Mason can pull Jorge's jacket, give us a better idea of this dude."

"He takes too long," said Jenny. "Dad gave us a lead, and the Hangman is getting bolder. We have to move on this."

"Right. So who's Sonya?"

"No idea, guess I'm supposed to ask him and find out."

"I asked Drew, he said this place is super shady," said Eliza. "Not for tourists."

"What about this guy?" Jenny pointed to Jorge's photo on the iPad. "Had he heard of him?"

Eliza shook her head. A concerning thought occurred. "We're sure Dad left that card for you?"

"Ilya said so, why?"

"It's just, that's the same kind of card that was on the doll body," Eliza said. "Not signed, though."

"The Stranger likes doing that," said Jenny. "But this was from him, trust me."

Eliza had another theory, very far-fetched, and Jenny would hate it, so she bit her tongue.

"Where are we on the room at the Crow's Nest?" she asked instead.

"I've got it down to three," Jenny said. "I tried calling and asking for a Johnathan or RJ in Room 237, but the Maître D' said there's no one by that name."

"Dad could have rented it under a nom de plume."

"Or it could be the wrong room."

"Did you try the other two?" Eliza asked.

Jenny shook her head. "The Maître D' is gonna know it's me if I keep calling. I need to wait a few days before I try again." Jenny reached for the door in the floor. "I should get going."

"Be careful. If you read between the lines, Jorge Lopez is a dealer, or worse."

"I'd say murdering little girls counts as worse." Her sister clambered down the ladder. "You be careful too."

"Sure," Eliza said, watching her sister's head disappear out of view into the floor. "Don't forget to send the car for Charlie," she added.

When Jenny was gone, Eliza closed the hatch and collapsed on the camp bed, a long sigh escaping her lips. There was a green seed of envy taking root in her soul, and try as she might, she couldn't bury it.

While she was in Sacramento, Eliza arranged to meet with one of her old friends, a fellow smart girl named Jessica Chen. She and Jessica had traded places at the top of every honor roll in grade school. They'd struggled together through puberty and periods in the hell that was seventh grade. Eliza thought they'd been tight once, but they hadn't seen each other in nearly three years.

They met at the La Fiesta in Midtown—which despite Jenny's crowing was still a better taqueria than any of the places her sister took her to in Glendale—and Eliza came prepared with a lie about having moved to Washington state. But Jessica could hardly be bothered to check her alibi. The lunch was awkward and stilted; her former friend spent most of the time buried in her phone. They had nothing in common anymore, Eliza realized. She'd made an excuse to leave early, and Jessica seemed relieved.

It hadn't even been a year since Nurse Bennet passed, and there was nothing left to go back to.

Eliza sat up with a mournful whimper and peeled off her sweater. For months, nearly all her public social interactions had been playing a role. Quite by mistake, due to crankiness and general irritation, she'd been herself in detention the other day, and Charlie... hadn't minded?

Standing, she regarded herself in the compact mirror taped to the wall above the sink. It was nice, having someone that made her feel pretty. Someone comfortable with Eliza's cool demeanor and lengthy silences she'd somehow grown accustomed to after so many years in near solitude. It's not like they were even friends or anything, but Charlie was *hers,* and now Jenny was taking that over too.

This Jorge fucker had better be the Stranger—or lead them to him—because Eliza didn't know how much longer she could do this.

Jenny studied the stranger looking back in the Lyft car window's reflection and had to admit it: Charlie was good. The Bitchy Brigader had gone wild with contouring, giving Jenny even sharper cheekbones, a rounder jaw, and a cute button nose. With a more mature, smoky aesthetic, fuller S-shaped eyebrows, and a cascade of sleek brown hair draped over one shoulder, she should easily pass for 21.

Provided she didn't fall over in her heels, that was. Charlie insisted on them for height, along with skinny jeans and a black leather jacket. She wore a plaid shirt tied at the midriff because, according to Little Miss Perfect Skin, "You have no sexy tops."

"You should really let Dinah dress you," Charlie said. "Or at least undress you."

Jenny made it clear that this had nothing to do with Dinah, and also that Charlie had best not breathe a word of this to her girlfriend. The makeup artist had only smiled shyly and used a brush to touch up Jenny's nose. If Jenny hadn't had her guard up, the amount of unblinking eye contact would have been dizzying. Not to mention the way her loose, unbuttoned collar kept falling open every time she leaned forward, giving Jenny an eyeful of her leopard-print bra and the hickey on her neck.

Maybe this explained why she flustered Eliza. Charlie seemed to delight in the power of her personal attention. Jenny had observed her making eyes at some boys who hung out with Jack and Mason, twisting them around her finger with the suggestion of future intimacy. It was an interesting tactic, one Jenny wasn't sure she had the sexual confidence to pull off.

For tonight's activities, she would just have to fake it.

"Bottle Shock," said the Lyft driver. The car eased to a stop on a dead-end street near the edge of town, far from the hand-crafted streetlights and piped-in jazz the tourists knew Blackbird Springs by. Sandwiched between an auto parts store and some warehouses was a seedy dive bar with a row of motorcycles out front.

She got out and adjusted her jacket, ignoring the attention of the bikers out front. It was after 10:00 PM. Because of the curfew, Jenny had to sit around for hours after Charlie did her makeup, waiting for Shelly to go to bed before she could hike to the highway to call a car. Her phone buzzed. It was Danger.

"How do I look?" she asked, answering.

"Like a sex crime," Eliza said. She would be near, watching Jenny. Her guardian angel. "You know, with different styling, and if you lost the wig: we could totally rock that look."

"Where are you?" Jenny asked.

"On top of the auto parts shop," Eliza said.

Jenny glanced to her left, scanning the roof, but couldn't see anything. The only light here came from the neon "Bottle Shock" sign above her. Rowdy rock music blared from inside. "Okay, I'm heading in. Stay sharp."

"You too, Trouble."

She kept one hand close to her purse—and the stun gun within—and reached for the door.

A burly man with a red beard and jaundiced eyes stopped her. "Identification?" he said.

Jenny passed him a Washington state driver's license for **Harmony Valentina**, 22 years old. Danger bought it on "the dark web." It looked... passable.

"Is Harmony your real name?" asked the bouncer, full of condescension.

Jenny reached for the card, passing a $100 bill to him as she took her fake ID back. "My friends call me 'Harm.'"

"I'll bet they do." He waved her in.

"Could've just handed him a graham cracker," she muttered. Crypto-coins 0, crisp American cash 1.

Jenny tried not to wince as the full force of the thumping heavy metal assaulted her ears. Winos crowded the bar, several of them smoking, laws be damned. Tobacco, weed, and rancid sweat burned her nostrils. She strode to the booths in the back, willfully ignoring the male eyeballs crawling all over her body. It wasn't hard to find Jorge Lopez; he was drinking alone.

She slid into the booth on the other side, sinking deep into the vinyl upholstery. Jorge had been staring straight ahead, nursing a pint of something nut brown. He gave no reaction to her arrival, but Jenny could see his eyes dilate. The word that instantly leapt to her mind was: *leathery*. His hands seemed permanently stained with carbon from forging. Sallow skin hung taut on his lean face, revealing too much of the shape of his skull underneath. When he raised his glass, corded muscles shaped by a life hammering steel rippled in his left forearm.

"Whadya want?" he growled.

"I thought we should talk."

"Do I know you?" Jorge cocked his head.

"I'm seeking information," Jenny said. "I hear you might have what I want."

His lip curled into a cruel smile.

"Oh, I got something."

It took all her strength not to wretch, but she forced a plastic smile and swallowed her disgust, trying to maintain that piercing, unnerving eye contact the way Charlie did.

"Good. Where were you on the night of August 10th, last year?" she asked.

It took him three heartbeats to react. His smile vanished, recognition blossoming on his face. "You."

"Me." Under the table, she withdrew the stun gun from her purse. "I figured I'd save you the trouble of following me around, *Jorge*."

He glanced past her, scanning the bar. "Lockhart put you up to this? Or that metal bitch?"

"It's just you and me."

"Then you're an even bigger idiot than I thought." He slapped a hand on the table, startling her. "This ain't a game, baby girl."

"Was it a game with Casey? Maybe that blonde hair caught your eye at the metal shop."

"I've been over this a hundred times," he said. "I was out of town! RJ couldn't prove shit then, and you can't now."

He rolled his eyes and raised a hand, signaling to someone behind her. Too soon! She wracked her brain for something appropriately threatening to keep him talking.

"Oh, you'd be surprised what I can prove," she said, forcing another phony smile.

Jorge made another gesture, waving someone away. "What the hell are you talking about?"

"See the thing is, I'm not some cop who needs a warrant, or a P.I.— or even a journalist." Jenny was fully bullshitting now. "I'm a multi-millionaire with an Axis I clinical disorder, and a lot of free time." She leaned closer to whisper, "I know about Sonya."

He swallowed a gulp of beer, eyes hardening to diamonds as he stared into his pint.

"I trimmed her early that day." Jorge took another healthy sip. "So I could get to Oakland before rush hour. Like I said, I was out of town."

"You're lying." Of this, Jenny was sure.

Then her watch started vibrating. Not three taps for *I'm Here*, or two for *Hide*, but five taps fast—her and Danger's code for *Get the Fuck Out of There*.

She glanced over her shoulder. It was all the distraction Jorge needed.

In a flash, he had her wrist in a vice grip, his calloused hands squeezing until she cried out. Then a knife was in her face, a wicked Bowie longer than her forearm.

"You think you can come in here—*in here*—and threaten me, you spoiled little twat?"

Her heart pounded, the massive knife an inch from her eye. She searched around for someone to notice and help, but there was some commotion over by the door that had grabbed everyone's attention.

"Yeah, that's right," said Jorge. "Your money ain't gonna help you here."

Her free hand found the trigger of the stun gun.

A window broke, and something metallic clattered nearby. This time they both turned to look. Several metal canisters were bouncing across the floor, spewing out thick blue smoke.

"The fuck—" said Jorge.

Jenny jammed the stun gun into his leg under the table and sent a jolt of electricity arcing into him—and her too, through his grip on her wrist.

It felt like being struck with a baseball bat, her vision going white-hot with pain. His grip on her recoiled, and they both spasmed uncontrollably as smoke filled the room. She tasted iron, hot blood pooling in her mouth, where an incisor had caught the edge of her tongue when the shock hit.

Heavy footfalls approached. Jenny's brain was screaming for action, but her body was frozen in place. She could only watch in horror as a tall figure dressed all in black emerged from the blue gloom. His head was a featureless black void under a fedora.

The Stranger.

Jenny couldn't move. She'd stunned herself at the entirely wrong time, messing around with some goon while the real threat waited patiently for her to fuck up.

He was almost to her. He was there—and then he was past her. The tall, dark, and strangesome menace halted at the next booth over, picked up a rocks glass off the table, and smashed it into the skull of the hooded figure cowering within.

Then the Stranger was dragging his victim toward the back exit. The man's hood slipped, and Jenny recognized with a shock that it was that skeezy reporter with the Warby Parker glasses being carried away.

Chaos reigned inside Bottle Shock. Bar patrons were fumbling and groping around for the smoke bombs. Glass shattered as tables upended. Someone was shouting, "Outside!" over and over. Jenny locked eyes with Jorge Lopez. It would go poorly if he regained motor control before she did.

Dimly, she became aware of sirens whooping close by—that was fast! Her watch tapped her with a two-beat code. It was like a switch being thrown in her nervous system.

Her fingers twitched, and suddenly she was moving again. She spit blood in his face and snatched up the bowie knife just as Jorge reached for her. In a panic, she slashed at him, opening up a big red gash in his forearm. He howled in rage as she fell out of the booth. Before he could murder her, she hit him in the ankle with another blast of her stun gun and scrambled to the back exit.

The reporter was moaning on the ground in the alley, holding his battered face. Red and blue lights flashed—a police cruiser pulling up to box her in on the left. She yanked off her heels and sprinted the other way.

Where was Danger? The plan had been to spook Jorge and then follow him, but they hadn't counted on the Stranger showing up.

She raced out from behind the warehouses and crossed Pine Street, heading right back into the alley on the other side. Adrenaline was wearing off, and now she was keenly feeling the pain in her wrist, her feet, and the dull ache in her tongue where she'd bitten it.

Shouts in the distance. Maybe they'd seen her. She ran on and made it to Oak Avenue just as a car raced up.

It was Eliza in the jeep, head covered with a black cap and sunglasses. Jenny leapt into the passenger side, and they sped away as fast as they dared, driving several blocks in the wrong direction, out of town.

"Ow fuck my thungue!" Jenny moaned, holding her jaw.

"We got a problem," Eliza said, focusing on the road, a troubled grimace on her face.

"What ith it?" Jenny asked.

"You first, what the hell happened in there?"

She did her best to explain the madness inside the bar while Eliza maneuvered them back to Highway 12 using side streets and alleys. The pain in her mouth gradually eased. She'd swallowed a lot of blood, though.

"You think Jorge will tell the cops?" Eliza asked.

"No," said Jenny as they turned onto Cellar Drive. "But that might not be a good thing. If he wasn't trying to kill me before, he will be now."

"Wonderful." Eliza eased to a stop at the dead-end where the path to the treehouse began.

"Okay, your turn," Jenny said. "What did you see?"

Eliza grimaced again. "The Stranger pulled that reporter out into the alley. It looked like he said something to him and punched him in the face. Then we heard sirens, and he ran off."

"Huh."

"I know I was supposed to follow Jorge, but with the Stranger... I went after him instead." This seemed reasonable to Jenny, but Eliza's face fell in a mournful frown. "He ran the other way behind the auto parts store, and when he got out to the street, he took his mask off."

Jenny's heart froze to the core. "Wait! Did you see who it was?"

Eliza nodded. "It was... Jenny, it was Jack!"

Chapter Thirteen

Reynard the Fox

Jack was the Stranger. It just couldn't be. And yet... The idea gnawed at Jenny all the next day at school. Or, rather, she gnawed at it, poking and prodding from every angle, hoping to find the key detail that would disprove the whole thing.

She'd barely noticed the silent distance between her and Dinah on the morning drive to school. How had Jack gotten away? Did he run all the way back to the Crow's Nest, or could he drive too? He probably hadn't even recognized Jenny underneath Charlie Zaleska's clever contouring.

The bell rang, and Dinah lightly brushed her lips over the corner of Jenny's mouth. It still counted—1,200 on the button.

There was, of course, the obvious explanation: Jenny put that reporter on her brother's radar, and this was about roughing up an interloper who had rudely barged into Jack's personal bubble of detached ennui. But if it was just about sending Warby Parker bro a message, then why the Stranger outfit?

"You're not mad about Alicia being in the band, are you?" Drew asked.

Jenny blinked. They were moving through the lunch line in the cafeteria. What happened to History and English? She grabbed a caesar salad kit she knew she'd never touch. "No, it's good, actually. We can use this. Get closer to her. Find out what she knows. Sleep with her, if you must."

She craned her neck around, searching for Jack in his familiar spot on the gym bleachers, not registering the pained smile on Drew's face.

"Do you remember the day we met?" she asked.

Jack was holding out his phone, posing for a selfie, and doing his best Byronic pout. Was this the disguise? The aloof, vaguely air-headed ponce who no one would ever suspect of cunning?

"At the sign of the Poison Pen?" Drew said. "Yeah."

"We almost died."

Jenny thought she'd seen the Stranger then, in the distance, when the stoplight almost crushed them. It happened right after she showed Drew her photo clue.

She'd definitely seen the Stranger in the Cellars when Declan Dillion talked about selling his clue to an outside party. Perhaps that was against the Stranger's own twisted rules. If so, it would make sense for him to target that reporter. The Stranger, by virtue of being the real killer, already knew Val was framed. If he wanted to blow Jenny's case against her, he could do it himself. No, he wanted to play, and the reporter wasn't invited.

Which all raised the question: if Jack was the Stranger, and the Stranger didn't like extra players, what would happen if Jenny caused another spare to cross his path?

"Jenny? Hey! Trouble!"

She snapped out of her reverie. Drew was waving a hand in her face, exasperated.

"Huh? What?"

"I said, 'Why do you ask?'" His eyebrows shot up, questioning.

"No reason." Another stray fact ricocheted around her cranium: it was only on Jack's word that RJ was unconscious when Jack found him. He was the only witness. Why were they all holding onto his version as the truth? "Are you free after school?"

"I have a baseball game. Preseason," Drew said.

"Clear your schedule afterward," Jenny said, her heart thumping in her chest. A dangerous plan was coalescing in her mind. A way to draw Jack out, if he really was the Stranger. "I'll need my sidekick tonight."

IT TURNED OUT SHE COULD HAVE USED HER SIDEKICK IN SHOP TOO. Mr. Howard gave them a woodworking project that Jenny's busy mind simply didn't have time for. She'd have to talk Drew into "helping" her make a napkin holder later. Jenny spent the entire class pretending to make measurements while texting under the table.

> **D:** For the record, I hate this plan.
> **T:** If I'm right, we could end this tonight.
> **D:** It could also get Drew or you killed.
> **T:** I trust you to protect me.

Eliza wasn't happy, but in the end, Jenny won out. The chance to catch the Stranger was too enticing.

Mr. White had no class for fourth period when Jenny was his TA, so he kept her busy working on a remembrance piece about Lily Geist. The Journalism students had collected a bunch of quotes from friends about Lily, and it was Jenny's job to weave them into a 500-word article. Mr. White gave her only 45 minutes and timed it. Practice, he called it.

Jenny finished in 30. She stewed with her feet up on the edge of

Mr. White's desk while he graded her work, shooting hateful glares every time his green editing pen dipped to make a correction. He was wearing a new Cam Newton jersey today, and his sartorial impertinence made every stroke rankle. When he was done, he tossed the stapled pages back to her.

She scanned over them, ignoring the typos for the meat of the critique.

"Meghan didn't say that," Mr. White said. "On page two."

"What do you mean?" Jenny asked, turning to the part with a quote from Meghan about the two of them playing dress-up.

"I've read all the quotes. Meghan said she would be the Princess, and Lily would be her Lady in Waiting, but you have her saying the opposite."

"Well—" Jenny flushed, annoyed that Mr. White had noticed. "I mean, throw the girl a bone. She's dead; let her be the Princess for once."

"Sometimes, the truth is inconvenient. It's not our job to hide it, though."

"But it's better this way."

"It's not about what's better, it's about what's factual," he said.

She crinkled her nose. "Fine. Besides that, though. Was it good?"

He hesitated. Jenny knew that look.

"Oh, fuck you."

"Language!" He gave her his sternest Man in Authority glare.

"I'll bet you never yelled at Tori," Jenny said, rolling her eyes and glancing at the plaque on the wall for "The Tori Award." Her step-sister was such a teacher's pet Mr. White named a goddamn award after her.

"Tori had a sense of decorum. Look, it's fine, okay. It's just... tonally—Jenny? Are you okay?"

"Has that always been there?" she asked.

With a shaking finger, she pointed to a drawing on the wall, pinned between old newspaper clippings, Celtics posters, awards, and movie tickets. It was a little man in a hat, peeking over a fence.

"Oh, him?" Mr. White smiled, his eyes brightening with some old memory. "Yeah, I've had Killroy for years. A little memento from your dad. Might even be the original."

Jenny's heart could start beating again. She crossed to the wall to pull aside the newspaper half-covering the drawing. It was actually the back of a coaster for some German beer. On the blank side, under the drawing, it read:

KiLLROY WAS HERE
À Votre Santé! -Renny

"Who's Renny?" she asked. "Is that your nickname?"

"No, it was his. We uh, we knew each other from way back."

"Renny?"

"For Reynard the Fox," said Mr. White. "John liked to think he was very clever."

"That's Jack's middle name," she said, frowning. Was Jack very clever too? As she pondered, the final piece of an old puzzle fell into place. "Wait. That's what the 'R' stands for?"

Much digital ink had been spilled on r/TroubleNovels debating what the R in RJ Valentine meant, as Johnathan Valentine famously had no middle name.

"Shhh," Mr. White said, a finger to his lips. "It's a secret."

"Right." Jenny blinked, filing this odd exchange away for later. "Sorry, what were you saying about my writing tone?"

"It's a little too Rita Skeeter."

"Who?"

"I thought you loved Harry Potter."

"I mean—sure!" Did Eliza ever shut up about those fucking books?

"Wow. Check out the fake geek girl."

"Oh, eat shit," she snapped back at him.

This time he let it slide, chuckling to himself.

"Okay, how about this, then? It reads like a story written in Trouble's Blackbird Springs. It's too pulpy." He must have noticed Jenny's face falling. "Lily's parents are going to read this. You gotta ease up on the purple prose. Let the quotes speak for themselves."

"So make it more boring?"

"There's a time for flash, this isn't it," he said. "Walk before you can run."

Jenny made a lewd gesture just as the door opened, and her aunt poked her head in.

"Hey, my kids are watching a video," Shelly said to Mr. White. "You wanna go make out in the service elevator?"

Mr. White coughed, scandalized.

"Real professional, Ms. Onishi!" Jenny yelled at her.

"I kid," said Shelly, her face turning grim. "The police are talking to all Lily's teachers, and it's my turn. Can you watch my class for a few minutes?"

"Yeah, sure," said Mr. White, standing up.

Jenny almost didn't catch it. Masked by the noise of his chair banging against the shelf behind him was a soft metallic click. Something silvery disappeared into Mr. White's right hand. He'd just locked his desk drawer.

Jenny kept her gaze dim and unfocused as Mr. White grabbed his coat. Once they were gone, she got to work picking the lock. If Mr. White had something to hide, then damned if it wasn't her job to find it. With one last satisfying click of the tumblers falling into place, Jenny was in.

Two items grabbed her attention. One was a cell phone. A cheap knockoff model. Why the hell did Mr. White have two phones? The other was one of those old-timey photo envelopes, the kind that real, printed photos came in.

She hesitated. Did she even want to see?

"Oh, God, please don't be gross."

She flipped open the flap. Inside were a couple dozen black and white photos of Mr. White and two little girls, all bundled up in Christmas sweaters for frosty weather. Maybe seven or eight years old. Shelly never said anything about him having daughters. Was this his secret family? She leafed through the photos with mounting dread, tracking what appeared to be a wintry father-daughters day at the ice skating rink and then mini golf at Scandia.

The last shot gave her pause. Mr. White and his girls were smiling in front of a bookstore. The older one was holding a copy of *'Tis the Season for Trouble*. But it wasn't the book that made Jenny's breath catch. Behind them in the photo was the storefront window, and in the reflection, Jenny could see the person taking the picture. It was Tori Valentine.

ALL HER CONCERNS ABOUT JACK HAD MOMENTARILY FLED HER brain. Like a photo negative exposed to light, the picture of Tori was imprinted on the back on her retinas, upside-down and backward and disgusting. Were those Tori's kids? Was she even really an alcoholic, or was the rehab a cover for her pregnancies?

Jenny despised Tori, but until now, she supposed she harbored a certain amount of grudging admiration for her step-sister. A worthy adversary with magnificent hair, at least. But sleeping with her teacher? What a cliché.

"What do you know about Tori Valentine?" she asked Dinah.

It was after school. They were bouncing a rubber ball back and forth in the gym, waiting for the student government meeting to start. Jenny wasn't strictly part of student government, but this meeting decided the destination of the Junior Class Trip this summer, and Jenny was determined to avoid a stuffy, boring trip to the Vatican and Rome. She had a line on a truly awesome castle in Austria that was perfect for them. If she had to pay for the whole class to make it happen, so be it. The castle sat high up on a crag, and there were rooms with balconies overlooking a deep ravine below. Jenny had already decided that this was where she and Dinah would go all the way.

"Do you know you ask me about her once a week?" said Dinah with an affectionate smile.

"I learned something about her today," Jenny said. She dribbled the ball, moving close to her girlfriend. "Come on, you always change the subject when I ask. I'm sure you've got an opinion."

"Honestly, she kinda reminds me of you," said Dinah.

"In what way?"

"Clever," Dinah said and pecked Jenny on the cheek, the ball rolling away who cared where. "Shady." Another kiss. "Pretty." Dinah nibbled on her ear. Jenny was intoxicated with her touch, her smell.

"Jeez, get a room," said Drew, clacking up on cleats in his baseball uniform. The Blackbirds wore bright white unis with purple and black trim and knee-high purple stirrups.

"Trying to," Jenny muttered, pulling away from Dinah but keeping a hand on her waist. "We still on for tonight after the game?"

"Oh? Should I be jealous?" Dinah asked with a smirk.

"It's Trouble business, ma'am," Drew said.

Over his shoulder, Jenny could see some other students arriving. It didn't escape her notice that Charlie Zaleska and Alicia Aaron were both watching them closely.

"Are they on the committee?" Jenny asked.

"Charlie is." Dinah scowled.

"She hates the sun; she won't vote for the cruise," said Drew.

"Sure, that's why. Hey Drew, your little Stevie Nicks is here," Dinah said, nodding to Alicia.

Drew frowned at Jenny. "What did you tell her?"

"Who's Stevie Nicks?" Jenny asked.

"Don't forget to say something nice to Thanh Trân," said Dinah. "She's the swing vote—"

"JENNIFER!!"

They all jumped with a start. Shelly was charging across the basketball court, her face livid.

"DID YOU DO THIS?!?!" Aunt Shelly stuck her phone in Jenny's face. It took a moment for Jenny to see that she was looking at a Ghostwriter post.

> Item! Mr. White and Ms. Onishi have been using the
> Humanities building service elevator to fornicate!

"Okay, that wasn't me!" Jenny said. "I would never use that word, ew."

Shelly pulled her aside, hissing in her ear. "Then who? You were the only one who—"

"Maybe there was someone outside who overheard. Come on."

"Heeey, Ms. Onishi!" Lai from the baseball team whistled at them.

Shelly snarled and went after him, muttering something about detention.

"I don't think that elevator even works," said Drew.

Dinah was blushing furiously.

"What?" he asked.

"Dryden Street," said Jenny to a perplexed Drew, blushing herself. "Hey Thanh, I love your iPhone case! Where'd you get it?"

"Online, I'll text you," said Thanh.

"Nicely done," said Dinah.

Jenny dropped her voice, speaking low to Dinah and Drew. "You know, I was just thinking today that Mr. White might be the Ghostwriter. I found a second phone in his desk. But I guess not."

"He still could be," said Dinah.

"Yeah, this would be a classic villain move to throw you off the scent," said Drew. "It's a secret he would know, and it makes him look like a target to have the Ghostwriter post it."

"Would he really embarrass himself like that?" Jenny asked.

"I mean…" Drew looked between Jenny and Dinah, biting his lip.

"What?" Jenny asked.

"Getting outed for hooking up with Ms. Onishi isn't exactly taking an L," he said. "You know what I'm saying?"

Jenny cringed. "Do you boys really think about Aunt Shelly like that?"

It was Drew's turn to redden. "She's got certain… you know… charms?"

"He means tits," said Dinah.

"Gross," said Jenny.

"You asked," said Drew.

"What you need to do is find some darker secret about Mr. White," said Dinah. "Something he wouldn't actually want shared, and send it to the Ghostwriter. And if it doesn't get posted, that's how you'll know."

"Huh," said Jenny, thinking of that photo of Tori and Mr. White she found. Maybe if she cropped the kids out… "Good idea."

Chapter Fourteen

Only the Good Die Young

I F ELIZA WAS REALLY GOING TO GO THROUGH WITH JENNY'S crackpot scheme to draw the Stranger out, she wanted something more than just a taser. Once school was out, she drove to the mall in Santa Rosa. The Sears here ought to sell throwing knives. A gun might make more sense, but Trouble didn't use guns.

She weaved through the afternoon crowd in the concourse, ignoring the kiosk sales pitches and making her way to the north end of the mall. A dozen yards ahead of her, Jenny's English teacher Mr. Hooke entered the Barnes and Noble bookstore. It seemed she wasn't the only one shopping a town over to avoid her fellow students. Maybe he could be of some use.

"I see you as an Erudite, myself," she said, sneaking up on him in the YA section.

He jumped, startled, and dropped the book.

"Miss Valentine! Um, hi!" He shook his head, collecting himself. "What a surprise—though I suppose a bookstore is your temple as much as mine."

She scooped up the copy of *Divergent* and handed it back.

"I'm Dauntless, obviously. Hey, can you do me a favor?"

"Uhh."

She didn't give him time to answer, hitting the **Call** button on her phone and switching it to speaker.

"Say you're calling for John or RJ in room 308."

The phone was already ringing.

"Wait—"

"Crow's Nest, how may I help you?" came a snooty voice over the speakerphone.

"Right, uh, can I get John in room 308?" said Mr. Hooke.

He was game, at least. There was a pause on the other end.

"Sorry, I think you've got the wrong number."

"He might be under RJ?" said Mr. Hooke.

"No, sorry. Thanks for calling."

Eliza ended the call.

"It was a nice try, at least. Thanks, Mr. Hooke."

"Miss Valentine, you're not in any—hah—*trouble*, are you?"

"Don't worry, I'm fine." She turned to leave, but couldn't resist getting something off her chest. "Hey. That thing with the Ghostwriter…"

His skin flushed. "If this is about your Saturday School…"

"No, never mind that. It's just—there's nothing wrong with missing your daughter. You shouldn't feel embarrassed about wanting to be closer to your family."

"That's um… very wise, Jennifer," he said, face flushing. "But I should probably keep my private life apart from my students."

"Sure sure, of course," Eliza said, holding up her hands in surrender. "No one will know I was here, promise. Not even the Ghostwriter."

164

Jenny's finger hovered over the **Send** button.

> "Dear Ghostwriter, you're not going to believe the tea I can spill about what this popular teacher has been up to after hours. Remember Tori Valentine? Well..."

If she was wrong, she'd be losing a great piece of leverage over Tori. On the other hand, she'd just badgered and cajoled the Juniors into choosing her Austrian castle for the class trip. Did she care more about leverage, or balconies and special nights with Dinah?

She tried feeling Eliza out, but when asked about Mr. White, her sister only replied with a bunch of devil emojis and, "Is that your final answer?" Fine. She'd hold off sending the email for now.

Instead, she spent the rest of the afternoon brooding about Jack. She wasn't sure what made her more nervous: that tonight would be a bust, or that it would work. When it came down to it, she didn't want Jack to be the Stranger, even if it meant solving the case for good. She just wanted him to be her brother.

"Should we maybe get it to go?"

Blinking, she snapped her head up to find Drew, giving her a judgemental stare across the table at Rosie's.

"Sun's almost down," he said. "You know, the curfew and all."

"No rush. The Crow's Nest isn't far. I have a room there, so it's technically home for me."

"Right." He waved a hand up and down at her whole body. "So, what's the occasion?"

Jenny glanced at her outfit like she didn't already know exactly what he meant. She was wearing a black tartan skirt and a white blouse under a purple Burberry trench coat. It was Trouble's exact look. She'd even gone the extra step of wearing the red fedora, which she usually found too theatrical for casual sleuthing.

"I thought I'd take some photos for the official Trouble Instagram account," she said.

"Huh, ok," Drew said. "Is that it?"

Jenny rapped her nails against the table before admitting it. "I may have a lead. It's—I have a test to confirm something. You'll know soon, I think. I'll just say, keep your head on a swivel."

The waitress arrived with her order, sparing her the need to explain.

"Avocado toast and grilled chicken with lemon?" the waitress said. Jenny directed the toast to her and the chicken to Drew. "Are you supposed to be Badger Berkeley? From *Here Comes Trouble*?" the waitress asked, looking to Drew, who was still in his baseball uniform, cleats and all.

"Is that why you told me not to change?" Drew glowered. Badger Berkeley was a Minor League baseball player who Trouble busted for steroid use. Most people considered his character a thinly-veiled shot at Barry Bonds. "But, he dies!"

"Humor me," Jenny said, turning to the waitress and holding out her phone. "Can you take a picture?"

"Oh, sure."

"So, not to be weird," Jenny said, "but I need it from high up. Get the food in the shot, not our faces. Well, maybe my cheek from behind. Make sure you can see the outfits. Maybe stand on that chair? Drew, look that way, and put your batting glove back on."

By the time Jenny got the shot she wanted, half the restaurant was watching them.

"I'm so sorry," Drew told the waitress. "You're going to get an amazing tip."

"Are you sure you want that tattoo in the shot?" asked the waitress. She was perched precariously on a barstool, aiming the phone camera down at them. Jenny glanced at her arm, palm up on the table, exposing her Ace of Clubs tat.

"Absolutely."

The waitress took a dozen more photos before Jenny let her go.

"I'm not on steroids," Drew grumbled.

On her phone, she was already assembling the Instagram post. "'Sometimes Trouble needs a sidekick. Hashtag Rosies. Hashtag First and Broadway. Hashtag mystery buddies.'"

Hashtag come and get me. If the Stranger didn't like it when she had help, this ought to draw him out.

"Mason might be." Drew shrugged.

"Posted!" Jenny said. "See, Stacy, I can post tastefully."

Dinner passed without much conversation. Jenny was too wound up with anticipation. About 10 minutes after she posted the photo, Jack liked it. He'd seen it then. If her theory was right, she'd be seeing him soon.

When dusk had fallen, Jenny tossed her napkin down and left a crisp hundred for the tip. They mingled outside, blowing on their hands as the night chill deepened. She popped a Xanax when he wasn't looking. Then another Adderall.

"Come on, let's take the alleys, just in case the cops are serious about this whole curfew thing," she said.

"Okay," Drew shrugged, following as she led them down a side-alley, making their way around to the Crow's Nest.

Maybe it was just her imagination, but the shadows hung heavier tonight. Impenetrable pools of darkness seeped out from every corner, tantalizing with the dread unknown. With each passing moment, her anxiety grew. Every footfall echoed louder. Her heart pounded harder. She became keenly aware of the noises and vibrations around her. The Doppler whine of an electric motor as a Tesla passed by at the other end of an alley. The light scuffle of tiny feet on pavement: a cat, maybe, or a raccoon. Drew's cleats clacking. Loose pieces of gravel under her Pumas.

It finally happened in the alley a block from the hotel.

A shadow detached from the wall to bar their path. Inky malevolence made flesh. Tall. Dark. Strangesome.

"Beware," Jenny whispered.

Three beats tapped her on the wrist. Danger was near. Jenny reached into her purse and brandished the stun gun. The Stranger had taken the bait, and now they had him.

She called out, "Jack? Is that you?"

A sickening giggle escaped from behind the Stranger's black mask. Bubbly and clownish, distorted into low octaves by some sort of electronic vocoder.

"Guess again!" the Stranger said.

He wasn't Jack? Jenny almost felt relieved, but now what? Her plan to ambush the Stranger—with Danger as backup above—didn't feel nearly as sound when he sprang at them, a silver knife flashing.

"Get back!" Drew shouted.

He yanked her behind him and charged the Stranger.

"No! Wait! Drew!"

Jenny stumbled backward. Something caught her ankle, and she fell, the stun gun sliding away across the pavement. In a panic, she looked back to see Drew and the Stranger entwined in a perilous scuffle, each gripping the other's wrist, that knife terrifyingly close to Drew's exposed neck.

Where was Danger?

Silver flashed again, and Drew grunted in pain. His legs churned, driving the Stranger into a dark corner of the alley. Another groan sounded—the Stranger this time, as he impacted the brick wall.

Jenny scrambled for the stun gun; more scuffling and a wet thud; the taser was in her hand now. She turned to charge just as Drew doubled over, flipping the Stranger off his back and tossing him head over heels into the street.

"Come on!" he shouted, rushing, nearly tackling her as he pulled them away from their attacker.

Jenny barely kept her feet underneath her as they fled. She glanced back to see a tall shadow scrambling out the other end of the alley. A blur of movement passed by on the edge of the roof overhanging them, light footfalls leaping from one building to the next.

"Wait!" she cried, trying to stop.

"Jenny, run!" Drew screamed at her and pushed her on.

THE STRANGER WAS FLEEING, AND ELIZA WAS RUNNING OUT OF rooftop. They were two wraiths in the night, he in the alleyway, and she on the parapets, racing toward Third Street with wanton haste. She could have sworn the knife she threw hit him, but he didn't seem affected at all. Still, she was gaining on him. If she could just get close enough for another shot!

The rapidly approaching edge of the roof demanded her attention. With another reckless leap, she flew over the gap and landed on the next building—the last before the wide Third Street intersection.

It wasn't supposed to go this way. Eliza was supposed to attack if it wasn't their brother, but then Drew tried to play the hero, the big idiot, and got in the way. That was an oversight. Jenny's oversight.

The Stranger broke out from the alleyway, and Eliza saw her chance: a U-Haul truck, just starting to move as the light turned green. This would be stupidly dangerous. She was born for it.

The last roof ended, and Eliza kept going, flinging herself out over empty space, just in time for the long cargo section of the U-Haul to slide underneath. For a brief moment, she hung in the air, a psychotic smile spreading on her face. She was going to make it.

With a teeth-rattling slam, she landed on the U-Haul's roof, ducking and tumbling as the truck's lateral momentum upended her. She rolled off the far side, her incognito baseball hat slipping askew, and somehow got a hand out to clutch the edge. Her grip held long enough to manage a semi-graceful second leap to the ground. Eliza stumbled onto the asphalt, doing another shoulder roll and coming up feral, searching for the Stranger.

There he was, diving into a pickup truck. She pulled her cap back down and ran.

Closer and closer. Her lungs were burning now. The pickup's engine started, and tires squealed burning rubber. For a second, she had the truck paced, but she was only human. With a last, desperate lunge, she reached out for the truck's tailgate—and missed by an inch.

Her hand clutched empty air. In the space of a few heartbeats, the truck was already far away. She slowed to a stop, clutching her knees to gulp down oxygen. It took her a few seconds to notice that the U-Haul driver had pulled over and was shouting at her. Nearby, a lady was on her phone, pointing at Eliza.

She ducked her head and yanked her hat lower, her adrenaline curdling in her veins. With a last, bitter surge of energy, she cursed the Stranger and took off down another alley.

They'd had their shot, and she missed it.

Jenny and Drew raced into the lobby of the Crow's Nest. There were a bunch of people standing around holding candles. It was a ceremony for Lily, Jenny realized, and they'd barged right into the middle of it.

"Excuse you," said Shani.

"Oh my God, breathe much?" said Meghan May.

She, Charlie, and Shani were sitting by the fireplace, dutifully holding little candles with wax guards.

"Yas queen," Drew said, his voice unexpectedly husky.

"Jenny?!"

Hands on her knees, Jenny's head snapped up. That voice—

Jack Valentine was standing nearby, sharing a candle with Penny. They both gaped in shock at Jenny and Drew.

"Drew! What happened?!" Penny cried.

"Is that your blood?" Charlie asked.

Murmurs rippled through the crowd. Drew straightened his back and looked down, still panting. He seemed to notice for the first time that his left hand was dripping blood. He held it up, his face full of wonder as he examined a nasty slash across his palm, red blood flowing freely down his forearm.

"Huh," he said. "That's gonna leave a mark."

"Are you okay??" Jenny asked.

He shifted and caught her eye, a dopey smile on his face.

"It's fine."

The smile faltered.

"I'm fine," he said again, less confident.

And then he swooned. The light switched off behind his eyes, and he dropped to his knees, thudding face-first onto the carpet.

On the back of his baseball jersey, PORTER was stitched in an arc across his shoulders. A black, steel throwing knife was sticking deep into the second R. Danger's knife. Drew's gleaming white uniform bloomed dark crimson.

Meghan screamed.

Chapter Fifteen

Nerve Damage

PEACHES AND CREAM. EVERY CORRIDOR IN BLACKBIRD SPRINGS General Hospital was lined with square, foot-long peach and cream tiles. The pattern was random, never repeating. Cream was the dominant color, with peach mixed in here and there. Jenny found that if she stepped lively and planned her path a few moves ahead, she could traverse the halls without ever landing on a cream square. It was a foolish superstition, of course it was, but with Drew's life in the hands of an E.R. doctor, could she ever forgive herself for being careless?

She pressed on with a drink caddie, weaving and side-stepping like a drunken knight on a chessboard, making her way back to the waiting room. Nuclear medicine thrummed on her left as she passed. A memory stirred...

She was out of her cage. Padded walls, restraints, sedatives: Trouble had defeated each in turn. She was unstoppable. They thought they could keep her prisoner in the Glendale Hospital psych ward, but she was about to show them all. She tiptoed in her gown; it was past midnight. Her ears strained for any warning that the night shift nurses were onto her.

What was that!?

Up ahead!

Footsteps around the corner, heavy footfalls. She pictured an overweight security guard, lazily making the rounds. Easy to evade, but if he sounded the alarm? She ducked into the first door she came to, pausing belatedly to worry about the sign she'd hurried past: Nuclear Medicine.

Was she about to get a lethal dose of radiation? Wait, who cared? She'd be outta here long before that became a problem. She crept through the back rooms, headed, she hoped, toward the stairwell at the end of the east wing. And then up to the roof... It was a shame she wouldn't get to see the look on Shelly's face. Jenny wanted this to hurt. Wanted them to regret forever what they did to her. The doctors, her scumbag principal, Shelly, and also... She couldn't bring herself to conjure the name. Pretended she'd already forgotten it. Forgotten her. The Girl. Would she even care? She'd better.

"Bitch, I'll haunt you."

It was freezing up on the roof. Must be the wind chill. Maybe she should go back and get a coat... No! Be brave! This was the moment—

As if on cue, her watch tapped her on the wrist. With arms full of coffee cups, she had to crane her neck to check it.

> **D:** Been patrolling for 2 hours. No sign of that truck. I'm headed over.

Jenny grimaced. This would only make things worse.

> **D:** Don't try to stop me. I'll be careful.

Eliza didn't need to say it: she was furious. It's not like Drew wasn't special to Jenny, but he was something else to her sister, and now he might die at her hand because of Jenny's catastrophic plan. Worse, the Stranger had escaped the trap.

The waiting room was just up ahead. Jenny paused on a peach square, balancing on one foot, only now remembering that she'd gone to get coffee in the first place to avoid a shouting match with these people. She buried her feelings, set her jaw, and stepped around to rejoin the others. Penny's attention snapped up at Jenny's entrance, mistrust plain on her worried face. She blamed Jenny for this. They all did. The worst thing was: this time, they were right.

Yvonne Griffin stood in the corner, speaking quietly with Officer Peña. Jack cradled Penny's hand in his own, offering a condescending sigh at the sight of Jenny's return. Hypocrite. Not 24 hours ago, he was rampaging into a hostile biker bar and roughing up some dodgy stringer. Who was he to judge her?

She stared him down for a few charged seconds before moving on to the others. Alicia and Mason sat in chairs nearby, buried in their phones. She'd told Dinah to stay away, which only made it more awkward that Charlie had tagged along to the hospital. Mutely, she passed out coffee to each. Lockhart was here too, brooding by the counter. She went to him last.

"Move your foot," she said.

"Hmm?" He grasped the cardboard cup, following Jenny's gaze down to his feet.

"Move it." She kicked his right loafer, which had the audacity to rest halfway over a cream tile.

"Hey!" he barked, pulling his foot back. Better.

"Got anything to make this Irish?" Jenny asked, sipping from her own cup and tossing the drink tray in the general vicinity of the trash can.

"Read the room, Valentine," said Lockhart.

"Fine. Any news?" she asked.

Ms. Griffin strode over to them. "He's still in surgery, but they downgraded him to serious."

"He's lucky," said Lockhart. "You shouldn't have pulled the knife out."

She'd had to, to wipe Eliza's prints.

"I know. It was a stupid reflex," said Jenny. "Someone should call his parents."

"Already did," Ms. Griffin said. "They're in Portugal, so it might take them a couple days to get back."

"I can cover their ticket, whatever helps," Jenny said, reaching for her phone.

"I'm sure they'll be grateful," Ms. Griffin said.

"Anything else we should tell them when they get here?" Lockhart asked, an edge in his voice.

Jenny pictured having to break the awful news to Mirai Porter and shuddered. "I told you everything. It was a mugger. Tall, dark clothing. Wearing a mask."

"Eyewitness says—" Lockhart paused as Mason leaned between them to grab a magazine. He squeezed his son's shoulder and continued. "Someone saw two people in black. One chasing the other."

"I only saw one."

He wanted to say more, but Aunt Shelly was here now, her arms full of takeout bags.

"How is he?" Shelly asked.

Lockhart stepped away, giving them space.

"I don't—" Jenny's voice caught, and she gazed down in horror. Somehow, both of her feet were standing on cream tiles.

"Jenny?" Shelly frowned.

It was too late. A man in black scrubs threw open the doors from the OR and stepped into the room.

"Your friend is going to be all right," he said.

Relief flooded the room. Penny let out a plaintive sob.

"Can we see him?" Penny asked.

"No, not until tomorrow, at least."

There were more questions for the doctor, but Jenny tuned them out, retreating to a chair in the corner. Her knees gave out as she sat, collapsing into the hard cushions. Drew would be okay. She hadn't gotten him murdered with her foolish plan after all. She fired off a quick text to Danger.

T: He'll make it.

Only then could she relent, finally letting the panic attack that had been lurking for the past two hours wash over her. It was agony. Her heart was beating so fast, so hard, she thought it might burst. It took everything she had to hold up her phone, hiding her face behind it and hoping no one would notice that Trouble Valentine was falling apart in the corner.

They noticed. One after another, they turned to her, their faces full of concern and pity and disgust. Fuck them, she was fine. She would not break.

If nothing else, it made for a good distraction. Not a single soul noticed—not even Alicia Aaron—when a bushy-haired brunette in hospital scrubs slipped by behind them and ducked through the restricted door.

THE NEAR-MURDER OF HER FRIEND BOUGHT JENNY SOME SYMPATHY from Aunt Shelly, but there was no way she was letting her stay home from school with potentially multiple killers on the loose. Lucky for her sister, Eliza was more understanding, even though she was still pissed at Jenny and had barely slept a wink.

She'd only peeked in on Drew briefly last night. Long enough to confirm he was alive and recovering. He'd been stupidly lucky, but the last sentence scribbled on his chart froze her heart.

Possible axillary neuropathy

In layman's terms: nerve damage.

Eliza would have it out with Jenny later; she wasn't going to kick a girl when she was down. Not when what happened was at least partly her fault, too. The way Jenny looked in the hospital… She'd only seen her sister like that once before.

Conflicting emotions roiled inside Eliza. Fury and compassion, locked in mortal combat. *Heartache.* That was the word. She'd read about it in dozens of novels, but only now understood. If anyone came at her sister right now, she'd claw their face off with her bare hands. Only she had the right.

"Hey," said Dinah, pulling her out of her thoughts.

Dinah was waiting by her car out front like always, a comforting smile for Jenny on her lips.

Eliza shuffled down the coral flagstone steps, squinting in the glare of the morning sun on a rare, cloudless winter day, and embraced her sister's girlfriend. The long, heartfelt hug wasn't a deception, wasn't a breach of intimacy, she told herself. This was allowed, this was genuine. And she needed it.

"Hi, Dinah," she said.

Dinah pulled away, studying Eliza's face. "Do you want to talk about it?"

"Just drive," she said. "I'll tell you on the way."

She didn't tell her everything, of course, but she explained the plan to lure out Jack after seeing him rough up the reporter in an alley. The idea that Jack might have been behind other attacks. Maybe even RJ's.

"So… you *don't* think Val did it, then?" Dinah furrowed her brow. Her hair tendrils were copper brown today. They were in a long line of cars waiting to pull into the school lot, backed up thanks to additional security checks at the entrance after another attack on a student.

"I don't know," Eliza said, choosing her words carefully so as not to reveal the frame job or, well, herself. "What if... What if Val was covering for Jack?"

Dinah crinkled her nose, nonplussed. "I just can't see—"

"I know, but pretend you could," Eliza said. "What do you remember about that night? Did you guys talk or text at all? When did you first find out about RJ?"

Dinah glanced up at the rearview and eased forward another car length as traffic inched along.

"I think it wasn't until the next day," she said. "Jack was doing homework. He'd signed up for this summer AP prep course—without even checking with me first, but we'll just file that under Dryden Street, right?"

"Sure," said Eliza, unsure of what she meant but even more intrigued now. "And you were at home?"

She nodded, craning her neck to look past the car ahead. "I don't remember what I was doing. Probably binge-watching Claire Saffitz videos. But Jack—I mean, he was a little distant with RJ, but not enough to hurt anyone."

Eliza nodded, lost in thought. It took her a few beats to realize that Dinah had asked her a question.

"Hmm?"

"You were in the hospital then, right?" Dinah asked softly.

Her mind flashed to that fateful night.

"Um, kind of, yeah," Eliza said. "The nurses were understaffed that evening. Snuck out of my room, went up on the roof. I had no idea that 400 miles away, RJ was... No one even told me. Not till I came here."

"The day we met." Dinah reached over and squeezed her hand. "Jenny, promise me you won't try something like this again," Dinah said, genuine concern on her face. "It could have been that farrier guy, or maybe Chuck Slater and the Carnegies had other accomplices."

She sighed. "I know, I know."

"Promise me," she repeated, giving Eliza the hard, demanding stare. "How am I gonna sleep at night if you won't?"

"Okay, okay. I promise I'll never try anything that stupid again," Eliza said. "It couldn't have been Jack anyway; he'd have to have teleported over to the Crow's Nest and changed clothes right after the attack."

"See?"

"Unless he has a twin." Eliza just couldn't help herself.

Dinah laughed. "I think I'd know if he did."

She smiled and sank back into the driver's side chair.

You're clever, Blondie, but not that clever.

They were almost to the parking lot now. Dinah said something about Mr. Hooke's class, but Eliza's mind was far afield. Jenny had done her best to teach Eliza the tricks of the *Trouble* trade in the months since they first met, with mixed results. She still couldn't pick handcuff locks, but she'd gotten pretty good at spying, and moving in silence. Trouble was much better at detecting when someone wasn't telling the truth, though Eliza knew the basic tells, at least.

Enough to know that Dinah had just lied to her about where she was the night RJ died.

It was well past noon by the time Jenny got out of bed for good. She'd wasted most of her day doing a lot of napping, a little bit of crying, and maybe a pinch of self-reflection. Today, she would be better. She swore it.

Eliza's FaceTime call came just as Jenny was getting out of the shower. She threw on a towel and retreated to her vanity in the closet to take it.

"Hey," said Jenny.

"Hey," said Eliza.

Her sister appeared to be in the back of the family town car, on the way back from school. Little beads of water dripped from Jenny's bangs onto her chest as they each regarded the other cautiously. Eliza went first.

"I don't want to argue with you."

"Really?" said Jenny. "I deserve it. If I'd listened to you—"

"If I hadn't thrown the knife with Drew that close," she replied. "Look, we both fucked up. I'm not saying you weren't more at fault, but I'm trying to let it go. We can't let this consume us. We've got work to do."

"Thank you."

Sometimes Eliza was so smart, so wise beyond her years. Jenny studied her face on the screen, appreciating the differences for once, instead of the similarities.

"Wait," Jenny said. "Is it my imagination, or did your black eye get worse?"

"Oh, right." Eliza's face flushed. "We uh, we've got Saturday School."

"I thought we already had Saturday School."

"Honestly, I've lost track," Eliza said.

"Who was it?" Jenny asked.

"Charlie called me—well, you—she called you the 'Angel of Death' at lunch, and I kind of lost it," said Eliza, rubbing the fingernail on her index finger. "Gave her a nasty scratch on the cheek. Think it might leave a scar."

"Damn, girl."

"I know. It was stupid. I shouldn't be taking it out on her," said Eliza.

"Yeah, not when you can take it out on me," said Jenny.

"I told you, I don't want to. But you should probably do the honors yourself," Eliza said, tapping her eye. "Anyway, Mr. Howard was up our ass about the Shop project, so we should get to work on that soon. And Mr. White was in a meeting all period, so I couldn't ask him anything else about 'Reynard.'" Her sister opened her mouth to say more but hesitated and bit her lip instead.

"What?" Jenny asked. "Is there something else?"

"Nothing. Just..." Eliza crinkled her face. She seemed to come to a decision, and her eyes softened. "Wear the red wig when you go to see Drew. It's his favorite."

JENNY SAW THIS IN A MOVIE ONCE. SHELLY'S EX, THE DREADED DAVID, was always forcing his Fincher obsession on them. It turned out to be a good thing since Shelly dumped his ass shortly after a spectacular argument that erupted while watching *Gone Girl*. She hefted the ball-peen hammer, making sure no one else was in the aisle at ACE Hardware. If it worked for Amazing Amy...

She swung the hammer at her face. The rounded steel hammerhead connected with a solid *thud* just below her eye.

Fuck! That hurt!

She stomped her feet, stifling a whimper, and tossed the hammer back on the shelf.

"Trouble?"

Jenny looked up with a start. An old woman was approaching. No, wait, not old. Though her hair was close-cropped silver, her features still bore the remnants of once youthful beauty. She was wearing a heavy plaid jacket, sauntering down the aisle toward Jenny with a box of grinding disks under one arm and a giant wrench in her hand.

Eliza had undersold Campbell Batori. She looked like Furiosa. Jenny was smitten.

"I didn't recognize you at first with the red hair. Are you okay?" she asked.

"Ms. Batori?"

"Campbell."

"Campbell, hi," said Jenny. "Yeah, I'm fine."

"Do I need to report whichever son of a bitch did that?" she said, frowning at Jenny's eye.

"Oh, it was a girl, actually," Jenny said. "It's okay, really?"

They made brief small talk, and Jenny tried not to let on how awed by the bronze carver she was. Aside from being Trouble Valentine, the living embodiment of a famous girl detective, Jenny had never felt like she fit into any of the boxes society created for girls. Looking at this woman, she suddenly realized that the boxes only existed if you let them. Campbell was butch but still feminine, confident and compassionate. She carried herself with the strength of someone who found her own center, even when the rest of the world was off-kilter. Two minutes after meeting her, Jenny decided that she wanted to be Ms. Batori when she grew up.

"You should come by the shop," Campbell said after Jenny explained her school project.

"Oh, I don't want to impose."

"No, I'd love it!" Campbell said, smiling. "Don't waste your money on this stuff, I've got all the tools you need."

"Okay, thanks," said Jenny. "Maybe tomorrow at four?"

"Ah-ah, no times," said Ms. Batori, a shadow passing over her face. "I can't—I don't do schedules. Just show up whenever you feel, I'll be there."

"Sure. Hey—actually, can you do me a favor?" Jenny pulled out her phone. "I'm trying to figure out if my dad had a room at the Crow's Nest. You know, before he…"

"Wasn't that months ago?" she asked.

"I think he might have paid for it long term, but the Maître D' refuses to tell me anything."

"That's annoying. What do you need from me?"

Jenny dialed the number on her phone and handed it to Ms. Batori.

"Just ask for RJ in room 525," Jenny said.

Ms. Batori held the phone up and waited.

"Hi, I'm trying to reach my friend in room 525," she said into the receiver. "He should be under RJ." She waited for a reply. "His first name? John? …Um, you know what? I'll just text him."

"No dice?" said Jenny, taking the phone back.

"I'm not sure," Ms. Batori said, biting her lip. "He hesitated on the initials and asked for a name. I think you might have the right room, but the wrong name."

"Interesting."

Jenny already had an idea about the name, but she wanted to be at the hotel before trying again. If she was right, this triggered a whole new set of questions, ones she hadn't dared ask until now. Chief among them: why did Dad need a secret hotel room? And what would she find inside?

PERHAPS IT WAS THE DAYLIGHT COMING IN THROUGH THE WINDOWS, but the hospital seemed a more hopeful place today. Jenny kept her hopscotch routine on the peach tiles going because clearly it was working. At least it was until she was five feet from Drew's room, and

Alicia Aaron walked out.

The wallflower girl had dressed to give Drew a show in a cleavage-revealing white scoop neck sweater. Jenny's eyes were immediately drawn to the gold chain around her neck and the skeleton key hanging from it.

"What are *you* doing here?" Jenny asked.

"He needed a friend. I know what he's going through."

It took Jenny a moment to get it. Her eyes reluctantly swept from the key to the smooth carbon fiber ankle of Alicia's prosthetic leg. When Jenny told Drew to get closer to Alicia, it hadn't occurred to her that Alicia might have had the same idea.

"I suppose you do," Jenny said, moving into Alicia's personal space to lift the key from her chest and inspect it. "A million dollars for this, huh? How bad is this book of yours?"

"It's good!" Alicia's face lit up in a rare, toothy smile. "It's a YA portal fantasy about a Dark Prince who—"

"Oh my god, I'm bored already." Jenny heaved a pained sigh. "Look, send me the manuscript, and I'll run it by my people."

"I'll think about it. Bye, Trouble."

Alicia shuffled away, leaving Jenny vexed and irritable. She paused at the door and popped a few pills before walking in to face Drew. He was sitting up in the hospital bed, his whole right shoulder wrapped in white gauze. Jenny wasn't sure how much he remembered, or how much he'd put together. He had a smile to greet her, at least.

"Does it hurt?" she winced.

"I mean, yeah!" Drew grimaced and clicked the little painkiller button they'd given him to bump his morphine drip. "It feels like someone's pressing a hot poker into my back. That's not the worst, though. It itches like a motherfuck."

Jenny reached out her hand with a questioning eyebrow. He didn't stop her, so she lightly ran her fingers along the gauze bandage, well away from the puncture site.

"Ooooooohhhhh yeah."

"All right, that's enough." She yanked her hand away.

"What? It's not sexual!"

"We're gonna put that on your tombstone."

They both laughed, even though Drew winced with every chuckle. He raised his head, catching her gaze.

"So uh, I was bait last night, right?" he said.

Jenny swallowed her mirth, icy tendrils gripping her heart once more.

"I'm sorry, Drew. I'm really sorry."

"I just. I want to understand," he said.

She took a deep breath.

"The thing is," Jenny said, picking at her cuticle. She checked behind her to make sure they were alone. "I think Valerie Valentine might have been framed. I think the real killer is still out there."

Drew bit his lip. "How?"

She spun a modified version of the truth: Bottle Shock and suspecting Jack, the threatening message left on the Big Board in RJ's study, and the other ominous notes she'd been receiving. She left out the fact that *she* was the one who framed Val. And Danger, naturally.

"You kinda know the rest from there," she said. "Do you hate me now?"

Drew was quiet for a full minute afterward, and Jenny worried he was about to explode in anger. His bandaged shoulder rose and fell with his deep breaths. The beeping of a nearby heart monitor was growing more insistent.

"It makes sense," he finally said. "Val seemed so shocked at the time. But then that means the guy who attacked us was—"

"The same guy who killed Declan Dillion," Jenny said. "The Stranger."

Drew shivered.

"Don't suppose the name 'Sonya' rings a bell?" she asked.

"Sorry," Drew said, furrowing his brow and repeating the words Jorge Lopez had told her. "'I trimmed her early that day.' Hedges? Oscar Manuel did those topiary statues down the road from Casey's house."

"Yeah." Jenny probed gently at her new black eye. "Maybe Jorge was covering for Oscar that day, trimming the statues?"

"What about a boat? You trim sails, right?"

"A boat named 'Sonya,' hmm. They did find Rita Thomas and Sarah Ortiz in the sloughs…"

"Is there a problem in here?" asked a harried female nurse, skidding into the doorway.

Her eyes were on Drew's vitals. His heart rate was still high but dropping.

"No problem," he said.

The nurse frowned. "We're not having another issue like this morning?"

"All good, I promise."

"What happened this morning?" asked Jenny.

"Apparently, you're not supposed to disconnect all this stuff if you have to use the restroom," he said, gesturing to the IVs and sensors snaking all over his body.

The nurse relented and held out a small potted cactus. "This came for you," she said, setting it on a nearby table.

"This is Jenny," said Drew. "She was the one—"

"He saved my life," Jenny said.

"That was very brave," said the nurse. "But don't be foolish. You're already at risk of permanent nerve damage. Take it easy."

Drew turned a shade pinker as she left.

"How bad is it?" Jenny asked.

"Three inches away from my parents picking out an urn, apparently." Drew ground his teeth. "They said if the nerve doesn't heal right, I might not be able to play ball."

"Oh. Shit, Drew, I mean it. I'm so, so sorry." Her voice caught, and she sniffled.

"I just wish you would have trusted me more to include me," he said. "I'm your sidekick, Jenny. But you always do this, you leave me out when I'm supposed to be helping you. I mean, I get that you and Dinah have your thing. But I hate feeling like a third wheel. It's already bad enough with Penny and Jack." It was his turn to sniffle a little. "I mean, I still woulda jumped in front of you. But at least I'd know what I was getting into."

"You're right. You're right." Jenny turned away, studying the little cactus on the table. It came with a small card. She peaked at the note.

"Knock knock?" said a voice at the door.

Jenny tucked the card into her hoodie pocket, turning to see Penny and Jack in the doorway.

"Can we come in?" Penny asked.

"Sure. Actually, I was just leaving." Jenny nodded to Drew. "To be continued?"

"Promise?" Drew asked.

"Promise." She paused as she passed Jack. "A word, please, baby brother?"

Penny gave her an appreciative nod for the one-on-one time with Drew. Jenny led Jack down the corridor to a quiet corner.

"What?" he asked.

"Bottle Shock," she said.

Her brother barely even twitched. Damn, he was smooth.

"What do you mean?"

"I get what you were doing, but you need to be more careful," said Jenny.

"*I* need to be more careful??"

"Yes. My fuckups do not excuse yours. And for God's sake, leave the mask on till you're well, well away from the scene."

His ears practically steamed. "Anything else?"

She heaved a weary sigh and gave him a big bear hug that he wanted nothing to do with. Jenny didn't care. She'd been so busy worrying about Drew that she'd hardly had time to appreciate that her brother wasn't the Stranger.

"Great. See you around, Trouble."

"Don't be a *Stranger*, Jack," Jenny said.

He shot her a quick wink before whirling around to return to Penny and Drew. She withdrew the cactus note from her pocket. It was almost too predictable. The little man in the hat and **KILLROY IS HERE** below.

On the other side was a terse message, not for Drew, but for her.

DON'T THROW A PARTY IF YOU'RE NOT READY TO DANCE

Chapter Sixteen
Room 525

LATER THAT EVENING, THE BILL WITH SHELLY FINALLY CAME DUE. Her aunt was crafty about it, waiting until Jenny was sated on seared ahi tuna, and they were both immobilized, feet soaking in little tubs of rosewater, before muting the TV and fixing her with an authoritative stare.

"Jennifer, we need to have a discussion about consequences."

It was hard to protest with a full belly, especially when zonked out on Xanax and muscle relaxers. She groaned and put her phone down. As far as Google knew, there were no boats named *Sonya* in the North Bay.

"Must we?"

"We must," said Shelly. "No more night bike rides. No more dinners out with Dinah and Drew. I'm going to tell the driver he is forbidden from taking you anywhere that is not to or from school without my permission."

"What?! I pay for him!"

"That's another thing," Shelly said, sipping her glass of 2013 Valentine Vineyards Pinot Noir. "Where did all those jeeps in the garage come from?"

"They're for the vineyard," Jenny said.

Her watch vibrated.

> **D:** I'm outside room 525. Sure you don't
> want to be here for this?

Jenny grimaced and replied.

> **T:** Wish I could, but no way is Shelly letting
> me out of her sight tonight.

She returned her attention to her aunt. "What is this? Did you and Paul fight or something?"

"You know his name is Peter. And no!" Shelly seethed. "This is because your friend was attacked, and you're sporting *another* black eye, and you sent poor Charlie Zaleska to the nurse's office. You're lucky they didn't expel you!"

"Mr. Carter can't expel me," Jenny said, her tongue looser than usual. "He needs me to catch the Ghostwriter."

"Hah," said Shelly. "Paul—Peter thinks you *are* the Ghostwriter."

"Let me guess, I get in one little fight, and now he thinks you're not being strict enough with me," Jenny said. "How very *Dryden Street* of him."

Shelly let out a long, rattling sigh.

"Stupid goldfish," Jenny muttered.

"It was a 'Celestial Pearl Danios!'" said Shelly, mocking her horrid ex.

"Yank yank." Jenny made a lewd gesture.

"Jennifer!" Shelly warned. "Anyway, I told Peter that if you were the Ghostwriter, the chaos would all be at least 10 times worse."

"Aw, Shelly!"

"He's not wrong, though. You've been taking liberties."

"Oh, I'll bet he's full of opinions."

"He's nice, really," said Shelly. "Things are still new, but it's nice."

"*Nice*. I know things about Mr. White you wouldn't believe." Jenny's mind returned to the email waiting in her drafts folder. That photo of Mr. White and Tori…

"Like what?" Shelly glared.

Jenny focused, trying to recall the right pronunciation for *never mind*. "Kinishinaide."

"Hmmph!" said her aunt.

A CONTRITE AND HUMBLED TWIN SISTER HAD ITS PERKS. JENNY set Eliza up with an evening spa package at the Crow's Nest. She'd been pampered and massaged and rested, and now she was ready for mischief.

Curfew had long since fallen. Eliza leaned against the wall across from room 525 and waited. Half a minute later, a phone started ringing.

Jackpot.

Goosebumps prickled on her forearms. She moved closer and stuck her ear to the door. The sound was coming from within. They'd found RJ Valentine's secret hotel room.

There was a tap on her wrist, Drew texting.

> **Drew:** No answer, it just rang. Now what?
>
> **Jenny:** Now I go to work.
>
> **Drew:** Who's Renny, btw?
>
> **Jenny:** If the ultimate Trouble fanboy doesn't know, I'm not telling 😊
>
> **Jenny:** Get some rest. Thx.

Eliza had to hand it to her sister. Finding out about Dad's old nickname from a coaster on the wall in Mr. White's class was some slick detective work. She'd save the question of why their Journalism teacher never brought up his close friendship with RJ for a later date. Right now, she had a hotel room to break into.

Briefly, she entertained the notion of some sort of Near Field Communication wizardry to pop the electronic lock, or applying a large sum of money to one of the night staff for a key. Her middle name wasn't "Hacker" or "Tiffany," though, was it?

Instead, she used her riches to slip the front desk guy a $50 bill so he'd change her room at this hour. 625 was already taken. Fine, wouldn't want this to be too easy. It was a half-hour drive to an open ACE Hardware store for supplies, and she spent another hour watching YouTube guides to make sure she didn't kill herself. Time wasn't a factor. The closer to Witching Hour, the better for this stunt.

Fortune was with her; it was a moonless night. No one would notice the wraith on the balcony, clad all in black, a dark smear across her eyes in lieu of a mask. The climbing harness hugged her waist and thighs, connected by a carabiner to a rope tied fast to the railing outside room 626. This was only the safety rope; she'd use the other to rappel. A little devil on her shoulder that sounded a lot like Trouble whispered that if she really wanted to impress, she'd do it free solo. Easy for her to say, it was her book.

With one last tug on all the knots for reassurance, she leaned out over the balcony rail and allowed the rappel line to take all her weight. Gusts of wind buffeted her body, pushing her around on the rope. She began to giggle.

"What are you doing, Elizabeth, you madwoman?"

The cold and the wind and her uncontrollable laughter had her shaking. She'd be 17 in a month, and this was her life now: hanging by nylon rope a hundred feet above the pavement, trying to break into her dead dad's sidepiece hideaway. Might as well take the plunge.

She kicked out and let the rope slide through her gloves. In an instant, her feet grazed the railing a floor below. From there, it was easy to walk herself sideways over to room 525. Tying off the rappel line and unhooking her harness, she peeked in through a gap in the closed drapes.

The room was barely lit, only a sliver of light spilling out from the bottom of the bathroom door. Eliza retrieved her trusty high-powered magnet from her knapsack. It made quick work of the sliding door lock—but wait. Was it just her imagination, or had a shadow flickered behind the bathroom door inside?

If someone else was in here, they'd know as soon as she slid the door open. No way to hide the change in air pressure. Unless... Hadn't RJ Valentine written about this? Yes, she remembered now, in *Trouble Eight Days a Week*. Trouble defeated this predicament by... She quickly checked the ebook on her phone...

> Trouble eased the door open a nanometer a second, her kinesthetic sense feeling the razor's edge between atmospheres melt away to nothing over a hundred heartbeats.

"So, go slow. Roger, Dad."

What the hell, she'd try it. Gripping the handle, she did as instructed, sliding the door as slowly as possible until she felt no resistance. Maybe it worked? There'd been no more movement inside. Time for the moment of truth. Despite Jenny's assurances, Eliza still sorta wondered if maybe, *maybe*, RJ was still alive.

Her shadow pooled into the room like a bottle of overturned ink. In six footsteps, she was at the bathroom door, gripping her stun gun and throwing it open.

There wasn't a soul inside.

She checked behind and between the shower curtains just to be sure, but no, there was no secret resurrection plotline hiding in here. Dead was dead. So much for that theory.

This bathroom wasn't just missing her father; it was empty entirely. No toiletries, no unwrapped soaps, no signs of life. She retreated to the main room, trading her taser for a flashlight. The bed linens were crisply folded, untouched. A quick search revealed only empty drawers and closets, nothing under the California king-size bed, or between the mattress and box spring. She checked the backs of framed paintings on the wall, ran a hand along the insides of lampshades, rummaged through the ice in the mini-fridge: no dice—

Except for that extremely obvious briefcase sitting out on the desk that she'd somehow missed until now. To be fair, the black snakeskin case had attracted a thin layer of dust, blending in with the furniture. Eliza wiped off the monogram.

R J V

Like he wanted her to find it.

The sliding door rattled from another flurry of wind. She tried the hasp releases. They wouldn't budge, locked in place. Just as she was calculating how long it would take her to brute force the combination, there was a scratching sound at the front door of the room, followed by the solid metal clunk of deadbolt engaged in a lock.

The hair on the back of her neck tingled. Someone was trying to break in.

Quickly she killed the flashlight and retreated with the briefcase to the balcony. Taking care to be silent, she pulled the drapes closed again, and the sliding door behind. Not a moment too soon. Inside, the front door swung open, and a dark silhouette entered. The Stranger?

Eliza didn't want to wait to find out, not when a knife slash and a push would make short work of her up here. She lashed the briefcase to her stomach with a bungee cord, slapped the safety line carabiner onto her harness, and swung back to the balcony next door. Going back up was much harder on her straining biceps. She'd just thrown a hand onto the railing of room 626 when she heard the sliding door open behind her and nearly lost her grip.

In horror, she peeked back over her shoulder to see a man step out onto the balcony she'd just left. Not the Stranger, only a man. He looked shorter now, from this angle, with dark hair and black frame glasses.

That fucking reporter.

He leaned on the rail, gazing out at the park. His floppy hipster bangs blew back, revealing a black eye and thinning hairline. Eliza held her breath, her muscles screaming. Somehow, the reporter never looked her way before re-entering the hotel room.

Eliza counted down a miserable 10 seconds before finally fixing her grip with her smarting hands and pulling herself up over the railing. She collapsed in a heap onto the floor, her panting breaths slowly morphing into an amused chuckle.

"You're too late, asshole," she said, patting the briefcase.

There was a clove cigarette hidden in her pack, bummed off of Alicia Aaron. She'd earned just one, hadn't she? Eliza lit up and leaned back against the railing, sending Jenny a long text recounting the night's adventure and her spoils.

Jenny's reply was brief.

> **T:** Nice work. Front doors are for basic bitches. Danger comes in through the window.

Chapter Seventeen

Colder

GUSTING WINDS HOWLED ALL NIGHT. *BANG!* WENT THE SHUTTERS outside her window, over and over. Jenny slept fitfully, her dreams beset by dark figures with glinting silver knives. Lily Geist was tearing at the noose around her neck, stumbling backward off a high roof. In a mirror, her reflection turned to bronze, a scream frozen on her metal lips—

Jenny snapped awake. She was in Mr. Hooke's English class, second period, and everyone was staring at her. Oh no, she must have fallen asleep.

"Miss Valentine?" said Mr. Hooke, leaning forward for an answer to a question Jenny had missed.

She looked over at Dinah to find her girlfriend grimacing in sympathy. Maybe taking one of Shelly's Ambien last night wasn't such a good idea.

"Well, I... guess it all speaks for itself, doesn't it?" Jenny said with a shrug. "That is to say, it is what it is. I'm sorry, what was the question?"

Sour silence hung in the air like bad breath.

"Douche chill," said Shani Wolf.

Meghan perked up. "When I was in Paris, that's what they called—"

"Sleeping in class will do you no favors," Mr. Hooke said. "Did you even do the reading?"

Crap. Eliza did the reading. They were supposed to talk about it, but in all the excitement about the briefcase, Jenny forgot.

"Let's assume, for the sake of the class, that I did not," she said. "Please, Mr. Hooke, teach me."

He wagged a scolding finger at her and paced down another row of desks. "I guess there weren't enough quidditch matches and invisibility capes in Jane Eyre for Miss Valentine."

"Cloaks," Alicia Aaron muttered.

"Rough night, eh, psycho?" Shani whispered with a snicker.

"I dreamt of Lily," Jenny said to shut her up.

"Penny," said Mr. Hooke. "Would you like to give it a try. Who is the madwoman in the attic?"

"Dinah, maybe let your girl get her beauty sleep," whispered Meghan May.

"Internalized misogyny," said Penny.

"See, I think there's another layer to the text there," Dinah said, shooting an evil eye at Meghan before turning back to the teacher. "We can see the madwoman as a feminist critique of the damage men do."

"Doubt they've even gone to second base," Charlie's poison tongue hissed behind her. "Not with those nails."

Jenny flushed crimson, spinning around with the dirtiest of looks. Charlie glowered right back, but there was a meekness—fear?—behind her pretty facade. Despite her makeup skills, the raised line of deep scratch marred Charlie's dewy left cheekbone, a gift from Eliza.

"See, I feel like you're attributing modern wokeness to a bunch of colonists," said Penny.

"Provocative!" said the teacher.

"Oh shit, you're right. Look at their faces, how embarrassing," said Meghan.

"Right?" said Charlie.

"Did you have something you'd like to add to the discussion, Charlotte?" Mr. Hooke asked, having come up behind them.

"I was just thinking about the woman in the attic," Charlie said, suddenly poised and chipper. "Do you think she had dissociative disorder, the way Jenny does?"

"I don't!" Jenny growled.

"I've seen that reading," said Mr. Hooke. "Has anyone here read *The Wide Sargasso Sea*? I think you might like it. It offers a very different take on Bertha, starting with her life in Jamaica."

Penny's hand shot up. "I have! It's a little problematic, but it's good."

"I read it on my summer trip to Yale," Dinah said with an icy smile for Penny. "Can't start looking at colleges too soon."

The conversation drifted away. Mr. Hooke bloviated on the archetype of the madwoman. Jenny's fingernails dug into the bottom of her chair, which she was gripping white-knuckled to keep herself from flying at the Bitchy Brigade.

"Dang, Jenny," came Charlie's low voice. Jenny could feel the girl's breath on her neck as she leaned forward with words only for her. "What are you gonna do when Dinah gets into an Ivy, and you're stuck here?"

Her soul entirely left her body. A ringing in Jenny's ears blocked out all other sounds. Somehow she managed to focus on her breathing and count to 10.

"Okay," she said to herself when the fury dwindled. Under her desk, she began tapping out a new email. "This means war."

SHE WASN'T BEING PETTY, JENNY TOLD HERSELF. SHE'D LET THE
Ghostwriter operate unimpeded for far too long; this was merely a
convenient way to flush the bastard out. She had her top suspects: Mr.
White, Charlie, and—because she just didn't trust her—Alicia Aaron.
And Dinah's logic was sound. The Ghostwriter wouldn't publish
something that was truly embarrassing about themselves. If Jenny's
plan humiliated Charlie Zaleska—and she wasn't the Ghostwriter
after all—well, oh well.

Jenny already had the email about Mr. White and his special
relationship with Tori Valentine queued and ready. It was easy to find
an app that would reverse-Facetune one of Charlie's selfies. Alicia,
though… After 15 minutes of debating various damning lies about
the little redhead, Jenny settled on a simple one: she smelled. She
knew it would hurt because it's what the mean girls back in Glendale
used to say about her. Self-consciously, she tucked her nose under her
collar and sniffed. Those bitches.

It was the matter of a few minutes to create some burner email
accounts. They were supposed to be reading quietly. Mr. Hooke was
at his desk, paying them little mind as he typed away on his laptop.
With a few taps, she sent her rage off into the digital ether. That was
that. The Ghostwriter would reveal themselves by not publishing their
own gossip, and Jenny could get back to focusing on nosy reporters,
the Stranger, and the Hot Springs Hangman.

They spent the last 20 minutes of class discussing the reading, and
Jenny had nearly forgotten about the entire business until the bell
rang, and everyone got their phones out.

"What the shit?" Penny said, staring at her screen.

"Great. More Ghostwriter bullshit?" Meghan asked, pretending
not to care, eyes darting to her phone screen in a panic.

Jenny hid her smirk as she gathered her bag and purse.

"Hah! Mr. White is so fucking canceled," said Charlie.

She blinked. The Ghostwriter actually published the thing about Mr. White. Which meant—

"Charlie, um, there's one about you," said Shani. "'Why Charlie Zaleska needs all that makeup.'"

The girl shrieked when she saw the photo Jenny had sent in, claiming to show the *real* Charlie Zaleska, without all the makeup. Jenny maintained a facade of clueless indifference, following Dinah out the door.

"Well, I guess it's not Mr. White," Dinah said. She bit her lip, giving Jenny a coy smile that drove her mad.

"Or Charlie," Jenny said.

Understanding blossomed on Dinah's face. "Oh, that's mean, Jennifer!"

"She had it coming," Jenny said.

"Try not to get in another fight with her," Dinah said. "It's what she wants, you know."

"What the hell did I ever do to make her hate me so much?" Jenny asked.

Dinah opened her mouth to reply but hesitated. "You really don't see it, do you?"

"See what?"

"Hey, Trouble, hold up!"

Jenny spun to see Alicia Aaron shuffling up. She braced herself. Now that it was done, she felt shitty sending that letter about Alicia.

"I'm going to see Drew after school," Alicia said. "Did you want to come?"

Jenny blinked.

"Um. What?"

"I just thought, since he's coming home from the hospital today..."

Alicia frowned and stared at the ground, overcome with shyness.

"That's very kind, Alicia," Dinah said.

Jenny fumbled for her phone and called up the Ghostwriter page. The stories about Charlie and Mr. White were there, but nothing about Alicia.

"Uh, thanks." Jenny managed a casual smile. "But Shelly wants me home right after school." She glanced at Dinah. "I'm sort of grounded, by the way." Alicia was nodding, already turning away. "Might come by his place later, though."

Alicia waved and slinked off.

"She's not so bad," Dinah said.

Jenny's lip twisted in a feral grin. "Sure she is. She's the Ghostwriter."

KNOWING THAT ALICIA AARON WAS THE GHOSTWRITER WAS ONE thing, but doing something about it wouldn't be easy. She couldn't exactly run to Vice Principal Carter and explain how she'd confirmed this information. Especially when, rumor had it, he already had his hands full with the Mr. White situation.

She fingered her locket, tempted to call Eliza, and claim victory in their bet. Nah, better to wait. Besides, her sister deserved her day of glory after her success in room 525. If only they could get the damn briefcase open.

When Jenny arrived at the Journalism Room for last period, the door was locked. Aunt Shelly waved from down the hall, calling her over. Mr. White had taken the afternoon off, so Jenny had to be her aunt's TA for the period. Shelly was remarkably calm about the scandal. Maybe she was just putting up a good front for the other students.

Jenny had been hoping to spend the period texting with Dinah.

She'd discovered a lounge called The Pink Umbrella in Napa, noted in their Yelp reviews for their WLW clientele, their pink drinks, and an all-ages area where minors could hang out. The real kicker: there was no curfew in Napa County.

Unfortunately, Shelly had no interest in letting Jenny slack off. She kept calling over to Jenny in her lecture, asking Jenny to explain a particular economic term or assist with an example. She was showing her off, Jenny realized after a while, and though she'd rather be texting, she was touched.

"Don't forget, I expect you to go straight home," Shelly said when the final bell rang.

"What about you?" Jenny asked.

"I'm going to go see Peter," Shelly said.

"You're not annoyed at the fact that he has a secret family with a former student?"

"Oh God, Jenny, you can't actually believe that nonsense?" Shelly rolled her eyes. "They're good friends, that's all."

"But I mean, if he never mentioned the kids to you before, can you really trust him?" Jenny asked frowning.

"Of course he mentioned them to me," Shelly said, shoving some worksheets into her bag. "They're from his first marriage."

"Oh." Jenny's face burned. "But you never mentioned them."

"We just started dating. It's hardly time to talk about stuff like—"

Aunt Shelly stiffened and glanced up from her messenger bag, realization dawning on her face.

"You little monster. It was you!"

"What?" Jenny squeaked.

"You're the Ghostwriter!"

"I am not, I swear!"

"Then you sent that thing about Peter to the Ghostwriter!" Shelly's eyes blazed as she yanked the zipper on her bag shut. Jenny remained silent. "Go on, swear to that!"

"I didn't mean—"

"Goddamnit, Jenny!"

"I'll fix it!" Jenny pleaded. "I'll tell Mr. Carter."

Shelly buried her head in her hands, rubbing her temples. It had been a while, but the sight was so familiar that it almost gave Jenny comfort.

"You can't," Shelly said with a groan. "After everything else—he'd just expel you for real this time. I ought to send you to one of those boarding schools after all."

"But I know who the real Ghostwriter is now!"

Jenny gave Shelly a slapdash explanation of her plan: sending the Ghostwriter damning info about her three suspects—and how only Alicia Aaron's dirt didn't get published.

"Alicia, she's the one with the…"

"She's differently abled, yes."

Shelly blanched. "Are you sure?"

"See, that's what I thought at first, but Jack is pretty sure you can't fake an amputation, and I have to say he's probably right this time."

"I meant about her being the Ghostwriter."

"What? Is my logic not sound?"

"You just accused my boyfriend of being a scumbag because you found a photo of him with a former student, in public, with his family."

Jenny twisted her face, searching for a retort but not finding one. "I'll prove it, then."

"No, please don't!" Shelly gripped her by both shoulders. "Please stop proving things. Can't you just—don't you have a girlfriend? Where's Dinah? She's a nice girl. Go hang out with her."

"I thought I was supposed to go straight home," Jenny said, sensing an opportunity.

Shelly furrowed her brow. "If you promise to go be a normal teenage girl and stay out of—"

"Heheheh."

"—Avoid situations that are unsafe or encourage bad behavior, I will permit you to see Dinah."

Jenny tried to keep the triumph from her face as Shelly locked up her classroom, and they walked across the quad.

"Do you think maybe I could stop in town first and get a manicure?" Jenny asked.

"Didn't you just do your nails?"

"Yeah, but they need a trim—" Jenny froze, the last word flashing in her brain.

Trim. "I trimmed her early that day."

Shelly looked back, tensing up. "What now?"

Jenny got her phone out and did a quick Google search:

farrier trim

Bingo. A manicurist trimmed nails. A farrier, besides shoeing, trimmed horse hooves.

"Shell's bells! Sonya is a motherfucking horse!" she proudly told Shelly.

"Maybe it's better if you stay home."

"It's fine! Really." Jenny smiled happily. "I'm fine. I'm turning over a new leaf. I'll be a good girl from now on, I promise."

AN HOUR LATER, JENNY WAS STANDING OVER A CORPSE.

"Well, I guess you're not the Hot Springs Hangman," she said, irritated beyond belief.

"How the fuck did I let you talk me into this?" Penny asked, swallowing hard like she might vomit.

"Don't puke!" Jenny snapped. "We can't leave any physical evidence."

Jorge Lopez was lying on his bed in his mobile home trailer at the Alkali Estates. His eyes were wide open in shock, staring blankly at the low ceiling above. Jenny reached out to tear away the note pinned to his chest by the Bowie knife sticking out of his ribcage.

"Don't touch it!" Penny whispered.

"It's all right, Pen," Jenny said. "It's for me."

Dried blood had seeped over most of the little cartoon drawing, and the **KiLLROY WAS HERE** calling card, but the message below was still legible.

You're getting colder.

Chapter Eighteen

It's Never Twins

JORGE'S TRAILER WAS AS NICELY APPOINTED AS MARY MANUEL'S—A stainless steel fridge, two flatscreen TVs, replica broadswords, and lots of leather furniture—but less well-kept. The linoleum was dusty around the edges, and the plug-in air fresheners Jenny spotted weren't completely masking the sour stench of stale sweat and cigars.

"I wanted this," Penny said in a mournful tone. "Jack told me about roughing up that reporter, and I thought: shit, that's hot. I could go for a little adventure. And now I'll never get into Pepperdine."

Penny had that thousand-yard stare, unable to tear her eyes away from Jorge's bloody wound as her college dreams evaporated. With Drew at the hospital and Eliza busy at Ms. Batori's working on their Shop project, Jenny'd had no one to tell about her Sonya-horse theory. Then who should she find in the school parking lot but fellow Casey Klein murder enthusiast Penny Griffin. Penny was intrigued, and more importantly, had a car. The plan had been to search Jorge's trailer while he was at work, but once again, the Stranger was a step ahead.

"You're still getting into Pepperdine," said Jenny, taking Penny by the shoulder and turning her away from the body. "I've already got an alibi, and Jack will say you were with him if anyone asks, okay? Now gimme one minute to look around, and then we'll make tracks."

Penny blinked and nodded, her panic fading. "What's the point? Doesn't that mean you're on the wrong scent?" She nodded to the note in Jenny's hand.

"It means..." Jenny said, sliding a black latex-gloved hand under the bottom of Jorge's small desk. "That someone would like me to think so."

She moved to check behind the headboard: nothing there either. On a whim, she lifted the side of the mattress.

"Psh. Amateur."

Jenny retrieved a crumpled paper bag with a small brick of cash inside.

"I'm guessing these aren't prescription," said Penny, holding up a baggy of multi-colored pills.

"MDMA," Jenny confirmed. Penny raised an eyebrow. "I was young and wild once."

Penny let out an incredulous titter. "Once. Leave the bag, it'll look like a robbery."

"Good idea." Jenny kept the cash and dropped the empty paper bag next to the body.

A quick scan of the kitchen revealed a staggering amount of Pop-Tarts, but nothing else of interest.

"Okay, it's been a minute, let's bounce," said Penny.

"Right."

Jenny peeked out the window. The sky was overcast, but it wasn't even 4:00 PM yet. Plenty of daylight to spot them by, if anyone was looking. She reached for the back door handle.

"Hold up," said Penny. She pointed to a calendar on the wall. "I found Sonya."

Every weekday in February had a few names listed in blocky but impeccable handwriting. Some were ordinary people's names: *Toby, John Mabry.* Others were odd phrases like *Summer of George. Sonya* was the third name on the first Monday of the month.

"Horses," Jenny said, lifting the calendar to see many of the same names repeated in March. "It's his schedule for trimming horse hooves."

She snapped a photo of the calendars for February, March, and April.

"He's got Sonya on the first Monday each month," said Penny. "Casey went missing on a Monday. April 3rd. Do horses live that long?"

"Some do," said Jenny. "This is as far as my dad got, I think. RJ thought there was some link between Casey and this horse. And Jorge Lopez."

"Except he's dead now," said Penny. "Jorge, I mean! Sorry."

"Right." Jenny blew out a frustrated breath. If Jorge was *colder,* then why kill him? Had the Stranger killed RJ Valentine for chasing the same clue? "We'll figure it out later. Come on."

They slipped out and walked as casually as possible back to Penny's car. Jenny couldn't shake the feeling that she'd learned something important. Something the Stranger missed. Jorge Lopez might not be the Hot Springs Hangman, but he was a piece of the puzzle, and as Trouble liked to say, *"There's no such thing as an extra puzzle piece."*

THE DESIGN OF THE NAPKIN HOLDER WAS STUPIDLY SIMPLE. JUST A nine-inch square piece of plywood, and a narrow bar in the center to hold the napkins down. Two carved dowels on each side held the wooden bar in place and let it slide up and down. Campbell let Eliza cut the plywood on her table saw while she turned the dowels on a lathe.

Watching the lathe shave away wood was oddly hypnotizing. Eliza wanted to get a closer view, but Campbell barked at her to stand well back.

"Gotta be careful with those hoodie drawstrings," she said. "If your shop teacher hasn't told you this, he's not doing his job. The most dangerous tools are things that can spin, draw you in. Something gets caught in the lathe, like a sleeve, or ties on a hoodie, and it can get ugly real fast."

Eliza reddened, suitably warned. For all she knew, Mr. Howard *had* told the class this, on one of Jenny's days. She took her hoodie off—Campbell kept the shop warm enough with a big propane space heater—and finished her plywood cuts before checking the new notification tapping her on the wrist. "Goddamnit, Jenny," she said under her breath. "You were supposed to stay in the treehouse."

"Everything okay?" Campbell asked.

"Yeah, fine," Eliza said, still bristling. "My... friend likes to do things on her own, and she doesn't always check with me first. Makes it hard to coordinate when we're supposed to do stuff together."

Campbell shrugged. "Sometimes, you just have to let a free spirit be free."

Eliza moved to the drill press to punch holes in her plywood for the dowels.

"Is that why you wanted me to just show up?" Eliza asked. "No appointments for free spirits?"

Per Jenny's instructions, Eliza had driven over unannounced, worried that Campbell wouldn't be home, or she'd be busy with someone else. Instead, she found the bronze carver working alone with her earbuds in, humming along and scraping away on a hunk of green wax. Not exactly a hippy, but she grooved to her own tune. Literally.

"Hmm," said Campbell, looking wistful. "I'm not sure I'd describe myself as a free spirit. I mean, I have a mortgage. No, that was about my allergy."

"What are you allergic to?"

"Waiting."

Eliza glanced up from the drill, expecting to find Campbell smirking. Instead, her expression was pained. It took her a few seconds to get it.

"Because you waited for Casey," she said.

"It was such a little thing," Campbell said, a sad smile blooming on her pale lips. "It's 3:30 PM. Maybe she stopped to talk with friends after school. 3:35 PM. Casey sure is taking her time. 3:40 PM. Wait, is my watch fast? 3:50 PM. Did she go over to Tori's? 4:10 PM. Valerie says Tori stayed home sick. 4:30 PM. I've walked the whole way back to Casey's school. Do I call Reed? What if she's at a friend's and I'm scaring him for nothing? 5:00 PM. I'm back at home. Casey's not here. I call Reed. It's 6:10 PM. Reed's home. I'm calling out for her as we walk the path again, but not too loud. I think: I don't want to embarrass her by overreacting. At 6:40 PM, I call the hospital. Has a little girl been admitted? No. We finally call the cops at 7:00 PM. It's getting dark now. It's 7:20 PM, and the sheriff is asking questions. I think: for sure she'll show up now. I can't wait to laugh about all this later."

Eliza bit her lip, sad that she asked. Campbell had slipped into an odd reverie, unable to stop reliving her trauma. She reached out and covered Campbell's hand with her own.

"It's 9:00 PM, and the entire neighborhood is out with flashlights. We comb the whole cemetery. We check the horse pasture. School janitors search every classroom. It's 10:00 PM, it's 11:00 PM, it's midnight, and the police call it quits. My narrative keeps changing. First, she's fallen and hit her head. No, what if she's been taken? Do the kidnappers have my number? Just in case, Reed, how much money do we have?

"It's the next morning, and she's still not home. We can do a million dollars. Maybe two if we mortgage the house again. We search all day. Nothing. Every time the phone rings, I think: this is it, one way or another, it's over now. But it's not. For the first week, I pray for a ransom note. I know the odds. I know she's gone. But I can't grieve when she could still be out there. So I wait and wait and wait. For five months, I wait."

Campbell blinked and snapped out of it. "Jesus, sorry. I haven't done that in a while."

"It's fine, really. Maybe we should take a break?"

They retreated into the house and took five in her cozy kitchen. Campbell poured Eliza half a beer—after she promised not to drive for an hour.

"Anyway, that's why I don't like waiting on people," Campbell said. "It's honestly kind of liberating. You just live your life, and if someone comes knocking, what a delight. Each day brings something new."

"What if you're, like, in the shower?" Eliza asked.

Campbell shrugged. "If it's important, they'll wait."

"What if they walked in on you?"

"I don't know, are they hot?" Campbell laughed. "Don't get me wrong, privacy is important. But we give up so much power when we let someone else's embarrassment become our own."

Eliza would remember the advice for a long time afterward.

"Speaking of embarrassment, do you actually still listen to CDs?" Eliza asked, holding up a jewel case of Vanessa Carlton she found on the counter.

"They do sound better, you know," Campbell said. "That was actually one of Casey's favorites—though I don't think she was old enough yet to understand about 'pretty-eyed boys you'd die to trust.'"

"No boys at school she liked? No crushes?"

"Not as far as I knew. Believe me, the cops explored that angle too."

"Hmm. Hey, can I ask you something? Did Casey have a horse or a pony?"

"Uh-uh," Campbell shook her head. "Horses terrified her. Tori rode. Tried to get Casey to come with her once, and the thing nipped at her. You would've thought it bit her arm off, she cried for so long. Still, she tried for Tori's sake." She swallowed the rest of her beer and stood. "Why don't you get to work sanding. Do, say, two minutes for each grit up to 240. It helps if you listen to music. Something with a good beat, lets you get in a rhythm."

Campbell vacuumed up wood chips while Eliza popped in her AirPods and scrolled through her music. Jorge Lopez was dead, and the Stranger seemed to be telling them the farrier was a red herring. By why trust the Stranger? On the other hand, Tori had a horse. But wouldn't RJ have known about that?

Eliza sucked in a breath, a new theory hitting her like Charlie's right hook to the face. She switched over to her Messages app and texted Jenny as fast as her fingers would fly.

> **D:** Crazy idea. What if TORI killed Casey, and RJ helped cover it up?

Jenny would hate it. Too bad. She'd hate Eliza's *other* theory even more. She finally settled on some Lizzo and switched over to the Find My app. The old iPhone she'd hidden in Dinah's car still had a 26 percent battery charge. Dinah was downtown, but the location dot had her car in the middle of a building. It took Eliza a moment to get it.

Dinah was parked in the garage underneath the Crow's Nest Hotel. Visiting Jack? Or Val?

WHENEVER ELIZA WAS OUT BEING JENNY, JENNY WAS TWO PARTS nervous energy and one part boredom. She lay on her fluffy comforter, trying and failing to make it through a paragraph in *Trouble Always Finds Me*. Finally, there was a knock at the bedroom door. Jenny slid off the edge of her enormous bed and scrambled over to answer. Mrs. Rivas had her Postmates from the taqueria.

"Ms. Onishi said you're not supposed to get food delivered anymore," the housekeeper said.

Jenny palmed Mrs. Rivas a $20 bill as she took the bag of food.

"Shelly says lots of stuff." Jenny dug into the bag and pulled out a foil-wrapped sandwich, a twin of the grilled chicken torta she ordered. "Take this to the chef, please, and ask him to study it. That way, I won't have to order out anymore, right?"

Mrs. Rivas shook her head ruefully. Jenny was two bites in, savoring the spices and flavors in the chicken when she got a text from Danger.

> **D:** Crazy idea. What if TORI killed Casey, and
> RJ helped cover it up?

Jenny scowled, a dozen nasty replies running through her head. Instead, she forced herself to wait, counting to 10 the slow way while she ate her dinner. It wasn't Eliza's fault. She just didn't understand Dad like Jenny did. When she was calm again, she texted back.

> **T:** He would never
> **D:** You sure?
> **T:** Yes.

She munched on, feeling a pang of regret when she dripped salsa on the cream-colored carpet.

"Crap."

She did her best to wipe it up with a sock, but there was still a pink splotch. Maybe she should order up a club soda.

The rest of the torta disappeared down her gullet in no time. Dead bodies made her hungry, apparently. She caught her reflection in the bathroom mirror while rinsing out that sock and spotted another dribble of salsa on her top. It was an old Trouble shirt, a little too threadbare and translucent to wear in public. Jenny grinned and snapped a risqué selfie for Dinah.

Jenny: Hungry tonight

After that A- in History, Dinah had insisted on keeping her weeknights devoted to homework, but a little text flirting wouldn't hurt.

Dinah: Stop, I can't concentrate! Save for tmrw babe!

Jenny flopped back on her bed. Fine. Kiss number 1,201 was going to burn a hole in her jeans.

Half an hour later, the nerves were gone, but the boredom remained. Dad's locked briefcase sat on her desk, taunting her. It was a unique model with linked three-digit locks on each hasp. Both had to be correct, or neither hasp would release. It could take weeks to work through the million potential combinations. She texted Eliza again.

T: We should just borrow a hacksaw from Casey's mom for this briefcase.

T: You done soon? Thinking of going over to see Drew.

D: Bad idea

D: On My Way! there now

D: Gotta update the big board

Jenny frowned.

T: 😣

She was the one who found Jorge's body. She should get to draw the red X over his face!

D: Come on. My first time seeing him while he's conscious.

T: I know I know. Maybe I'll go see Jack at the Crow's Nest.

She peeled off her shirt and went hunting for clean workout clothes. It didn't escape her notice that her Messages app showed the (•••) of Eliza typing a few times, but no response came for a full two minutes.

D: Better not, just in case. Gotta be careful.

Jenny bit down on her cheek, wanting to protest, but knowing that Eliza was probably right.

T: OK fine. Say hi for me 😌

D: o/

T: \o

Well, that was that. She gave up looking for her sports bra and pulled on a hoodie and leggings instead. Maybe Shelly wanted to watch a movie.

Drew's father, Arturo, answered the door and let Eliza in. He was tall and affable. Bronze skin, pressed shirt and slacks, vice-grip handshake.

"Is it all right if you're here after curfew?" he asked, raising his right eyebrow. His voice was deep but soft-spoken.

"It's fine," Eliza lied. "My driver is around the corner."

He relaxed his inquisitive brow, but only by half. There was an air about Mr. Porter that she couldn't place until she picked up a family photo from the mantle to look at and then put it back. Thirty seconds later, he nonchalantly leaned over and rotated it a half-inch to the left. This was a man who liked everything to be *just so*.

Mirai Porter, in contrast, wore a knit sweater dress, her hair in a messy ponytail, and a wine goblet dangling on her slender fingertips. With no prompting at all, Drew's mom embraced Eliza in a bone-crushing hug and pressed a glass of table red into Eliza's hand.

"Thank you for taking care of my boy," Mirai said, unfamiliar raw emotion in her voice.

Eliza nearly flinched, overcome with guilt.

"I didn't—he took care of me. He saved my life," she said.

Mirai waved her remorse away, stroking the silky red wig Eliza was wearing.

"So brave, just like his father," Mirai said.

Eliza glanced at Drew's dad. He smiled sheepishly.

"Two tours in Afghanistan, one in Iraq. Culinary Specialist."

"We met at the Army rec center in Edelweiss," said Mirai. "Supposed to be a summer job for me. Arty got me pregnant so fast!"

Eliza's cheeks went as red as the wine.

"I'm not hearing that!" Drew called from the hall, mortified.

He shuffled in wearing a loose Kelly green A's shirt with one arm cut away to make room for the mass of bandages around his shoulder.

"Don't overdo it," said Mirai.

"He's not," Mr. Porter said, mostly to himself.

Neither teenager spoke a word until they were alone in the garage.

"Can I ask you a personal question?" asked Eliza.

"Shoot."

"Did the nurse have to, you know, wipe for you?"

Now that she saw he was up and moving around all right, and didn't appear to be in danger of immediately dying, she had an uncontrollable desire to bust his balls.

"No, there was a bathroom," he said with a glare. "I managed. Actually, the toilet had a little hose thing."

"Hah! That was our deal: 10 percent and a bathroom with ass-jets! *Monkey's paw curls a finger!*"

They both laughed until he winced.

"Shit! Sorry."

"It's all good," Drew said, swallowing the pain. "Come on, let's get to the Big Board."

She tried to leap up and grab the handle to roll the screen down but kept missing by a few inches.

"I guess we know it's not Jack," Drew said, pulling down the screen with his good left arm.

"Oh, we know a lot more than that."

Eliza relayed all the new shit that had come to light. Well, except for the adventure at the Crow's Nest. The briefcase reminded Eliza too much of the dossier she found on herself when she followed Dad's map to the treehouse. Better to know what was inside, first. She told him the rest, though, and when she got to the part about the note on Jorge's body, Drew perked up.

"Like the note the metal shop guy gave you, right?" he asked. His gaze went unfocused, the wheels turning upstairs.

"No signature on this one," Eliza said, showing him a photo of it that Jenny had texted her. "When they're like that, it's from You Know Who."

"Hmm." He looked at her warily, like she might bite. "Okay: theory. Hear me out. What if RJ isn't dead?"

She tossed her crimson bangs in annoyance. "He is. Jen—Jesus, I held a mirror to his face for minutes at the funeral: no breath. Also, the Undertaker personally embalmed him, said so at Pinefall. Believe me, what a fantastic twist that would be: all some big fun game with no real stakes, but that's not how it is."

"Is it possible he had a twin?" Drew asked.

"Psh. It's never twins," Eliza bit down hard on the inside of her cheek. "How about this: what if it's Tori? She was Casey Klein's best friend, but mysteriously home sick the day she disappeared. And according to Campbell, Tori rode horses."

"Interesting." Drew mulled it over. "Maybe an accident while playing?"

"And RJ covers it up."

"What? Like he sets up Oscar Manuel?" Drew frowned. "Then why would he go to all that effort afterward to exonerate him? That'd be pretty cruel to Oscar's mom, right? Unless that was all part of the cover—which actually would be genius."

"Yeah, I don't know," Eliza said. A new thought occurred. "Tori's tall. With heels on, she could be your height, maybe. Could that have been her who stabbed you in the alley?"

"Not unless Tori's secretly yoked," Drew said. "They didn't seem *super* strong, but they weren't weak, either."

"Maybe Tori killed Casey, and the Stranger knows," said Eliza.

"Well, the Stranger should open a window if he's gonna close a door, you know what I'm saying?"

"For real." Eliza walked over to the MIDI synthesizer and hit a few keys. "You could probably play this one-handed."

"Alicia and I were talking about that," Drew said quietly.

"And how is *that* going?"

"Going fine." He was no good at hiding his bashful grin.

Eliza gave him a big, broad smile back, even as her stomach plummeted. It was never going to happen between them. It couldn't happen, she knew that. While he was single, she could still dream on it. But if Drew and Alicia became a thing, that was just one more unit that she wouldn't be a part of.

"Okay, you need rest, and I smell like linseed oil." She stood up. "Let's sleep on the clues and regroup."

Eliza texted Charlie on the walk with Drew back to the house.

> **Jenny:** Any makeup tips for a black eye?

The response came in seconds.

> **Charlie:** Yeah, fuck yourself with your mom's rusty dildo
> **Jenny:** My mom is dead
> **Charlie:** I hope you join her!!!

That could have gone better.

"Oh, shit," Drew said. He was checking his phone too.

"What?"

"Valerie Valentine's lawyers are holding a press conference tomorrow," Drew said, reading from his phone. "Says they have 'new evidence that will go a long way toward exonerating their client.'"

Eliza's arms rippled with goosebumps. "Fuck. I gotta go."

"Hold on, we should strategize—"

"Can't! I'll call you!"

She fled, racing back to the jeep she'd parked around the corner and practically diving into the driver's seat. Please, please, please let her get back before Jenny did anything rash.

Chapter Nineteen

Night Callers

J ENNY THOUGHT SHE WAS HANDLING THE SITUATION VERY WELL;
thank you very much. She was sitting in Dad's study in a blonde
bob wig and fake glasses, a pen behind her ear, war-dialing every
private investigator on Yelp. The conversation went the same way each
time: Jenny wanted someone to find out what Val's attorneys had. The
private investigator told her to call a lawyer instead.

She already had a lawyer. Sort of. But she couldn't use Mr. Webb
for this. If Val had somehow dug up new evidence, or—more likely—
paid someone off to give her an alibi, then the executor of Dad's will
wouldn't be able to advise her, conflict of interest and all.

"Can't you just sneak into their offices, get a peek at their files?"
Jenny asked the 12th guy down the list, a 3-star private dick from
Vivero Security Services.

"Breaking and entering is still illegal, even for licensed investigators,"
the guy said.

"How do you guys even work?"

"Ma'am, if I may, you're going about this the wrong way," he said.
"Stop thinking about the evidence they have and start thinking about

leverage on Valerie Valentine. You should be investigating her—hell, you should have hired someone to keep tabs on her months ago. I can give you full-service surveillance. I'm talking the platinum package. Wiretaps, credit checks—"

"Yeah yeah, thanks for the up-sell."

She thumbed **End Call** and sighed. Were any of these private dicks worth a damn? Just as she swiped back to Yelp, her phone vibrated with an **Unknown** number.

"Oh God, are you calling back? How embarrassing."

She declined the call. A moment later, Shelly poked her head in.

"Hey, I thought we were gonna watch that movie?"

"I mean, he's obviously a ghost, right?" said Jenny. "You go ahead, some stuff came up."

Her aunt cocked her head, hands on her hips.

"Stuff?"

"It's just teen girl drama, don't worry about it."

"Sure, why would I ever worry," Shelly muttered to herself, wandering away.

Jenny made a face and got up to shut the door. The phone in her hand buzzed again. Another **Unknown** calling. Oh, fine.

"Hey, so in case I wasn't clear—"

"Stop calling people," purred a voice on the other end. A low, male voice. Velvety soft, vaguely foreign.

"What?"

"Stop calling investigators," the voice said, taking care to emphasize every T. "You will put a target on your back."

"Get in line." Jenny puffed a loose strand out of her face. She really needed a haircut. "Who is this? Did I call you?"

"Lambert," he said. "And no."

"You're French?"

"Austrian, long ago. I shall consider the message delivered. Good evening."

"Wait!" Jenny said. "How did you know I was calling other P.I.s?"

"It is my business to know my competitors' business," Lambert said.

"Nice." Jenny sprang up, remembering her predicament. "I want to hire you."

"I'm afraid I must decline," said Lambert. There was an odd chirp in the background on his side of the call. "The others are correct; you need a lawyer."

"I don't have time for a lawyer," said Jenny.

"That is what lawyers are for. They create time, if you can pay, which I'm sure you can."

"You sound old. Are you?"

"Impertinent. Be more specific. *Hic!*"

That chirp again.

"Was that a hiccup?" Jenny laughed. "Are you drinking?"

"It is my dinner time," Lambert said in a low growl.

"I'm scandalized."

"We all self-medicate," said Lambert. "You have amphetamine/ dextroamphetamine. I have… grape juice—*hic!* I must go. I cannot help you with your current predicament, but if you wish to discuss other business, you may find me most days at the Winchester during lunch hour. My fee, if I take your case, will be a bottle of *Ressort Rouge*. Au revoir, Miss Valentine."

The line disconnected. Jenny gave her phone a dubious frown. "Was that real?"

She called Drew.

"Hey, are you all right?" There was worry in his voice.

"Fine. Did you just prank call me?"

"Uhh, no."

"K."

"Wait—"

She hung up and rapped her nails on her vanity desk. Maybe Jack would talk to her if she played it real casual.

The intercom squawked. "Miss Valentine?"

It was the security guy she'd hired. Jenny slapped the talk button. "Yeah?"

"There's a man at the front gate asking to see you," the guard said. "Are you expecting someone?"

"No. Who is it?"

"Wouldn't give me a name. Says he's a reporter."

"Wait, does he have hipster glasses, drive a white Hyundai?"

"Bingo."

Jenny chewed her lip.

"Does Ms. Onishi know he's here?"

"Negative," said the security guard.

"Gimme 15 minutes and then bring him around to the Conservatory. Search him first. No phones, watches, nothing in his pockets."

A minute later, she was tip-toeing into the map room. One of the display cases contained a pirate cutlass along with a fake treasure map and some plastic doubloons. The steel sword was authentic enough, though. Heavy, but if Warby Parker tried anything funny, it would poke real good. She eased back into the western hall, tucking the cutlass to her hip.

"Jenny? What are you up to?" Shelly called from the screening room. She could feel her aunt's sour glare through the wall.

"Nothing, just getting a book."

Jenny walked stiffly past the door, concealing the sword behind one leg until she was inside Dad's study. Moments later, the bookshelf in the corner slid open. Danger stepped out of the secret passageway.

"Sorry," her sister whispered. "Got home as fast as I could, but there was a cop. Had to go the long way to avoid him." Eliza registered the cutlass in Jenny's hand. "What's up?"

"That reporter is here. He wants to talk. I think he might know something about what Val's up to. Come on."

Jenny caught her up to speed as they headed back through the passageway to the Conservatory.

"There's something I should tell you," Eliza said when Jenny finished. They were at the other end of the hidden corridor.

"Later. How's Drew?" Jenny asked.

"He's okay. Alicia Aaron's been helping him." A flurry of emotions ran across Eliza's face. She reached out and pulled the blonde wig off Jenny's head and fixed her collar. "By the way, not cool going to Alkali Estates when I was with Campbell. You gotta at least keep me in the loop."

Jenny waved her concern away. "I know, I'm reckless. Sorry. All right, keep watch from in here. I need your keen eyes, smartypants."

Would Eliza be an insufferable asshole if she'd known her entire life that her name was Danger?

Jenny was doing that thing she'd warned Eliza about: sensing she was on thin ice and making it 10 times worse. If self-destruction were a sporting event, Jennifer Valentine would burn down the stadium. Eliza understood this, intellectually, but goddamn did she have it coming sometimes.

Inside the passageway, she shuffled into a little alcove built into the corridor. The wall would be brick on the conservatory side, but cleverly concealed peepholes allowed a sneaky person to spy from within the passage. Eliza pressed her tired eyes to a hole in the wall. The warm, fragrant air from the greenhouse cushioned her skin, and she watched.

Jenny sat on a bench between two slouching cherry trees, waiting silently with that ridiculous sword draped across her lap like some sort of Japanese pirate princess. Shortly, the security guard appeared, escorting in a thin man wearing skinny jeans, a brown blazer, and black frame glasses. When she'd first noticed him, Eliza took the reporter for some kind of young, hip blogger. Now, with a black eye courtesy of Jack, he was revealed for the slippery weasel that he was.

"Leave us," Jenny said to the security guard. "Wait out front."

Once security left, a hard, mean grin spread across the reporter's face.

"What an audience, your majesty. Should I be impressed?" he asked.

"You should be grateful I didn't have security do the other one," she said, pointing to her unblemished eye.

"Looks like we're twins."

"Don't mistake my injury for empathy," Jenny said. "Start talking."

"You should know I've taken precautions—"

"Literally, I don't care. I'm kinda busy tonight, so let's just skip past all that. I promise I won't murder you."

"Okay, sure," he said.

"Who are you, really?"

"Oh, I'm nobody. Just a humble stringer, looking for a big scoop."

"'The Stringer,' huh?" Jenny chewed the name over. "No, that won't do. It's too close to the Stranger. Gimme a name."

Eliza's lips parted in a grin she couldn't fight. Sometimes, Jenny, swear to God.

"You can call me Jeffrey," the reporter said. "I just came from

225

Valerie Valentine's penthouse."

Ice gripped Eliza's heart. That's where Dinah was tonight. Had she sold Jenny out?

"It's blackmail, then. Okay, Jeffrey, tell me what you've got, and we'll see if it's worth anything."

His eyes darted around like a nervous squirrel.

"Am I being recorded?"

Jenny shook her head and got her phone out. With a few taps, she had a bouncy Carly Rae Jepsen song blasting from hidden speakers all over the greenhouse. So much for following along with the conversation. Eliza flexed her cramping leg; these peepholes were made for someone taller. Her father, she supposed.

The music wasn't right for it, but Eliza imagined a dance between Jenny and the reporter. For the first steps, she let him lead. His manner was grave and self-important, all straight-backed gravitas like he was the bearer of stupefying news. It was a put-on, though. His hands gave him away, the way he gestured, almost unconsciously, as he talked. There was a smug insouciance hiding within, feet tapping to the wrong beat.

He seemed to be building to a big revelation when Jenny cut him off at the knees. His teeth bared, he retreated, frowning spitefully. She'd scored some point, gotten to the punchline early. Jeffrey spat out a mouthful, talking fast, his mask of solemnity slipping.

Jenny shook her head. She was unconvinced. So he changed the steps, swooping in with a flourish to reveal a folded up page from his jacket pocket. He dashed the paper in front of Jenny's face before yanking it back and retreating from a swing of Jenny's cutlass that looked a little too much like she meant it. The reporter stomped his foot, wagging a finger at her, and tucking the page safely away.

"Those are sealed!" Eliza heard Jenny yell over the music.

"Not from me," his thin lips appeared to reply, with a lizard's mirthless smile.

He went on, speaking fast, all his control fallen away, his harsh movements incongruent with the serene cherry blossoms that framed his face. This was the real Jeffrey: calculating and cruel.

When he was finished, Jenny turned to regard the patch of daisies, calling a question over her shoulder. His answer was curt and quickly followed by something sharp to twist. Jenny steeled herself and turned back to him. Now they danced in time, both familiar with the steps. A negotiation was happening. The reporter was smiling; he was getting his way. Jenny produced a brick of cash from inside her coat.

Eliza sucked in a breath. Was Jenny seriously thinking of paying this guy off? And where'd she get the cash?

Before she gave it to him, Jenny returned to the flowers. The reporter couldn't see, but Eliza could, as Jenny plucked a daisy and smeared the pollen all over the stack of $100 bills. He greedily accepted the cash, making a show of counting it as he rattled off another monologue, shamelessly pleased with himself.

Jenny rolled her eyes, but Eliza guessed it was false bravado. That worried her. Finally, she tapped her phone to switch off the pop music.

"I think I can make that happen," the reporter said. "It's been a pleasure doing business, Trouble."

He took a step toward the door, and Jenny called out.

"Jeffrey."

The reporter turned, that shit-eating grin still plastered on his face.

"You should know," Jenny hesitated, her wild eyes darting around. "There's someone else who's been playing this game with me. He uh, he doesn't like it when guys like you—guys who *aren't canon*—try to play too. It hasn't gone well for the ones who do."

"Is that a threat?"

227

"No. Just a warning. Maybe you should take that money and call it a win."

He scoffed and jabbed a finger at her. "You have till Tuesday, or I give Val and her lawyers the rest of my dirt."

Her shoulders sagged, and she seemed almost sad when she held up her phone to snap a photo of him.

"Don't say I didn't warn you."

The reporter sneered and left. Through the glass, Eliza could see the security guard escorting him back across the grounds to the front gate. She waited until they were out of sight, then touched the hidden release and swung the passage door open.

Jenny yawned, stuck the sword deep in the soil, and ran her fingers through her hair. After a count to 10, she slipped back into the passage with Eliza.

"Well, thoughts?" Jenny asked.

You're pretending to be tough and in control, but you have no idea what you're doing, and you might be in over your head.

Eliza didn't say it, but Jenny nodded, as if she somehow understood, anyway.

"He's a real shitheel," Eliza said instead. "What's he got?"

"So, Val's lawyers have a sworn statement from someone who claims—claimed to be the one who sent the note to Val the night of Dad's attack." Jenny flapped her arms. "It was Jorge Lopez."

"Bullshit."

"Obviously. He thought he'd help Jorge get revenge after Bottle Shock, but I was way ahead of him. It doesn't matter, since Jorge's dead now, but the reporter saw Penny and I leaving Jorge's place today. He hasn't told anyone yet, but one call to the police…"

Eliza rolled her eyes. "Unless he was killed right before you got there, Newton's Law of Cooling will clear you. But what did he really have? What was that paper?"

"Shift report from the Glendale Hospital psych ward for August 10th last year."

The day everything changed.

"Says I was missing during bed checks for half the night." Jenny shivered. "And he claims he can buy off the only nurse who worked that afternoon."

"You were on the roof," Eliza said softly, remembering that fateful night—*oh fuck!* Her stomach somersaulted. She'd told Dinah about that the other day. Dinah, who was at the Crow's Nest tonight. "You never left the building."

"Says who?" Jenny's voice caught, and she swallowed. "Apparently, the math works out where I could have driven up here, snuck in and hit Dad, then drove back."

"It's six hours each way," said Eliza. "I'd say that's doable."

"Whatever. Assuming that's true, Val doesn't know anything about this hospital stuff. He's holding out on her, trying to get more money. I gave him the cash as a retainer, so he'll get her to delay the press conference until Tuesday. He wants $1 million a year, after taxes, run through Trouble, Inc. like a real consulting job."

"Worst case, I could always testify," Eliza said.

"If it ever gets to that, we're way beyond worst case," said Jenny.

"That reminds me, I looked over all the paperwork we got from Mr. Webb. If Val gets cleared and they take 90 percent back, we're about $7 million in the hole."

"Oh, is that all?"

"It'd be more, but the new earnings don't count against the inheritance. If we can hang on and bank another good quarter, we could maybe get in the black, should the worst happen. Anyway, what's with the daisy pollen on the money?" Eliza asked.

"Oh. It occurred to me that this could all be a setup," Jenny said. "So I added a little 'fuck you,' in case he runs back to Val with the cash. She's allergic to daisies."

"He won't, he's desperate. And greedy. What'd he say at the end? It made you nervous."

Jenny shook her head, avoiding eye contact. Eliza knew Jenny well enough by now to know that this look meant she didn't want to acknowledge a particular facet of reality.

"He claims to have some dirt file on Dad. Says it could hurt Dad's image, hurt Trouble. I think he's bluffing."

"I wonder." Eliza shifted her jaw, considering. "He was there the night I broke into Yvonne's place. What if—what if she kept some kind of burn file on RJ? And he found it?"

"We can't worry about that now," Jenny checked her watch. "I've got security stalling him, dragging their feet bringing his car around. Where's your jeep?"

"I parked it at the end of Cellar Drive."

"Think you can go follow him?"

Eliza huffed a frustrated breath. "You need to learn how to drive."

"I know. What was it you wanted to tell me?"

"It can wait." Eliza bit her lip.

"Careful out there," Jenny called, as Eliza stepped out into the conservatory and jogged to the side exit.

Not yet. Eliza couldn't tell her sister about Dinah yet. Not until she had proof, or Jenny would never believe her. Without proof, Jenny would side with Dinah, and Eliza would be left alone all over again.

Eliza told herself it was just the shock of the crisp night air after that warm greenhouse atmosphere that had her blinking through blurred vision as she ran, but the icy chill that ran down her cheeks told the truth.

Chapter Twenty

T.G.I.F.

KISS NUMBER 1,201 WAS A QUICK PECK ON THE CORNER OF HER mouth. Dinah was late to pick Jenny up, apologizing in a rush and driving white-knuckled back into town.

"Guess we don't have time for Starbucks?" Jenny asked.

"Hilarious," Dinah said, running a yellow light. "Missed my first alarm. I *hate* it when that happens. Now I'm all out of my routine, and my hair's a mess."

The car ahead of them slowed way down for a turn, and Dinah had to jam on the brakes.

"Come on!" Dinah yelled, gunning it again as soon as the way was clear.

"Hey." Jenny moved to place a hand on top of Dinah's to calm her but overshot and got her knee instead. Suddenly the car got much warmer. "It's okay. I'm the one with Val's lawyers up my ass, not you. And they're gonna postpone their dumb press conference, anyway."

"I'm sorry, it's just..." Dinah swallowed hard. "You're acting like everything's fine, and it's not. And when you don't feel things, it's like—it's like I have to feel them for you."

"Pull over," Jenny said.

Dinah ignored her.

"Seriously, pull over!"

Dinah quailed and pulled into a fire lane, two blocks from the school. She put her hazard lights on and glanced sidelong at Jenny.

"Why am I so lucky to have you?" Jenny asked, reaching out to cradle Dinah's lovely cheek. Dinah burst into tears, so Jenny kissed them away, counting each one. "1,202, 1,203, 1,204…"

"You're still counting," Dinah said with a hiccup.

"Yeah, so?" Jenny blushed. She should never have told Dinah about the numbers.

"Are you shooting for a certain number?"

"I'm shooting for a castle in Austria, with minimal adult supervision," Jenny said, nibbling on Dinah's ear to change the conversation.

Dinah let out a soft moan—that somehow morphed into a high-pitched *neigh!*

Jenny yelped, and they broke apart, startled. A big, russet-faced horse head was fogging up Dinah's driver-side window. Deputy Calderon looked down from his saddle, pointing for them to move it along. She leaned over and rolled down the window.

"Hey, do you know a horse named Sonya?"

Calderon blanched. "Good girls go to class, right, Ricochet?"

He did something to the horse to make it nod its big horsey head.

"I just got boxed out by a fucking horse," said Dinah.

"We're late anyway."

They were. Second bell was already eight minutes rung when they got to campus.

"We're still on for tonight, right? Pink Umbrella?" Jenny tugged at Dinah's fingers, not ready to break apart as they stood in the hallway.

"Totally," Dinah said. She frowned, though, eyes averted. "If I wear a dress, will that be, like, gauche?"

"Wear whatever makes you feel good," Jenny said.

Dinah nodded, pressing her soft lips one more time to Jenny's knuckles.

"Do you count those?" she asked with a sly smile. "Or only kisses on the mouth?"

Jenny felt her cheeks redden. "You can kiss me *anywhere*, and I'll count it."

She ran away like a scamp, reveling, if only for a moment, in emotions that had nothing to do with the Stranger, Casey Klein, blackmail, or murder.

ALL ELIZA WANTED TO DO WAS SLEEP IN, BUT HER PHONE WOULD not! Stop! Buzzing!

She'd spent hours watching the reporter get dinner at a Chili's, try and fail to pick up on the waitress, fail again at a swankier lounge—like, dude, with a black eye? Read the room—go back to his crappy motel, and finally fall asleep after three reruns of SportsCenter.

Bzzzz!

Eliza shrieked and threw off the covers, lunging for her phone next to the camp bed. It was Trouble, naturally. She'd be in Mr. Hooke's class right now.

    T: Hey

    T: Hey!

    T: Wake up ho

    T: Did the Stranger get you?? 🌚

    D: WHAT?!??!?!

    T: Do you pronounce the b in subtle?

D: No

D: Seriously?

T: WELL CONGRATULATIONS GENIUS

T: Any luck with the briefcase? I've tried all the birthdays and significant Trouble numbers I can think of.

To be honest, she'd been mentally leaving that part to Jenny. She did her job and got the damn thing, didn't she?

Eliza sighed and took a moment to ponder. The way the briefcase felt like it was just waiting for her... They'd only found it because of the Fortune Teller, and they only found her because of Declan's Tarot card. Had Dad planned on Jenny following the Tarot card all the way to it?

D: Maybe something with the Tater card?

D: Tarot

T: 🪦

T: Sounds like we need to study up on Death 💀

T: We're still switching at lunch, right?

D: Come on, I was up till 3

T: Plz?? I forgot the woodworking thing for Shop, so you need to bring that, anyway.

Eliza cursed. She and Campbell had worked hard on that damn thing. She couldn't let that go to waste.

D: Goddamnit fine

With a belabored sigh, she tugged her jeans on.

THE WAY THE MORNING HAD BEEN GOING, JENNY FELT LUCKY TO make it to lunch. Mrs. Cortez sprung a surprise test on them in

History. Fill-in only, no multiple choice. What a monster. In English, Mr. Hooke made them all take turns reading aloud. Everyone laughed when Jenny pronounced the 'b' in 'subtle.' The Bitchy Brigade spent the rest of the period working extra 'b's into words, which they found extremely hilarious. Rather than defend her, Mr. Hooke said it was nice to see them smiling through their grief over Lily. He even added a saucy 'b' into "throttle." That would have been bad enough on its own, but then Alicia Aaron said "troubable" to the biggest laughs of all.

She got her revenge when Vice Principal Carter called Alicia to the office before lunch. He had intel (from Jenny) that Alicia used a bitcoin app on her phone and might be the Ghostwriter. If she wasn't, Jenny promised herself she'd make it up to the girl by taking a look at her manuscript, which had arrived in her email in the middle of the night.

When the Lunch bell rang, Danger was still on her way, so Jenny loitered in the cafeteria, munching on a container of trail mix she'd brought from home. Jack and the boys lounged in their usual spot.

"Where's your girl?" Penny asked, walking up with Thanh Trân.

"Studying," said Jenny. "Your fault."

Penny hid a sly smile as they sat with the boys. Mason gawked at Jenny's snack.

"Nice CoolWhip container," said Mason. "Aren't you rich now?"

"It's an Asian thing," said Thanh, snaking JeRay's pudding cup and sitting at the Bitchy Brigade's table.

Jenny nodded. "True story. If your dad wants back in Shelly's good graces, he should find a way to be conspicuously washing used Ziploc bags the next time he sees her."

"I could watch that," Thanh said.

"My God, the DILF energy," said Jack, playing with his mashed potatoes.

"Nah, she seems happy with Mr. White the Pedo," Mason said.

"He is not!" said Penny.

As if in support, a grape bounced off Mason's forehead.

"Ooop! Sorry!" Meghan yelled, laughing with her friends. She and Shani Wolf were "smiling through their grief" by playing a lascivious game that involved tossing grapes into each other's open mouths. They would giggle after each failed attempt and shoot coquettish smirks at the boys.

"Don't bite it," Meghan said to Shani. "Catch it in your mouth, not your teeth."

"Oh my God, in Paris, you don't bite it, you just catch it in your mouth," Penny said to Jenny in a simpering Valley Girl voice.

They both snickered. Mason laughed too. Several phones vibrated at once.

"Ghostwriter?" Jack asked, checking his phone.

"That guy sucks now," said Charlie, who was abstaining from the grape game and looking glum at the end of the table.

Shani and Meghan stopped their game to abuse the mysterious Ghostwriter on Charlie's behalf.

"Didn't like your 15 minutes, Charlotte?" Jenny said.

Charlie's micro-bladed eyebrows narrowed, and she bared her teeth at Jenny.

"Look at this shit," Shani said, reading from her phone. "*The Ballad of Jaybird and the Last Winter Queen*. He's trying to be all literary. Like he's trying to impress with his writing or whatever because his gossip dried up. Dude, no one cares."

"He could at least do us the favor of tagging his fic," said Jack.

"Is there Trouble fanfic?" Mason asked no one in particular.

"Ew, she's like 11," said Thanh.

"I mean aged up, jeez," Mason said, blushing. "13 at least!" he added with a lecherous grin, his hand up for a high-five that everyone left hanging.

Jenny elbowed him. Meghan glared at both of them.

"We do not look for, or acknowledge any non-canon material," Jenny said officiously.

"God forbid the girl ever go through puberty," Charlie said. "No wonder you're so fucked up."

The others winced like they might come to blows again, but Jenny just shrugged and rolled her eyes.

"It's not that kind of story," was her standard reply. She did not need this on her mind before her date tonight.

Thankfully, her watch tapped three times.

"TGI-fucking-F," she said, rising. "Ladies, gentleman, Mason, a pleasure as always."

Mason gave her another queer smile as she put away her trail mix and hurried to the quad bathroom. Thankfully, the stalls were all empty, except for the last one where Eliza was waiting. Jenny gave her a quick debrief as they swapped clothes.

"So what's that do?" she asked, looking at the wooden square Eliza brought with her.

"It holds napkins. Dude, did you see the file Alicia sent you? It's 200,000 fucking words!"

They both laughed.

"What's it called?"

"*Hands of—*"

Jenny hushed her. The restroom door had just opened.

Heavy footfalls entered—boy footfalls. The door closed, followed by the sharp metallic clink of a bolt sliding into a locked position. Eliza silently stepped up onto the toilet seat in a crouch. The footsteps moved closer; softer now, someone trying to keep quiet. Jenny retreated from the stall door.

The steps halted; a shadow loomed in front of their stall. Eliza had her stun gun out, ready to strike. Everyone held their breath.

The shadow moved away. Jenny was about to exhale when the door burst inward.

Mason Lockhart had kicked it open.

The colossal asshole was standing there in shocked chagrin. He'd *seen* them. Had them cornered.

"I knew it!" he shouted in triumph.

Chapter Twenty-One

Mexican Standoff

HEARTBEATS POUNDED IN HER EARDRUMS. THERE WAS A GREAT rushing sound; Jenny thought she might collapse.

"Wait! You can see her?" was all she could think to blurt out.

Mason hesitated, momentarily stupefied by her last, desperate con. Eliza leapt off the toilet seat and charged.

The big oaf was sneaky agile. His confusion vanished, and he easily swiped the stun gun aside, doing a twisty wrestling grapple to get Eliza in a headlock. She ducked out of it—and right into his meaty left hand. Jenny cried out as he bodily lifted her sister into the air by her neck.

"Not this time," he said.

Eliza writhed in the air. Mason used his other hand to grip her wrist and squeeze. She yelped and dropped the stun gun. Jenny had her collapsible riot baton out now. "Stop it!" she screamed.

"Easy," said Mason. He retreated, using Eliza as a shield.

"Let her go," Jenny said, inching closer.

"Or what?"

"Or I'll fucking kill you and everyone you love."

"Jesus! You must be Danger." Mason let Eliza down and pushed her toward Jenny, holding up his arms in surrender.

"No, that's me," Eliza said, rubbing her neck.

"How did you find out?" Jenny demanded.

He chuckled. "You know, it's kind of a funny story."

Someone tried to enter the restroom—and slammed right into the door when the sliding bolt stopped them.

"Ocupado!" Mason growled.

Jenny pulled Eliza close, embracing her with one arm while the other held out her baton in what increasingly seemed like an empty threat against this big, beefy hulk of a boy.

"You can relax, I'm not here to hurt you," he said. "The way I see it, we're even. Actually, you might owe me a favor or two now."

"Who else knows?" Jenny asked.

"No one."

"You sure? Not your dad, or your baby mama?"

"This is just between you and me—and you, I suppose," he added, turning to Eliza. He studied them both. "Uncanny."

Her sister placed a hand on Jenny's baton and pushed it down. "It's okay," she said. "We can work something out. He doesn't want people finding out about his daughter either, right?"

"We've been respectful so far," Jenny added. "But it would be trivial for us to figure out who Lilah's mom is." She glanced at Eliza. "Do you think it's a teacher? Shelly did get hired super late for that Econ teaching job."

Mason struggled to adopt a poker face.

"Something tells me your secret is more valuable," he said.

Thwack! A small throwing knife embedded itself in the wall a few inches from Mason's stunned face.

"Tell us how you knew," said Eliza, brandishing another.

"You started this, you know? You sent that shit about me to the Ghostwriter. I had to get you back! But then you got real touchy about your birth certificate. And I thought: huh, maybe she really *isn't* RJ's."

Jenny groaned and rubbed her face.

"So I spent a few afternoons at the Calistoga County public records office. Even got my dad to pull some strings to get me special access. He thinks I'm researching our genealogy. Heh."

"There's nothing on my birth certificate about her," Jenny said.

"There isn't, you're right. It took me an entire day to find that damn thing and nothing," Mason said. "Sure enough, there's Johnathan Valentine listed as the father. Still, something didn't feel right. Why so protective? So I went searching for your mom's death certificate instead."

Eliza hissed.

"That was another day, and another big waste of time, right?" Mason said. "But still, I didn't believe. I was just flipping through random death notices, unsure what I needed to see, and then there it was: Elizabeth Danger Valentine. Born March 10th, died March 14th. And I thought: no way, right? But what if? Jack's always saying Jenny has a split personality. How is she always one step ahead? How can she get a concussion and then ace her worst subject while high on pain pills? How can she drink three screwdrivers and pass a breathalyzer? Believe me, Dad was fucking flabbergasted at that. He thought he had you. And why is she always checking her watch and then running to the bathroom? Most people wouldn't notice, but I know a thing or two about living a lie. For a while, I thought it was drugs or something, but I saw that death certificate and I knew. It was right there in front of me the whole time."

"Fucking bravo." Jenny turned to Eliza. "We need to destroy that death certificate. Should have done so already." She regarded Mason warily. "Can you get us back in there?"

He let out a loud guffaw. "Why would I? Why do you even care?"

"If it gets out, it puts us both in danger," said Jenny.

Eliza tittered.

"Wait—did *you* kill RJ?" Mason gaped at Eliza.

"No, of course not," Eliza said.

"Hmm." Mason leaned back against the sink counter. "Well, it looks like we got us a real Mexican standoff here. That's when everyone's got shotguns pointed at each other's balls. Now you don't have any, but—"

"We take your meaning," Eliza said. "Seems like it's in all our best interests to do nothing. Pretend this didn't happen."

"Nah, I'm gonna need more than that. You know, day care's a real bitch, and expensive."

"Fine," said Jenny. "We'll get you a nanny."

"A French nanny," Eliza added.

"How about a house?" Mason asked.

"Don't push it," said Jenny.

Mason rubbed his hands together, delighted. Jenny felt sick. Any girl detective knew that you could never buy silence, only pay for it on installment. Hopefully, full-time care for Mason's daughter would be enough. On her phone, she tapped the contact for Mr. Webb.

"Jennifer, how are you?" the lawyer said on the first ring.

"Still kicking. Hey, you know that concierge service we used to hire security? Do they do child care? I need an Au Pair on super short notice."

"Intriguing." She could hear Mr. Webb's Cheshire cat smile through the phone. "I'll text you the number."

Jenny hung up. "Expect her at the cabin by this evening."

"You might want to hurry home and clear out your little weed farm," Eliza said.

"Might as well, my buyer woke up with a knife in his ticker," said Mason.

"Wait—Jorge Lopez?" asked Eliza. "What did you know about him?"

"With Jorge, the rule was the less you knew, the better. Scary dude." He looked back at Jenny. "I'm gonna be a little light now. Don't suppose I could get some weekend fun money?"

She grimaced and dug in her purse, already knowing she'd come up light herself.

"I'll text you some cash later. Here, have these," Jenny said, handing him the baggy of MDMA pills she found in Jorge's trailer. "But I want to be real clear: not a word about Eliza to anyone, or it all disappears, and I will make it my mission to make your life a living hell."

"A fucking pleasure as always," said Mason. "Now, how do we do this?"

"I'll leave first," said Jenny. "Let's skip switching today," she told Eliza. "Mason, you get in that stall and stay there. Don't come out until at least 10 minutes after the last lunch bell."

"I'll be late," he protested.

"The school lunch didn't agree with you. When's your birthday?"

"Why?"

"Just tell me."

"April 12th."

"I'll get you box seats at the Giants' game," Jenny said, perking Mason up. "I can be a real good friend or a real bad enemy. Your choice."

"Right," he said, plucking the knife from the wall and handing it to Eliza. "Well, nice meeting you."

Once he was inside the stall, Jenny rummaged in her backpack and tossed her sister a curly brown wig.

"I'm sorry," Eliza whispered.

"It's not your fault," Jenny said. "We'll talk later."

Her sister left first, slipping out while Jenny waited in the second stall. It wasn't Danger's fault, Jenny knew, it was hers. She'd been lazy. Reckless. Taken her eye off the prize, and it had nearly cost them everything. Just tonight, she told herself. Let her have one decent night with Dinah, and then she'd be back on the hunt.

AS MUCH AS SHE WANTED TO GO HOME AND SLEEP AGAIN, ELIZA WAS wide awake now. Mason's discovery was a disaster, for sure. There was another part to it, though. It was the first time she and Jenny had ever been together with someone else. It had felt… electric. She knew she shouldn't think it, but to be seen like that—as herself—was intoxicating.

These were dark thoughts. She fought them off by keeping busy. By the time school got out, Eliza had finalized the arrangements for Mason's nanny. She also visited three different ATMs downtown, withdrawing the max amount of cash each time. If Val should suddenly go free, she wanted to make sure they had some emergency funds that were off the books.

> **D:** You can tell Mason the Au Pair will be there at 7:00 PM tonight.
>
> **T:** Fucker even gets a date night out of this. I'm with him now. Headed to the records office to destroy any traces of you.
>
> **D:** Cool

Eliza swayed, her exhaustion threatening to overtake her. She hurried back to Valentine Manor and napped in the treehouse for a few hours, dreaming darkly of nooses and knives.

The sun was dipping low when she awoke, filling the treehouse with golden light. Dinah would be over in a little while, but Jenny had texted, asking to talk. Shelly was in the City to see a play with Mr. White, so they met up in the mansion.

Jenny was sitting with RJ's briefcase in her lap and a big smile on her face. She had a photo of Declan's bloody Tarot card open on her iPad.

"Figure it out?" asked Eliza, her pulse quickening.

"You were right. The Roman numeral XIII, and the Mark of the Beast," Jenny said, pointing to the number's on Death's flag.

"Ten. Three. 666. 103 and 666."

With a snap and a pop, Jenny flipped the hasps open.

"Did you already peek?" Eliza asked.

Jenny shrugged. "Guilty."

Eliza joined her on the bed to look. Inside was a large photo print. A young RJ Valentine and their mother Laura were huddled close, entering one door of many in a long hallway. A hotel room. His secret room at the Crow's Nest, Eliza realized, recognizing the carpet pattern. She flipped the photo around; there was nothing on the back this time. It was the only item in the briefcase.

"I gotta be honest, I was expecting more," Eliza said.

"Right?" Jenny chuckled, unconcerned.

Eliza released a moan of frustration. She risked her life for *this?*

"I guess Dad's showing us that they were being watched and followed?" she said. "In case we didn't get that from the heirloom photo?"

"If we can figure out who Val hired to take these, they might know if she hired someone to run Mom off the road," Jenny said. "Hell, they might have been the ones who did it."

"Sure, just find the haystack this needle was in, 17 years ago." Eliza blew a lock of hair out of her face. "We'll call this plan B."

She glumly snapped a picture of the print on her phone, feeling the end of this case drift further away with each new clue.

"Cheer up, the news about Lily Geist is even worse," said Jenny. "While you were napping, the police connected Jorge Lopez to her murder. There was a lock of her hair in his trailer. And maybe Sarah Ortiz's too."

"Convenient."

"Isn't it?" Jenny shook her head. "Perfect, if you're the real Hot Springs Hangman."

"Or the Stranger," said Eliza. She still hadn't told Jenny about her newest suspect. It was hard to when Jenny was about to go on a date with the person. Dinah was too young to have killed Casey Klein, but she was up to something and couldn't be trusted.

"Maybe you were half-right about Tori," Jenny said. "Maybe she killed Casey, but Dad never knew about it."

"So, what, Tori and Casey are fighting over a barbie or whatever, and oops, she accidentally chokes her to death? And somehow hides her body for five months and frames the gardener?"

"Maybe. Okay, so Tori's home sick that day. She goes riding in the morning, hence the horse hairs. Later, she's poking around the mansion and somehow discovers that the books aren't written for her. Or—Oooh! Maybe Casey is with her. Tori could've sent the driver to pick her up after school. And they find out about me: the real Trouble. A pureblood Valentine, not her adopted ass. And she just loses it."

"You're such a Slytherin," Eliza said.

Jenny's eyebrows arched sky-high in umbrage. "Fuck you! I am not!"

"It's not an insult!"

"You basically called me evil!"

Eliza groaned in revulsion. "There are good Slytherins. Honestly, Trouble, if you would only read—"

"I've seen the movies. Slytherins suck." She raised her chin, feeling superior. "I'm a Gryffindor."

"You are *so* not a Gryffindor."

"Oh, and you are?" Jenny asked.

"Obviously, yes." She placed a hand to her chest. "Courage, bravery. I mean, hello, Danger is my middle name."

Jenny's eyes narrowed. "If it wasn't, you'd be a Hufflepuff."

"You know, you say that like you think Hufflepuffs are just a bunch of duffers, but they're not."

"That's exactly what a Hufflepuff would say."

Eliza flopped back on a pile of pillows, trying and failing to keep her next words from exiting her mouth. "I mean this with love, Jenny—and no offense to dear old Dad—but seriously: read another book. There's more out there than just *Trouble*."

"Sure, because *Harry Potter* is totally branching out."

"It would be a start."

"I've read other books," said Jenny.

"Were they for school?"

"Not all of them."

"What's the last book you read for fun that wasn't written by RJ?" Eliza asked.

"Are you gonna make me read some fuckin' *Lord of the Rings* book to prove my bonafides?" Jenny replied.

Eliza scoffed. "You wouldn't make it past the second chapter of *Fellowship*."

"For your information, I read *all* of *Gravity's Rainbow*."

"Because RJ said it was his favorite!" Eliza was shouting now. She didn't mean to, but she couldn't help herself. All her caution and mistrust that she'd buried deep within, held against that day that this sisterhood would splinter, was rushing to the surface.

"So?" Jenny asked.

"And how was it?"

"Fucking incomprehensible!" Jenny said. "Are you happy?"

"I should write a fake article where RJ says he loved... I don't know. *Pride and Prejudice* or something. At least you might enjoy it."

"That's actually Dinah's favorite book," said Jenny.

"*Really.*"

"What?"

"You don't seem like much of a Darcy," said Eliza.

"What's that supposed to mean?"

Don't say it. Don't say it.

"It means I don't trust her."

Jenny only blinked, stunned.

"She's happily dating Jack until you show up and win the inheritance," Eliza said, holding up a finger to count.

"That wasn't how it happened," Jenny muttered.

"She knows *way too much* about this family," said Eliza, gesturing with finger number two.

"She was Jack's girlfriend," said Jenny.

"And she's lying about where she was the night Dad died!"

The antique clock on Jack's bedroom wall ticked between them, each tock a crack in the foundation they'd built this alliance on.

"I don't want to hear this," Jenny said.

There was nothing to be done now. If they couldn't get past this, they were always going to break. "Well, you need to listen. I asked her about that night," Eliza said.

Jenny gaped.

"Casual-like, not like I was accusing or anything. Just, 'Hey, what do you remember? What was it like to find out?' She said she was at home—and honest to God, Jenny, it was a fucking lie. One even I could spot. She knows something, and she's not telling. I'm not trying to hurt your feelings, I just want you to be careful."

"Oh, I'm sure that's it! Just your *concern!*"

"I hid a phone in her car."

Her sister had gone scarily silent. Eliza's eyes stung. They were full of tears.

"You want to know where she was last night when Valerie Valentine was cooking up a plan to screw us? At the Crow's Nest! I checked!" Eliza held up a screenshot on her phone to prove it. "Do you think that reporter just lucked into shift logs that said you missed bed checks? Dinah told him because she knew you were on the roof that night. Because I mentioned it to her, like an idiot!"

"You've never liked her," Jenny said.

"How could I?" Eliza said, swallowing a sob. "We were a team! Now I'm just your errand girl!"

Jenny opened her mouth to speak but hesitated. Her jaw moved wordlessly, as though she were auditioning and rejecting the appropriate cutting remark.

"Lizzy…"

"You know I don't have anyone, right?" Eliza said in a small voice. "Nurse Bennett moved me away from all my friends, and I had to watch her disintegrate in front of my eyes for three years. And then she was gone. I had no one until I found you. I don't get to have Dinah or Jack or Shelly or Drew or Charlie or even fucking Alicia Aaron. Because I don't exist to them. Only you do. And you don't even want them half the time! So fuck me for caring, right?"

"It is not fair for you to take this out on Dinah when you're really mad at me," Jenny said.

"That's not what this is about at all."

"I can't have this conversation right now. I'll say something I'd regret." Jenny rose and walked to the bathroom. "I'm going to take a shower. Dinah will be here soon."

Jenny didn't need to say it. The unsaid command was clear: leave. Eliza searched her sister's eyes, hoping desperately for pity, but finding only pain. The foundation split asunder, and she plunged into icy despair.

"Fine," she said. "Don't come crying to me when Bi-Curious Barbie sells your gullible ass out and runs back to Jack."

She hurled a bottle of silver nail polish at her sister and stomped out of that goddamned room, believing in her heart that she might never return.

Chapter Twenty-Two

Brave or Chicken?

THE PINK UMBRELLA WAS A HALF-HOUR DRIVE AWAY IN NAPA. Jenny and Dinah talked the whole car ride over; it was the snappiest, airiest conversation they'd ever had. Jenny was on her game. They were *vibing*. No trouble in this paradise. She and Dinah were doing great; thank you very much. 1,249 and counting.

For her look, Jenny stripped it down to basics: black stretch pants, purple Keds, a thin white v-neck t-shirt, and a black bra underneath. She was trying out a new wig today: silky black, shoulder-length, with all the tips dyed purple. She was still a little self-conscious about her jacket. It was denim and tiny, barely came down to her mid-riff and had "Trouble" spelled across the back in purple and white rhinestones. Now that they were walking up to the Pink Umbrella, she wondered if people might make fun of it behind her back.

Not that she should worry, no one would even notice her, standing next to Dinah. Her girlfriend was a sultry vision, from the purple feather in her canted Kentucky derby hat on down. She'd kept her tendrils snowy white, styling her hair to drape in blonde and silver waves down her bare right shoulder over a strapless white cocktail dress. The A-line skirt barely reached her knees, flaring out from the purple ribbon belt she'd tied above her hips. Her legs went on for days, even before the strappy Miu Miu heels gave her an extra 3 inches.

"I'm overdressed," Dinah mumbled in her ear as they got in line for the door. She pulled on a matching purple cardigan to keep from shivering in the chilly February air.

"Who cares? You look amazing."

1,250, for courage. She gripped Dinah's hand tight, fingers entwined, waiting their turn. Muffled bass beats vibrated through the walls. The Pink Umbrella was situated just off the corner of a four-story building in downtown Napa. Jenny knew from researching online that most of the bar was upstairs, in a big loft on the second floor. The bouncer scanned their IDs and gave them orange wristbands because they were underage, then they were hustling up the steps. Jenny shot a nervous smile at Dinah, who had just turned to do the same right back. They both giggled and leapt up onto the landing.

It felt like every eye turned their way, but in reality, it might've been like two people. It was impossible not to compare the warm smiles she received here to the leering male gaze that surrounded her at Bottle Shock, or the drug-laced trance of those clubs in LA from the bad old days. These people were... her people. She took a deep breath, inhaling Dinah's vanilla perfume, the sour smell of beer foam, aloe, sweat, leave-in conditioner. Pictures wouldn't do. She needed to build a sense memory for this moment.

They drifted further inside, navigating by the soft yellow sconces and pink Christmas lights running all over the exposed brick walls. Top 40 music thumped, but not too loud.

"Let's do a lap!" Dinah said in her ear.

Jenny grinned, pointing out a Ms. Pac-Man machine. Some cool college chicks were playing shuffleboard and darts. There was a row of booths in the back for some privacy, and lots of little clusters of chairs and stools for people to socialize on. Through an archway, they found themselves in the dining area. The menu was pub food, and Jenny couldn't imagine eating anything with her stomach aflutter, but maybe a street taco would be good later. Running through both areas was a circular bar, backed by glowing neon pink umbrellas, and televisions playing *A League of Their Own*.

"What'll it be?" asked the bartender.

Jenny was standing there slack-jawed.

"How about some pink drinks?" Dinah said.

"Virgin?"

Jenny flushed.

"I mean no alcohol," the bartender said with a laugh. She was older, a few streaks of grey in her brown hair, wearing a Stone Brewery shirt under a flannel with the sleeves rolled up.

"Oh, yeah, sure," said Dinah.

They both watched speechless as the bartender mixed the drinks in a blur of motion before pouring them into martini glasses. As far as Jenny could follow, there was grenadine, seltzer, pink lemonade, and some other stuff in there, topped by a maraschino cherry and a pink glow-stick drink stirrer. Jenny paid with her Black card.

"Open a tab?" the bartender asked.

"Sure," Jenny said. A thought occurred, perking her up. "Actually, drinks are on me tonight. For everyone. Tell 'em, when Trouble's in the house, their money's no good."

"Okay," the bartender shrugged.

Dinah smirked. "You're incorrigible." They were about to clink glasses when a familiar voice called from across the lounge.

"Hey Heather, when you're done with those baby gays, can I get a White Claw? And a Diet Coke?"

Jenny frowned, turning. Was that—?

It was. Officer Peña was sitting at a booth in the corner. Jenny almost didn't recognize her out of uniform, wearing low-slung jeans and a scoop neck shirt falling off one shoulder.

They blinked at each other.

"Well, well, well," Jenny said, strolling over.

Officer Peña bit her cheek, grimacing.

"She 100 percent drops the ball on purpose," said a familiar voice from the opposite seat. She was tucked way back into the booth where Jenny couldn't see a face from this angle. Her boots were thousand-dollar Guccis, though.

"You only say that because you're a big sister," Peña said, reluctantly turning to greet Jenny. "Hello there. Who's your friend?"

"This is Dinah," Jenny said, pulling Dinah closer. "Fancy meeting you here, Officer."

"It's just Darcy tonight," she said. "I believe you already know—"

One of the pricy Gucci boots kicked out sharply at Darcy under the table.

"Oh, give it a rest, are you gonna hide all night?" said Darcy.

Jenny tilted her head, curious, and came around to get a look at the booth's other occupant. She nearly dropped her drink.

Tori Valentine was seething in the corner, wearing a beanie and a corded knit sweater like some townie.

"Yeah, we've met," said her stepsister.

"Hi Tori," Dinah said sweetly beside her. Tori's eyes shifted, roving over Dinah. Did they narrow a bit?

"Hey, Di. How's Lancer?" Tori said.

"Old and lazy."

"Good dog," said Tori.

"Wait. You and her?" Jenny was still trying to catch up to this new paradigm shift. How had she never noticed the silver Tiffany ring on Officer Peña's finger before, a twin of the one Tori wore? "How long has this—you're too good for her!"

"Hey!" Darcy said, flashing Jenny a warning glare. "Be nice, Girl Detective, we're here to enjoy ourselves."

Tori looked like she wanted to disappear into the booth's deep cushions.

"But you and Mr. White?" Jenny gaped at Tori.

"Are just friends!" Tori flashed her teeth. "Jesus, how did someone so clueless ever put my mom in jail? Peter is *45*."

"*Peter*," Jenny repeated.

"Do you guys want to sit?" Darcy asked, a devilish grin on her face.

Tori's whole body clenched like she just sharted.

"We probably shouldn't intrude," said Dinah.

"You guys seemed awfully close for a student and teacher." Jenny couldn't let this go.

"Because everything's a *Trouble* book to you," Tori snapped. "Right? It's *Trouble Eight Days a Week*: the Professor and his scheming teacher's aide. What a weird self-own by Dad, by the way. This is what happens when you build your whole life around fiction." Some real bitterness was dripping into her mocking tone. "You keep looking for those same cliches everywhere, and it's blinding you."

Darcy had a knowing smile for Dinah. "Can't take these Valentine girls anywhere."

"*We were a team!*" *Eliza sobbed.*

Jenny blinked, forcing the memory away. Her sister's treachery could wait. She would have hated it here anyway.

"Maybe you could show me the ladies' room," Dinah said to Darcy.

The cop nodded and stood up, but not before reaching across to squeeze Tori's hand. Jenny made sure to do the same with Dinah.

Before they left, Jenny couldn't help notice Dinah glancing at Tori. Something passed between them, some silent command or request.

"She knows something, and she's not telling."

Their girlfriends left, leaving Jenny standing awkwardly over Tori. Her step-sister stared ahead, picking at the label on a bottle of Tapatío hot sauce. Jenny slapped her hips, shrugged, and took Darcy's seat across the table.

"This place is cool," Jenny said. "We could have met here, instead of the Bad Egg. You know, when you tried to get me drunk."

"Oh please, you knew what you were doing, you just couldn't handle your liquor."

"I guess you would know."

"Insolent," Tori said, leaning forward and adopting her most condescending tone. "Look, you're probably thinking this is some sort of common ground, a way to bury the hatchet, whatever. Please let me disabuse you of that notion immediately. You and I are not cool."

"Ya know, there are a lot of people out there who have good reason to hate me," Jenny said. "I'm just not sure what I did to earn it from you."

"You don't think framing my mother for murder and stealing the family fortune is enough?" Tori asked.

Before Jenny could reply, a waitress with a big afro and killer sleeve tattoos approached with drinks. She put the Diet Coke in front of Tori but hesitated with the White Claw.

"This is for Darcy, and Darcy only," the waitress said.

"I have my own drink," Jenny said, sipping on her Pink Drink.

"Wasn't talking to you," the waitress said, eyeing Tori.

"Thanks, LT. I'm good," Tori said, pushing the White Claw to the corner, far away from her.

Jenny snickered. They sipped their drinks in silence for what felt like a long time.

"You hated me before I won the game, though," Jenny said.

Tori didn't reply.

"They sure are taking a while."

"If I know Darcy, she's probably in there telling Dinah her whole life story," Tori said, allowing a private, almost sweet smile to cross her lips. "That, and she loves torturing me." Tori rapped her fingers on the table. "I need a cigarette. You still smoke sometimes, right?"

"You know I don't have anyone, right?"

"Uhh, trying not to," Jenny said, even as she got up to follow. Eliza said she quit, but Jenny was beginning to realize there was a lot that Eliza had been keeping to herself.

THE PINK UMBRELLA HAD A SMOKING AREA OUT ON THE VERANDA IN the back that overlooked the parking lot. In this chilly weather, they were the only ones willing to brave the cold to dirty up their lungs.

Tori tapped a pack of cigarettes against her palm. They were cloves, the same kind Alicia Aaron favored.

"You haven't laced them with arsenic or something, have you?" Jenny asked. Tori's lips curled in a wicked grin. She handed Jenny the one she'd already lit and lit another for herself. Jenny tried not to inhale but still ended up coughing. The oily warmth made her lungs sizzle. "Been a while. These'll kill you, ya know?"

"Of all the ways I've tried to kill myself, this is taking the longest." Tori took a long drag and slowly exhaled.

Jenny couldn't help picturing the hospital roof. The windchill was freezing then, like tonight.

It was only four stories down, but that would be enough. Hopefully. She didn't want it to hurt. She had one foot up on the ledge when she heard three sharp knocks behind her—

"I'm so fucking angry right now," Jenny said aloud.

"*Right now,*" Tori repeated with a laugh. "As if you aren't the angriest girl I've ever met. It's the only thing we have in common."

"Well, maybe not the only thing," Jenny said with a sly smile, glancing back at the door to the lounge. Something clicked for her. "Oh. Now I get it."

She took another drag of the clove cigarette, disgusted and also proud to do so without coughing this time.

"What?"

"I'd been kicking around this theory that maybe you killed Casey Klein," Jenny said.

"Hah!" said Tori.

"But you would never. She was your..." Jenny closed her eyes, banishing the painful memories of her own first crush.

"She was mine," Tori said. Her affected Mid-Atlantic accent had vanished.

"Did she, you know?"

"I don't know. Never got a chance to find out," said Tori. "Maybe she's at peace now. Now that Jorge Lopez is dead."

Jenny frowned. If she were nice, she'd let Tori have this. But she wasn't nice; she was Trouble. "It wasn't him."

"How do you know?"

"I just do." Jenny held the clove cigarette away, afraid if she took another drag she'd like it. "Don't suppose Dad had any other suspects?"

"Darcy should be back by now," Tori said, shields slamming back into place. She flicked her cigarette out into the void.

"Yeah, better find them before they run off together," Jenny said, trying to coax a smile out of her step-sister.

Tori snorted. "Darcy isn't rich, you've got nothing to worry about."

"What's with these homies dissing my girl?"

"It's a small town, Trouble. We call 'em like we see 'em."

"You saying I shouldn't trust her?" Jenny asked, hating that Eliza had ever incepted this idea into her head.

"I could say something," Tori said, opening the door and waving to Darcy and Dinah, "But I'd rather not and let you tear yourself to pieces doubting."

Dinah greeted her with kiss number 1,251. This kiss was deep and aggressive and full of searching tongues and heat. Was Dinah trying to distract her?

Stop it!

"They've got a karaoke room," Dinah said when they broke away. "Wanna go watch?"

"Yes, but if you try to get me to sing, I'm Lyfting home."

She let Dinah pull her into the main bar area, unable to resist looking back in time to catch the evil smirk on Tori's face. Reflexively, she reached for her phone to text Danger and ask her to follow Tori when she left. But that wasn't an option right now. Maybe never again. Damn her.

"Brave?" Dinah murmured in her ear, "Or Chicken?"

They were sprawled on Jenny's bed, sunken deep into the new comforter Mrs. Rivas had changed after the other one ended up covered in nail polish. She owed the housekeeper a week off for cleaning up Eliza's mess. Coming home to the fresh bedspread, it was almost like the fight never happened.

"Brave," Jenny said into her pillow.

She was lying prone with Dinah at her side. Shelly and Peter were still at their play, which meant Jenny and Dinah had the house mostly to themselves. Dinah took full advantage, sliding her hand from where it was resting on Jenny's calf up the back of Jenny's leg to her thigh. It was her turn to say something now, to tell Dinah something she didn't already know about Jenny.

"You know that reporter?" Jenny asked. "The one Jack roughed up?"

"His name is Jeffrey Jordan. He was fired from *The Intercept* last year. Before that, he worked for *Gawker* until they shut down. I found some of his old tweets he deleted. Real piece of garbage." Dinah leaned closer. "You're not the only one who can snoop. What about him?"

"He's blackmailing me. Your turn."

"Oh, come on, that's all I get?" Dinah pouted.

"You know how to get more."

"Okay, Valentine," Dinah squeezed the back of Jenny's thigh. "Brave? Or Chicken?"

"Brave," she lied. Danger was the brave one.

Dinah slid her hand higher—but then lifted it up and moved to the small of Jenny's back.

"No fair!" she cried.

"Never said I played fair," Dinah purred.

"He's working with Valerie Valentine," Jenny went on. "He's gonna try and make it look like I killed my dad."

She wasn't sure why she was telling Dinah all this. If her girlfriend really had betrayed her, she was doubly a fool for continuing to trust her.

"That doesn't seem very plausible," Dinah said. She encouraged Jenny to go on by slipping her hand under Jenny's shirt, lightly rubbing her back.

"He knows I was out of my bed at the psych ward the night of the attack. He has documents that can prove it, I guess."

"Hmm. What's this?" Dinah asked. She'd ignored the revelation and was running a finger over an old scar a few inches below Jenny's bra.

"Brave," Jenny replied, waiting for those fingers to slide under her bra strap to continue. "When I was eight, I got in a fight at the park. There was some broken glass in the sand that I somehow fell right on top of."

"Ouch!"

"Luckily, it was more of a slice than a puncture," Jenny said. "Lots of blood, though. Shelly freaked the fuck out. I got nine stitches."

"Feels nasty," Dinah said, her fingers returning to the smooth ridges of the scar.

Jenny shrugged. "I honestly forgot about it, I never really see it myself."

Without either of them acknowledging it, Dinah had slid a leg over Jenny's thighs and was sitting up now, on top of her, massaging her shoulders.

"Such a feisty girl," Dinah said with a conspiratorial laugh to make Jenny ache.

"I told you about how I was on the roof that night, right? At the hospital?" Jenny asked.

"Oh, I think so, yeah," Dinah said.

Maybe she was just a fantastic actor.

"I went up there to kill myself."

Dinah froze as the words hung in the air. She'd never said it aloud before. There was no need with Eliza, no good reason with Shelly, no trust with her court-appointed therapists.

"Why are you telling me this?" Dinah's voice was soft. Caring.

Jenny shifted, rolling over underneath Dinah's legs to look up at her. Her white dress pooled over Jenny's lap, steady pressure keeping her balanced on Jenny's hips. She'd thought about this vantage point quite a lot lately, but hadn't expected to arrive here like this.

"I don't want there to be any secrets between us," she said.

Dinah's eyes were wet. She smiled sadly down at Jenny.

"Jenny…"

In that moment, she was ready to tell Dinah everything. *Everything*. But she needed a question answered first.

"Where were you really that night? The night my dad got attacked?"

Dinah leaned down, hot breath nuzzling Jenny's ear.

"Dryden Street," she whispered.

Chapter Twenty-Three

A Light in the Mist

THE NERVE OF THOSE MOTHERFUCKING BLACKBIRDS. HOW DARE they sing? They were following her, tormenting her, punishing her. Was this Karma's way of telling her to call Eliza and apologize? Fuck that, she started it.

Jenny had barely slept. Tossing and turning all night, unable to shut her brain off and just feel *nothing*. Xanax hadn't helped, and she'd be damned if she went back on her other meds over this.

She rose early with a splitting tension headache, unable to stand her bedroom any longer with those damned birds chirping outside her window. How did they even know the sun was out in the pea soup fog that had rolled in overnight? The treehouse was empty, so Jenny pretended she'd walked all the way into the woods to get Eliza's bike. No, she wasn't checking on her sister. Fuck her.

Everything got kinda fuzzy after that. Eventually, she found herself in front of Woodhall Elementary School on MacArthur Street, clothes damp from the thick mist that blanketed the town.

It felt like fate—or at least something else to occupy her mind—to follow Casey's Walk again. Except this time, she stopped to see Dad

263

on the way.

Black Rock Cemetery was suitably spooky in the hazy morning light as she walked to RJ Valentine's grand tomb. It felt right; it should always be foggy here. An angry part of her—a part she refused to acknowledge—was hoping to find Eliza here. But RJ was alone.

"'Dryden Street!'" Jenny said to Dad's grave. "What the shit is that, right? 'Well, we agreed. No questions asked, I'm allowed to change the subject.' I feel like that is a violation of the faith in which that rule was instituted, but I guess that makes *me* the asshole!"

She let out a savage shout of rage and frustration, so strong it hurt her throat. The blackbirds didn't mind. They went on singing. Laughing at her.

The intercom had saved Dinah. Before Jenny could even mount an argument, Shelly was home, calling upstairs. It was all the excuse Dinah needed to book it. One last peck on the cheek—1,348—and a plea for Jenny to drop it, to trust her, and she was gone. Dinah was in such a rush to get out of there that she didn't realize Jenny was having a panic attack. To be fair, she'd never seen Jenny have one before. Until then, Jenny had always felt safe around her.

"Do any of those clues point to Dinah?" Jenny asked the grave. "Not the noose, she'd have been a toddler then. I don't get it. I know the reason for the heirlooms was because you didn't know for sure who was after you but was Jorge Lopez really your theory this whole time?" She closed her eyes, searching her memory for the exact words in the will. "'To Blake Something Lockhart, I give you a reminder of our disagreement and a plea to reconsider.' Reconsider what?"

She waited, half-expecting to get some sort of sign. Maybe the blackbirds would chirp out a suspect's name or something. That kind of happened in *Here Comes Trouble*. A lightning strike started a fire, which revealed the secret passageway inside the haberdashery. It was the only time Dad really went the deus ex machina route. People didn't like it, so he never went there again.

"No hints, huh? Fine." She got back on her bike. "See you around. If you see Lizzy, tell her... I don't know. I'll leave that between you two."

On wheels, the rest of Casey's Walk flew by. She stopped at Brett Klinger's house for a few minutes, but no inspiration struck, so she went on to the old Klein house and ditched her bike in the leaves. By habit, her eyes scanned the ground for more of Alicia Aaron's cigarette butts—or perhaps they were Tori's. Either way, she found none.

The blackbirds still sang in the trees above. Jenny walked a ways down Denmark Street. Open fields ran on for some way into the fog on the right, but surely those had all been searched. There were a few houses on large lots on the left. One of them even had a small vineyard in the front yard.

She headed back to Casey's house, plopping down on the sidewalk next to a yard gnome. Breathing in deep, she counted to 10, trying to exhale all her anger and frustration. She just needed to focus. Those damn birds. Her hand found its way into her backpack, digging for the cocktail of pills she'd been taking. She needed silence.

A memory flashed from their awful fight the night before. *"You need to listen," Eliza said.*

Jenny slowly withdrew her hand, a funny feeling tickling her brain. A rooster had joined the birds. If she breathed in and out, kept her eyes closed, let her other senses drift off, she found she could hear other sounds too. A woodpecker in the distance. Bees buzzing. Sprinklers, a lawnmower, the whinny of a horse, some large truck grinding gears on the road across the field, chickens clucking, dogs barking. The line between suburban and rural was always narrow in Blackbird Springs.

Her head dipped. Sleep had finally found her. Would the new

owner of Casey's old place mind if Jenny took a nap on the grass?

The horse neighed again—clip clop.

Goosebumps were forming on her arm before her brain even put it together. With light feet, she rose from the sidewalk, following the sound.

Clip clop.

It might have been coming from behind the houses. Hard to tell. The heavy mist made it seem like the sounds came from all over.

Jenny walked east on Denmark Street, stopping at the next house. She waited. A horse neighed again, definitely behind these houses. Between this one and the next was a narrow path, really a drain culvert. It ran between both lawns, back into a tiny alley created by the wooden fences that walled off each backyard. Jenny followed the culvert between the fences, each step amplifying the sensation that she was on the verge of a breakthrough.

Past the little alley was a small pasture to her right, enclosed in low, wire-mesh fencing. A ray of sunshine had burned through the fog in the clearing, allowing Jenny to make out the outline of a battered wooden stable. Two chestnut brown horses ambled about.

She swung her legs over the low fence and took a wide, arcing path to the stable, ambling so as not to disturb the horses. She could relate to Casey's fears now. Up close, they were almost twice her height.

"Easy, horsies."

One of them whinnied, staring straight at her.

Jenny froze, hardly daring to breathe. After a spell, it got bored and looked away. She went slower. The stable doors were open. Inside were spacious stalls for the animals, and above each, wooden plaques with their names carved in. A full-bodied shiver rippled up Jenny's spine when she read the plaque on the right.

Sonya

"We meet at last," Jenny said. "Tell me, Mrs. Horse, did you kill that poor little girl? Yea or neigh?"

It was a neigh.

Jorge Lopez had been here that afternoon, trimming Sonya's hooves. He'd lied and said he trimmed them early. Had he seen something? Done something? Or perhaps he'd merely been eager to claim an alibi far away, given his extracurricular pursuits.

Jenny retreated to the edge of the pasture and checked her phone. On the map, she was just south of Brett Klinger's house. There was a tall stucco wall hemming in the pasture on the northern side. In the morning haze, it gleamed white. Too white. Either it got power-washed recently, or it wasn't there 13 years ago.

An older memory stirred, of an apartment she and Aunt Shelly lived in for a year when she was nine. It was backed up to a dormant construction site, one Jenny would always cut through on the way to the park. Would Casey cut through here, despite her Equinophobia?

"So if that wall wasn't there…" Jenny trailed off, turning south and retracing the culvert path, back to Denmark Street. She glanced at the map. "Casey's mom goes around the corner on Eastin here, because she's expecting Casey to come that way."

The culvert dumped her out onto Denmark with the Klein house 50 yards away on the right. If Casey came this way, Mrs. Klein wouldn't see her. They could have been that close and just missed each other. But then who could have grabbed her? And silently? It would've had to be someone Casey knew or trusted.

In answer, a siren whooped on her left. A familiar Chevy Tahoe Police Cruiser headed her way. Sheriff Lockhart pulled up sharply and rolled down the window, a puzzled look on his face.

"Got a call about a hot prowl," said Lockhart, regaining his asshole implacability. "Figures it'd be you. Get in."

"Would you mind, terribly, if I didn't?" said Jenny. "I'm sort of in the middle of something here."

"Yeah, I mind. The Dude minds, man," Lockhart said.

"Huh?" Jenny blinked.

"Oh come on, that's an easy one," he said, an odd familiarity in his tone.

"Yeah, sorry, just in the middle of… brain thing right now." Jenny tapped out a quick entry in her Notes app about the horse pasture.

"Lotta ins and outs, lotta what-have-yous," he said.

"Mmhmm. Is this another one of your old man references?"

"To think, I thought you could actually not be a complete pain in the ass."

Feathers tickled the back of Jenny's neck. This happened sometimes, Danger would talk to someone without Jenny knowing about it.

"The name on the tin ain't lying. Bitch." When in doubt, just be a little stinker. But when the hell was her sister talking to Lockhart? Last night?

"So, no more 'new you?'" he asked.

"I'm adaptable." Jesus Christ, Eliza. What had she told him?

"Sure. But seriously, get in," he said.

"I rode my bike here," she said.

"Leave it, you can pick it up later."

"What if someone steals it?"

"Then you can buy another one, moneybags."

Jenny made a gagging face and reached for the passenger door. It was locked. "Seriously?"

"You know the drill." Lockhart thumbed at the back seat. His right hand, she noted, was bandaged.

Jenny grunted and pulled herself into the seat where the perps went. Lockhart drove off before she'd even shut the door, heading back toward the center of town. For once, the Sheriff's stubborn arrogance, always forcing her into the perp seat, would help. He couldn't see when she got her phone out and googled:

the dude minds man

"Look," he said, grinding his teeth. "Sorry about last night."

"It's cool," she said, curious as hell now. "So what do you want?"

The line was from a movie called *The Big Lebowski*. She tapped on the search suggestion for:

The Big Lebowski quotes

"Did you give any consideration to what we talked about?" he asked.

She shrugged and read the first quote on the list. "'Obviously you're not a golfer?'"

He rolled his eyes. "You should at least talk to Webb. As long as Val's foundation is spending major cash in town on park statues and Valentine's Day events, the mayor will be looking for a way to drop those charges. You've got the money, start your own foundation."

"Jenny's Fund for Girls in Trouble," she suggested, piecing together what he must have discussed with Eliza. The mayor wanted Val's murder charge to go away. Lockhart was telling her this, which meant... "So, what kind of favor do you need?"

"Two, actually." He cracked a tiny smile.

Of all the times Jenny couldn't text Eliza. Well, she could, but— no, it shouldn't be on her. Eliza had to make the first move.

Lockhart turned onto the highway, heading east.

"Wait, where are we going?" Jenny asked.

"I'm leasing some property I own. Need to go have a look at the tenants."

Jenny kept her face placid, casually asking, "Uhh, where's this property? Is it far?"

"Not far. Off Castle Road."

He could only mean the family cabin in the woods, where Mason and his baby mama had been hiding their child. If Lockhart learned about the kid, Mason would have no reason to keep Danger a secret.

Fuck.

Chapter Twenty-Four

French Farce

J ENNY STUDIED THE SHERIFF CLOSELY. HIS FIVE O'CLOCK SHADOW was a couple days old, and his aftershave couldn't entirely mask the stale scent of booze on his breath. But he kept his eyes on the road, wasn't even looking back at her. His hands were light on the wheel. Very lackadaisical. If this was a put on, and he was fucking with her, he was a hell of an actor.

Which meant Mason was about to get a very unexpected visitor.

"How do you afford another house, anyway?" she asked while switching to her Messages app to text Mason. "You've barely touched the money I gave you from the will."

Jenny: 911 Your dad is on the way to the cabin.
Don't ask. You need to hide!!!

Lockhart had gone quiet. Jenny glanced up to see him faking a cough into his bandaged fist.

"It's in the family," he said.

"Lilah's?"

"I asked you not to say that name!" he said sharply, eyes blazing.

"Sorry! I just… It always makes me smile when Shelly mentions my mom, but I guess it's different for you."

He softened a little. "Yeah. It is."

Her watch tapped.

> **Mason:** wtf?
>
> **Mason:** r u serious?
>
> **Jenny:** Yes I'm fucking serious! Hide!

"So what's with these tenants? They late on a payment or something?" Jenny asked.

"No, they're on time," he said, scratching his stubbled chin. "The property management company says they've been using a lot of juice recently. Way more than expected. Probably leaving the flue open with the heater on or something."

> **Jenny:** fuck do you still have your weed farm set up?

"If they keep it up, I'm gonna get hit with extra fees," Lockhart said.

They were on the gravel road now, only a minute or two away.

> **Mason:** No. Got rid of it for the nanny.
>
> **Mason:** Shit, what about her?
>
> **Jenny:** Good.
>
> **Jenny:** Give Lilah to nanny. Have nanny say you're both out. Hide in the closet or something.

"Who you texting back there?"

"Dinah. We're sexting."

She winced at her own joke. Oh, Dinah... With one last turn, they were pulling up to a familiar cabin. It was a Scandinavian design: steep roofs with long overhangs. Basically, just a big box with a chimney on one side. It seemed cozy in the morning light. The last time Jenny had been here, it was dusk, and the Stranger had cut her brakes and tried to kill her.

"Right, so what's this favor I'm doing here?" Jenny asked.

Lockhart parked on the gravel next to an old Subaru. Thank god Mason hadn't driven up here.

"Might not be as simple as an open flue," Lockhart said. "You're the Girl Detective: detect."

They both hopped out, Jenny's feet crunching on the loose gravel as she followed Lockhart to the front door.

Jenny: Have nanny open flue

Lockhart knocked loudly with a big, meaty fist.

After what seemed like too long—he raised his fist to knock again—the door finally opened. It was the nanny, with a bundle of joy tucked to her chest. She was young, mid-20s, maybe. Not super cute, but her French accent sure was.

"Bonjour?" she said, doing a double-take at Lockhart. Because of his uniform, or his chiseled good looks, it wasn't clear.

"Bonjour, je m'appelle Trouble," said Jenny.

The nanny frowned, "Trouble?"

"Ah… difficulté?" Jenny tried.

"I speak English," she said, frowning harder. "I don't understand, though. Are you saying I'm in trouble?"

"Let me handle this," Lockhart growled. "I'm the owner; she's Trouble."

While he explained their presence to the nanny, Jenny perked her ears for signs of Mason. So far, nothing. She smiled at little Lilah, who smiled back at her. The nanny explained that the tenants were out, but let them in to look around.

Her free hand was shaking. Too nervous.

"Can I hold her?" Jenny asked, stepping between Lockhart and the nanny.

"Oh, um…"

Jenny reached for Lilah before the nanny could stop her.

"Ooof," she said, sagging under the weight. "She's heavy."

It was so weird. This was Mason's freakin' kid. Lockhart's granddaughter.

"Here, you take her!" she spun, passing off the baby to Lockhart.

He tried to protest, but she practically shoved the little one into him, and some ingrained dad-instinct took over, and he scooped Lilah up and held her properly.

Jenny smiled for the first time since her date last night. Blake Lockhart had no idea, but that baby was his family. She was about to cry, so she hastened to the hallway.

"I'll check the back rooms," she said, her voice gone husky.

She stomped down the hallway—another odd sensation after all the sneaking she did last time—hoping to give Mason plenty of warning. The door on the right was a bedroom. The nanny's, from the look of it. She made a cursory effort at snooping around, looking for clues.

Back in the hall, Lockhart had passed his granddaughter back to the nanny and was headed to the back rooms. Jenny ducked past him and took the master. Inside, the bed was disheveled and unmade. She ran a hand over the sheet. Still warm.

"Anything?" Lockhart called, peeking his head in through the doorway.

"No," Jenny said, casually pulling the comforter up over the sheets.

"Check the closet. Look for anything plugged in."

He withdrew into the hallway. Jenny made a show of sliding open the closet door—then quickly shut it.

"Nothing in here. Did you check the flue?" she called.

"On it right now," he called back from the living room.

Jenny eased the closet door back open, face to face with Mason and his baby mama: Meghan fucking May.

"You!" she whispered. "The blonde hair-dye, of course." In her blackmail video, the mom's face had always been turned away, hidden by blonde hair. The better to keep raven-haired Meghan's presence in town a secret, she now deduced. "You should just use wigs. All that shit about Paris…"

Belatedly, she took in their current appearance. They were both in their underwear, grinning madly at their predicament and looking rather flushed.

"Were you guys…?" Jenny glanced down—and instantly regretted it.

Mason was somehow still sporting an obscene erection, straining against his silk boxers. Jenny clapped a hand over her mouth and spun away, mortified.

"Oh, my God."

"We took some molly," Meghan whispered, silently shaking with the giggles.

Jenny spotted the little baggy of pills on the nightstand now, next to a condom wrapper. She pocketed the remaining pills, hid the wrapper, and forced herself to turn back around, keeping her eyes locked straight ahead. Meghan reached out to paw at her.

"Trouble," Meghan said. "Naughty girl."

Jenny allowed a tight smile as she dug in her purse, handing Meghan her water bottle.

"Stay hydrated, but take it slow," she said, ignoring the electric tingle she got when Meghan reached out and stroked her cheek. "Now be quiet. Oh—do you have an extension cord here?"

Back in the hallway, she eased the door closed.

"Just some cell phone chargers," she said, joining Lockhart in the kitchen. "I think the wife's on her period. That's neither here nor there, I guess. Find anything?"

"Flue was open." He grimaced at her.

"Oh, well, there you go."

"Not so fast," he said, holding out a hand to stop her. "Do you see it?"

He pointed to the living room where the nanny was sitting on the couch with Lilah. Was he testing her?

Jenny walked onto the ugly orange shag carpet, searching for whatever clue she was supposed to get. She almost missed it. Not bad, Lockhart.

"Soot on her hands," Jenny muttered softly, rejoining him in the kitchen. "She just opened it."

"It's not very cold in here, and the heater's not on."

"Maybe she was just about to build a fire."

"Then where's the firewood?" said Lockhart.

Jenny motioned for him to follow her back into the hall.

"Check her room again," she said, pointing into the first door on the right. "I'm gonna look around the veranda."

As soon as he entered the nanny's room, Jenny snuck out the back door, working fast.

It took longer than expected; the cord was all tangled up. She ended up dashing back through the front door, knowing she'd cut it too close. The nanny was still on the couch, but where was the Sheriff? She hurried to the back rooms, and her heart plummeted when she found him in the master. He was just reaching for the closet.

"Hey!"

He glanced back, his hand on the door.

"I think I figured it out," Jenny said. "Come on."

"Okay. Let me—"

"Leave it!"

He frowned, suspicion growing on his fair features. Without a word, he yanked open the closet door.

Jenny winced, clenching her fists.

There was nothing inside, just some women's clothing.

"I told you, there's nothing," she said coolly. "Come on, you're gonna want to see this."

She waited for him to leave first before kicking Mason under the bed.

Outside, there was a big patch of poured concrete where the other cars parked. Jenny led Lockhart over to an extension cord that ran back to the side of the house.

"I asked the nanny, she said one of 'em has a Tesla."

"Can they charge off a regular house plug?" he asked.

"I guess so. Okay, mystery solved. Now, what's the real favor you want?"

He twisted his lip and motioned for her to follow him back to the police cruiser. In the back, there was a locked evidence box. From it, Lockhart withdrew a stun gun, encased in a plastic bag. It was Eliza's, a twin of the taser in her own purse.

"An illegal search, I know, but I was curious," he said. "You want to explain why this piece matches the taser burns we found on Jorge Lopez's body?"

"Did you know about Sonya?" Jenny countered. "You must have, right?"

"I asked first."

"I didn't kill him if that's what you're implying. I'm sure your medical examiner can tell you those burns were a few days old."

"How'd he get them?" Lockhart asked.

"He thought he should keep holding onto my wrist," Jenny said. "I disagreed." She grabbed the evidence bag. "What are you playing at?

You know this would be inadmissible."

"The mayor's got my ass hanging in the wind over these killings. He wants a bow on Jorge Lopez, nice and tidy, and you keep getting in the way." The vein in his temple pulsed. He took a step closer. "People around you keep getting stabbed. I'd like to know why. Not to mention the sudden reappearance of the Hot Springs Hangman, who seems rather fixated on you. That's right, Calderon told me all about how you found Lily Geist's body."

"It comes with the territory," she said. There it was again. A clue was tickling her, just out of reach.

"This is where I remind you that if you know something about these crimes—like maybe you've got a whole arts and crafts board full of evidence—and you're not telling, it's obstruction of justice."

Lockhart was going for maximum intimidation, but Jenny was lost in thought, remembering the epiphany he'd interrupted back at Casey's old house. A tenuous new theory was taking root.

"Justice. That's rich, coming from you of all people."

"What are you talking about?" he asked. There was worry in his angry glare.

"I think you know," said Jenny. "I think this is what Dad wanted you to reconsider, but you hid behind your thin blue line instead. There's a certain type of person who little girls are taught to trust." She poked at the badge on his chest. "No matter how little they deserve it. Someone Casey Klein would have gone along with, no questions asked. Someone who could direct search parties away from damning evidence. Someone who would know how to point police to the body, once a frame job on Oscar Manuel was all set up."

The vein in Lockhart's temple was throbbing now.

"Tell me something," Jenny said. "The day Casey Klein went missing: where was Deputy Calderon?"

The sheriff burst out laughing. Not exactly the reaction she was fishing for.

"Swing and a miss, Valentine," said Lockhart. "Miggy didn't even work here then. He would've been up in uh Windsor, I think. But by all means, ask him yourself, I'm sure you won't take offense."

"I was just asking, jeez." Jenny could feel her cheeks burning.

"Word of advice, Truffle: you need to stop being so impatient. Learn to nibble around the edges, so your suspect doesn't see you coming. You know, pretend you want to interview people who worked that day and ask me who would have been on staff. I'd still tell you to get bent, but at least your motive wouldn't be so obvious."

He closed the back of the Tahoe and headed for the cab. Jenny remained rooted in place, struggling to stay calm. That Lockhart's advice was good only made him extra abhorrent. Listen more, observe more, react less: those were not Trouble's ways. But Dad wasn't writing the story anymore. It might not hurt to expand her toolkit. Trouble was all about adaptability, wasn't she?

"Fine," she said, exhaling all—well, most—of her hatred. She hopped back into the perp seat behind him. "I could strike up an innocuous conversation, maybe ask him how long he's been riding that horse."

"Mmhmm. And he'd say he's been with Ricochet since he moved to Blackbird Springs and took over my beat nine years ago. Then you could cross him off your list without tipping him off."

It took a full five seconds for the alarm bell in her mind to sound.

"Wait, was your beat riding the horse too?" she asked.

"Six years on that damn horse. My ass is still sore." He glanced back in the mirror, and Jenny's heart froze to the core. Could he tell? "Betcha didn't know that about me," he added with a grin and locked all the doors.

Chapter Twenty-Five

White Houses

13 hours earlier

THE FIRST THING ELIZA DID WAS DRIVE TO THE SANTA ROSA MALL and buy a whole new outfit. She was sick and tired of being Jenny fucking Valentine. Nordstrom had a low-cut yellow and red floral print dress that Jenny wouldn't be caught dead in, and some fuck-me black Prada ankle boots. She changed at the store and threw her old clothes in the trash.

Same deal for her purse, ditching the double of Jenny's larger Bebe handbag for a svelte Louis Vuitton clutch. She had to toss out the baggies and latex gloves, lock pick set, bottle of rubbing alcohol, and tube of plaster of Paris. There just wasn't room, and it's not like she'd need them. She kept her stun gun, though, just in case.

At the wig store, she found some new hair as close to her old style as she could find: silky black, shoulder-length, with some volume. She was about to put it up in a braid when she stopped herself. Fuck it, she knew what she was about tonight. Instead, she paid for a session at Sephora to cover up her black eye, sharpen her cheekbones, and give herself sanguine, bee-stung lips.

Eliza regarded herself in the mirror. She could pass for 21, maybe. 18, at least. Perhaps she'd follow the Russian River to the coast, look for a beach bonfire, and throw herself at the first pretty-eyed boy she'd die to trust. It's what girls her age did, or so that Vanessa Carlton song went. It'd be nice to be kissed, at least.

After tipping the makeup girl, she did a lap around the upper level, watering her parched self-regard with leers and stolen glances from miscellaneous dudes. On the way back to the valet, a sudden, basic urge forced her to stop at Cheesecake Factory and get a slice of White Chocolate Raspberry Truffle to-go. There were a dozen orders ahead of hers, so she killed time at the bar, skimming through Alicia Aaron's mammoth manuscript, studying those clue photos of Mom and Dad, and people-watching. So many young couples on Friday night dates. Between them and Alicia's purple prose, the yearning in her chest was only growing stronger.

Eliza forced herself to look away, focusing on some pathetic bastard dining alone. He was pretty hot to be single—

"Holy shit!" She blinked twice. "Blake?"

The Sheriff of Blackbird Springs was out of uniform, a goddamn snack in tight jeans and a faded Third Eye Blind shirt that his biceps were doing their best to destroy. He was way too old for her, but the Danger part of her brain briefly wondered what those forearms would feel like against her back.

Shut it down! The Eliza part commanded. The burden of being the smart one. Still, it wouldn't hurt to go say hello.

"Come here often?" she said, taking a seat across from him.

It took him a moment. He'd been staring blankly into oblivion, waiting for his food. Anger, confusion, then embarrassment flickered over his chiseled face.

"Didn't even recognize you in a dress," he said, unusually chill.

"It's the new me. For tonight, anyway—are you drunk?"

"Not yet. What are you doing out? There's a curfew."

"Not in this county."

"Something tells me your aunt wouldn't see it that way if I called her."

"Well, lucky for me, she doesn't take your calls." Eliza bit her cheek. She should go. She should go, she should go. But something about Blake's manner told her he'd be talkative tonight. And it wouldn't hurt to find out what was on the Sheriff's mind. "What are *you* doing out? Shouldn't you be hunting the Hot Springs Hangman?"

"Tonight is—" Blake hesitated, catching himself and masking an old pain. "—None of your business."

She tossed her hype beast titanium credit card on the table.

"Let's get a couple Tequila Sunrises in you first, and maybe we can renegotiate."

"White Russians, but you're under 21."

"I'll be having seltzer," Eliza said. "Damn, you *are* in a mood. Trouble at work?"

He chuckled grimly. "Drinks first."

She smiled. See, Jenny, it paid to not be a total mercenary sometimes.

FROM GENTLE PROBING, SHE LEARNED THAT BLAKE WAS A vegetarian, ambidextrous, and extremely touchy about any mention of his late wife, Lilah Lockhart. He was also worried about his job. Local business owners weren't happy with the mayor because of the curfew.

"And shit rolls downhill," Blake said. "I'm the one who put Oscar Manuel away. If he didn't do it, I make an easy scapegoat." He killed the last of his first White Russian. "But if I say Jorge Lopez did it, maybe that takes the heat off, the mayor says. A known drug dealer? We have enough to put Lily Geist on him already, and Jorge's dead now, so it's not like he can protest. The threat is gone, the curfew can lift, and the locals are happy. No more need for a scapegoat."

"Until the real killer strikes again," Eliza said.

He nodded like a proud teacher.

A waiter approached. "Truffle?"

Eliza waved, clearing a spot for her cheesecake. Lockhart laughed. "What?"

"They messed up your name," he said, starting on his second drink. "'Truffle.' It suits you. It's like 'Trouble' and 'Trifle' all in one."

"White chocolate raspberry truffle." She pointed to her dessert.

"Truffle," he repeated.

She rolled her eyes. "Tell me more about the mayor."

"You're not getting it, think bigger."

Between healthy sips, Blake unfolded a tale of how Valerie Valentine used the Foundation as a patronage system to curry favor. As long as Val was dumping a bunch of money into the local economy, the locals were happy. Which meant the mayor really didn't want to prosecute her for murder.

"No one else will tell you this, so consider it a favor," he said. "You're not competing at Val's level. She's going to outmaneuver you."

"Sounds like you want me to be just as corrupt as she is," Eliza said, peeling the label off her bottle of seltzer.

He shrugged. "Welcome to the real world."

"So you're saying that Val draws a lot of water in this town, and I don't draw shit, huh?"

He cracked a tiny smile, catching the Lebowski reference.

"I got a nice, quiet B&B community here, and I aim to keep it nice and quiet."

283

Blake reached a clumsy hand for his drink and knocked it over, sending a wave of booze across the table.

"Fucking fascist!" she yelled, snatching her phone up just ahead of the mess.

"Shit, sorry."

"I'm cutting you off," she said.

"I'm fine."

"Ugh, hold on. Lemme get some napkins."

She hurried over to the bar, looking for a waiter to flag down. Blake had hit on something that had been worrying her from the start: that there were things she and Jenny didn't know, adult things, that would end up biting them in the ass. Even hearing it now, she didn't know what to do with the information. She and Jenny didn't know the first thing about running a charity foundation.

When she returned to the table with a busboy, Blake was sitting calmly, unperturbed by his mess.

"What is it with you?" she asked, once the mess was cleared. He raised an eyebrow. "I know all about self-destruction, Blake, so you can stop pretending."

"You don't know shit about shit, Valentine."

"I know Mason's worried about you," she said.

Blake's neck twitched. He had no retort, but was saved when the waiter arrived with his food: a bacon-wrapped filet mignon.

"I thought you said you didn't eat meat," Eliza said.

"I still did, back then," he said, mostly to himself.

An awkward silence descended. He left the steak alone and ate some mashed potatoes. Eliza noticed it then: the flash of gold on his ring finger. The waiter returned with a new White Russian.

"Let's play a game," Eliza said. "Drink if the words are true, right?"

"I'm not doing this with you," he said.

"Humor me."

"Fine. I didn't plant that chess piece in Val's purse," he said, eyeballing her.

Poor choice of words. Technically, that was Jenny. She sipped her seltzer. Blake scowled and took another belt of his White Russian.

"I'm not the Hot Springs Hangman," she said.

He almost seemed impressed by her nerve. They each took a sip.

"I blew it with Shelly," he said, drinking again immediately.

"You did. But I can always put in a good word." She left her seltzer alone.

"I'll pass," he said. "Your turn."

A theory had been bubbling in the back of Eliza's mind for the last few minutes.

"Jorge Lopez wasn't RJ's only suspect," Eliza said. "Dad had another."

He glared at her; the tumbler gripped tight in his hand, but not rising.

"Who was it?" she asked, drinking herself.

The glass exploded in his hand, spraying her with droplets of vodka, cream, and Kahlúa. His palm was bleeding freely, a twisted, animalistic rage on his face. He was on his feet in a flash. Eliza winced as the other patrons stared.

As calmly as her shaking hands would allow, she wiped her face and stood, getting right up in the sheriff's face.

"Let's call that strike two," Eliza said, glancing at his sliced hand. "I'll get the check and send someone over. I gotta go."

She grabbed her cheesecake and left him there, stewing in his grief and rage. Eliza's instincts were right: RJ had another suspect, maybe someone close to Blake. It was late, but Campbell did say to come over any time, and she had a couple questions for the ex-Mrs. Klein.

Briefly, she considered texting Jenny. But no, like Blake, her sister needed to handle her own issues first. When she was ready to talk, Eliza would be there. And maybe, if things went well tonight, she'd have already solved the Casey Klein murder.

Not only was Campbell Batori up, she was still in her workshop, hunched over a flaming forge. Maybe Eliza ought to be Danger instead of Trouble more often. Everything was falling into place.

The workshop doors were thrown wide, spilling bright radiance onto the yard outside from the heavy-duty work-lights mounted all over the shop. Campbell looked deep in thought, brooding with her headphones in, poking at the forge with what looked like a long, skinny metal ladle. Eliza approached from a wide angle, so as not to startle her.

"Hey!" Campbell exclaimed when she spotted her, looking up and pulling off her earbuds. "What's up?"

"It's not too late, is it?"

"Not at all," said Campbell. "Actually, this is perfect, you can help me with the crucible. The big pours are way easier with a second pair of hands."

She paused her iPod and stood up, ushering her over. There was a glowing red canister set deep into the forge: a crucible, Campbell explained. The fire inside the forge burned yellow, too intense to look at for more than a moment. Eliza leaned back, letting the winter air cool her face.

"What's in there?" Eliza asked.

"Bronze." Campbell used the ladle thing to skim another layer off the top of the molten metal within the crucible. "The oxides tend to float to the surface. You want as few impurities as possible before you cast. I'm doing the head piece tonight, so I want it to look good."

She waved over at a half-assembled statue of a portly baker holding a cake. It was split down the middle on the side, and the head was missing.

"They're hollow?" Eliza asked.

"Oh yeah."

"For some reason, I assumed they'd be solid bronze. Like you just make the cast and pour a ton of metal in."

"You could," Campbell said. "I've done that for a few small jobs, but it would weigh a ton on something this big. Really, it's a waste of metal. A quarter-inch of bronze will do you just fine, and it's way easier to do this in pieces, in case you fuck a pour up—but I'm sorry, I haven't even asked you why you came. What's going on? Shouldn't you be out chasing girls?"

Eliza laughed bitterly. "It's uh, it's one of those days," she said. "I thought, maybe I'd come and do something with my hands, maybe ask you a few questions?"

"Oh sure. Here, put this on so you don't get burned."

She took off her heavy flannel coat and handed it to Eliza. The lining was cool inside as she slipped it on. She wondered if there might be kevlar or some other protective material woven in.

"This is pretty dangerous, huh? I like that," she said with a grin.

"Well, a little. Not like a lathe. Fortunately, our bodies are pretty well trained when it comes to heat. You touch that hot stove once, and you learn."

Together they moved a big boxy plaster cast—Campbell called it "investment"—over to the lawn just outside the shop. There was a large hole in the top where the bronze went in, and other holes to vent. While Campbell lit a compact portable blowtorch and casually waved it over the investment to heat it up, Eliza broached the topic of Casey as delicately as she could.

"So, I've been doing some research. I think my dad might have had a second suspect," she said. "Did RJ ever mention any other theories to you?"

"Hmm," Campbell said, thinking back. "I don't think so. I remember, one time, he came over with a few questions about the initial search, but he never mentioned anyone else."

"What kind of questions?"

"It was like: where did Reed and I look first, where did the first cops on the scene search, then the search party. He was really keen to figure out the search patterns."

"Hmm."

"All right, let's do this," Campbell turned off the blowtorch and clapped her hands together. "Crucible goes in there, then we both lift and pour."

By the forge, there was a six-foot-long metal bar with handles on both sides and a circular ring in the center. Campbell used some heavy tongs to lift the crucible out of the forge and place it into the ring.

"Okay, lift!"

The ring held the crucible in place while they lifted from both sides and carried it to the investment cast. Eliza let Campbell set the pace as they tilted the bar and poured molten bronze in. Flames shot up everywhere the liquid metal landed. It was fascinating to watch, and Eliza felt weirdly satisfied by the whole process.

After the pour was over, they backed off and put the bar down. Eliza wiped her forehead.

"That was awesome!" she said. She could feel the dopey smile on her face, but so what? Campbell wasn't the type to tease like the Bitchy Brigade—or even Jenny.

"Investment's nice because it's water-soluble," said Campbell. "We'll let this cool a bit and then dunk it in a tub, and it'll just crumble right off the bronze."

They went back into the shop, and Campbell turned the forge off.

"Search patterns," Eliza said, picking up the earlier thread. "I—I think I might know what he was after. Like, if someone knew what places would be searched when, it would make it easier to hide something. Do you remember who the first cops on the scene were?"

"Yeah, the cute one, Blake."

"Heh," Eliza forced a laugh, her heart beating a mile a minute. *Blake?* He would never, would he?

Campbell killed the forge and peeled off her work gloves. "Whew, I could use a beer. Want one?"

"Sure," said Eliza.

"Hang tight."

Campbell retreated into the house. Eliza was only half there, still thinking about Blake. It seemed impossible, but she'd gotten a peek at his dark side tonight. She sat down by the forge to collect herself, stuffing her hands into the heavy coat's pockets for warmth. Something metal and curved was in the left one. Curious, she pulled it out.

It was Campbell's ancient iPod. "White Houses" by Vanessa Carlton was paused onscreen. Eliza was just thinking of that song! Campbell was always going on about listening while she worked, and every maker having their own special playlist to get in a groove. Apparently, Early-2000s piano songstress was her trade secret. Would she mind, terribly, if Eliza had a listen?

Campbell was still inside. Fuck it. Eliza unwound the earbud cables, popped them in, and hit play.

It wasn't music she heard.

For a second, it sounded like static or distortion. She turned the volume down a little, and the sonic chaos morphed and shifted until her brain could put a name to the sound. It was screaming. A high-pitched voice. A little girl. Screaming for help. Screaming in pain.

Dread flooded her veins, her stomach somersaulting from a great height.

The screaming subsided, and there was a discordantly warm laugh on the recording.

"Now, now, be a good girl and take your medicine," said a voice. "You don't want to anger Mommy, do you?"

It was a familiar voice. It was Campbell Klein née Batori's voice.

Eliza's hand darted for her purse, searching for her stun gun—

"Shit. You weren't supposed to listen to that," came Campbell's voice again. Not in her earbuds—behind her.

Her hand frantically sought for the taser, but it wasn't there! She was sure she'd put it in her new purse—

A white rope dropped over her head and yanked tight, choking the life out of her. Her hands shot to her throat, but before Eliza could kick out and fight, Campbell pressed a breathing mask to her face. The smell was sweet and full of chemicals, and she knew no more.

Chapter Twenty-Six

Hooke and Webb

Casey went home. It was so obvious, now that Eliza considered the clues from her new perspective. No one had ever questioned Campbell Klein's story, least of all Eliza. Who would have guessed that the rich, beautiful blonde mother, frantically searching for her lost daughter, was lying?

It was probably the next day. She'd awoken slowly in a dark room, a splitting headache overriding all other thought until she tried to rub her temples and found her wrists were bound behind her back. Her shoulder blades shrieked in pain. Her legs burned with numb, neural fire. The memory of Campbell's voice on that iPod came rushing back.

"You fraud. You fucking monster," Eliza said—or tried to say. It might have come out like a bunch of incoherent moaning. Her throat burned where the noose had strangled her, and she was still hazy from the chemicals Campbell had forced her to inhale. Whatever the Fortune Teller had given her, this was much, much worse.

A dank wetness hung in the air. Somewhere underground, Eliza guessed. Her eyeballs darted around, slowly adjusting to the dark. She was in a large, low-ceilinged room with no windows, and it was eerily quiet. After what felt like an hour, a voice spoke softly behind her ear.

"I know," said Campbell Batori, her tone still so maternal and calm. "This isn't how I wanted things to go either."

Jesus Christ, had she been there the whole time?

Campbell stepped around in front of Eliza, flipping a switch on the wall and blanketing the room in blinding white light. Eliza winced in pain, sure that her skull was about to explode out her forehead. She screamed until her throat was raw. No one came.

When Eliza's voice gave out and her eyes recovered, Campbell was sitting too. They were in a windowless room, covered in white hexagonal tiles.

"Obviously, the room is soundproof, so you can scream all you like, it won't do you any good," Campbell said. "But if you annoy me, I'll get the noose again."

"You torture them," Eliza managed with a rasp. "And record it!"

Campbell shrugged. "It soothes me."

"You sick fuck!"

"It's not a fetish or anything, it just helps me clear my mind. Every maker has their own playlist."

Eliza wretched, vomiting down her front. Campbell shook her head.

"Hence the tile. This will be cold, sorry."

She got up and leveled a hose at her. The icy chill was almost a relief. Campbell sprayed the puke away, leaving her clothes soaking. She walked behind her and returned a moment later with a plastic cup and two brown pills.

Eliza shook her head violently.

"It's just water and ibuprofen, relax," Campbell said. "It's not like I need to trick you. Not anymore. God, what a disaster. I was so looking forward to molding you, shaping you—in a way I never had the chance to with Casey."

"You won't get away with this," Eliza said.

"I already have. I ditched your phone and your jeep; they'll never find you."

"How did you do it, with Casey?" Eliza asked, hoping to keep her talking while she strained for the watch on her wrist. Damn! Campbell had taken it too.

"My darkroom," she laughed. "I'd just built a false wall in the back. Much smaller than this place." She waved her hand around her murder-torium, so pleased with herself. "That's where the sawdust in Rita's lungs came from. How sloppy of me, but they never figured it out."

"I get it now, the daylight savings time thing," Eliza said, feeling no joy in her deductions. "It was *your* clock that was off, the one in the darkroom. You thought it was only 2:20 PM. That you still had an hour before Casey got home, and then she barged in and caught you with Rita Thomas. You panicked and strangled her, hid her inside the false wall with Rita, and went outside and pretended to wait for your daughter. Your own fucking daughter!"

"Well done, Trouble," Campbell said, offering polite applause. "I warned Casey so many times not to come in when the red light was on!"

"You waited it out, moved the bodies, and framed the poor gardener for it." Eliza couldn't believe she ever liked this woman. Her smile was so disturbingly unaffected, like they were talking about the latest Taylor Swift album.

"It was real touch and go there, those first few days when they searched the house, but they barely gave the darkroom more than a once-over." Campbell shivered. "What a rush! To lie over and over and have them all eating out of my hand. They triple-checked my idiot husband's alibi, and never once questioned mine."

"All that shit about PTSD from waiting," said Eliza. "You don't hate waiting. You *like* getting surprised. You get off on it, don't you?"

"Guilty," she said with a smirk. "But leaving that iPod with you, that was a mistake. Seriously, my bad. I'm not prepared at all."

"Prepared for what?" Eliza asked, the bile in her stomach rising again.

Campbell giggled. "You'll see."

JENNY STEELED HERSELF. THERE WOULD BE NO PANIC ATTACKS. NOT today. They were on the highway, but she had Eliza's taser. Wherever Lockhart was taking her, she would be ready.

Except, where he took her was back to her bike on Denmark Street.

"See, it's still here," he said, getting out and unlocking the back doors.

She scrambled out, holding up Eliza's stun gun, nerves on a hair-trigger. Lockhart just stared at her.

"What??"

"You're him, you killed Casey Klein!"

"Jesus, would you give it a rest, Truffle," Lockhart said. "I'm honestly starting to feel a little insulted."

"The horse hairs! You found her body because you knew where you hid it!"

He grimaced and rubbed his face. "You know what, I was gonna offer to put your bike in the back and give you a ride home. Instead, I think I'll take that—" He snatched the stun gun right out of her hand. "—and go get a French omelet at Rosie's. Good day!"

Lockhart actually had the nerve to look disgusted with *her*. He climbed back into the police cruiser without another word.

"Wait! Seriously?"

In answer, he peeled out and raced away, leaving her alone in front of Casey's old house. Prick. After spending a half-hour staring up and down the street, wracking her brain to fit her Sonya discovery into a new theory, she finally admitted defeat and rode back home.

The treehouse was still empty. She'd barely been back in her room when Aunt Shelly stormed in.

"Where the hell have you been?" Shelly cried. "You missed Saturday School."

Jenny's stomach plummeted. Crap. She'd written that off as Eliza's thing, and of course, her sister didn't go today.

"Shit, I totally forgot," Jenny said.

"You're going to get expelled! Mr. Carter isn't going to let this slide."

"I'll fix it," Jenny said. "I was helping Lockhart with something, the Vice Principal can't object to that, right?"

Not that the sheriff was liable to back her up after she'd accused him of murdering a child.

Shelly narrowed her eyes. "What are you doing spending time with him?"

"Nothing, really. He just needed a little mystery solved about his family cabin. It was low stakes, I swear, no danger at all."

The word brought on another pang of guilt. Where was her sister?

"I don't want you leaving this house again today," Shelly said. "Not even for Dinah."

Fat chance of that. Dinah wasn't texting either, not that Jenny had tried to reach her. She had no idea what to say to her girlfriend. How was she supposed to just move past this, when it could involve her father's murder?

She tried to busy herself with homework, taking hours to complete a simple assignment, and doing a sloppy job of it. By 7:00 PM, Jenny finally caved and texted Danger. She wasn't apologizing, but they needed to talk.

> **T:** New shit has come to light
> **T:** (how is it you have in-jokes about 20-year-old movies with Lockhart?)
> **T:** never mind just text me. It's important

All evening and night she waited for a reply. None came. Sometime around 4:00 AM, she fell asleep from sheer exhaustion. It was nearly noon when she awoke, groggily pawing for her phone under her pillow. Nothing from Eliza or Dinah. Only a reminder notification about her impending deadline with the reporter. What was she going to do?

"Now, now, it's all going to be fine," said Campbell, lowering a metal mask onto Eliza's face. "In a way, you'll live forever, and people will like you better this way."

Without knowing it, Campbell had dredged up the perfect psychological horror for Eliza: to be encased in a bronze statue of Trouble.

"Lucky for you, I'd already cast most of the parts on spec. What a delightful addition this will make to the park for the Valentine's Day parade."

They were back in the shop. Eliza was propped upright inside the metal sculpture, which Campbell had clamped onto her one piece at a time. Her brain raged at her limbs to fight back, but her captor had injected her with something that rendered her paralyzed. She could only watch in horror as the statue took shape around her. She was going to die with her left foot forward, head titled, holding up a fucking magnifying glass.

"Thanks, I hate it," Eliza managed, her tongue slow to react, and her words muffled inside the metal tomb. Campbell had left holes in the statue for the eyes and mouth. Not for Eliza, she knew, but because Campbell wanted to enjoy her victim's panicked screams and fear.

"I'm really going to miss our talks," Campbell said, using another clamp to hold the metal mask in place. "You were so hesitant to bring up Casey when I just love a chance to perform."

Keep her talking. That was how Trouble defeated the Undertaker. She kept the idiot talking until an opportunity presented itself. Maybe, just maybe, the drugs Campbell dosed her with would wear off. She just had to keep her talking, because it would all be over once the welding began.

"Tell me about your first time," Eliza said. "And I don't mean with Reed."

The psycho actually blushed.

"'A rush of blood, oh, and a little bit of pain,'" she sang, before breaking into a fit of laughter. "Okay, okay. I was 22, living in the city. You know, just a girl and her dreams…"

JENNY WALKED THE STREETS OF BLACKBIRD SPRINGS WITH NO EXACT destination in mind. The treehouse was still empty. Their room at the Crow's Nest was empty. Eliza had vanished.

Thunder rumbled in the distance where patches of dark clouds rolled over the horizon. Three minutes later, it was pouring.

Jenny cursed and hurried for an overhang. She was halfway there when she spotted a familiar face with an umbrella: Mr. Hooke, her English Teacher.

"Hey, Mr. Hooke!" Jenny called, waving and jogging across the street to meet him.

She was sure he saw her, but the bastard abruptly turned around and power-walked in the other direction. When she got to the corner, there was no sign of him.

"Asshole!"

She hung her head, all hope washing away with the rain. Jenny's girlfriend was avoiding her, her sister hated her, and the townspeople ran the other way when they saw her coming. At least the downpour would hide her tears.

But then the rain stopped.

Not everywhere, just above her. Jenny spun, confused, to find a man with a hawkish nose holding out an umbrella over them both.

"Miss Valentine, what a pleasant surprise," said Mr. Webb.

His features seemed sharper today, his cheekbones more pronounced, his hair wet, and the collar of his coat flipped up against the weather.

"Oh! Hi." Jenny sniffled. "I almost didn't recognize you. No glasses today?"

"They're such a bother in the rain, don't you think? Is everything okay?"

"Um, yes. No. I don't know."

"Should be an interesting press conference from Valerie Valentine on Tuesday," he said. "I hope you won't hold it against me if the trust has to repossess RJ's assets."

Jenny thought she couldn't feel worse. She was wrong.

"Let's hope it doesn't come to that," she managed.

"You're a clever girl, I trust you to see that it doesn't."

A valet pulled up with his car, a black beamer. Mr. Webb handed her the umbrella and stepped out into the rain.

"Thanks," she said.

"Oh, I meant to tell you," said Mr. Webb, pausing with one foot in his car. "Got a call from LoJack. They found one of your jeeps at the Napa Greyhound Station. You know anything about that?"

Jenny frowned. Did Eliza take a bus somewhere? Why not drive?

"Uh, it's fine. I'll pick it up."

Mr. Webb nodded and drove off. Jenny pulled out her phone. She'd resisted doing this until now, trying to respect her sister's privacy, but if LoJack was involved, this had already gone far enough. Using the Find My app, she checked Eliza's location. It had her at the Napa Greyhound Station too. Strange. Shelly had restricted her car privileges, so she ordered a Lyft to Napa. It was time for her sister to get back in the game.

THE STORM HAD BLOWN PAST BY THE TIME SHE EXITED HER LYFT at the Napa bus station. She was across the river, not far from a public market she and Eliza had lunch at once, over Thanksgiving break. The jeep was parked in the back of the lot, the keys still in the ignition. There on the passenger seat were Eliza's phone and Apple Watch. Had she really just run off and left her?

A wave of revulsion slammed into Jenny. She'd done this. She'd driven her own twin away. They were a team! Jenny sagged against the car door, despondent. Did Eliza even leave a note?

When she grabbed the phone to check. Something shiny flashed underneath: her sister's locket.

Jenny shuddered, a piece of her very soul crumbling. Was she really that unlikeable? That unpleasant to be around? Her own twin... She picked up the locket, staring numbly at it. This was supposed to be a forever gift.

Her other hand found her own locket. She squeezed tight, accepting the pain, promising the gods that she could do better, if only she got another chance. When she let go, the locket popped open, and a folded up scrap of paper fell out.

A memory clicked. Eliza had written down the supposed identity of the Ghostwriter on this. She'd be a total ingrate to peek, right?

Jenny sighed. Fuck it, if her sister already hated her this much, what was one more line to cross? She unfolded the piece of paper, no longer really caring who the culprit was.

Mr. Hooke.

Her English Teacher? Seriously, Lizzy? But he was the first one the Ghostwriter went after!

Jenny mentally reviewed the evidence. Obviously, Mr. Hooke knew about his own sad divorce and custody situation. He would've been there to take that picture at Saturday School. He might've even heard Shelly's flirtatious remark to Mr. White through the wall between their classrooms. But why hadn't he published the Alicia Aaron story she sent him?

Whatever. Creep. Jenny couldn't feel any joy over the revelation. It had been Danger's discovery, not Trouble's. She was the smart one; probably traced the email headers or some hacker shit. Still, she was getting that prickly feeling—like when she was just on the verge of figuring something out. About Mr. Hooke? No, but related. Something about his being the first victim...

Casey was the Hot Springs Hangman!

No, that was ridiculous. But the nagging sensation grew. Not Casey, but close. The way she'd looked past Mr. Hooke as a suspect...

Whose alibi had Jenny never questioned? Not Reed Klein's. Where would Casey run to if she'd been frightened when petting Sonya, the horse? Not Brett Klinger's house. Who would Casey have trusted implicitly? Not Jorge Lopez. Who lived near a creek that ran down to the North Sloughs, where Sarah Ortiz was found? Not Tori Valentine. Who was the only person who had willingly inserted themselves into Jenny's investigation? Not Blake Lockhart.

And who would abandon Jenny after one regrettable fight? Not Eliza Valentine.

It clicked.

Mother. Fucker.

Chapter Twenty-Seven

Trouble Always Finds Me

THE APPROACH TO CAMPBELL BATORI'S FARMHOUSE YIELDED several red flags that Jenny should have caught earlier. Eliza had mentioned them, but Jenny, like everyone else, had never put Casey's mom on her suspect list and didn't give her the scrutiny she deserved. First: Ms. Batori's house was up in the hills, with a long, private driveway and no close neighbors. Second: the farmhouse was only a half-mile from Huichica Creek, which ran all the way down to the North Sloughs, where the body of Sarah Ortiz was found.

Third, and most damning: all these bronze statues were just fucking creepy. It wasn't hard to picture them belonging to a woman who preferred the cold, metal facsimile of life to the genuine thing.

She was driving Eliza's jeep, having no better option to get back from Napa in a hurry. Navigating the narrow dirt road was tricky, but Jenny made it to the farmhouse without incident. Once parked, she swallowed a handful of pills and chased them with water from her officially licensed *Trouble* AquaFlask. It was time. She took a big breath, feeling much less confident now that she was here, and gripped her own taser in her purse as she got out.

The front door was around to the left. Jenny had taken three steps in that direction when she heard loud hissing and popping from the back of the farmhouse. It was an odd noise, like frying bacon, but with a distinctly electric sizzle to it. She reversed course and headed to the back of the farmhouse to find the big barn doors thrown open. With one last focusing breath, she stepped around the door and peered into Ms. Batori's shop.

HER TIME WAS UP. ELIZA HAD COAXED EVERY LAST MORSEL OF information from Campbell, from her first brush with death—witnessing a car accident when she was seven years old—to her botched killing of Sarah Ortiz, where Campbell had misjudged a tranquilizer dose on her victim, who promptly fled once her legs could move. Campbell had chased her across the meadow and into the woods. It was the middle of the night, and the poor girl plunged into the creek and got swept away before Campbell could reach her.

"I'm gonna miss that wig," Campbell said wistfully. "Not all the girls got to wear it for their fittings, just the pretty ones. You could have worn it," she added like it would cheer Eliza up.

"Is that why you killed Lily Geist?" Eliza asked. "To cover your mistake with Sarah?"

"You were supposed to tie her to Jorge Lopez and take the heat off," she said nodding. "What happened with that, anyway? Did you kill him?"

"People who cross me rarely make out too well," said Eliza, keeping the Stranger to herself. Where was that bastard when you needed him?

"That's the spirit," said Campbell, rising to admire her creation.

All the pieces of the statue had been clamped in place, except the front of the headpiece, which Campbell was still tweaking with a hand file.

"Should I leave your wig on?" Campbell asked. "Or maybe it could be my new trophy."

"You can keep it," Eliza croaked out. "My scalp itches like crazy."

"Oh, well, in that case, we'd better leave it on," she said, wandering back to her workbench. A car engine sounded in the distance. Campbell froze, listening intently. "What the—?"

She scrambled back to Eliza, pressing the headpiece onto her face.

"Wait. Shit." She pulled the piece off, shoved a rag into Eliza's mouth, and then clamped the headpiece on again.

The rag tasted like the Undertaker had smelled: of death and chemicals. If she tried to talk, she might gag and drown in her own bile. Through the pinprick eye holes, Eliza watched Campbell throw the doors to the shop open before scurrying to the welding table where she donned her face shield and pretended to splice two steel bars together. A shadow moved outside, and Eliza's heart stopped.

Her twin sister had just walked into view.

Campbell pulled off her welding mask and froze in shock. Her head angled over to Statue Eliza, unable to resist double-checking what her own eyes were telling her.

Surprise, psycho, there's two of me.

Campbell recovered after a moment and turned on the charm offensive.

"Jennifer? Jennifer. I love your new hairstyle!"

"Why thank you," said Jenny, a lively smile despite her smeared mascara and bangs plastered to her forehead.

"Come on in," said Campbell.

Jenny stepped forward, eyes roving over all the power tools and equipment. She'd never been here herself before. Did she know? Or was this just another house call to ask about Casey? Eliza prayed for her sister to glance her way.

"You all right? You look like you've just seen a ghost," Jenny said.

Campbell pretended to laugh and grabbed a tarp, tossing it over Eliza. *Damn it!*

"I wasn't expecting you," Campbell said. "I hope I didn't ruin the surprise."

"Is that *me?*" Jenny asked. Footsteps.

"Ah-ah, no peeking," Campbell said. Eliza pictured the woman moving over to cut Jenny off. "Val wanted this to be the big reveal at the Valentine's Day parade. Trouble and RJ: together again."

"Funny how she didn't ask me," Jenny said. "Whatever, it's fine. Money to you is less money for her lawyers."

"As you say. So what's up? To what do I owe the honor?"

Three sharp clanks sounded from Jenny's direction: a hammer hitting an anvil.

"Heh. Sorry, couldn't resist. I was hoping to get your advice," Jenny said. "Do you have tea?"

"Sure, you want to come inside?" Campbell asked. "I'll put a kettle on."

It was only after both pairs of footsteps had trailed away and entered the farmhouse that Eliza realized what Jenny had just done. Those three hammer strikes: that was their signal. *I'm here. I'm with you. I love you.*

Eliza blinked through tears three times in silent response. Jenny knew she was here. But what the hell was her plan?

WHATEVER DOUBTS JENNY HAD ABOUT MS. BATORI VANISHED THE moment the bronze carver saw her. That freeze, that look of shocked bewilderment—it could only mean one thing: she'd just realized there were twins. Jenny prayed she wasn't too late and that her sister was still alive.

They moved inside Ms. Batori's homey kitchen, Jenny taking care to always keep the woman in front of her. She made small talk about the weather as Ms. Batori prepared the tea, pretending not to watch her too closely. In her purse, the stun gun comforted her twitchy fingers.

"Here we are," said Ms. Batori, bringing two mugs of tea over and placing them on the table. Jenny reached for hers and pretended to sip.

"Oh, do you have any honey, Ms. Batori?" Jenny asked.

"Please, call me Campbell," Ms. Batori said, the words coming out on reflex. She hesitated then, a grin blossoming on her face. "Um, I think so."

Campbell rummaged in her cabinets. The table between them was wide and round, with a heavy barrel in place of legs. Hard to tip over or knock aside, Jenny wagered. She stirred her tea, watching Campbell hunt in her cupboards—

—and switched mugs when her back was turned.

"Here we go," Campbell said, holding up a golden bottle. "It's organic."

Jenny made a show of dumping massive amounts of honey into her tea before taking a big sip. Only then did Campbell sip her own tea.

"Mm, thanks," Jenny said. "So, let me tell you about my problem."

Campbell leaned forward, eager.

"I'm being blackmailed."

"Blackmailed?"

"Blackmailed," Jenny confirmed. "He's this freelance reporter. The Stringer! He's trying to make it look like I killed my dad."

"Hmm," said Campbell, utterly baffled.

"Now, as I'm sure you're aware from my meltdown at Declan's

memorial service last fall, this is impossible, since I have an alibi."

"I wasn't there, actually. What happened?"

"Hah, funny story." Jenny recounted the tale of her Winchester embarrassment in agonizing detail, strangely unbothered to revisit one of her lowest moments. Could this be some kind of poison acting on her now? Loosening her tongue? Maybe it was merely that she was sharing a cup of tea with a mass murderer. Next to that, rehashing an embarrassing incident just didn't move the needle.

"Anyways, the doctors say it's like there's two of me, the Jenny part and the Trouble part. Ironic, really." Jenny smiled, relishing the confused horror on Campbell's face. "God, I should call Dinah right now."

"Sorry, what?"

"Do you mind? I'll be quick." Before she could reply, Jenny had her phone out, calling her favorite contact. Campbell gawked with visible unease as Jenny listened to it ringing. "Voicemail. Figures." She took a deep breath. "Hey, Dinah. It's me. Um… I know we made promises, and I'm not asking you to break them, but I really need to talk. I need your help to get past this. It's hard, and I'm trying. But I need help. I gotta go. See you tomorrow? Text me. Bye."

"Girl trouble?" Campbell asked.

"Phew, that's been eating at me all weekend," Jenny said, putting her phone away and once again clutching the taser. "So, the mental hospital thing. Yes, I got committed. But I wasn't actually in my room that night, and this reporter asshole has the shift logs or whatever to prove it. He's gonna spin that into me having enough time to drive up here, attack my dad, and drive back."

"Where were you, really?" Campbell asked. "Just out of curiosity."

"I was up on the hospital roof," Jenny said.

It was only four stories. She wouldn't fall for long. She forced herself to raise one foot up on the ledge.

Three sharp knocks sounded behind her.

"I wouldn't do that if I were you," said a familiar voice.

Jenny looked back, furious at this rude intrusion—and caught her breath when she saw her own face smiling back at her. The hair was longer, the frame maybe a tad leaner, but it was her.

"You're just getting to the good part," her doppelgänger said.

"Are—are you real?" Jenny asked.

"Of course." She walked forward and took Jenny by the hand, pulling her back from the edge.

"Lizzy," she whispered, remembering the name her aunt seldom uttered.

Her twin nodded with glassy eyes.

"I'm Trouble."

"I'm Danger," Lizzy said.

Oh, it was perfect! She'd never been so happy in all her life, and they'd only just met.

"Someone found me up there," Jenny said, shaking off her reverie. "Someone dear. She saved my life. Changed my life. But now this reporter is trying to use that moment against me. And that just feels… abhorrent. So I don't know what to do," she sniffled and checked her watch. They'd been talking nearly 20 minutes. Any time now. "Do I pay the guy off? Let him shoot his wad and hope it doesn't hold up?"

"I guess they say the only thing you can do with a blackmailer is beat them to the punch," Campbell said, rubbing her head. "Get it all out there, so their dirt is useless. And you've got a whole PR machine, he doesn't."

Jenny snapped her fingers. Or tried to. Her hand was going numb. Oh yeah, she'd been drugged, all right.

"You just gave me a capital idea!" She fished her phone out and pulled up the *Trouble* Instagram account. Now, where was that photo she'd snapped of the reporter? She pulled it up and drew a little black box over his eyes, so Stacy in PR wouldn't totally crucify her. Then she tapped a quick message, reading aloud as she typed with clumsy thumbs.

"'See this guy? He thinks he's got some dirt on RJ and me, and he's trying to blackmail yours truly. What he doesn't realize is that the hashtag TroubleHive is bigger than any one person. And if he thinks he can shame me about my mental health, he's in for a big surprise. I'll be donating the million a year he asked for to the National Immigration Law Center instead. XOXO Trouble.' Hold on, let me clean up these typos."

She glanced up at Campbell, who didn't seem to realize that she was compulsively stroking her own face.

"Sent." Jenny chuckled. Her breathing had slowed, sapping her energy. "Oh. Wait. One more."

She snapped a photo of Campbell. This time she didn't read the caption aloud.

> The Hot Springs Hangman isn't even a man.
> #YasQueen? No, seriously, it was Casey's mom the
> whole time. #911

"There we go." She stashed her phone, the effects of the drugged tea coming on strong now. "Good talk. Eliza was right; you are a good hang. Well, mostly."

Campbell's mask finally slipped.

"God, I thought you'd talk forever," she said, a lipless grin spreading on her face. The smile even reached her eyes—what a complete nut job.

"I'm impressed, you put the poison in your cup," Jenny said, pointing to the tea she'd been drinking. "What's in this?"

"Some heavy sedatives. Was that your whole plan? To switch glasses on me?" Campbell giggled—and struggled to stop. "How adorable."

Jenny brought the taser out with her right hand. "If you've hurt her…"

"She's still breathing, but not for long," said Campbell, now staring at her hands in a daze. "Hate to break it to you, but that taser won't make it through this welding coat. In another minute, you won't even be able to stand, let alone lift your arm."

"We'll see," Jenny said, struggling to maintain her concentration, buoyed beyond measure to hear that Eliza was okay. "Switching drinks wasn't my only plan."

"Let me start my recorder first," Campbell said. "I love to hear you scream."

"See, I swallowed a bunch of activated charcoal pills before I walked in," Jenny said. "So your sedatives might not be as effective as you think. At least, that worked in *Trouble on the Orient Express*. Maybe Dad was full of shit. Let's find out."

Jenny stood.

Slowly, and on unsteady legs, but she could still stand. Score one for Dad. She straightened her back and took a confident step around the table. Campbell leapt to her feet, backing away.

"You're probably wondering what's going on with your… whole shit, right now," Jenny said, waving a hand over Campbell's body, which the woman was pawing at in wonder and horror. "I didn't just switch mugs, I put four doses of MDMA in your tea."

Campbell's eyes had glazed over, but panic kindled from somewhere deep within.

"Thanks, Mace, I owe you," Jenny said.

Campbell made the first move, but not at Jenny. She bolted for the garage, running away like a frightened rabbit.

It felt like an eternity. Eliza could just make out the barely audible buzz of conversation within the house. What the hell were they talking about? The minutes stretched on. Panic pressed in on her shoulders.

No, wait! That wasn't panic! That was the bronze shell she'd been encased in! And it wasn't pressing on *her*, she was feebly straining against *it*! Enough to make the tarp Campbell had thrown over her fall away! Feeling was returning to her limbs at last!

There was a crash, and Campbell Batori stumbled into the shop. She looked disoriented, holding her hands out like she might fall over.

Trouble followed a moment later, falling on Campbell with her taser. It connected with her shoulder, but the shock did nothing, blocked by Campbell's welding jacket. She spun and knocked the stun gun away, leaving Jenny open to a kick in the solar plexus.

"You crazy little rat!" Campbell shouted, still stumbling around as Jenny slid across the floor.

Eliza strained harder, the bronze plates creaking under the clamps. Campbell picked up a heavy sledgehammer. *Get up, Jenny!*

The murderess lunged, bringing the hammer down in an overhead strike.

Jenny barely rolled away in time, the hammer smashing into the concrete where her head had been only moments before. Campbell shrieked. Jenny kicked out, catching the back of her knee and sending her sprawling. She scrambled away, but her sister's movements were lethargic and strained now.

To only watch, unable to help, was agonizing. Eliza bit down on the rag, channeling all of her fear and rage and hope into one desperate headbutt.

Clank!

The metal mask fell away, clattering on the ground. Jenny and Campbell both looked up in surprise to see Eliza, revealed within the Trouble statue at last.

"Lizzy!" Jenny screamed and stumbled to her side. She kissed her on the cheek and yanked off the gag.

"Look out!" Eliza shouted.

Jenny spun, a pair of iron tongs in her hands, and deflected another of Campbell's overhead hammer smashes just in time, forcing the swing into the big fume extraction machine next to her. It sparked, causing Campbell to blink and shield her eyes, punch drunk.

The opening was enough for Jenny to weakly push Campbell back. She dropped the sledgehammer and flailed to the far side of the shop, knocking over a tool chest. White rope spilled out of a dislodged drawer: the noose.

"Blow torch!" Eliza suggested, spotting the little hand torch gas canister rolling Jenny's way.

Her sister snatched it up and turned on the gas, but no flame emerged from the spout.

"Shit, I need a lighter," Jenny said.

"Right hip!" Eliza shouted, watching nervously as Campbell steadied herself, gripping the welding table.

Jenny detached more clamps and tore off pieces of the bronze plating, uncovering Eliza's legs.

"Oh my God, this has pockets?!"

"Right?"

Jenny fished inside the right pocket that Campbell had never noticed to search and pulled out the slim Zippo lighter Eliza still held onto, despite her vow to quit smoking.

With one click, flames erupted from the blowtorch.

"Ha-hah!" Jenny shouted in triumph, waving the flame around.

Campbell hadn't been idle, though. She pulled on her welding helmet and sparked the plasma cutter. The fuel hose would limit her range, but it was a long hose.

Eliza struggled harder inside the statue, more strength returning to her limbs, as Jenny and Campbell faced off in the center of the shop. Campbell advanced, a lunatic laugh emerging from under the hood.

"This should help with the trails," Campbell said, tapping her opaque face-guard. "And you're only growing weaker."

"Yeah? How about now?" Jenny asked, waving the blowtorch in a figure eight.

If that was supposed to stop Campbell, it failed. They danced around each other, exchanging blasts of heat, and dodging fiery lunges.

"You've only got a few more minutes of gas," Campbell said, charging with her plasma torch again. Jenny retreated further into the far corner, spraying flames everywhere in defense.

"It's okay," Jenny said. "I'm just the distraction."

"From what?" Campbell asked, adjusting the beam on her plasma cutter.

A rounding hammer smashed into the side of Campbell's helmet and sent the woman flying.

"Me," said Eliza.

Not a bad throw for a numb arm. The welding hood bounced away.

Jenny pounced, dropping the blowtorch and tackling Campbell. She got her hands on the noose spooling out of the upended tool chest and slipped it over Campbell's neck. She gasped for air, fighting against the rope as Jenny throttled her. Eliza shrugged off the rest of the bronze and picked up the slack to help. Together they dragged Campbell across the shop, their combined but weakened strength just enough to overcome her wild, bucking defiance.

They were running out of room, though, and out of leverage.

"Tie her down!" Jenny screamed.

Eliza looped the rope around the lathe spindle and yanked down hard, using it like a pulley to draw her in until she had no choice but to stop fighting or asphyxiate.

"Okay, okay!" Campbell cried out.

Eliza let the rope slacken just enough for her to breathe. "Careful of the fire," she warned Jenny.

Her sister collapsed, crawling on her hands and knees to snatch up and extinguish the blowtorch and plasma cutter. Only then did she sag back on her elbows, panting, bruised, and bloodied, to stare down the Hot Springs Hangwoman.

All the fight had gone out of Campbell. She sat with her legs splayed, arms slumped at her sides.

"How could you kill your own daughter?" Jenny asked when her breath returned.

Campbell shrugged, a sad smile still plastered to her face. "She saw. Told her not to bother Mommy in her darkroom. Was it really so important to tell me she pet a horse?" She glanced at the Valentine girls. "No one who sees can live. You understand, don't you?"

"You're a monster," said Eliza.

Campbell cocked her neck to lock eyes with Eliza.

"Don't," Campbell said. "You're not like her. Not some rabid, feral gremlin. Lizzy, was it? You're special. I saw it from the start. I could have taught you! That damned iPod! So sloppy! My mistake, my mistake. I had so much to teach you, Elizabeth. I still could."

"Thank you for believing in me, Ms. Batori," Eliza said. "Consider the lesson learned."

She flipped the switch on the lathe.

Rope wound around the spindle with terrifying speed, wrenching Campbell back into the machine. She barely had time to grasp at the noose before the rope dug into her neck. The lathe gears whined in protest, and the Hot Springs Hangwoman's head popped right off in a gruesome gush of arterial spray.

"Holy shit," said Eliza.

Hot red blood splattered them both. Campbell's head bounced across the floor, coming to rest next to the Trouble statue's faceplate. Her eyes were still open, that eerily benign grin frozen on her face, looking back at them.

"Dark, sis," Jenny said, a repulsed, thousand-yard stare hanging between them. "And here I thought you were the good twin."

Reflexively, Eliza retreated into her wounded shell. Despite their present circumstances, they hadn't parted on good terms.

"How did you find me?" she asked, studying the floor and her grimy feet.

"You were right. I am a Slytherin," Jenny said, pulling a scrap of paper from her purse. It was the stationary from her locket, with Mr. Hooke's name on it. Jenny grinned. "I cheated."

Chapter Twenty-Eight
The Mistress of Metal

THERE WERE SO MANY QUESTIONS JENNY HAD FOR HER SISTER, BUT if the cops weren't already on their way, they would be soon. They agreed to meet when it was safe; Eliza deserved a two-hour shower, a soft bed, and a Double-Double right now.

The rest of Jenny's Sunday was lost to endless questioning by multiple law enforcement agencies. Someone from TMZ was early on the scene, and soon bloodthirsty reporters mobbed the hillside meadow, trying to get a peek. Shelly had to force her way past the crime scene tape, relieved and furious to find Jenny alive. There was no sign of Jeffrey Jordan, Jenny noted. Some of his Twitter cronies were trying to cancel her for posting his photo, but they were no match for Stacy from PR, and an army of teenage girls posting Trouble memes.

Eventually, everyone lost interest in her, busying themselves with cataloging evidence and searching the grounds. As dusk fell, Lockhart found Jenny and Shelly sitting on an ambulance bumper, sharing a Clif Bar that her aunt had in her purse.

"Can you just lock her up until she's 25?" Shelly asked.

"How'd I do, Sir?" said Jenny.

"The legend fucking grows," he said, disgusted. "Half the internet wants my badge, the other half is delighted to learn that the real Sheriff Lockhart is just as bad at his job as the one in your dad's stupid books, and is demanding I keep it."

"Don't sell yourself short," Jenny said. "Dad's Lockhart was written to be an idiot, you get there all on your own."

She could feel Shelly tensing next to her, but Lockhart played it off like he was in on the joke, even as he ground his teeth behind his smile.

"Someone should call Mary Manuel," Jenny said, lost in thought. "And Tori."

She'd forgotten to ask, but Campbell gave no indication of having anything to do with RJ's death. Lockhart seemed to read her mind.

"I did some checking. Campbell was out of town on August 10th. Unveiling a statue for ILM at the Presidio. Another swing and a miss for John's heirloom clues." Lockhart's gaze drifted to the shop. "You almost ended up a lawn ornament yourself. You're lucky that business with the charcoal pills worked, and you broke free before she could weld you in."

Jenny shivered. "She said I would be a delightful addition to RJ's bench in the park. For Valentine's Day."

"Disgusting," said Shelly.

"Wait," Jenny said, locking eyes with the sheriff as a hideous thought occurred to her. "You don't think?"

Lockhart's brow furrowed, face twisted in revulsion. His hand darted to his radio. "Mack, we got anything that will cut metal?"

CAMPBELL BATORI HAD PLENTY OF POWER TOOLS, BUT THEY WERE all evidence. Ultimately, it was the new municipal worker, Tyrone, who got called in to assist, using a handheld angle grinder.

"This is on your orders, right?" he asked. "I don't want Valerie Valentine up my ass."

The sheriff's reply was lost in the noise of a car horn. They turned to see Penny Griffin's Civic pulling up to the curb next to the ring of construction barriers. Perfect timing, they were just about to begin. Drew carefully levered himself out with one hand and helped the passenger in the back seat. Lockhart immediately protested.

"Hey! Uhn-uh! No way! This is not a spectator event."

"She deserves to be here!" Penny replied.

Mary Manuel spoke in a brief burst of Spanish, calm, but resolute. In her arms was a thick black binder.

"She's not here for your badge, she just needs to see this through," Drew translated.

"I know what she said." Lockhart made a point of pushing the orange and white safety barrier another foot outward and glared at Jenny. "Who else did you tell?"

"No one, and she should be here. Tori too," Jenny said.

"If we don't get to it soon, the press is gonna get wind," Deputy Calderon said.

They'd decamped to Town Square: Shelly, Jenny, the sheriff, and a few cops. A small affair, in case Jenny and Lockhart were wrong.

"Darcy can fill her in," Lockhart said and waved to Tyrone. "Do it."

With one last shrug, Tyrone flipped on the angle grinder and began sawing into the statue of RJ Valentine. He made it about a half-inch in before he recoiled, dropping the power tool and holding his nose from the stench. Shelly wretched. The air went out of Lockhart, deflated by the grim truth.

"Call the coroner," he said. "And call the FBI."

"I knew there was a reason I hated that statue," said Jenny.

That was enough for Shelly. She didn't need to witness the extraction of the body from inside the RJ sculpture. The theory was proven, and now it was time to go home. For once, Jenny obeyed.

Drew and Penny hung around so Penny could interview Oscar Manuel's mother for the school paper. She was, technically, the first and only reporter on the scene, and the glint in her eye suggested she knew just how to exploit it.

With help from Mary Manuel's binder, dental records and DNA tests would later confirm the identity of the remains as a girl who'd gone missing from Marin County four months ago.

She wasn't the only one. Campbell had kept meticulous business records. In the weeks to come, FBI forensic units, working in a joint task force with local law enforcement, would discover the bodies of 36 girls inside various bronze statues fashioned by Campbell Batori, giving her the most confirmed kills of any female serial killer in the history of the United States. Everyone forgot about the Hot Springs Hangman. In time, she'd come to be known as the Mistress of Metal, a soubriquet courtesy of Penny Griffin—though Drew tried and failed to make Murderangelo happen.

None of that mattered to Jenny tonight. All she knew, back at home and fully showered, was that despite her voicemail, despite the evening news, despite her Instagram posts going viral—even after Stacy and the lawyers deleted them—Dinah still hadn't texted.

JENNY WOULD HAVE STARED AT HER MESSAGES APP ALL NIGHT IF Eliza hadn't interrupted with a soft knock at the bedroom door after midnight.

"Can I come in?" Eliza whispered in the dark.

"Please."

Her sister entered glumly, pausing just inside.

"I'm sorry about the bed," Eliza said, staring at the carpet.

"Oh my God, that was like a million years ago, get over here!" Jenny scrambled out of bed and embraced Eliza in a big hug, practically tackling her and pulling her back onto the soft comforter.

Eliza laughed, burying herself deeper into the mound of pillows. "Mmmm, I could sleep for days," she said. "Tell me it's not my turn tomorrow."

"It's not," Jenny lied. "I'll make sure Mrs. Rivas doesn't clean the room, so you can sleep all day."

They each lay there, side by side, staring at the ceiling. At some point in his youth, Jack had decorated it with little glow-in-the-dark stars and moons. Jenny glanced over at her sister, her eyes shimmering in the faux starlight.

"None of this is worth it without you," Jenny said. "I'm sorry if I never said it. And you were right, Dinah *is* hiding something. She told me as much. She wants me to trust her, but I'm a little short on that these days."

"Maybe you should," Eliza said.

"I thought you hated her."

"I don't, really." Eliza rolled on her side to face Jenny. "This game we're playing, all these secrets and lies, switcheroos and spycraft: it's making us harder, meaner people. Everyone becomes an asset. Every kindness a calculation. No weakness we won't exploit."

"You're the one who said we should let Val die. And then frame her."

"I am. And maybe it was easy, because I wasn't the one who had to look her in the eye when you did it. I just know that none of this is worth it if we lose ourselves to win, either."

Eliza's words reminded Jenny of an idea that had been nagging her.

"Speaking of winning, I don't know if you saw, but I made some promises to give some of our money away," said Jenny. "And I think we could even do more. A lot more. If that's okay with you."

"What about Val and that reporter?" Eliza asked. "What if they get the charges dropped, and they take our inheritance away?"

"Practically speaking, what's the difference between being $10 million in debt, or $100 million? I just know it felt really good when I posted it. Like helping Sarah Ortiz's parents out with immigration. We've got all this money, let's use it. And it's like Lockhart said, having our own foundation wouldn't hurt, either."

"Okay." Eliza smiled. "Yeah, let's do more. See, being nice can be fun too."

"I'll be sure to let Campbell Batori know that," said Jenny, unable to bite her tongue.

"I didn't know it would take her head off!" Eliza whisper-shouted. "I did that for us, you know."

"I know."

For a while, they listened to the wind, declining to consider Campbell's death further.

"Guess who Mason's baby mama is," Jenny said.

"Someone's wife."

"Meghan May."

"No shit!" Eliza was delighted.

"Wait till you hear how I found out," said Jenny.

They talked deep into the night, catching each other up on their weekend of horrors and revelations. Eliza eventually succumbed to her ordeal, falling asleep mid-sentence. Jenny tucked her in and allowed herself a moment of deep relief before drifting off herself.

IN THE MORNING, SHE THREW ON A BLACK TURTLENECK AND capris—they both agreed hiding her neckline was preferable to duplicating the red bruises Eliza had suffered from the noose—and hurried downstairs.

Shelly had already left for school, but there was a note in the kitchen from her to eat breakfast and call the publishing company. It seemed they weren't entirely happy with Jenny's Instagram posts. She took her parfait into Dad's study and joined the video conference from his desk, munching on her breakfast as a bunch of lawyers yelled at her over Zoom.

"Aren't you PR peeps always saying it's better to get out in front of stuff?" Jenny asked after they'd tired themselves out.

"I don't believe so, no," said Stacy.

"Hmm, maybe that was *Scandal*. Whatever, he's not gonna sue, and even if he does, we can counter-sue, right?"

"We have many options," said a stuffy lawyer with a giant painting of a sailboat behind him.

"We could've had more options if she'd come to us first," said another.

"If you're worried about PR, I *did* just stop a serial killer."

"Yes, and we're all relieved to hear you're okay," said Mr. Webb, looking sharp in a dark void. She could swear he was lit by a ring light. "Let's also not forget about the charity initiative Miss Valentine announced."

"This is just a very different landscape for us," said Stacy. "Blackmail and serial killers in the books is one thing. It's something else when it's real. The *Trouble* image is usually more PG, you know?"

"Well, Trouble grew up," Jenny said. "Her readers will understand, they all did too."

"We still have to think about new customer acquisition," said the lady from Penguin, surrounded by books. "A lot of those older readers are moms now, and they might not want their kids getting into this New Trouble."

"Maybe we can chase another audience," Jenny said. "Did anyone read that manuscript I sent over?"

The call erupted at the mention of Alicia's novel.

"*Hands of Adamant*?" Mr. Gregory scoffed. "It's lurid trash!"

"Where did you get that?"

"We are *not* publishing that under the *Trouble* shingle!"

"I had to have a very embarrassing conversation with my wife!"

"Is that title supposed to be romantic?!"

"It is if you're nasty," said Stacy.

"Still, I could sell it," said Mr. Gregory.

"Look, we can do it under a shell company, so we don't sully my good name," Jenny said. "But I'm sorry, this is happening. Draw up a contract with a million-dollar advance for Alicia Aaron."

More groans. She muted them.

"I know, I know. I'll cover it."

Mr. Gregory had his hand up, so Jenny let him speak.

"If trash is your new market, I can get you trash for a lot less than that."

"Do you honestly think I'm paying her that much for her writing?" Jenny replied. That shut him up. "Consider it essential research for the next *Trouble* book."

The Penguin lady raised her hand. Jenny unmuted her.

"So, there *will* be a new book?" she asked.

"Absolutely," Jenny said.

Faces brightened.

"When I find my dad's manuscript."

Faces fell.

Mrs. Rivas peeked in from the hallway, tapping her wrist.

"I'm gonna be late for school. I promise from now on, the *Trouble* Instagram will be rated E for Everyone. Thanks, Mr. Webb, guys." She disconnected the call and looked up at the housekeeper. "Is the town car out front?"

"No, Dinah is," Mrs. Rivas said.

Jenny blinked. She'd already talked herself into the idea that Dinah wasn't coming this morning. This should be interesting.

"Oh, um, I've got some personal stuff out in my room right now. You can just skip cleaning it till tomorrow, okay?"

Mrs. Rivas nodded. Jenny grabbed her backpack in the foyer, pulled on some big, white-rimmed Bebe sunnies, and opened the door.

Chapter Twenty-Nine
Number 1,349

Dinah stood in front of her Acura, arms crossed, her face unreadable behind giant sunglasses of her own. She'd dyed her hair tendrils black today, to match the black dress and leggings she wore under a white denim jacket. Jenny knew she was in trouble when Dinah nodded and walked around to the driver's side as soon as she walked out.

"We need to hurry," she said when Jenny got in. "There's a lot of press back in town."

They drove in silence. Despite her sour mood, Dinah wasn't wrong. Traffic was backed up for several blocks when they got closer to school.

"Did um, did you get my voicemail?" Jenny asked, when she couldn't stand it any longer.

"Yes," said Dinah frostily.

"I could have used someone to talk to yesterday."

Dinah had her phone out in an instant, shoving yesterday's Instagram posts in her face. "You sure about that?"

"I—yeah," Jenny said. "Why are you mad at me?"

"You promised!" Dinah said, her voice catching. "You said after

Drew got hurt that you'd stop doing this! And you're never going to."

"I didn't—" Jenny hesitated. She'd been about to repeat her "official" story that she'd told the cops. But no, she couldn't stand one more lie between them. "I'm sorry. But it couldn't be avoided. A lot of girls are safer today."

"Don't pretend that you did this for them," Dinah said. "I know you, Jenny. You like this."

The car inched along. Jenny could feel her temper rising.

"Hold up," Jenny said. "You lied about your alibi the night of my dad's murder. You asked me to trust you, then avoided me all weekend, and somehow I'm the asshole here?"

"Is that what this is? You're punishing me?"

"I'm not—Dinah, I'm not even mad at you, though I'm starting to get there. I just want you to talk to me, be honest with me."

"Oh sure," said Dinah. "Because you're always so forthcoming."

She slammed the brakes at another slowdown.

Jenny's lip quivered. "I—I told you something the other night that I've never told anyone before."

"Uh-huh," said Dinah. "And I finally get it now, all the hot and cold with you, pulling me close and pushing me away. All the insane risk-taking: you never dealt with it, you just found a different outlet for your self-destruction."

"I KNOW!" Jenny roared.

Dinah recoiled. The fright on her face filled Jenny with shame.

"I can't—I don't want this." Jenny reached for the handle and opened her door.

"Hey! Stop!" Dinah reached over, but Jenny was already getting out.

"I'm sorry, I'm sorry," she said. "I'm trying, but not now. I never dealt—? Why do you think I told you? Forget it. I'll see you later."

Jenny stomped away before Dinah could see the hot tears on her cheeks, unsure if she was more pissed at her girlfriend or herself. She hadn't even made that promise to stop sleuthing, Eliza had. But did Dinah just expect Jenny to *not* solve crimes?? It wasn't an avenue of thought she wanted to explore right now, or ever, so she wiped her smeared eyeliner, swallowed her emotions—and a Xanax—and hurried to school.

The mob of press in front of campus meant Jenny had to hike all the way around and hop the fence to avoid them. By then, she was 10 minutes late to History, and Mr. Carter was waiting for her at Mrs. Cortez's door.

"Miss Valentine," the Vice Principal said. "I've been looking for you."

She heaved an exasperated sigh. "Maybe keep looking?"

"I hope you don't think your recent heroics in any way make up for your truancy on Saturday."

"I wasn't feeling well," Jenny said. "Did you talk to Shelly?"

"I did. Your aunt said you would be most willing to make up the Saturday detention you missed."

"Uh-huh."

"But we might have to add a few," Mr. Carter said.

"How many?"

"Oh, how about for the rest of the school year?"

Jenny's eyebrows shot to the roof. "Oh, come on! Can't you just suspend me?"

"I could expel you. I hear Ms. Onishi has some nice pamphlets on private schools for delinquents."

"Wait, what if I tell you who the Ghostwriter is, will you shave some months off?"

"Do you mean to tell me that Alicia Aaron wasn't the Ghostwriter?"

he asked, an authoritarian timber creeping into his voice. "And that I suspended her, on your word, for nothing?"

"Ehhhhh. That's on you, man. I just said to check her phone. But I'm right this time."

"Still, what is power if it can't be used, I suppose..." He trailed off, cocking his head in thought. "Hmm. Nah."

"Nah, what?"

"The Ghostwriter," he said. "Whoever they are, they seem to have worn out their welcome, and that woman is all kids will be talking about today. No one cares about the Ghostwriter anymore. There's a moral there, maybe. So, we'll be seeing you on Saturday?"

Jenny nodded crisply and yanked the door open before she said something that would definitely get her expelled.

Dinah's desk was empty when she got to English. Instead, she was greeted by disconcerting smiles from the Bitchy Brigade.

"I was about to be mad when you didn't show at Lily's funeral," Shani said as Jenny took a seat. "But I guess you had your reasons."

Meghan May stayed quiet, unable to hide her pink cheeks. Jenny was never not going to picture her in her underwear now.

Someone squeezed her shoulder. Jenny looked back, eager for Dinah's touch. Instead, it was Charlie Zaleska, giving her some kind of knowing nod. Whatever. To distract herself from Dinah's absence, she spent the class watching Mr. Hooke with fresh eyes. He was clever about it, but yes, he definitely watched them too, even getting up to linger closer when the Bitchy Brigade talked in hushed whispers. What a creep. She was tempted to expose him right here, but no, he was Eliza's trophy to collect.

At lunch, Jenny found Jack in the cafeteria. He was eating with

Penny, who was typing away on her MacBook, her feet draped over Jack's lap. Mason and the boys were nearby, playing some sort of game that involved eating packets of hot sauce.

"Jenny, come do the challenge!" Lai Saechao called, holding up a packet of Tapatio.

She ignored him and kicked Jack in the shoe. "Have you seen Dinah?"

"No, why?" he said brusquely.

"Nothing, forget it."

Penny glanced up from her work to shoot a curious glance at Jack. He let out a heavy sigh and returned to his lunch. Penny shrugged and went back to writing. The curfew and closed campus restrictions had been lifted, and Jack had taken full advantage, getting pasta from the Winchester delivered.

"Isn't Chicken Alfredo a little basic for you?" Jenny asked.

"It's pheasant. And this is marsala sauce, you prole," he replied. But the corner of his lip tugged, so very RJ-esque, to let her know he was just messing with her.

"Have you talked to Tori?" she asked.

Jack's smile disappeared. "No."

"You're worried about her," Jenny guessed.

"She's going to blame herself for not seeing it in Casey's mom," said Jack.

"No one saw it."

"You saw it."

Penny smiled grimly. "My mom said she'll let me co-write a new end to *Casey's Walk* if I can get an exclusive with you."

"Gladly," Jenny said. "I always support my local journalists. Don't suppose I could get a peek at *The Stranger of Sausalito* in return, though?"

329

"I wouldn't hold my breath," Penny said.

Her phone buzzed, so Jenny excused herself to take it. Drew was FaceTiming from home.

"So is school crazy today?" asked Drew. His shoulder was still bandaged, but not quite as heavily. It looked like he was in his garage.

"Nah, it's the same old shit. How's the shoulder?" she asked.

"It's coming along," he said, and Jenny detected a bashful smile lurking behind his terrible poker face.

"Coming along with your new nurse?"

He was fully blushing now. "This is your fault, you know. You're the one who got her suspended. Now she has some extra free time, and it so happens that I do too."

"You're welcome. She's not there right now, is she?" Jenny made a face.

"She went out to get lunch."

"Okay, I have to ask, and I'm not trying to pry, but like, what's the status here? Is this more: Drew likes a girl and follows her around like a puppy and never makes a move, or?"

"Well…" Drew hesitated. That shit-eating grin was back again. "At the hospital, she was massaging my shoulder, said it was good for the wound. Then she kind of reached down and started rubbing my—"

"Okay, I get the idea!"

"My *forearm!* And her face was kinda real close to mine, and I looked over and, you know."

Drew pantomimed giving Alicia a kiss.

"Aww, that's adorable. I'm disgusted," Jenny said. "Just remember who you're working for."

"Yes, ma'am. Maybe we can double-date with you and Dinah." She must have made a face because Drew quickly asked, "What?"

"Nothing. Check this out. I think Mason just swallowed a whole thing of habanero sauce on a dare," she said, changing the subject and switching cameras. Mason was stomping around, his face bright red, begging someone for milk.

"Amateur," Drew laughed. "Hey, what's up with your camera? Is it cracked?"

"Wait, really?" Jenny flipped her phone around. Sure enough, there was a hairline crack across the camera lens. "Goddamnit. Fucking Campbell!"

"Is it true she got decapitated? All the news reports are calling it 'massive head trauma.'"

"Well, that's the polite euphemism." Jenny bit her cheek, an idea forming. "Hey, I gotta go. I'll come by to visit after school. Oh, and tell your girl to call me."

"Who? Alicia?"

"Yeah. We've got shit to discuss. Not about you."

Jenny ended the call and pulled up the photo they'd found within Dad's briefcase. Maybe it wasn't so useless after all.

SCHOOL WAS NEARLY OUT WHEN ELIZA WOKE UP. HER WHOLE BODY ached from being crammed into that statue. Wincing, she rose and relieved her bladder, then stripped off her clothes and took a long shower, followed by a bath. Once in the tub, she put on some music and forced her mind to go blank—it needed cleansing too. When she was good and pruned, she reached for her phone to text Trouble.

> **D:** Where you at?
>
> **T:** Drewboo's. Catching him up. Be home soon.
>
> **T:** PS we have Saturday school till we're seniors now.

D: Oh shit

D: I forgot

T: We can split them

D: I'm going to hide under more bath
bubbles now

She did just that, sinking low and letting water seep into her ears and distort the music.

"Hey Siri, play 'White Houses' on repeat."

The song played. One time or five or 20, she wasn't counting. She rocked her head slowly from side to side to let the water seep in and out of her ear canals.

"Is this therapy?" Jenny asked, knocking on the open door.

"I'm reclaiming it. I keep thinking over our conversations, Campbell and me. Looking for the hidden poisoned tongue, the bad advice, the malevolence. But there wasn't any. Not until…"

"I know," Jenny said, a sad smile on her lips. "She was really cool, except for that one little thing."

"Hey Siri, play something else." Eliza sat up, her ears going *whoop!* when the water drained.

"Damn, your neck!"

"That bad?" Eliza asked, tenderly probing the bruises on her neck.

"You'll just have to use lots of foundation," said Jenny. "Check this out."

She held up their two photos of Mom and Dad. The heirloom clue of them kissing in front of the old Poison Pen, and the briefcase photo of them entering a hotel room. Jenny handed Eliza a magnifying glass and tapped the lower-left corner of each.

"Look closely, do you see it?"

Eliza peered through the magnifying glass.

"Hmm. The little black spot?" She went back and forth. There was definitely a black shape next to a thin squiggle line in the same spot on both photos. "Probably a speck of dust or a scratch on the lens."

"Yep!" Jenny was grinning ear to ear. "And these photos were taken months apart. Mom is barely showing here. Which means this is the same P.I., same camera, and he doesn't clean his lens very often."

Eliza got it.

"It's a photographic fingerprint," she said. "If we can find other pictures that have this, we can figure out who the P.I. was."

"Exactly."

"Great, now we just need to get our hands on a bunch of local P.I. photos from 17 years ago."

"I have some ideas for that," said Jenny, putting the photos away.

"In more immediate concerns, what are we gonna do about that reporter? Val's press conference is tomorrow."

Jenny shrugged. "Maybe the Insta post scared him off."

The intercom crackled in the bedroom.

"Spoke too soon," said Eliza.

"Jenny, are you there?" It wasn't security this time. It was Dinah. Was she here?

Her sister frowned and hurried to the intercom controls.

"Dinah?"

"Can you come downstairs to the study?" Dinah asked. "I need to talk."

"Um, okay," Jenny said before killing the intercom.

"How did she get in?" Eliza asked, scowling.

Her sister peeked back into the bathroom, grimacing. "Sorry. Um—"

"I'll get out, just in case," Eliza said. "Just don't bring her up here."

Jenny scurried away. Alone again, Eliza dunked herself entirely one last time before climbing out of the tub. They were meeting in the study. Maybe she ought to slip down into the passageway through the conservatory and watch, just in case.

THE SUN WAS DIPPING LOW IN THE EVENING, MAKING THE VIEW through the study windows sumptuously picturesque. Golden light bathed the courtyard, the grapevines on the ridge beyond glowing with a lush orange nimbus. Jenny found Dinah mixing herself a drink at the minibar. Shelly had previously locked all the booze into the cabinet underneath, but it seemed Dinah had a key.

"Hey," Jenny said.

Dinah turned, holding two pink, sparkling drinks. The ice clinked as she pressed one into Jenny's hands.

"This is a La Paloma. My mom says everyone has one bad tequila experience in their youth and then they never touch the stuff again. Drink."

Jenny took the fizzing glass, raising an eyebrow.

"Should I be nervous?" she asked.

She was hoping for reassurance. Instead, Dinah's lips compressed into a thin, dour line.

"Drink," said Dinah.

Jenny drank, and Dinah followed. The citrus sweetness helped the pungent liquor go down easier. After a few sips, warmth began spreading from Jenny's belly to all her appendages, and Dinah spoke.

"I got into a car wreck this morning. Totaled my Acura."

"How?" Jenny frowned. "It was bumper to bumper."

"I'm fine, by the way," she said, blue fire flashing in her eyes. "I turned around, was on my way… I don't know where. On the highway. There was a traffic slowdown, and I didn't brake fast enough."

Jenny wanted to reach out, to embrace her girlfriend, but Dinah had taken a few steps back, keeping her distance.

"You're going to hurt tomorrow. Trust me."

"I'm hurting now," she said, a tear running down her cheek. "Jenny... I can't do this anymore."

"What do you mean?" Jenny asked, casting around for something to hold on to. Deep down, she knew exactly what.

"I mean, I can't be your girlfriend anymore."

"What are you talking about?" Jenny said, her voice pitching higher as she spoke too quickly. "It was just a stupid fight. I'm an idiot, and I'm sorry. People don't have to break up just because of one fight. They talk it out and make up."

"You know, right before the accident—granted, I was distracted about a lot—but right before, I heard this buzzing like a phone vibrating. I knew it wasn't mine, and I looked behind me and—" She ran a fist into her palm, grimacing. "Boom. Afterward, when we were waiting for the CHP, I looked around in the backseat—and I found this."

Dinah pulled out an old iPhone.

"It was vibrating because the battery was almost dead," she said. "Did you put this in my car? Were you tracking me?"

Jenny's heart plummeted. She didn't plant the phone, but Danger did.

"I swear to God I didn't put that there," Jenny said.

"I don't believe you," Dinah said, her mouth contorted in sorrow. "I wish I did, but I don't. I can't handle this, Jenny. I've tried, and I've tried, but I can't. My grades are suffering, I'm getting in car wrecks, I can't sleep at night. My therapist wants to put me on anxiety meds. Have you even noticed how skinny I've gotten?"

"So this isn't about the phone," Jenny said. "Come on, what's really the matter?"

"Us, Jenny. Us is wrong. We're not communicating, not really. You're so hot and cold, I never know which Jenny is gonna show up, and I always feel like I've done something wrong."

"You haven't!" The tears were flowing freely now.

"So you say, but you don't know what it's like, being on my side of the 'Trouble experience,'" she said, with mocking air quotes. "People are trying to kill you. Killing people connected to us, and you just go on like it's all part of a game. That lady got fucking decapitated in front of you, and you're posting viral Insta stories." Dinah took a ragged breath, nearly sobbing. "This isn't healthy, and I don't want that to be us! Maybe you can mentally compartmentalize, but I can't. I feel it all."

"This is all because I asked you about that night," Jenny said. Her mouth had gone dry, so she took another heavy belt of the tequila cocktail. "It's not fair to put this on me when you're the one keeping secrets."

"We both are!" Dinah said. "I know you framed Val, Jenny. I *know* it. And I'm trying to help you, trying to find out what Val's team knows, and you put a tracker in my car! Well, fuck you! You want to talk about secrets? Then you go first!"

Jenny's mouth dropped, hesitating.

"See!" Dinah said, jabbing a finger, a joyless smile on her lips. "You can't. Fuck it, I'm easy. Tell me you love me, and we'll say it together on three. Can you do that?"

Jenny sniffled. She took another sip of the cocktail as her heart burst asunder.

"I can't."

The light died in Dinah's eyes. She'd been holding out this whole time, Jenny realized. Hoping in vain that Jenny would level with her. An alert tapped on her wrist. She stole a glance.

D: You know you can't tell her.

"I know," she said aloud, dismissing the alert. "I can't. I'm sorry."

She had to turn away. Her chest heaved with wracking sobs.

"I guess I can't either," Dinah said.

"Is this real?" Jenny asked, looking back with pleading eyes.

Dinah nodded.

"It wasn't all bad, was it?"

"Not at all. What'd we make it up to, anyway? 1,300?"

"1,348," Jenny said, closing her eyes and letting the alcohol numb her soul.

"Next time, you don't need to count," Dinah said. Jenny's heart fluttered as Dinah's hand graced her cheek.

"There was a girl. Back in LA," Jenny said, hiccuping from another sob. "*The girl*. She kissed me five times."

"The one from the club?"

"Different one," said Jenny. "I—I don't like bringing her up. She kissed me five times, and then she said it wasn't real, and she was just practicing, and it didn't mean anything. She and her friends all made fun of me after. It really messed me up."

Dinah cupped her face with both hands and brought her lips close.

"This was real," she said. "This meant something."

She kissed Jenny. One last kiss, her cinnamon-spiced lips burning with angry passion. Dinah put everything into that kiss, her ravenous mouth and fearless tongue celebrating their entire history. Jenny was just as fierce, parting her lips, devouring Dinah's mouth, refusing to breathe, wanting it to last forever.

But it couldn't. Dinah finally pulled away, dazed and gasping for air.

Jenny wiped her mouth. A trace of blood came away on her finger.

"No fair."

Dinah licked her lips and shrugged as if to say, *who said anything about fair?*

Jenny could only stare as Dinah Black walked out of her life. 1,349 kisses and done. Why did it have to be the best one?

Chapter Thirty

The Ghostwriter Unmasked

Jenny never mentioned the phone. Never blamed her for anything. Eliza hated to admit it, but she couldn't deny the relief she felt in her little goblin heart, now that Jenny and Dinah were over. She wished her sister all the love in the world, but until the game was won, and Eliza didn't have to hide, this was probably for the best.

When her sister returned to the bedroom, she handed Eliza two bottles of pills. Her Xanax and Adderall.

"I need you to keep these for a while," Jenny said. She looked as miserable as the first day they met but was stubbornly holding it together. "You can decide for how long."

"Okay. I can do that."

Eliza kept her distracted that night, ordering up dumplings and watching YouTube videos about Trouble. Jenny put on a brave face. She cried later when she thought Eliza was asleep.

Someday. Someday, I'll get the chance to have my heart broken like this too.

Well after midnight, Eliza woke from a restless sleep to soft knocking at the door.

"Jenny?" came Aunt Shelly's voice in a whisper.

Jenny was still sleeping soundly. It would be cruel to wake her, so Eliza moved some pillows to hide her and crept over to the door, keeping the lights off as she opened it a crack.

"Yeah?"

"Just checking," Shelly said, her face sagging with relief. "Security says there's a problem at the gate."

"What kind of problem?"

"I don't know yet."

"Let's go find out," Eliza said. "Hold on."

She closed the door and ran to the closet, pulling on Jenny's purple Burberry coat over her pajamas. A minute later, they were meeting the night shift guard in the foyer.

"What is it?" Shelly asked him.

"It's a car," he said. "At the gate. There's nobody in it. Just sitting there, engine still running. I called two of my guys from the service. They're on their way now."

"I'm calling Blake," Shelly said, getting her phone out.

The security guard looked to Eliza. "It's that same car from the other night. The reporter's."

Her spine tingled.

"Is the house locked down?" she asked.

He nodded.

"Let's go see."

Shelly tightened her kimono, and they switched from house slippers to Uggs. The guard led them down the long driveway, softly illuminated by golden lamps in hidden fixtures on either side. Sure enough, there at the front gate was a white Hyundai with the engine still running. Milky exhaust billowed out of the muffler into the frigid air. The driver's side door was open, a warning chime still rhythmically beeping within.

"Have them search inside the fence, too," Eliza said when extra security arrived. The side gate she used going to and from the treehouse lay heavy on her mind. "Just in case."

A few minutes later, a familiar Chevy Tahoe police cruiser pulled up. Blake hopped out, clad in loose basketball shorts and a tight, *tight* muscle shirt. In the light from his truck, vapor radiated off his broad shoulders.

"Nice outfit," said Shelly.

"You caught me in the middle of a set," he said.

Eliza thought she detected her aunt's gaze lingering on his ripped abs. Blake conferred with the security guard, grabbed his own huge flashlight, and took off into the vines. After a half-hour, they had covered the grounds twice. There was no sign of the reporter, or anyone else.

Blake studied the gate entrance. "Do you have any cameras out here?"

The guard shook his head.

"We should really get some," said Shelly.

"Found something," said one of the other guards.

He walked forward, holding up a pair of broken, black frame glasses. Warby Parkers.

"They were in the grass, just a few feet off the road," the guard said.

Blake held out a pen to lift and examine the frames without touching them. After a moment, he shot a glance at Eliza.

"You know this doesn't look good after your little Instagram stunt," he said.

She held up her hands. "I've got nothing to do with this. It's probably some trick of his, like he planted a bug in the car or something."

Blake's expression darkened. He bagged the glasses and searched the area where the guard found them again, but there was nothing else to see. The reporter, Jeffrey Jordan, had *vanished*.

ELIZA HAD AN EARLY ALARM THE NEXT MORNING, RISING LIKE A zombie so she could apply copious foundation to hide her bruises. She put on the red and black tartan coat that Jenny had bought but never worn, with a black scarf to match the belt, since her makeup skills were only so good. There'd be no rides from Dinah anymore, so she left with Shelly in the town car.

"Let's get coffee," her aunt said, yawning and instructing the driver to stop at Starbucks. "I don't know about you, but I could barely sleep."

"I got like three hours, I could def go for a mocha," Eliza said.

Her aunt frowned but said nothing.

They'd eventually called a tow truck to move the reporter's car. With nothing else to do, Shelly and Eliza went back inside for the night. Blake said he'd keep an eye out for any news about Jeffrey Jordan.

"So uh, my sources tell me you and Dinah had a fight."

"Sources, eh? It's the chef, isn't it?" Eliza said, guessing the likely snitch. "He's still mad Trouble insulted his tacos."

It came out before she could stop herself, but Shelly only raised an eyebrow and said, "I can't handle Third-Person Jenny until I get my latte. You're dodging the question."

"It wasn't actually a question," Eliza said, doing her best to dredge up some emotion. "I don't really want to talk about it. We're taking a break."

Shelly sighed and patted her leg. "Okay."

Armed with a nonfat mocha, Eliza powered through Mrs. Cortez's class. She had her endgame for Mr. Hooke all planned out, but she wanted to get him alone to ask a few questions first. English class also meant seeing Dinah, unfortunately. Her sister's ex was withdrawn, avoiding eye contact and small talk, which made Eliza's role as Trouble easier, for once. Until the incident at lunch.

She was walking through the cafeteria when Penny called from behind.

"Hey, Trouble, you hear the news?"

What followed must have looked hilarious from afar. Eliza looked back, still walking. Penny's eyes widened, shouting, "Ooh! Look out!" Eliza glanced back to see Lance Ashcroft backing right into her, taking a selfie on his phone. She dodged to the right, arms flailing out for balance—and her hand slammed right into the purple smoothie Jack was sipping. The sticky liquid went flying. Not onto Jack, but straight into the face of Charlie Zaleska, sitting at the table nearby.

Oh, how the Bitchy Brigade howled in laughter, even their new recruit, Thanh Trân. Except for Charlie. She sat there, stunned, as Eliza lamely apologized. The whole cafeteria was watching now, in hysterics. Charlie's face collapsed into tears. She got up and speed-walked to the bathroom.

"You owe me a raspberry kombucha smoothie," Jack said.

Eliza glared daggers at Meghan and company, but they made no move to help.

"You guys suck!" she said and hurried to the bathroom.

Inside, Charlie hovered over the sink, washing her face, and crying. Eliza tipped the trashcan over so it blocked the door.

"I'm sorry."

"Go away!"

"It was an accident, I swear," she said, moving closer.

"Don't!" Charlie squeaked, hiding her face.

"What? What is it?" Eliza moved closer, despite her protestations.

"It's okay, I won't tell."

Timidly, Charlie lowered her hands. Gone was the dewy skin and sun-kissed complexion. Without her makeup on, Charlie's skin was ghastly pale and blotchy, her chin covered in scars.

"Oh, Charlie," she said.

"Why are you so horrible to me?!" Charlie sobbed.

"I really don't mean to be," she said, guilt making her sick as she replayed the last month's interactions with the girl. "I thought—you're just so confident all the time. I thought you liked a little back and forth. I'm sorry. I'm not a bully. Or I shouldn't be."

Charlie sniffled. "Sometimes, it was fun, but you can be so cold."

Eliza grabbed a bunch of paper towels, wondering if she or Jenny was the cold one. "Let me help."

"It's fine, I got it," Charlie said, drying her face and getting to work with some RMK liquid foundation. There were no mirrors in the cafeteria bathrooms, but that wasn't stopping her. "I used to have bad acne. The girls never see me without my face, I can't go back out there like this."

"How are you doing that without a mirror?" Eliza asked.

"Years of practice."

Eliza watched, fascinated, as Charlie made all her scars gradually disappear with expertly applied foundation and concealer. Her skill with a makeup brush was impressive—beautiful, even. Like watching an artist paint. When she got to the scratch Eliza had given her a week prior, Eliza clutched her hand to stop her. They both shivered, Charlie's touch sending a chill up her arm.

"Leave that one," Eliza said.

Their faces drifted closer. "Why?"

"Because it's mine."

Charlie glanced at her lips, their foreheads almost touching now.

Does she want this? Eliza felt her stomach tumble. *Do I?*

Before she could find out, one of the stall doors flew open, and out came Dinah Black.

Eliza instantly put a foot between herself and Charlie. Dinah gaped, then gave her a flippant eye roll that failed to mask her disappointment and hurt. She kicked the garbage can aside and walked out. Charlie had eyes only for her shoes.

"Hey, hey," Eliza followed her sister's ex outside. "That wasn't what you think."

"Oh, and what do I think!?"

"I swear to God, there's nothing going on there," Eliza said.

Jenny was going to kill her.

"I don't care. Do what you want. We're over, remember?" Dinah pivoted on her pink Keds and stomped off.

"You didn't wash your hands," she couldn't help adding.

"Now how did you fuck that up, Valentine?" asked Jack, striding up with Penny.

"I guess it runs in the family," Eliza said. "Hey, what were you going to tell me earlier, Penny?"

"Oh, Valerie canceled her press conference," Penny said. "It seems her new evidence wasn't so solid after all."

"Hmm, imagine that," Eliza said. "Guess Dad's fortune is staying with me."

Jack was scowling, as usual, at the mention of his mother.

"I wouldn't get too attached," he said. "My mother is innocent. We both know it."

Eliza turned to Penny because she knew it would annoy her brother. "You should tell your boy if he really believes that then he should be working *with* me. I'm three clues down already."

"What do you think, Junior?" Penny asked, playfully hip-checking him.

"I remain dubious," he said.

"Fine," Eliza checked her watch: still 13 minutes of lunch left, it should be enough. "Hey, you wanna see a magic trick?"

"What kind?" Penny asked.

"I'm about to make our English teacher disappear."

MR. HOOKE WAS EATING ALONE AT HIS DESK WHEN ELIZA LET herself into his room.

"Ah, Miss Valentine," he said, wiping his mouth. "I normally take my lunch in private."

"Shoulda locked the door then," she said, hopping up to sit on the desk closest to his. She kept her body pointed at him, so the camera lens on her phone, peeking out of her pocket, would capture all this.

"Um." He set his jaw, projecting a stern facade.

"I know you're the Ghostwriter," she said.

Mr. Hooke blinked, his mouth hanging loose in a daze.

"No, I'm not," he managed a full three seconds later. "That's absurd."

"Your poker face is absurd."

"Young lady!"

"Relax!" Eliza said, waving her hand to Jedi mind-trick him. "I'm not gonna tell, we just need to talk."

She could see it in his face, the longing to trust her, to hope that he would get out of this.

"About what?" he asked.

"Don't you want to know how I figured it out?"

His body sagged. "It was the post about your aunt, wasn't it?" he asked. "I knew I was tempting fate with every story I ran about you."

"What can I say, I'm good copy." She beamed, thrilled to get his admission on camera. "But no, that's not how I figured it out."

Anticipation hung in the air.

"Oh, go on, do your thing."

"Gladly!" Eliza bounced off the desk, strutting back and forth in her best impression of Trouble. "Right from the start, it was all wrong. The writing, the *email*, and then using Facebook? I was like: ok, boomer."

"I'm Gen X!"

"You were definitely some old dude pretending to be a student. And who would care about school gossip if not a teacher? I combed through all your guys' LinkedIn profiles; yours stuck out. See, you listed 'writing services' under skills. You know, like editing, consultations. Or ghostwriting. But still, that's a giant leap. So I did a deep dive on your social. You've heavily implied on multiple forums that you ghost-wrote one of those Bronte-but-with-dragons books. Seemed to be a sticking point with you. Betcha wanted credit. Am I getting warmer?"

"They said I took too long, and they could hire a grad student and pay them peanuts and get the work in faster," Mr. Hooke said scowling. "Philistines. *Wuthering Heaths* was of an entirely higher caliber than the rest of that dreck."

"I mean, it was okay," Eliza said. "You got a little aggressive with the gory wound descriptions, and somehow managed to make Heathcliff a Gary Stu, but whatever. Still, this wasn't enough to prove anything, was it? But now I was onto you. I dug deeper, searching for other uses of that 'gh0stwrit3r' handle."

"I scrubbed anything connected to me," Hooke said.

"You missed one. The Internet Archive is a bitch."

Eliza savored the moment while her shitty teacher buried his face in his hands. She could see why Jenny loved this part.

"At least it took you a month to figure it out," he said into his palms.

"It took me two hours," Eliza said. "I just didn't say anything because I had a bet going. Sorry, Vice Principal Carter, but you shouldn't have given me Saturday detention."

"Great. Trouble wins again. What do you want?"

"How many people sent you bitcoin not to post about them?"

"Just two," he said bitterly, collecting himself. "Cheap assholes. They all just started using me to spread gossip. I knew it was lies, but I wasn't getting any good stuff, so I had no choice."

"Their names," Eliza said, sliding a pen and paper over to him, then shifting her hip so the camera didn't pick up what he was writing now. When he was done, she snatched up the paper and glanced at it. The first name was Alicia Aaron and the second... "Figures."

She pocketed the names for later and backed away toward the door.

"Is that it?" Mr. Hooke asked. "You're really not going to tell?"

"Don't have to," Eliza said, pulling her phone out and aiming it at him. "You told on yourself."

"Wait!" he shouted, his face draining white. "I can pay you!"

"I have money."

"Tutor you?" he tried.

"I'm the smart one."

"I could help you with new *Trouble* books! Ghost-write them for free. I've got some great ideas, honestly."

He was casting about with his hands, desperate now.

"Sorry, Harvey, but we're not doing that. And your writing style wouldn't match RJ's," Eliza said. She flipped the camera around for a selfie. "Anyway, this is a livestream, bitch. You're on the official *Trouble* Instagram. Say hi to all the Troublemakers."

Eliza winked at the camera and killed the stream.

AFTER SCHOOL, MR. WEBB PICKED HER UP IN HIS BEAMER. HE HAD Alicia Aaron's deal ready for a signature.

"Well done today," he said, taking them downtown. "That's more the kind of excitement the publisher is looking to see from Trouble online. Though their latest market research is rather curious."

"How so?"

"Well…" Mr. Webb hesitated. "People don't seem to think you're entirely real."

"I am too!"

Alicia's place was a cavernous loft apartment, a block from Town Square. When she answered the door, she stepped out into the hallway, barely giving Eliza a peek at the bare walls and floors inside.

"Just moved in," she said. "They're still doing renovations."

"Well, aren't you the happy little shithouse rat?" Eliza said

Alicia ignored her, skimming over the contract Mr. Webb handed to her. "What about film and TV rights?" she asked.

Eliza couldn't stop herself from bursting into laughter.

"Shut up, you never know!"

"The publishing company takes 10 percent," Mr. Webb said. "Then 45 to you, and 45 to Miss Valentine."

"What is this book even about, again?" Eliza asked.

Alicia stuck her chin out, indignant. "The Dark Prince seizes power when the King and Queen are away on a trip. Meanwhile, in our world, a poor, homeless orphan girl gets sucked through a magical door and discovers she's the only one who can fight him. And they hate each other, but secretly they share a connection—"

"Are you a fucking Reylo?" Eliza interrupted.

Alicia went bright red. "Shut up! So? Jack is too!"

Her eyes got even wider as she realized she'd said too much. She grabbed the pen from Mr. Webb and signed in a huff.

"Excellent," Mr. Webb said, snapping the contract folder shut. He withdrew a thin envelope from his coat pocket. "As agreed, one million dollars."

Alicia reached out to take it, but Eliza grabbed onto the other end. "The key," she said.

Alicia withdrew her heirloom clue from a chain around her neck and placed it in Eliza's hand. Eliza released the envelope and stared at the skeleton key. It was just a simple piece of brass. It had better be worth it. She turned it over and peered closer. There was writing engraved on one side.

Before you use me, give the world a spin. Home and home and home again.

"What's this?" Eliza asked.

"No idea," said Alicia.

"Congratulations, Miss Aaron," Mr. Webb said. "You're officially an author."

The redhead glowed, a dorky smile plastered on her lips. Eliza noticed now that she'd recently gotten braces.

"So what secret were you afraid the Ghostwriter would share?" Eliza asked.

Alicia's smile faltered, and she retreated into her loft. "Pleasure doing business, Trouble," she said and slammed the door in her face.

Eliza turned to Mr. Webb. They both shrugged at each other.

"Who knows," he said, cleaning his horn-rimmed glasses on his tie. "Maybe people will read it."

They both laughed and headed for the elevator.

"Do I get to know the other name?" Jenny asked when Eliza recounted the story later.

She hesitated. They were both up late, drinking daiquiris in Jenny's bathroom. Eliza sensed this wasn't Jenny's first drink of the night. "You're not going to like it," she said.

"Just tell me."

Eliza handed over the slip of paper Mr. Hooke had written the names on.

Alicia Aaron

Dinah Black

Jenny was silent for a while, staring at the skeleton key that now hung around her own neck.

"There could be a totally innocent reason for this," she said at last.

"There could be," Eliza replied.

Neither of them believed it.

The next night, Jenny finally visited the Griffins for dinner. She arrived early for the interview, which they conducted downstairs in the offices of the *Blackbird Times*. Eliza had typed up a few pages of notes and reflections on the whole Campbell Batori affair, which Jenny passed off as her own and gave to Ms. Griffin before sitting down to take questions.

"You're not bullshitting me on this, are you?" Yvonne asked when Jenny got to the part about the activated charcoal. "I can't publish tall tales. Especially after that stunt with your teacher."

"That was all true, he confessed!"

"I know, but to a lot of the internet, this is just some weird, viral marketing campaign."

"Well, you can ask Sheriff Lockhart to confirm," said Jenny.

Yvonne's eyebrow remained raised, but she moved on to the next question. Jenny spent the next half hour filling in the personal detail, trying to inject as much of her own humanity as she was capable of. Trouble was never much for pathos; she just sort of *did stuff*. When Yvonne was satisfied, they adjourned upstairs to her and Penny's apartment.

"LET'S SEE HOW DINNER IS COMING ALONG. PENNY?" YVONNE CALLED, stepping to the side so Jenny could squeeze into a narrow hallway lined with portraits of young Penelope Griffin. The photos tracked her growth from infant to toddler to little girl to teenager. In all of them, Penny had a wide smile for the camera. Confident and loved.

"You coming?" Yvonne called from down the hall. Jenny blinked and caught up.

The Griffin home was new to Jenny; a tidy two-bedroom apartment full of old, ramshackle furniture that smelled of Pine-Sol and steamed vegetables.

"Hi Jennifer," Penny said, getting up from the couch to greet her. "Look who's here." Jenny followed her nonplussed gaze to the kitchen where Drew was chopping carrots—left-handed, and rather ineptly— while Alicia Aaron watched. "I invited him over, and she came too."

"We can't complain, can we?" Jenny said.

A knowing chuckle passed between them.

"Girls can always complain," said Penny. "Wanna play Zelda?"

"Uh, maybe in a little bit. I can't watch this anymore," Jenny said, moving to the kitchen and taking the knife from Drew's hand.

Drew shrugged, pleased with his male ineptitude, and joined Penny on the couch to play video games.

"He needs to practice," said Alicia.

"He can practice with you," Jenny said, with a wink that sent Alicia's ears aflame.

She made quick work of the carrots and tossed the salad. While she was cleaning the knife, she noticed a little row of books on a shelf above the sink. Cookbooks, by the look of them. But wouldn't this be a brilliant place to hide *The Stranger of Sausalito*? Jenny was just reaching for one when—

"It's not there," Yvonne said, stepping to her side.

"Where is it?" Jenny asked.

"Somewhere safe."

"You had a break-in recently," Jenny said, turning away from the shelf. "I'm fairly certain it was that reporter, Jeffrey Jordan. Is there any chance he took the book, or something else?"

"Not the book," she said. "Someone was in my files downstairs, though. They crowbarred the lock on the cabinet."

Jenny furrowed her brow. "When he tried to blackmail me, he implied that he was in possession of some scandalous material about RJ. Did you keep some kind of burn file on my dad?"

"Well, not exactly." Yvonne grimaced. "But after the will reading, I did some research on my own. You know, for the game. The hard copy of my notes is missing."

Jenny munched on a cucumber slice, pondering the information. "What was in them?"

"It's probably best not to say," Yvonne said.

The doorbell rang before Jenny could probe further. It was Mr. White and Shelly, bearing a bottle of Ressort Rouge.

"Hey, that's not the last one, is it?" Jenny asked.

"There's a few left," Shelly said. "Why?"

"No reason. Mr. White, I've been meaning to ask, why do you keep a second phone in your desk?"

The room fell silent, but Mr. White only smiled and rubbed his goatee.

"Well, I wouldn't say keep," he said. "If you're talking about the time you broke into my drawer, that was Danny Pham's phone. I confiscated it for texting in class, but he has it back now. You can ask him."

"Hmm. Maybe I will."

"Come on, Jenny, give it a break for a night," said Drew, walking up with a glass of sparkling cider. "We're celebrating. Penny sold her story on Mrs. Manuel to *The Atlantic*."

"No shit, really?"

Penny blushed. "It wasn't for much, but the exposure could be pretty good."

"I still think you should have gone with 'Murderangelo,'" said Drew.

"Pepperdine, here you come," said Jenny.

They both grinned, and Jenny retracted her claws. She could do this, she could be nice. She wished Eliza could be here too, though.

Dinner was pleasant enough, even with Alicia and Mr. White there. Ms. Griffin made Chicken Parmesan to die for, and Shelly let her have several healthy sips of wine.

The rest of the week passed in a blur, and Jenny focused on her classes for once. With Mr. Hooke fired, the new English teacher let her move to the other side of the room. Annoyingly, Charlie took her old desk next to Dinah. Mason and Meghan May "officially" started dating; only Jenny and Eliza knew they'd been banging for over a year already. At some point, she'd have to get Mason to explain why keeping their child a secret was so important. Jack was quietly pleased to see Mason and Drew preoccupied, putting 33 Percent Mike on hiatus and saving him from secondhand embarrassment. There was no sign of Tori, but a dozen purple tulips arrived at the mansion with an unsigned note that read:

Thank you

The penmanship was exquisite. And then, before Jenny knew it, Valentine's Day had arrived.

Chapter Thirty-One

Valentine's Day

THE PARADE WOULDN'T START UNTIL SUNDOWN, BUT *TROUBLE* fans were already crowding into Town Square. Everywhere Jenny looked, adorable little Trouble cosplayers scampered around in their purple trench coats and red fedoras. They bought cotton candy and corn dogs from the street vendors and reenacted their favorite scenes from the books with their friends. She was particularly impressed with one girl who had the whole killer reveal monologue from *Trouble and Treble* memorized.

Jenny waited in the park, in the exact spot where RJ's cursed statue once sat. She checked her watch, frustrated.

"They should've been here by now."

"Relax," Mr. Webb said, checking his phone. "They're just around the corner now."

Sure enough, a delivery truck rounded the corner, inching through the throng of fans who saw street traffic as a mere suggestion.

"Hmmph!" said Jenny, adjusting her hat. Honestly, she hated wearing the fedora with wigs, but today sort of called for the full regalia. Eliza had suggested she play it too cool for school and show up in simple black, but she was Trouble, goddamnit. Instead, she shipped her twin off to Napa for a well-deserved spa weekend and talked Charlie into doing her makeup for the parade.

"I gotta pee," Charlie said. "I'll find you later."

Jenny nodded, puzzled. After the makeup session, Charlie had just sort of hung around. Were they friends now? What *did* Eliza get up to with Jenny's identity?

The truck finally eased to a stop, and the work crew got out to unload the package: a simple slatted-wood and cast-iron park bench. Tyrone from the public works department was on-hand with some power tools. He had the bench bolted to the patch of concrete in no time.

"We surely didn't want another statue, but it still feels like something is missing," Mr. Webb said.

"I'm working on it."

Jenny plugged a wood-burning iron into Tyrone's extension cord. With her phone out, she started another livestream and filmed herself as she slowly burned small letters into the upper left corner of the bench back.

"For the record," she said to herself—and the 8,496 people already watching online, "the statue wasn't my idea. Everyone knows he hated having his picture taken."

She paused to admire her work.

For RJV

"I want this to be for all of us," she continued. "When this bench fills up, I'll find a spot for another."

For RJV & LKO

357

Jenny glanced around, looking for a volunteer. A little girl, maybe nine years old in an oversized purple coat, was watching nearby. She waved her over and showed her how to use the tool.

"Be careful, it's hot."

Jenny filmed a while longer as more kids—and many older girls—gathered around and formed a line to wait their turn. Mr. Webb had disappeared somewhere, so she went for a stroll, still filming as she passed through the crowds of little Troubles and a fair amount of black-clad Strangers. There were even—hilariously—a few Sheriff Lockharts with big fake paunches.

She paused in front of Bella's Boutique; their mannequin dressed up like Trouble in the window. In the reflection, her lips smiled behind her phone. "Bye guys. Have fun tonight." She waved and killed the stream.

A shadow passed by. Jenny looked up to see a new reflection in the window: Valerie Valentine, looking once again flawless in a silky white gown.

"I can't believe that weasel of a judge is letting you out of your cage for this," Jenny said.

Deputy Calderon waved, clip-clopping up on Ricochet, nominally to escort Val, but keeping his distance.

"It pays to put down roots in the community," Val said.

"What do you want?"

"I see you've gone and solved another heirloom clue."

"Three for three," said Jenny. "Plus you."

"Jorge Lopez was going to help me with that," Val said. "And then Jeffrey Jordan. And yet, it seems you keep getting lucky."

"Maybe you're just unlucky."

"I thought so for a while," Val said. "But now I see the bright side. The real killer won't bother with me, now that you're the much more enticing loose thread."

"Casey Klein's mom bothered with me. Now she's a foot shorter."

"I'm talking about escalation," said Val. "RJ had his detractors. I'm guessing the next one won't be a pretentious soccer mom who thought her arts and crafts made her smarter than she was. You're on their radar now. The book, the photo, the blackbird, or the key: which one will come for you first, I wonder?"

"Is there like an offer somewhere in here?" Jenny asked, yawning.

"I underestimated you. Mea culpa. I can still help you, though. Even after you framed me, I'd still help you. But not with this on." Val stuck her right foot out, flashing her ankle bracelet.

"But you wear it so well. Sorry, Val. I admire your ingenuity in finding novel ways to threaten me, but you can't talk your way out of getting caught with the murder weapon and no alibi. Do the crime, do the time." Jenny turned to the deputy. "Mr. Calderon, I believe we're not supposed to come within a few hundred feet of each other. That works both ways, right?"

"That's true," Calderon said. He motioned for Val to march in front of him. "Giddy-up, Valerie."

Her nemesis departed, leaving Jenny to register the change in the crowd behind her. It was dusk, and the streetlights had come on. Everyone was hurrying to stake out a spot on the sidewalk as the street emptied for the parade. Jenny hopped over a few fans and strolled down the center of the road, shooting another livestream video.

"Excuse me, miss," said some dude in a black "STAFF" windbreaker, holding up his palm to stop her. "We're clearing the street for the Trouble parade."

"I am Trouble," she growled and kept walking.

After another block, she tired of filming and signed off, yawning again.

"Time to be a basic bitch and go get a latte," she said, angling for the Starbucks on the corner. "Oh God, I'm talking to myself now, and I'm not even streaming. Don't become one of those awful people, Trouble."

If only she'd thought ahead, the line for coffee was out the door. Jenny ordered from the app on her phone and took a seat at an empty table outside to wait.

> **Jenny:** I'm at Sbux. You want to hang, or are you stuck with AA all night?
>
> **Drew:** Ummmm TBD. 😵 I'll let you know.

Ugh, boys. She was debating which gif to send him when someone sat down at her table.

"Oh, um." Jenny looked up, blinking in surprise at the tall, dark, and strangesome menace seated across from her. "Nice costume. I was kinda planning on sitting alone, though."

There were lots of people in The Stranger outfits here tonight. Most in just an oversized black coat and black hat, but some, like this one, went the extra step of covering their faces in a black stocking mask.

He shook his head. Jenny sighed.

"Are we gonna have to do the whole 'arch-enemies' thing before you leave me be?"

He nodded.

Jenny rolled her eyes—

—and in a flash, had her stun gun out, lunging at the man across the table and trusting her instincts.

She was right. It *was* the Stranger—the real one.

Who else could have caught her stun gun in his left hand, the immobilizing volts sparking harmlessly on his thick black glove?

Jenny's eyes widened in horror as he twisted his wrist and snatched the taser away from her. Something flashed, and a small card appeared in his right hand. On it was a handwritten message in blocky letters.

DON'T!

"I'll scream," Jenny said.

He produced another note, shifting a deck of them fashioned like playing cards into his other hand.

I WOULDN'T IF I WERE YOU.

Fans and patrons laughed and cheered around them, eagerly anticipating the parade. What would he do? Was it worth risking them to find out?

"What do you want?"

Another card. In the distance, brass horns wailed as a marching band played.

DON'T YOU THINK IT'S TIME WE TALKED?

She studied his figure, searching for a weakness. Darkness enveloped him. He must have worn some sort of shield underneath the black mask, making his face a rounded, featureless orb.

"Is that what this is? You somehow got a card prepared for anything I say?"

He dealt another from the middle of his deck.

YES. I DO.

Her spine tingled.

"Okay, we're talking. I want my book back," she said, thinking of her copy of *My Name is Trouble*, signed by her father, that someone had stolen from her last fall.

The Stranger only rumbled with laughter, deep and ominous.

"Fine. What's on your mind, Killroy?"

He rifled through a few cards before turning one over.

YOU'RE ENJOYING THE LIMELIGHT. I THOUGHT I MIGHT HAVE THIS DANCE.

Jenny swallowed. "What does that mean?"

She could sense the smile behind his blank void of a face.

BUT FIRST, I'D LIKE TO PROPOSE A TRADE.

"Hold up, I've got some questions first," Jenny said.

He spread his hands, motioning for her to continue.

"That reporter, Jeffrey Jordan. Did you do something to him?"

Even with his large frame, the Stranger somehow managed a coquettish shrug.

"It bothers you when other people get involved, doesn't it?" Jenny said. "That's why you went after Declan and Drew."

The Stranger dealt two cards from the bottom of the deck.

HE SUCKS.

NO SIDEKICKS.

"No, that's not it. You're all alone, and you want me to be too."

He turned his head, looking into the coffee shop through the window. Jenny followed his gaze and felt her stomach drop when she spotted Jack and Tori at the counter.

NO.

YOU'VE GOT SOMETHING TO LOSE.

"What about Campbell Batori?" Jenny asked, hoping to distract him. "Did you know she was the killer?"

He re-dealt an old card.

YES. I DO.

"You could have stopped her! All those poor little girls!"

He violently flipped over another card.

WHO DO YOU THINK YOU'RE TALKING TO?

"The Stranger didn't kill little kids."

His shoulders flexed in frustration. To her right, the marching band paraded down the street, followed by a giant float overloaded with girls in Trouble costumes. How tacky, Val.

After a moment, a pen was in the Stranger's left hand, scrawling something on the card in block letters.

I POINTED YOU IN THE RIGHT DIRECTION, DIDN'T I?

"Well. Now I know something about you. And I think you're full of shit! You didn't know about Campbell. You just heard about the wig. So maybe you're someone on the force? Or you've got access to Napa PD's case file?"

He returned to his deck, pulling out another card.

YOU'LL NEVER GUESS.

WHEN PUSH COMES TO SHOVE, YOU'LL ALWAYS SACRIFICE YOUR FRIENDS TO SAVE YOURSELF. I RESPECT THAT.

They stared at each other as the seconds ticked by.

"You mentioned a trade," Jenny said at last.

DID YOU KNOW ALLERGIES ARE HEREDITARY?

He angled his head again, looking inside at Jack and Tori. They'd found a table and were sipping their coffee, deep in a private conversation.

VALERIE VALENTINE BREAKS OUT IN HIVES AT THE MERE WHIFF OF DAISY POLLEN. LET'S SEE WHAT HAPPENS WHEN HER CHILDREN INGEST A CONCENTRATED DOSE, COURTESY OF THE FLOWERS FROM YOUR GREENHOUSE.

Jenny's heart froze to the core. Inside, Jack was coughing.

"What do you want?" She was out of her seat, watching helplessly as her brother pounded on his chest, a stitch in his throat that wouldn't go away.

The Stranger held up another card.

GIVE ME THE KEY, AND I'LL TRADE YOU AN EPIPEN.

He produced a bulky yellow canister from inside his coat. Tori was trying to help Jack, but coughing herself now.

BUT YOU MUST CHOOSE WHO TO USE IT ON: THE IDIOT BROTHER YOU CARE ABOUT, OR THE MEAN STEPSISTER WHO

HAS INFO YOU NEED.

Jenny blinked, the bitter choice dawning on her. A *frisson* was rippling through the crowd inside; other patrons were noticing her brother's distress. Jack sagged to the ground, clawing at his throat.

"Why do you want it?!" Jenny screamed, pounding on the window in horror as Tori collapsed too. "What's so special about Alicia's key?!"

He set one final card on the table.

I COULDN'T SAY. I JUST WANT TO PLAY.

"Fine!" Jenny yanked Alicia Aaron's key out, breaking the necklace that held it, and slammed it onto the table. "Gimme the EpiPen!"

The Stranger laughed again. A low, distorted, rumbling laugh that made her teeth chatter. Alicia's key disappeared into his palm, and he tossed her a life-saving syringe. She snatched it out of the air and ran to the coffee shop entrance, scrambling inside and elbowing her way through the crowd of onlookers who only stood and watched while Jack and Tori choked to death on the floor.

"Get out of the way!" she shouted.

"I called 911!" a woman said.

Falling to her knees, she tore the EpiPen out of its sheath. Tori looked up at her with wide, scared eyes.

Jenny hesitated, the EpiPen clutched in her fist. The Stranger expected her to let Tori die. Did that mean she was the key to unmasking him? Or was this all a con, knowing she'd want to make the smart choice, and tricking her into sacrificing Jack for nothing. This was the heartless majesty of his machinations: a game she had to play and could only lose.

Tori wouldn't let her.

Her hand darted up and grabbed Jenny by the wrist.

"Fuck. You," Tori gasped. With desperate strength, she wrenched Jenny's hand down and plunged the syringe into Jack's thigh before collapsing beside him.

Jenny couldn't move, awestruck and horrified at Tori's sacrifice. Another low, modulated chuckle cut through her shock. Jenny whirled, just in time to see the Stranger tip his cap from the doorway and spring away into the night.

In a heartbeat, she was on her feet, charging through the crowd with reckless abandon; vengeance the only thought left in her mind.

TROUBLE SPED UP THE ROAD. THE TALL FORM OF THE STRANGER bobbed in and out of view in the fading light, both of them negotiating the packed crowd. Valentine's Day revelers poured into the street behind the giant parade float, caterwauling along in tuneless cacophony as the marching band played "Sing a Song of Sixpence." She dove between two cosplayers, stumbling for 10 feet before tucking and rolling on the hard asphalt, springing up, careening off a false Lockhart and shouting "STOP HIM!" with a desperate howl that none paid heed.

"...Four and twenty blackbirds / Baked in a pie..."

Sung by that creepy specter in *Here Comes Trouble*. not a ghost, just a lonely albino—

Inspiration sparked, and Jenny leapt up onto the float platform, ignoring the annoyed cries of the dancers as she clambered up to the top.

From this vantage, along with some vertigo, she gained a view of the whole square. Her eyes ricocheted around, searching for The Stranger in a crowd full of them.

"...Hanging out the clothes. / Along came a blackbird / And snipped off her nose..."

There he was! Moving across the park.

"KILLROY!!"

Somehow, he heard her and stopped to look back.

Jenny sprang down, a sharp pop in her knees as she hit the pavement. As she ran, lungs burning, she whispered a silent "thank you" to her hightops for keeping her ankles intact. Parents honked in outrage as she tore through the toddlers' play area. That Strangesome Menace was making for the edge of the square on First and Broadway.

The sidewalks were packed tight here, with fans still waiting for the marching band to round the corner. A score of Trouble dancers twirled batons in formation. Jenny weaved through them and into the crowd. Her small body ducked and dodged, squeezing between fans until she found herself hemmed in by a portable fence at the rear.

Officer Peña stood guard, a Police SUV blocking the way behind her.

"Did you see him!" Jenny shouted. "Did anyone come through here?!"

"What?" Darcy said. "No one gets through this way, Jenny. You gotta go around. Blake's orders."

"Fuck!"

She jumped as high as she could, craning her neck to see over the crowd, searching in vain for the Stranger. The bitch of it was, she spotted several of him.

New plan. Unmask them all!

Jenny squirmed back to the street and ping-ponged between every black-clad rogue she could find, ripping off hats and masks, searching for a familiar face, or a sign of recognition.

"Jenny?!" called a voice. It was Dinah, standing in uniform with her cheer squad.

"Which way?!" Jenny pleaded. "Did you see anyone running by?"

"Um, I think that way?" Dinah pointed to her left.

Jenny was away in a blink, unable to make out what her ex shouted after her. Every few steps came a new Stranger to unmask. It was never him. Hope slowly drained from her soul as each potential suspect turned out to be some dad, some boyfriend, some tall chick—even two kids, one on the other's shoulders under the black trench coat. But never *him*.

"Mason!" she said in surprise, finding a certain big oaf dancing around under a black hood. "Seriously?"

"Danger! I'm high as balls!"

"Ugh!" She pushed him away, but already her feet were slowing. It had been minutes now without a sign of the Stranger. Night had fallen, making it harder to see. More and more people were staring. Unbidden, she glanced up. There was Valerie Valentine at the Parade Judge's table, jabbing a finger at her and shouting to her event staff.

She didn't even know about her kids.

Jenny swallowed the bitter pill. It was useless now. The Stranger was gone.

She hurried to a swarm of Troubles, doffing her fedora and coat amidst them, and slipped out the other side in a black t-shirt and jeans. The cool air was a balm to her flushed skin. Glumly, she headed back toward the Starbucks.

Halfway there, it was clear the paramedics had arrived. In time for Jack? She dared to hope.

Sirens chirped, an ambulance inching forward as the crowd around the coffee shop cleared.

"What's going on?" Charlie asked, joining her as she reached the edge of the scene.

"I—" Jenny held her face in her hands. "I can't right now, Charlie."

She pushed on, finding Alicia and Drew at the curb. He had made a seat for the little redhead with his left bicep, holding her up on his good shoulder to see over the crush of rubberneckers.

"I think I see Jack Valentine," Alicia said.

"Is he okay?" Jenny asked.

Drew nodded at her, but when he read her mournful expression, his face fell.

"What happened?"

"Penny's with him," Alicia added.

It took a lot for Jenny to resist knocking Alicia off Drew's shoulder and taking her place.

"I heard some chick straight up choked so hard on a biscotti she keeled over. This is why no one goes to Starbucks in Paris," Meghan May was telling Thanh and Shani.

Jenny's knees wavered. "Someone should go get Val," she said to no one in particular, falling to a crouch on the sidewalk. A minute or an hour later, Shelly and Mr. White found and collected her. None of her friends could say why she was so shaken up. None of them knew how badly she'd failed.

Chapter Thirty-Two

Zip Me Up

Miraculously, Tori lived. She was in a coma, still unresponsive two days later, but a faint hope remained that she would pull through.

Jenny found out afterward that Tori went without oxygen for at least five minutes before another customer with chronic allergies had used his own EpiPen to save her. Even if she awoke, there might be permanent brain damage. A horrible voice in the back of her mind wondered: *what if she forgets the information I needed?*

Val refused to let Jenny near Tori's room at Blackbird Springs Memorial Hospital, but Val was still technically awaiting trial for murder and had to go back to her gilded cage. On Sunday, Jenny headed into town to visit her stepsister. But first, she had an errand to run.

The Winchester was packed with the brunch crowd. Jenny weaved her way through the dim ambiance to a small corner booth. An older man, 60 at least, was dining alone. His gray hair was tucked under a newsboy cap, and he wore a shabby, wool-knit vest.

"Lambert, I presume," Jenny said, taking a seat. "Ich bin ein

Trouble."

"Not quite, but well met, Miss Valentine," said Lambert in his odd accent. "Is this business or pleasure?"

Jenny replied by setting a bottle of *Ressort Rouge* onto the table. Lambert's eyes were suitably ravenous.

"You're lucky, this is my last bottle."

A lie, but Jenny guessed he was the type to enjoy exclusivity.

"Sic transit gloria mundi," he said. "Although, I hear Blackthorn Vineyards purchased the old Pinefall lands. Perhaps we'll have a *Ressort Noire* in a year."

Jenny forced a smile. Yet another thing Dinah had never mentioned.

"Perhaps."

"I was just reading your story in *The Atlantic*," he said, nudging a dog-eared magazine across the table. "Did you enjoy it?"

Jenny glanced at the lede Penny wrote, even though she had it as good as memorized by now.

> "Trouble Valentine dances between raindrops, driven by an almost solipsistic need to Solve Mysteries. Mary Manuel doesn't have that luxury."

"It's not really my story," Jenny said. "My friend Penny wrote it."

"Interesting. And do you agree with it?"

"Well. I don't always miss the raindrops."

Lambert took his time chewing on a bite before wiping his mouth with a napkin and fixing her with an inquisitive eye.

"So. What would you have me investigate?" he asked.

"Not really an investigation," Jenny said. "More of a research project."

She paused to gauge his mood.

"Go on—*hic!*"

"Might want to take it easy on your…" She glanced at his plate.

"Beef Stroganoff. And I shall go as I please."

"Whatever. I need a census," said Jenny. "I need to know every private dick who operated in the North Bay between, let's say, 15 and 20 years ago."

"And what do you wish to do with this census?" he asked.

"Let's call it research for a book. Better yet, call it none of your business. Can you do it?"

He took another spoonful of food, chewed, swallowed, and washed it down with the table red.

"It would take some time," he decided at last.

"That's fine. This is more of a long-term project. Will you do it?"

His eyes fell greedily on the bottle of *Ressort Rouge*. Jenny yanked it back and gave him a look.

"Yes, fine," he said, snatching up the bottle when Jenny slid it back his way. "Was there anything else, or just the census?"

"I may require a few other things when you finish," she said, deciding to leave out the photo search for now. "I'd like to think this buys me some runway. Enjoy your Beefaroni or whatever that is."

Jenny headed for the exit, waving at Mrs. Porter. If she thought she was going to get out the door without a hug and a kiss on each cheek from Drew's mom, she was mistaken.

"How is he?" she asked Mirai.

"Spending an awful lot of time with that little goth girl," Mirai said, eyes narrowing. "She dotes after him, and he plays his keyboard one-handed to still be in her band. Should I be worried?"

"I don't want to alarm you, but yes."

Mirai bit her lip. "I shall spy further."

They said their goodbyes, and Jenny stepped outside, breathing deep after the musty atmosphere in the restaurant. If she was lucky,

Lambert's research would take her one step closer to the P.I. who spied on—and maybe killed—her mother. And if she was really lucky, they wouldn't see her coming.

Seeing the peaches and cream tiles of the hospital again, Jenny reflexively reached for the Xanax bottle in her purse. Her pills were gone, though, held by Danger until Jenny could be trusted not to abuse them. Her twin had rationed her one Adderall pill per day while she was at the spa. Usually, that kind of control would annoy her, but it felt different when she knew Eliza had her best interests at heart.

Come to think of it, maybe she shouldn't give her aunt such a hard time after all. She pulled out her phone and texted.

Jenny: Excited for tonight. I hope they like me.

Shelly: They will. 💜

Jenny: 💜

She smiled and walked to Tori's room, forcing herself not to look at the tiles she was stepping on. Her stepsister lay peacefully in a sun-filled room, her face looking younger and softer in her ceaseless slumber. Jack was here too, keeping vigil. Deep hollows had formed under his eyes, those Valentine cheekbones looking gaunt and razor-sharp.

"Hey," said Jenny, taking the other chair in the room.

For a while, no words passed between them. The rhythmic pulse of the heart rate monitor counting each beat that remained in Tori's willful heart.

"This is what it was like with Dad," Jack said in a tired voice. "Three weeks of hoping he'd wake up, and then…"

"She'll make it," Jenny said. "This bitch is too stubborn to go out like that."

"Hey."

"Okay, this princess of a young lady." Jenny sighed. "I can't talk. She made the hard call when I couldn't. I couldn't even catch him or stop him when he was right there." She held up her taser. "This thing is fucking useless."

"What did he want?" he asked.

"To make me choose," said Jenny. "The Stranger always loved dangling moral quandaries in front of Trouble."

"Dad's ham-fisted way of forcing a moral on the story. But hold up, you really think this guy is real?"

"As real as I am," Jenny said. "Someone who's read the books and wants to play with Trouble."

"This is the guy who attacked you and Drew."

"Declan too." She nodded.

"Didn't you say the Undertaker confessed to that?" he asked.

"When I asked him..." Jenny paused, crafting a new lie, now that the old one was unviable. "When the Undertaker took us to the Haunted Vineyard, he said, 'Fuck Declan, he owed me eight grand and wasn't paying.' I suppose that's not exactly an admission of guilt, now that I think about it."

"Mmhmm." Jack pivoted to address her head-on, his cool blue eyes boring into her. "And you still think my mother killed Dad?"

"That's up to a judge, not me," she said, returning as much fire as she could muster. "And she'd be a lot more trustworthy if she wasn't constantly hunting for new lowlifes to help her pin his murder on me. All I know is this: someone out there thinks they're my arch-enemy, and they don't like it when other people try to play the game. So if your mom is innocent, she should stay in her fancy penthouse and leave me the fuck alone."

Jack looked down, and she could see the wheels turning in that inscrutable brain of his.

"Well, in that case, we're going to need to keep this on the DL."

He reached down and hefted his backpack. Jenny leaned closer, curious, as he unzipped the main pouch and pulled out something bulky, wrapped in a towel from the Crow's Nest. The white cotton fell away, and there, at last, was the Onyx Blackbird statue. Jack's heirloom clue.

He handed it to her gently. Jenny's fingertips tingled, finally touching the smooth black surface of the fragile statue.

"Do you trust me?" she asked him.

"You're the girl detective. Detect."

"What if *you're* the Stranger?" She narrowed her eyes.

"*How?*"

"I don't know. Mirrors?"

"Then I trust you to kill me," he said.

"Okay. Just remember, you asked for my help."

Jenny raised the Onyx Blackbird over her head.

"What do you—wait!" he cried.

She smashed the statue into the peaches and cream linoleum, exploding it into a hundred black shards.

"WHAT THE FUCK!?" Jack yelped.

"'To my dear son Johnathan Renard Valentine, I leave the Onyx Blackbird he has almost broken so many times running up and down the hall,'" Jenny quoted from her father's will. "He hid something inside. He wanted you to break it."

She crouched down on the floor, sifting through the pieces of onyx. Jack's mouth was still agape in horror.

"There's probably like a note or map or something…" Jenny ran her hands over the rubble, careful not to cut herself.

"Are you fucking shitting me?" Jack whispered.

"Maybe it went under the bed," Jenny said, ducking down low and hoping she was right. She could feel her face flushing bright red. She spotted a few more shards, but...

"There has to be something!" she said.

"Jennifer," Jack said, his voice oddly calm.

She refused to look at him, still doggedly searching for the clue Dad must have hidden within.

"Sister."

That killed her. Her eyes rose to meet his wintry face.

"I don't want to be mean," he said through his teeth. "So I have to ask that you get away from me for a while before I lose my temper."

Jenny rose, feeling physically repelled by his aura of icy rage. "I'm sorry," she said at the door. "Just keep looking. It'll be there."

"Go."

"Oh, and if Tori wakes up, tell her I bought her that animal shelter!"

"Go!" he shouted at her.

Jenny ran off, dancing to each peach tile on the floor, thoroughly mortified. An empty statue. What could it mean?

"You couldn't have like, shaken it, first?" Eliza asked later, upon hearing her sister's story.

She had her eyes jammed shut, so she couldn't gauge Jenny's expression.

"I figured he taped it to the inside or something," Jenny said, her breath on Eliza's face.

They were both seated in front of Jenny's vanity in her massive closet, her sister attempting to do Eliza's makeup by following one of Charlie's YouTube videos. Tonight was the long-awaited dinner with their grandparents on Mom's side.

"Go easy on the raccoon eyes," Eliza said, sensing that Jenny had been doing her eye shadow for too long.

"Relax," Jenny said with a snicker.

"Maybe you're supposed to, like, grind up the statue and burn the dust, and then the smoke from the fire will flicker in morse code with a message of the next clue."

"Would that work?" Jenny asked.

"No, of course not." Eliza shook her head. "He is never gonna talk to us again."

"He'll get over it. I have another plan for that clue, anyway."

"Do I get to know about it, cause I definitely would have cautioned against your last one."

"All in due time," Jenny said with a maniacal laugh.

"You know what? Fine. I could use a break."

She felt Jenny lean away. "Okay, open," Jenny said.

Well, they weren't raccoon eyes, at least. Jenny had really gone for it, giving Eliza some bold crimson wings below her lashes.

"I was going for sort of byojaku look, with my own twist," Jenny said.

"Looks dangerous, I like it."

Jenny chewed on the end of her brush. "I still can't get Charlie's whole dewy skin technique down."

"That's her specialty—oh shit!" She shot up, ramrod straight.

"What?" Jenny asked, hand darting into her purse.

"We forgot to go to Saturday detention again!" Eliza winced.

Jenny sagged in relief, a cackle escaping her lips. "Ahahahah! You're right!"

"Mr. Carter is totally going to expel us," Eliza said.

"You know what, family emergency!" said Jenny.

"I hope you like boarding school."

"You're the one with the Hogwarts fetish."

"That's true. I could adopt an English accent there, and no one would be the wiser…" Eliza sighed, warm feelings spooling out of her as she imagined herself at Wizarding School.

The intercom chirped. It was a new feature Eliza had security install, which notified them whenever a car approached the front gate. There was a video screen now, too, showing the feed from the gate camera. Jenny leaned into the bedroom to get a look.

"It's Shelly," she called. "I'd better get going."

"Are you sure about this?" Eliza asked. Jenny had decided at the last minute that Eliza should go to dinner instead. "Shouldn't it be you that meets them first?"

"I got to meet Jack first, it's your turn," said Jenny. "You crushed your Rosetta Stone, you'll be fine. You can make a good first impression for us."

Eliza waved goodbye to her sister, waiting for a count of five before moving to the bathroom to wet a sponge and ease up on the hangover eyeshadow just a teeny bit.

Ten minutes later, she finally admitted to herself that she was only making it worse. Her grandparents were going to think Jenny was a coke fiend. Oh well, there was a decent chance they already did, anyway. Eliza returned to the closet to pick out an outfit. Initially, she'd planned on wearing the tartan coat dress again, but that would be far too much red with this makeup. Nothing else was working for her either, though.

"Jenny? Are you almost ready?" Shelly called from down the hall. "I need to stop at the store first."

"Almost!" Eliza lied.

She was close to settling on boring jeans and a t-shirt when she spotted her aunt's little black dress in the back of the closet. "Ooh!

Perfect."

Eliza stripped quickly and slipped into the silky black number. The neckline was modest enough. Elegant, even. If it was good enough for RJ's funeral, it would have to be good enough for Toshi and Catherine Onishi.

She stepped into some casual black flats, struggling with the low zipper in the back.

"Jenny?" Shelly called from the doorway.

"In here," Eliza called. "Can you gimme a hand?"

Her aunt peeked in from the closet door, sizing her up.

"Oh, that looks nice," Shelly said. "Except for your face."

"Wow, thanks. Zip me up?"

Shelly allowed a sly smile and spun her around. "Can't wait to see the look on your..."

Eliza waited for her aunt to finish the sentence, but she'd gone awfully quiet and stiff, still clutching the zipper at the small of her back.

"What?" she asked.

"...On your grandparents' face," said Shelly, almost like a question.

"Are you all right? You're not gonna start crying, are you?"

"Nothing," Shelly said. "Just thinking. Do you remember that time you got in the fight at the park? You cut yourself on that bottle?"

"Um, I guess," Eliza said, suddenly wary. "Why?"

"Just thinking... Those were happy times, weren't they? That place on Dryden Street?"

"We had our moments," she said, her pulse rising. "You *are* gonna cry, aren't you?"

Silence.

"Shelly?"

Still no response, though she could sense her aunt's presence. Eliza forced herself to turn around, apprehension mounting with each fluttering heartbeat.

All the color had drained from Shelly's face. Her eyes were wet, shock and terror, and other intense emotions rolling off her in waves.

Eliza's mouth hung open, at a loss for how to fix this.

Shelly blinked in realization, letting the tears stream down her cheeks.

"Lizzy?"

To be continued...

ACKNOWLEDGEMENTS

Thanks are due, right at the top, to everyone who read and enjoyed the first book, *My Name is Trouble*. The positive response and encouragement kept me going when it seemed like drafting was taking forever. It was scary putting Book 1 out into the world, not knowing if it was good, or if people would hate it, so every tweeted photo of the cover you sent us, every star rating you left on Amazon or Goodreads or Apple Books, was immensely appreciated.

Brainstorming with my writing partner is one of my favorite activities, and I will always cherish the countless hours we spent talking and discussing and brainstorming the story for *Trouble Always Finds Me*. Sometimes we'd cover a huge chunk of the mystery in one session; in others we'd spend an hour just trying to come up with a character's name. Thank you, as always, to Marco, for reigning in my worst ideas, and finding the right bit of humor a scene is missing.

This time around, I was a bit more restrained with my beta readers, not spamming all my friends' inboxes with new chapters every week, which made friend of the pod Ally's feedback on the second draft absolutely invaluable. When Ally tweeted a photo at the Trouble account showing Book 1 indexed with dozens of color-coded post-it notes, I knew we had a Spencer Hastings-level intellectual as a fan. I am in Ally's debt for giving me such detailed notes on every chapter. I could not ask for a more helpful reader.

As he did on the previous book, Michael Manuel once again provided excellent cover art, working tirelessly to capture the mood we were thinking of, and bring Jenny to life with his stylus. I can't wait to tell him about my ideas for Book 3's cover. It might break him.

Many thanks are due to Karen Crain, who once again provided proofreading and a final polish for the book. Someday I will remember to stop using the British spellings of words. JJ Allendorf's willingness to read the first draft as it developed was similarly irreplaceable. Kudos to JJ for always asking the important continuity questions to keep the mystery honest.

Thanks are due as well to my other beta readers: Dan Grayson, who always loves a good Harbor High reference, Alex Rühl, who's excitement is infectious, and my sister Rachael, who is the actual talented writer of the family, and reminded me that I should probably do something about Jenny's frankly alarming pill abuse.

My parents actually read the first book (sorry for all the foul language), and my mother even posed on the park bench in Sonoma, CA for the cover concept. My sister Sara organized a local book club meetup for *My Name is Trouble*, which was surreal and delightful. Thanks are do as well to Marco's family, and his two cats, Harry and Sally, who keep him sane, and like to make noise during podcasts.

We hope you liked Book 2, and we're hoping against hope for a Covid-19 vaccine soon, since we'd really love to travel to Europe for research on Book 3. Yes, as you may have guessed, for her next adventure, Trouble will be taking a holiday.

—James Taylor

ABOUT THE AUTHORS

JAMES TAYLOR is a writer, podcaster, and jack-of-all-trades media producer. During the pandemic he's perfected ground turkey tacos and losing hours of conscious thought whilst putting together 1000-piece puzzles. He's an excellent liar, though he prefers to tell the truth. Sometimes he has to remind himself that other people are real, and not merely robots sent to test him. He lives in the Golden State.

MARCO SPARKS is a writer living in California. He's suspiciously tall. His fiction and non-fiction can be found in various dark corners of the internet. He is the co-host of several podcasts, particularly focused on teen murder shows. Also, he has the kind of cats where, when he suddenly ends up dead, no matter how much it looks like it was an accident, they were behind it.